THE
ROYAL
REBEL

ELIZABETH
CHADWICK

SPHERE

SPHERE

First published in Great Britain in 2024 by Sphere

1 3 5 7 9 10 8 6 4 2

Copyright © 2024 by Elizabeth Chadwick
Map artwork by Stephen Dew
Rose chapter ornament by Lucy Rose Illustration

The moral right of the author has been asserted.

A CIP catalogue record for this book is available from the British Library.

Hardback ISBN 978-1-4087-2980-9
Trade paperback ISBN 978-1-4087-2981-6

Typeset in BT Baskerville by Palimpsest Book Production Ltd, Falkirk, Stirlingshire
Printed and bound in Great Britain by Clays Ltd, Elcograf S.p.A.

Papers used by Sphere are from well-managed forests and other responsible sources.

MIX
Paper | Supporting
responsible forestry
FSC® C104740

Sphere
An imprint of
Little, Brown Book Group
Carmelite House
50 Victoria Embankment
London EC4Y 0DZ

An Hachette UK Company
www.hachette.co.uk

www.littlebrown.co.uk

Character List (in order of appearance in the novel)

Jeanette
Known to history as Joan of Kent, daughter of Prince Edmund of
Woodstock (executed while Jeanette was an infant), the uncle of King
Edward III

John of Kent
Jeanette's brother, younger by three and a half years and heir to the
wealthy earldom of Kent

Margaret Wake, Dowager Countess of Kent
Jeanette's mother

Hawise
Jeanette's maid, daughter of a yeoman and slightly older than Jeanette
but still a young woman

Otto Holland
Thomas Holland's younger brother and knight of the royal household

Thomas Holland
Young royal household knight of military and logistical skill, making
his way in the world but with many rungs to climb

King Edward III
King of England, twenty-five years old at the outset of the novel, strong, fierce, romantic, warlike and ambitious

Philippa of Hainault
King Edward III's Flemish wife, twenty-five years old, mother to their growing brood of children

Isabelle
Edward and Philippa's eldest daughter, a child of six at the outset of the novel

Joan
Edward and Philippa's second daughter, a child of four

Katerine, Countess of Salisbury
One of Queen Philippa of Hainault's chamber ladies and a woman confident in royal circles; Jeanette's chaperone and tutor in the absence of Jeanette's mother

Joan Bredon
One of Queen Philippa's chamber ladies and Jeanette's particular friend

Lady St Maur
The lady with overall charge of the royal wards and children

Petronella
One of Queen Philippa's ladies

Henry de la Haye
A knight attached to Thomas Holland's household

Lionel
Edward and Philippa's second son, born in November 1338

William Montagu Senior
Earl of Salisbury, Katerine's husband and a close friend of King Edward III

Walter Manny
A senior-ranking household knight

Paen de Roet
A chamber servant of Queen Philippa's

Bernard and Armand d'Albret
Gascon nobles, father and son

John de la Salle
Falconer and yeoman servant to Thomas Holland

Duncalfe
Thomas's yeoman and manservant

John (of Gaunt)
Edward and Philippa's third son, born in March 1340

Donald Hazelrigg
A knight often in the company of Thomas Holland and later, outside the novel's scope, to marry Joan Bredon

Father Geoffrey
A Franciscan friar (imaginary)

Maurice of Berkeley
Thomas's superior and royal household knight

Hannekyn
A chamber servant in Queen Philippa's household

Isabel Holland
Thomas Holland's sister, mistress of John de Warenne

John de Warenne
Earl of Surrey and Warenne, a friend of the Holland family

John Crabbe
King Edward III's senior ship master

Samson
An archer belonging to Thomas Holland (imaginary)

William Burgesh
A royal household knight

Prince Edward of Woodstock
Eldest son and heir of King Edward III

William Montagu
Son and heir of William Montagu, Earl of Salisbury, and Katerine, his countess

Elizabeth de Montfort
William Montagu Senior's mother

Raoul de Brienne, Comte d'Eu
French nobleman

Thomas Wake
Jeanette's uncle, her mother's brother

Agnes
A chamber lady in the Dowager Countess of Kent's household (imaginary)

Ralph Stratford
Bishop of London

Mary
A servant in Katerine of Salisbury's household (imaginary)

Edmund of Langley
Edward III and Philippa's fourth surviving son, born circa May/June 1341

Maude Holland
Thomas, Otto and Isabel Holland's mother

Costen de Roos
Flemish knight (imaginary)

Godwin and Joss
Two more of Thomas Holland's archers (imaginary)

Edith
Mistress of Prince Edward of Woodstock

Robert Beverley
An attorney experienced in dealing with the papal court in Rome, representing Thomas Holland

Isabella of Juliers
Philippa of Hainault's niece and wife to John of Kent

Nicholas Heath
An attorney employed to represent Jeanette at the papal court in Avignon

Robert Adhemar
A papal cardinal

John Holland
An attorney experienced in dealing with the papal court in Rome, representing William Montagu

John Vyse
Another attorney employed to represent Jeanette at the papal court in Avignon

Clement VI
The Pope

Bernard d'Albi
A papal cardinal

Amerigo di Pavia
An Italian mercenary captain serving in Calais

Geoffrey de Charny
A French knight with a reputation for high chivalry

A guide to the places mentioned in the novel,
in order of appearance

Castle Donington
Jeanette's family caput and where the novel opens. The castle is no longer there, but the environs are now famous for motor racing and festivals.

Orwell, Ipswich
Where King Edward III embarked for Flanders and his campaign to conquer the French in 1338

Antwerp, modern day Belgium
Where King Edward III landed after sailing from Orwell and where the court spent some of its time

Ghent – modern day Belgium
Where Queen Philippa was domiciled while the court was in Flanders

Hertford
A royal palace not far from London

Reading

Another royal palace with an important abbey

Langley

Another royal palace often visited by the royal family. Now called King's Langley

Bisham

A family manor and mausoleum of the Earls of Salisbury. One of the places where Jeanette may have been incarcerated. Now a national sports centre and wedding venue.

Windsor Castle

Needs no introduction. Site of St George's Chapel and the Knights of the garter and many a tournament and moment of chivalry. Jeanette and Thomas were very familiar with Windsor.

Caen

French town seized by the English and where Thomas took Raoul de Brienne prisoner and set himself on the road to securing the funds necessary to his court case

Calais

Port on the French coast taken after a long siege by the English during the ongoing warfare with the French

Avignon

French city, home to the papal court at this time

Eltham Palace

Another royal home on the outskirts of London

Otford

A royal palace in Kent

Broughton

A village in Northamptonshire where Thomas Holland had a manor and where he and Jeanette lived in the early years of their marriage

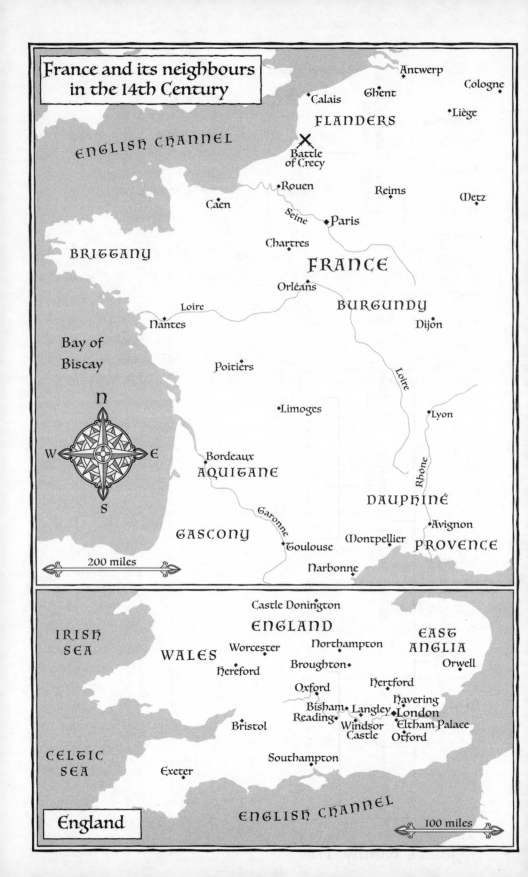

France and its neighbours in the 14th Century

ENGLISH CHANNEL

Calais

Antwerp

Ghent

Cologne

Liège

FLANDERS

✗ Battle of Crecy

Rouen

Reims

Metz

Caen

Seine

Paris

Chartres

BRITTANY

FRANCE

Orléans

BURGUNDY

Loire

Nantes

Dijon

Bay of Biscay

Poitiers

Loire

N

W   E

S

Limoges

Lyon

Bordeaux

AQUITANE

Rhône

DAUPHINÉ

GASCONY

Garonne

Avignon

200 miles

Toulouse

Montpellier

PROVENCE

Narbonne

IRISH SEA

Castle Donington

ENGLAND

EAST ANGLIA

WALES

Worcester

Northampton

Hereford

Broughton

Orwell

Oxford

Hertford

Bisham

Havering

Langley

Reading

London

Bristol

Windsor Castle

Eltham Palace

Otford

CELTIC SEA

Southampton

Exeter

ENGLISH CHANNEL

England

100 miles

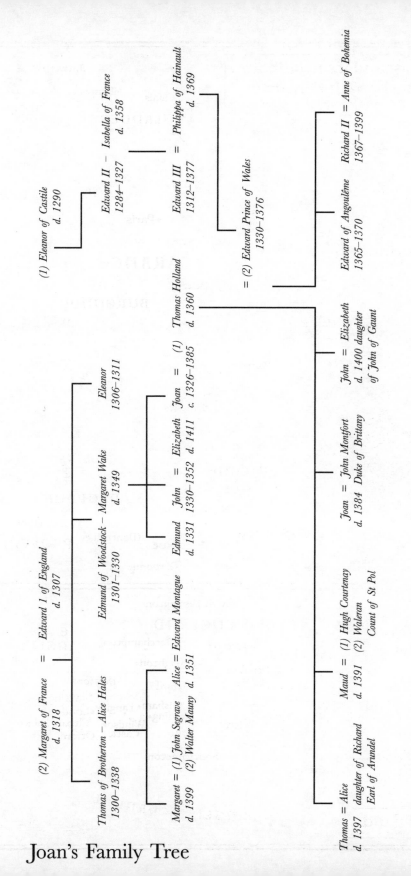

Joan's Family Tree

1

Donington Castle, Leicestershire, June 1338

Sitting at the river's edge, enjoying the sun on her face, Jeanette was watching Grippe hunting water voles among the reeds when she heard her brother's shout, and turned to see him running towards her.

The terrier splashed over to greet him, whiskered muzzle dripping, and John fended him off with laughing protests. 'Mother's looking for you,' he announced.

Jeanette observed the antics of dog and boy, her amusement edged with irritation, although not at either of them. 'What does she want now?'

John shrugged his narrow shoulders. 'Things to do with returning to court and crossing the sea. She's not happy you gave your maids the slip.'

Jeanette rolled her eyes, knowing she would be lectured on her appearance, her deportment, her attitude. *Walk don't run. Think before you speak. Listen to your tutors and your elders. Don't stare. Don't be so forward. Remember the duty to your blood, and to your father's memory. Remember you are royal.* Every time she came home from court it was the same. She always hoped it would change, but it never did.

'I wish I was going to Flanders.' He was nine years old to her twelve, and eager for adventure.

Jeanette tossed her head, irritated by his envy. 'You'll be in Prince Edward's household with your friends and training with weapons. You'll be allowed to go riding and camping while I'll be cooped up sewing with the women.' All under the watchful gaze of the ladies of the court, including Katerine, Countess of Salisbury, who was her mother's close friend and whom Jeanette heartily disliked.

'But you will be crossing the sea on the King's own ship and seeing new things!'

There was that, Jeanette conceded, although how much of Antwerp she would actually encounter was another matter. Queen Philippa was expecting her fourth child in the late autumn, and would keep to her chamber even if she did entertain guests. Opportunities to roam further afield would be few, unless they were clandestine – Jeanette had developed a certain expertise at absconding when driven by the desperation of boredom.

Sighing, she stood up and shook out her skirts. Grippe immediately sprang at her, leaving two perfect muddy paw-prints at knee-height on the pale rose velvet.

'Hah, you're in trouble now.' John grinned, although without malice.

'When am I not in trouble with Mama?' Jeanette said impatiently, and with a sinking stomach, turned back to the castle.

John darted in front of her and practised running backwards. 'She's proud of us and scared for us – that's all. She wants us to do well.'

'Then she will forever want, because I always disappoint her.'

'She's just worried about you.'

Jeanette eyed his earnest, bright face and shook her head. Perhaps their father's execution ten days before his birth, and the uncertainty and hardship of house arrest in the months afterwards, had imprinted upon his being and given him a different insight. As far as Jeanette was concerned, her mother's worry was all about the family lineage and reputation, not her daughter's well-being.

Jeanette often imagined herself as a caged hawk, eager to fly but thwarted by the conventions of her sex and the expectations of her rank as the daughter of a prince and cousin to the King. Next thing they'd be marrying her off to some flabby old baron as a sweetener to a peace treaty or a pact of war. She knew how it worked and wanted no part of it.

On her return from court a fortnight ago, she had been desperate to run to her mother, hug her warmly and be hugged in return, to have that contact and acceptance, but the moment had been as stilted as usual. Her mother's embrace had been brief, her fingers hard and thin, patting Jeanette's back, her kiss a cool peck, before she remarked how much Jeanette had grown and would need money for new gowns. In the next breath she had been asking how her lessons were progressing. It was about appearance and achievement, nothing of the heart.

Stiff with apprehension, Jeanette beat at her stained skirts to no avail, tucked a wayward strand of thick blonde hair inside her coif, and approached her mother's chamber.

Margaret Wake, Dowager Countess of Kent, widow of Edmund, Earl of Kent, uncle to the King, was poring over account ledgers with her clerk, two deep frown lines scored between her brows. Glancing up at Jeanette's arrival, she pursed her lips, her taut expression more eloquent than words. She dismissed the clerk with a brisk command, and after he had bowed from the room and closed the door, she regarded the paw-prints smirching Jeanette's velvet skirts and sighed.

'It's nothing,' Jeanette said defensively. 'They will brush out.'

'It is not "nothing",' Margaret snapped. 'That velvet cost seven shillings an ell. We are not made of money – and are those grass stains? For a certainty they will not brush out!'

Jeanette pressed her lips together and stared at her feet, feeling mutinous.

'You must learn to be responsible for your possessions and your expenditure,' Margaret said with exasperation. 'You are of an age now to marry. Certain standards are expected of any bride that joins a family. I do not want to hang my head in shame at your behaviour. Your actions reflect on me, and also back to your father, God rest his soul.'

Jeanette blinked hard. She wanted to love the memory of her father, not have it used as a constant rod for her back. Her every action was measured against propriety these days. She had a vivid memory of playing at hobby horses with her brother and Prince Edward, and being told it was no longer seemly for her to straddle a pole – that she must be a lady, not a hoyden. Protests had been met with a day of bread and water, and the fierce, thin pain of a willow rod across the tender palms of her hands. It wasn't fair; nothing was fair. And she certainly didn't want to marry anyone.

'You might have a position at court, but it costs silver from my coffers to equip you. That money is hard won by my toil, and not yours to fritter.'

Jeanette looked up. 'I do not fritter!'

Margaret's stare was relentless. 'You would improve matters by not running wild with the dogs, letting them jump all over you, and by not riding through thickets, losing your headdress and tearing your sleeves. There is a difference between being lively and being wayward.' Her mother's frown deepened. 'What am I to do with you? You pass the time of day with kitchen maids and servants as if it is an acceptable thing for a lady to do. Yesterday I found you sitting with the bee-keeper, licking honey from the comb and letting it drip all over your clothes.'

Jeanette jutted her chin. 'I wanted to learn about the bees,' she said. 'A lady should know about such management.'

'Do not be impertinent with me,' Margaret said frostily. 'You went out riding with your merlin earlier this week – astride, with only a single groom for company – the youngest one and no fit escort. Have you no sense of propriety? You are becoming a woman and it is neither safe nor respectable to behave in such a wise. In faith, daughter, you make my head ache. How is it that I can manage the affairs of an earldom and yet find it so difficult to deal with you?'

Jeanette sent her mother a resentful look. 'I know what is set upon me, mother. I am good at my lessons. I can read anything you ask of me in French and English, and even Latin – *anything* – and understand it well. I know animal husbandry and estate management. I can curtsey to match any woman at court and play chess to rival any man. Why not praise me for those things?' A lump was growing in her throat, tight and painful, attached to her heart. 'I'll never be good enough for you to accept me, will I?'

'It is not a matter of being good enough,' Margaret said, her knuckles blenching. 'Until you heed the rules and boundaries of your sex and your position, all the learning in the world will avail you nothing.' She rubbed her temples. 'Why do you not understand? You are coming to womanhood and men are beginning to look at you in that light. It is not meet to smile at them and flirt, for it will encourage them to take liberties that will sully your reputation and mine.'

Jeanette folded her arms, pressing them around her body in a gesture of self-defence and defiance at the same time. There was nothing she could say or do when her mother was in this kind of mood. The words were like blows, and with each verbal slap she felt the sting and then the numbness.

Her mother sighed heavily. 'My first husband died in battle, when I was little older than you are now,' she said. 'Your father was executed for alleged treason a few weeks before John was born. I was confined at Arundel under house arrest, not knowing what would become of us. You had to stand as godmother at John's baptism because I had no one to turn to. I lost your brother Edmund when he was just five years old. What would have happened if I had spent my time in frivolity and running amok instead of doing my duty? Every day that dawned after your father's death, every breath in my body, every heartbeat, I was engaged in a bitter fight for your inheritance. One day John will be Earl of Kent and he has a position with the King's oldest son. You are being raised at court, in Queen Philippa's household. You are the King's cousin with a dowry of three thousand pounds to your name and that makes you a highly valuable marriage prize. You will not squander all my striving because you want to kick and rebel like a spoiled brat. People will look at you and see a girl who has been given too much liberty and has turned to wanton sin. Is that how you would repay your family? How can anyone take such wilful disobedience to their heart?' Running out of breath, a pink tinge in her cheeks, Margaret pressed her hand to her throat.

The moment hung between mother and daughter like a bloody sword. Jeanette dropped her arms, and the tightness that she had been containing inside her chest surged painfully upwards. 'Then do not love me, for I certainly do not love you!' she cried. Spinning on her heel, she ran to the door, fumbled the latch, and fled the chamber, tear-blind, furious, distraught.

Jeanette paced her chamber, wiping her eyes with a piece of scrap linen and sniffing. The initial storm, verging on a tantrum of grief and rage, was spent, cried into her damp bed pillow, but tears kept leaking, and her throat was still tight. She had dragged off her headdress and her thick blonde plaits were messy with wisps of loose hair straggling free, and she was still wearing her smirched gown. If she was a hoyden, then so be it. She would show her mother! But she didn't want it to be like this between them, and she felt horrible – sick and angry, and defiant.

She turned to the baggage bags and chests that were being readied for her return to court in the morning. Gowns and undergowns, shoes and two cloaks. Combs and veils. Cloths for her fluxes which had been coming regularly for six months now.

And the jewel box. It stood on the empty chest at the foot of her bed – a beautiful thing enamelled in blue and scarlet and gilded with gold. The finest work of Limoges craftsmen. In a moment of defiance, she had taken it from her mother's chamber and brought it to her own, for it belonged to her by her father's will. The father she had known but could not remember because he had been executed when she had been too small to have such cognition. But this – this box – at least was tangible.

She unlocked it with the golden key, also purloined from her mother's chamber, opened the lid, and gazed at the contents.

Her father's rings of ruby and emerald. A cross on a gold chain set with pearls and sapphires and crystals, various brooches, but most wonderful of all, a belt of embroidered gold silk, featuring an enamelled white doe on the buckle plate, with a crowned chain around the base of its neck. Jeanette had always loved this piece, and she stroked the image for a moment before restoring it gently to its designated place and closing the lid.

The door opened and her mother walked in. Her face too was blotched, but her eyes were bright, although that might be from the wine she always drank when she had one of her headaches.

Margaret's gaze fell on the enamelled box in Jeanette's hands. 'What are you doing with that?' she demanded.

Jeanette's cheeks burned beneath her drying tears. 'I am taking it with me. It's mine!'

'You took it from my coffer without permission – how dare you!' Margaret snatched the box smartly from her hands. 'This might be your father's legacy to you, but they are part of the estate and not to be worn frivolously. They are jewels for a grown woman who has accepted responsibility and position. When the time is right, you shall have them, but that time is certainly not now.' She opened the lid to inspect the contents and make sure they were all still present; then she snapped it shut and fixed Jeanette with a hard stare. 'You may think me harsh, but when you show me you are trustworthy, then we shall discuss the matter. Your father would agree with me in this, I am certain he would, for I was his wife, and you might be his child but you were barely in the world when he died – and that is my grief as much as it is yours.'

This time she was the one to leave the room, holding the box to her breast in a way that she had never held her daughter.

Empty now of tears, Jeanette turned to the waiting baggage chests and wished she was already on the road.

The next morning, Jeanette was ready soon after daybreak to set out on the return journey to court. She had an escort of two stalwart men at arms, her personal maid, Hawise, and a staid, middle-aged groom for the horses. The sunlit morning beckoned, drenched with all manner of possibilities as soon as she was out of these gates and away from her mother's scrutiny. The bridle bells jingled as her black mare tossed her head, as eager to be off as her mistress.

'Write to me, as I shall write to you,' Margaret said stiffly. 'I shall keep you in my prayers.'

'Yes, mother.' The words were easier to say from Ebony's back. They had barely spoken since the jewel-box incident. 'I will pray for you too.' The words sounded more like a retort than a beneficence.

'Remember your family,' Margaret said. 'Remember your lineage, and be humble before God.' She folded her arms inside her cloak.

Jeanette's brother lightened the moment with a gift, his grey eyes bright as he handed up a linen cloth, tied at the top in a rabbit's ear knot. 'Almond tarts for the journey,' he said. 'Don't eat them all at once or you'll get fat.'

Jeanette laughed. 'As if I would!'

'Hah, as if you would not!'

She made a face at him, but his gesture had lifted her mood. 'Be a good boy,' she said. 'Look after Grippe – talk to him about me every day – I don't want him to forget me while I'm gone. And tell Edward I shall miss him!'

'My word on it, sister.' He stooped to pat the dog leashed at his side. 'Grippe will be waiting your return to muddy your dress

9

again. And I promise I'll remember you to the Prince. Come back safely.'

Smiling through a sudden sting of tears, she blew a kiss to him and Grippe, nodded brusquely to her mother, and reined Ebony to face the castle's open gates and the road back to court.

2

Port of Orwell, Ipswich, July 1338

'You're being watched,' Otto warned his brother.

Thomas Holland looked up from securely stowing his baggage pack and cast a glance over his shoulder at the group of ladies who had recently joined the cog bobbing at anchor, awaiting the tide. The King was still ashore talking to a group of nobles, with Queen Philippa roundly pregnant at his side, but some of the ladies had been sent aboard to ready her quarters for the journey, including the girls and young women who were royal wards of her household, and the two little princesses, Isabelle and Joan, aged six and four.

Thomas was more concerned with seeing to the safety of equipment than paying attention to the women's flurry. He preferred to keep his distance, although the green livery of a household knight was a beacon when it came to being recruited to perform little tasks by the more formidable ladies in the Queen's entourage. They seemed to think that when not on active military duty, the King's knights existed to attend their every whim.

A party of older girls, flighty with excitement at the prospect of a sea voyage, stood in a giggling huddle. One in particular had fixed her gaze on him. She was tall and willowy, with a coil of plaited hair in mingled tones of honey, cream and gold. When he met her stare, she held the contact for a long moment, before looking down, a smile curling her lips.

'Be wary of that one,' Otto warned, his tone amused but pointed. 'She's after you.'

Thomas shook his head, smiling, but unsettled by the girl's candid regard. He resumed his own concerns, but remained aware of her scrutiny. If she was with the royal party and among the Queen's women, then she was of high status, and therefore a dangerous prospect. More giggles flurried his way, and a louder shriek of laughter, followed by a sharp rebuke from one of the older ladies that resulted in semi-silence, punctuated by muffled titters.

'Don't worry, I'm not going to play with fire,' he said. 'There will be plenty of women in Antwerp without becoming embroiled with one of the royal wards.'

'Henry says he knows a drinking house where they will take out their combs for three groats.' Otto nodded at one of the other young knights, currently out of earshot. 'Imagine lying with a woman with her hair down and her legs up round your waist.'

Thomas could more than imagine. He had enjoyed several such encounters on the recent Scottish campaign, including one in Berwick that still gave him sinful dreams. Otto hadn't been with him then. 'Best keep your mind above your balls until we get there,' he said, and nodded towards the gangway. 'Here are the King and Queen.'

At Lady Katerine's sharp rebuke, Jeanette tore her gaze from the handsome, raven-haired knight. Her stomach was fluttering and she felt the urge to giggle even more and had to clap her hand over her mouth.

She was saved from herself by a fanfare of trumpets as King Edward and Queen Philippa boarded the cog with the rest of the Queen's entourage. Jeanette dropped in a deep curtsey, her skirts creating a pool of tawny silk on the decking. She dared an upwards glance. The royal couple wore garments dripping with jewels and embroidery. The Queen's gown was loosely cut to encompass her pregnancy and she walked with care, but she had a smile for everyone and an adoring look for her tall husband with his straight, fierce nose and keen blue eyes.

A cushioned, luxurious shelter awaited her behind the mast, protected from the wind and waves by a decorated canvas cover. Once she had been escorted within and settled in comfort, the King kissed her hands and departed to his own ship, for it was unwise for them both to embark on the same vessel, even if the weather was set fair and the voyage only a day and night's sail. Their son and heir, ten-year-old Edward, was remaining behind as a ruling figurehead guided by counsellors until their return.

Jeanette was delighted that the knight she had been admiring was staying aboard their own cog as part of the Queen's guard. Several other girls were eyeing him too, whispering behind their hands while the older women were distracted seeing to their royal mistress.

Beneath Jeanette's feet the cog shuddered as the crew loosed her mooring ropes and raised her anchor. Like a horse released from its halter, the ship bucked and pranced on the tidal drag. The Queen's chaplain stood at the prow, voice and staff raised in blessing, exhorting God to grant them a safe, swift passage.

Jeanette crossed her breast and momentarily forgot the knight as she absorbed the new experience of leaving dry land. A stiff breeze blew a belly into the striped sail, turning it into an ale-drinker's paunch, and above it at the pinnacle the lions of England rippled out, fierce gold, tongued with long red streamers. The waves slapped beneath the cog's strakes and burst white spume against her sides.

Jeanette detached herself from her companions, suddenly irritated by their laughter and shrieks as the cog bowed to the waves. Going to stand at the side on the upper deck, she watched the vista change as they furrowed through the greater waves of the open sea. She didn't want to be confined inside the deck shelter with the other ladies. She could sit on a footstool and gossip any time, but this was her first sea crossing and the experience tugged at her soul. She wanted to remember this for the rest of her life.

The port shrank to a vista of tiny buildings standing on a hemmed colour block of ruffled blue and green. Jeanette lifted her face to the wind. This was what it was. This was how it felt. Absorbing every sensation through her young body, she relished the moment and laughed with joy when a larger wave buffeted the ship, sending up a sparkle of silver spray. The horse was energetic now, eager to chase. When her friend Joan summoned her to eat and drink with the others, she didn't want to leave her position, but obeyed rather than face a reprimand. Once she had made an appearance and behaved meekly, she could escape again to her wave-watching.

She curtseyed to the Queen, to Lady Katerine, Countess of Salisbury, and to Mistress St Maur who had overall responsibility for the royal wards. Supposedly, eating dry bread would stave off the *mal de mer* as they sailed into heavier seas. Jeanette had noticed some of the ladies looking peaky, but her own stomach growled with hunger and she had to stop herself from wolfing her portion lest she attract censure. Nibbling daintily, she concealed her exuberance, and eventually, when everyone had finished, offered to throw the crumbs overboard.

'Let the servants do that,' Katerine said sharply. 'It is not your place.'

'Oh, leave her, Kate,' the Queen intervened, smiling at Jeanette with a sparkle in her eyes and handing over her own napkin. 'Do not throw into the wind, or it will blow back upon you.'

'No, madam.' Jeanette curtseyed, flashed Katerine a triumphant glance, and returned to the ship's side. Mindful of Queen Philippa's warning, she made sure to shake the cloths in the right direction. Now she truly had cast bread upon the waters.

In the corner of her eye she saw Lady Katerine beckoning her to return and considered ignoring her, but eventually complied because it wasn't worth the scolding she would receive otherwise. As she turned, a boisterous wave smacked the ship's prow. Caught off balance, she staggered, and would have fallen except for the support of a firm hand under her elbow.

'Steady, demoiselle,' said the raven-haired knight. 'It takes a while to acquire sea-legs.'

His eyes were a rich peat-brown and his smile sent a lightning jolt through her body. 'I am all right,' she replied, flustered but determined to recover her dignity.

He released his grip and bowed, and when he stood straight, his expression was full of indulgent humour. Jeanette swept him a haughty look, and with head high, returned to the ladies, although inside she was quivering. A swift backwards glance revealed that he had turned away and was already going about his business.

'Come and sit by me,' Katerine instructed. 'It is unseemly to go wandering about the ship bothering others.'

'I stumbled, that is all,' Jeanette defended herself. 'I wasn't "wandering" and I wasn't bothering anyone.'

'No, but you lingered when you should have returned immediately. You must learn decorum.'

Jeanette puffed out her cheeks to show what she thought and received a prim glare.

Queen Philippa called for one of her ladies, Petronella, to read from a book of romances – an Arthurian tale of a grand tournament held to find the most valiant and chivalrous warrior in the land. As Jeanette listened, her imagination made the hero into the knight who had caught her arm to steady her, and her heart filled with a hollow yearning.

The wind freshened and the motion of the ship became frisky as they approached the mid-crossing. Jeanette listened to the creak of the ropes and timbers, the shouts of the sailors, and wished she could run up the rigging to the lookout platform where the banner flew. Lady Katerine started to turn green and had to go and lie down. Unaffected, Jeanette turned to her friend Joan Bredon, who was two years older than she was and knew a great deal about everything, and enquired nonchalantly about the knights sailing with them.

'I know the one you are really asking about,' Joan said, not in the least fooled, and shook her head as Jeanette started to protest. 'You would be wise to leave him well alone.'

'If you know his reputation, then you must know his name,' Jeanette persisted.

Joan rolled her eyes. 'If you have to be curious, he is Thomas Holland, one of the sons of Robert Holland of Thorpe. The fairer one with him is his brother, Otto.'

'Why would it be wise to leave him alone?' The idea that this Thomas Holland might be dangerous sent a delicious shiver up Jeanette's spine.

'Because your rank is far above his and the King will want to arrange your marriage for advantage to the crown.'

Jeanette sniffed in disgust. 'That's exactly what my mother would say. It's not as though I'm about to marry him!'

'Even more reason to keep your distance!' Joan leaned in closer and lowered her voice. 'His father betrayed his sworn lord, Henry of Lancaster. He was supposed to come to his aid in battle and he stayed at home instead. The King pardoned him all past transgressions, but his enemies bided their time, and they ambushed and beheaded him for his want of loyalty.'

Jeanette thought of her own father who had also been executed, caught out by the shifting sands of court politics. She had been too young to remember him, but she had been told the story, and knew he had been wronged. She didn't judge – she had learned not to believe everything she was told. Besides, a child was not its parent, God forbid. People always had their reasons for what they said and few were pure of intent. 'But he is a household knight,' she said. 'He's guarding the Queen, so King Edward must trust him.'

'He and Otto have proven themselves in loyalty and battle,' Joan replied, 'but you should still keep your distance. Being loyal to the King and fierce fighters does not mean they are like lap dogs. Imagine wolves instead.'

Joan's warning only stoked Jeanette's interest, not least because she and Thomas Holland shared a common bond regarding the fate of their fathers, and she could add sympathy for him to her curiosity. The notion of him being untamed was an intrigue, not a deterrent.

The sun set behind their ship and the moon rose in a broken silver path across the sea. People wrapped themselves in their cloaks and went to sleep. Jeanette dozed, but could not settle for her mind was still buzzing like a midsummer hive, and eventually she rose and tip-toed from the deck shelter. The sea had calmed from its earlier choppiness and was an undulating black glint. The heavens were an endless vista of stars, and she felt herself expanding to join all that space. This was what mattered in the world; this was beauty, this was God – not that deck shelter of petty rules enclosing the mounds of sleeping women amid aromas of wine and vomit.

In the darkness a shape moved quietly to join her, and she gasped in alarm before she recognised the knight she now knew as Thomas Holland.

'Mistress, should you not be soundly asleep with the Queen's ladies?' he asked, his voice pitched low.

She heard the soft clink of his sword hilt against its fixings and the faint creak of leather. The feel of him so close raised the hair on her nape and she had to strive to control her voice. 'Are you going to send me back there?'

'I am not your guardian, demoiselle, but it is my duty to ensure the safety of all during the voyage. If you fell overboard now, who would know until the morning?'

'I am perfectly safe, as you can see,' she replied pertly, 'unless you think a sea monster is going to rise up from the depths and snatch me off the ship.'

'No, but there are far worse fates than sea monsters, mistress, believe me.'

She shivered, feeling his breath against her cheek, but she wasn't afraid. The sensation was as new and exquisite as the voyage itself. Lady Katerine was always warning her about worse fates, although she was never specific as to what they might actually be. 'No one will harm me on this ship,' she said. 'Their lives would be forfeit – a single scream would be enough.'

'You would not have time to scream,' he answered. 'You are fortunate that I am honourable and diligent in my duty.'

Unable to think of a fitting retort, Jeanette lifted her gaze to the night sky. 'Why would anyone want to sleep rather than see and feel all of this?' she asked. 'One is being alive; the other is not.'

'True,' he said, after a hesitation, and leaning beside her, loosely clasped his hands. 'Have you sailed before?'

'Only on rivers and inshore,' she said. 'But this is like riding a horse – a wild one. Have you, sir?'

'Many times, demoiselle, enough that I would rather roll myself in my cloak and value sleep above novelty. But you remind me of that first sense of wonder, and you are right about riding wild horses – although I wouldn't encourage it on land,' he added with a smile in his voice. He straightened and stood with legs planted to keep his balance. 'But sleep is also a necessary thing. You should bid me goodnight, and return to the ladies, for whether you are safe or not, you will be reprimanded if they find you gone.'

She gave an uncaring shrug. 'I am always being scolded for this or that. I shall tell them that I wanted to be sick, and better over the side than in their shelter.'

He gave an amused grunt. 'You have a good excuse at hand, but in truth, I cannot go to my own slumber unless you are safe with the other ladies, for it is my sworn duty, and I am sure you would not want me to be wakeful the night long.'

His tone was light and teasing, but it kindled a flame in the pit of her belly. 'No,' she said untruthfully. 'I would not want to be the cause of that.'

She remained a few moments more beside him to make the point that she could stay as long as she wanted, but he was right, and since he was being courteous rather than issuing a blunt command, she was more disposed to cooperate. 'Then I will bid you goodnight, messire, and I shall sleep well, knowing you have my best interests at heart.'

'Demoiselle,' he said, bowing.

Returning to the women's shelter, she eased in beside Joan, who was awake.

'Where have you been?' Joan hissed.

'Nowhere,' Jeanette whispered in reply. 'I felt sick, and did not want to wake everyone or make more of a stench than there is.'

'Really?' Joan's voice was sceptical.

'Girls, hush, what are you gossiping about?' Katerine's head rose off her pillow. 'Jeanette, I might have known. Be silent, you will wake the Queen.'

Jeanette murmured an apology, but under the blanket stuck out her tongue in Katerine's direction.

She thought it would take an age to fall asleep, but slumber washed over her in swift, smooth undulations with the motion of the ship, and in moments she had left the world.

Thomas returned to his own part of the deck, for, as he had said, he was not her keeper. That was up to the women. The passion with which she had spoken about experiencing the voyage rather than sleeping had, however, surprised him, for he would not have expected such a profound thought to occupy the head of a flighty young girl, and she was indeed flighty, no doubt of that – but so very alluring.

Otto was dozing, arms folded behind his head, but cocked an eye at his return. 'You were gone a while.'

'One of the Queen's damsels was out of the nest – watching the stars if you please – never been to sea before.' Thomas unhooked a leather wine bottle from a peg on the ship's side and took a swig before telling Otto what she had said.

'This was the one who was watching you earlier?' Otto accepted the bottle from Thomas and put it to his own lips.

Thomas sat down and drew his cloak over his long legs. Earlier, judicious enquiry had informed him that she was the King's cousin, daughter of Edmund of Woodstock and a considerable marriage prize. 'Yes, but I only happened on her – it wasn't an assignation if that was what you were thinking.'

Otto passed the bottle back to him. 'No, you wouldn't be so stupid when we are clawing back our family's reputation,' he said pointedly. 'What was she doing wandering the ship in the dark?'

Thomas adjusted himself to a more comfortable position. 'She wasn't "wandering the ship", she was standing at the side to take it all in. She made me remember what it was like to experience something for the first time and to be full of wonder at the world.'

Otto snorted. 'Well, that is fine for a squire, but not for a royal ward. Mark me, she has the potential to cause trouble.'

Thomas said nothing. He liked high spirits in anything, be it horse or falcon, man or woman. In girls of her age and status, the flame was fleeting, stamped out by life's brutal practicalities, but he sensed an underlying tenacity in her. A bright, fiery lack of compliance. He recognised the danger, but as a soldier he lived with danger and balancing risks every day of his life. The trick was not to fall. Otto was right: she did indeed have the potential to cause trouble – and that made him smile.

3

Antwerp, Flanders, July 1338

In the house where the royal family were lodging, having arrived in Antwerp earlier that day, Jeanette sat with her maid, Hawise, and Joan Bredon listening to a musician singing a lai of King Arthur and felt irritated when Lady Katerine ordered them to retire to bed. The story had just reached the part where Sir Gawain had arrived at the castle of the Green Knight. Jeanette knew the tale by heart, but was always enthralled by the clandestine, forbidden kiss between Gawain and the Green Knight's lady – the perfect knight resisting the ultimate temptation, until brought to the point of his downfall by a beautiful woman. However, it was useless to argue with Lady Katerine who was still in a sharp and queasy mood after their crossing, especially when Lady St Maur was backing her up.

They were lodged in a fine house by the river while more permanent quarters were made ready and the royal household was cramped together in more proximity than usual, although the soldiers were camped under canvas in nearby orchards.

Jeanette, Joan and Hawise left their places, curtseyed goodnight to the gathering, and climbed the simple ladder stairs to their sleeping quarters on the floor above which had a trap door that could be bolted to increase the women's security. The King and Queen were housed in a more luxurious chamber on the other side of the building.

A series of pallets stuffed with straw lay the length of the room, each one covered by a linen sheet, with a blanket folded on every bed. It was hardly the height of luxury, but Jeanette was accustomed to such when travelling, and this was only for a night or two.

Without space for major disrobing, the girls helped each other to remove their shoes and outer gowns, and loosened each other's laces. Hawise helped Jeanette to take the gold pins from her hair and softly plaited it for comfort. A swift wash of hands and face, a prayer to God and His Holy Mother, and it was time to snuff the candles.

Jeanette listened to the other girls and their attendants settling down. Joan was sneezing from the straw in her pallet. Petronella had an irritating dry cough. Jeanette wondered if she would be allowed to visit the markets of Antwerp with their interesting array of goods, many from exotic lands filled with strange creatures. Perhaps she would buy John a monkey, which she would train and feed almonds, or instead a green popinjay in a cage with a belled red collar around its neck. A fan of peacock feathers, a new hood for her hawk. Silk belts, hair combs set with pearls. She closed her eyes, imagining the stalls, and the cries of the street sellers. She saw a man balancing a tray of hot pies on his head. Indeed, they were so hot that they were burned and smoking from the oven, and as she tried to avoid their acrid stench, she awoke to Joan shouting in her ear and shaking her.

'Get up, Jeanette, get up! Quickly! Fire!'

She sat up with a jerk; the acrid scent of burning was real and powerful and she could taste smoke in her mouth. Some of the girls had begun to scream and cry out in panic.

Petronella ran to the trap door and yanked it open, but smoke roiled through the hole, and she reeled back, choking. Jeanette darted forward and slammed the door down, then turned back into the room, coughing hard, her heart hammering. Everyone knew about stray sparks in summer heat and how swiftly a small fire could become a deadly conflagration. Dear Holy Virgin, she wasn't ready to die with her life unlived.

'Enough of this!' Lady St Maur's voice rose above the wails of panic and distress. She banged a candlestick upon a coffer to draw everyone's attention. 'You are like a gaggle of foolish poultry. The next girl that screams, I shall slap! All of you, gather your things together, and return to me in good order. Quickly now!' She nodded to Katerine of Salisbury, who stood a little to one side, her eyes wide and lips tight. 'My lady, if it please you, will you unbar the window shutters?'

Katerine went immediately to work with her maid, ramming the latches back and drawing the shutters wide. The window arches were narrow, with perhaps just enough width in them for a person to squeeze through.

Jeanette hurried to her bed, swept her cloak around her shoulders and bundled up her gown, headdress and jewel coffer in the sheet, tying a knot in the top. Although focused and tense, she was not terrified, but instead was filled with a strange, fierce exhilaration. Several girls were weeping and stumbling about, foolish with terror. A sharp snapping sound came from the room below, and then a roar as the flames took hold of some object. Tendrils of smoke began seeping up through the floorboards, and Lady St Maur's palm cracked across Petronella's cheek with a savage admonition to stop screaming.

Jeanette darted to the windows and shouldered up against Katerine's maid, making room to peer down. Torches wavered underneath, where a party of soldiers had gathered. Someone had set a bucket chain in motion, and people were passing pails from hand to hand and beating at the fire with brooms. Several more soldiers arrived at a trot carrying a long ladder, and heaved it up against the window. One man climbed up while another held the base of the ladder. Jeanette twisted to look round and saw the thickening fog of smoke rising through the floor cracks, and the taste of smoke thickened in her nose and throat.

The soldier arrived at the top of the ladder and spoke through the window. 'There's a ladder to the ground, ladies,' he said briskly. 'You must make haste. I will come down beneath you, and guide you, but I pray you be swift.' He gestured to Katerine of Salisbury. 'You first, madam, if it please you.'

Katerine firmed her lips, but without hesitation and setting an example, she gathered her skirts, eased through the aperture and stepped out on to the ladder, barefoot. The soldier took her bundle and threw it down to be caught by one of the others. Her maid followed, and then two of the girls. Petronella backed away, shaking her head like a wall-eyed horse, until Lady St Maur roughly grabbed her arm, gave her a cuff worthy of a fishwife, and almost pushed her out. Her cries as she stepped down the rungs carried up to the other girls.

'Oh God, oh God, Jesus and His Mother save me, save me!'

Jeanette was next. She tossed her bundle out and squeezed through the window arch on to the ladder. It wasn't that far from the ground, little more than the ladders she had scrambled up and down in the orchards at Donington when picking fruit – work for servants, her mother said, and no place for a lady, but she hadn't cared a jot. Tucking her chemise between her legs and stuffing her shoes inside the top of the garment, she made her way down the shaky rungs with confident agility, and even jumped the last one to the ground.

Thomas Holland was standing near the base of the ladder and gave her a brief smile, although his eyes were already on the next lady descending. 'Bravely done,' he said.

'I'm not scared,' Jeanette said proudly, then flicked a superior glance at Petronella who had collapsed in a weeping huddle. God help her indeed if she ever had to face the fires of hell.

'I do not imagine you are,' he answered. 'I hazard you would pass any test.'

She could not tell if he was mocking her for his face was turned away as he helped Joan Bredon to the ground, followed by Hawise. Jeanette removed her shoes from her bodice and put them on her feet.

Holland gestured to another knight among the group. 'Sir Otto will take you all to safety.'

Lady St Maur was the last to descend the ladder, coughing, but still intrepid. Smoke drifted from the window above her like the trail of an autumn leaf burn.

Otto Holland opened his arms in a shepherding gesture. 'Come, ladies. We shall find you accommodation for the rest of the night. Stay together, stay with me.'

Two more household knights joined him to escort the women a short distance to an open area where tents had been emptied of soldiers to make room for the King and Queen and others displaced by the fire. The King had a comforting arm around his wife's waist, but Philippa's expression was brave and calm. One hand was cupped protectively over her womb. Nearby, her two small daughters sheltered under the wing of a nurse's cloak.

Sir Otto placed a cup of hot wine in Jeanette's hand, and as she sipped the steaming liquid, excitement fizzed inside her like small sparks. She gazed round, all her senses heightened. She had survived potential death and was standing outside under the stars at midnight, drinking wine. Some of the other girls were still crying, but they were milksops. Sir Otto escorted the ladies to the tents that had been made ready, and in due course took his leave with a bow, while another knight, Sir Henry de la Haye, remained behind on guard.

The girls gathered in their tent and chattered for a while. Jeanette joined in at first, but eventually retreated to the soldier's pallet that was to be her bed for the rest of the night. Stroking the coarse cover, she wondered what it would be like to be a knight and live like this, camping in the open, with all the perils and freedoms of being male. To wear armour and ride a warhorse through the streets, harness jingling, people casting flowers under her stallion's ringing hooves. Or she might not return from battle, of course, but perish in brave and tragic nobility. That particular notion, born of the tales that she had been hearing at the Queen's feet, felt romantic and poignant, with an aching sensation that almost brought her to tears, but at the same time held their own sort of perfection.

At dawn, the court moved to the guest house of the Abbey of St Bernard several miles upriver from the main dock. Jeanette was last into the covered cart, having wandered off to look at the devastation wrought by the fire. The King's soldiers and neighbouring households had eventually managed to douse the blaze, but not before great damage had been done to the lower room where the interior was pitch-black with soot and scorched half-eaten beams. That no one had died was being touted as a miracle. The fire seemed to have been caused by a broken candle that had fallen from a table into a basket of dry kindling and gone unnoticed as people retired to their sleeping quarters.

Gazing at the destruction, Jeanette's previous excitement was flattened by reality – how easily they could have suffocated in their beds.

She had seen the household knights from a distance that morning, breaking their fast in the open as the carts were readied to take the royal entourage to St Bernard's. Lacking sleep, filthy from their efforts, they were joking together nevertheless in tired but tight camaraderie. No glances were spared for the ladies; everything was business, and she was a little envious.

'Jeanette, come, come, girl, we've been looking all over for you!' Katerine of Salisbury raised her velvet skirts fastidiously above the puddled ground as she joined her. 'Why are you the one who always goes missing? What in God's name are you doing here?' Her sapphire eyes were fierce with censure.

Jeanette turned to face her frown. 'I wanted to see what the fire had done,' she said. 'I wanted to know.'

'Well, now you do,' Katerine snapped. 'Let that be a lesson to always check the candles – never trust the servants. Make haste, everyone is waiting – and hold up your gown! The laundresses will never be able to remove that mud.'

As if that was what mattered, Jeanette thought irritably. Katerine of Salisbury was reckoned a great lady and exemplar for the young girls in the household. She was beautiful in the glittering way of a hard, stone jewel, and as the mother of several sons and daughters had provided her husband, Lord William Montagu, with the required dynasty. She was an accomplished military wife, efficient in all things, and courageous, as she had demonstrated last night. Her husband was one of the King's closest friends and rode in high favour at court, as did

Katerine herself. Jeanette was wary of her, especially when she got that sharp brightness in her eye.

Sighing, she followed Katerine to the cart, and hoped their journey wasn't going to be long. She hated the idea of being cooped up with the other women like so many hens in a cage. She wasn't a hen and never would be.

4

Antwerp, Flanders, December 1338

The sun cast stripes across the frosty grass, glittering the silver with icy gold and gilding the pavilions of the lords and knights who had gathered to tourney in celebration of the birth, four weeks ago, of the King and Queen's new son, baptised Lionel after one of King Arthur's knightly heroes.

Jeanette had never seen so many depictions of lions in one place before. They decorated banners and shields and barding. People sported lion badges on their clothes and woven into the fabric itself, or embroidered on hems and cuffs and belts. There were hats decorated with lions, and garters and shoes. The wafer sellers and hot pie vendors were hawking lion-shaped confections and pastries, all to celebrate the baby prince.

The King had been absent from court well into the autumn, busy about the matter of gathering allies and raising funds to aid his war with France and seeking support for his claim to the French throne, but had returned to celebrate his son's birth and to spend the Christmas festivities with his family.

Jeanette sat in the stands that had been erected for the eager spectators. Her breath emerged in puffs of white vapour, but bundled up in her fur-lined cloak she was not cold, and extra warmth rose from the hot stones placed beneath the benches occupied by the Queen and her household with a clear view of the lists. A squire sent a basket of sweetmeats down the line and Jeanette selected and nibbled on a delicious morsel of almond marchpane.

She was tingling with anticipation, for although she had attended tourneys before at court, she had been younger – a child. Now of marriageable age, she could take part as an eligible damsel of the court. A basket filled with artificial flowers crafted from fabric and wire sat in her lap, ready to be cast at the heroes as they rode on to the field. Having spent most of the autumn cooped up in the Abbey of St Michael, attending on Queen Philippa while she awaited Lionel's birth, Jeanette's anticipation was as keen as a knife. Of course, she adored the baby. He was so sweet with his huge blue eyes and a coppery glisten to the hair beginning to grow on his little round head. She loved to hold him, sing to him and rock his cradle, but even so, there were many more things in the world to see and do that did not involve babies and sewing.

Occasionally, she had managed to escape when the older ladies were preoccupied with the Queen or too comfortable around the fire with their hot wine to bother about her, but she had had to choose her moments wisely and not abscond for too long, lest she be reined in and forbidden to go out at all.

Her greatest success was spending time in the mews visiting her merlin, Athena, which was at least viewed as being a legit-imate occupation. The small, creamy-brown falcon had been a gift from Queen Philippa when Jeanette was six years old, and she had learned the art of falconry and hunting with her. Athena had already been fully grown when she came into Jeanette's keeping, and she was overdue a new bird, but she remained fiercely loyal to the little merlin, and loved her with every fibre of her heart. She whispered her thoughts to her, her secrets and desires. Who she liked, who she didn't. How much was unfair and unworthy and boring.

Now at last with the King's return, the court was a different place, sparkling with danger and possibility. And a tourney was a magical thing – it was like the sugar pinnacle on a subtlety, and Jeanette was ready to devour every moment to the last sweet sliver.

A blare of trumpets heralded the parade of knights on to the field and she craned her neck to watch them ride past in their gorgeous array. The King led them out, clad in the red and snarling gold of England, trimmed with the blue and gold fleur de lys of his claim to the French throne. Heralds and squires, men at arms, accompanied him, their pike-tips flashing in the winter sun. The steam clouds rising from the horses made the array appear otherworldly. Indeed, some of the palfreys were decked out like unicorns with false golden horns twizzling from their brow harnesses.

Jeanette's heart swelled with joy. The knights rode past the stands in their glittering parade armour and the ladies tossed their flowers over them in a bright shower. She cast her eyes avidly over the procession until her gaze lit upon a jet-black stallion barded in blue and gold, a coppery chestnut pacing in tandem. Here were the brothers Thomas and Otto Holland. Half rising, she threw her lapful of flowers, and watched them tumble against the men's armour. One of the blooms caught between the mane of Thomas's horse and the rein guard, and stayed there, the same rich blue as his surcoat.

He looked up, found her with his smile, and her cheeks burned as he saluted her. Lips parted, she followed him with her gaze, until her stare was interrupted by a warning hiss from Lady Katerine, who waved at her to sit down. She obeyed, but had to tap her toes and wriggle, unable to stay still.

The ensuing sport was so exciting that Jeanette spent her time on the edge of her seat, and only the threat of being made to leave the stands for indecorous behaviour kept her from jumping up and down. The knights rode at each other headlong and she gasped at their speed and skill. Even if much of the display was theatrical, with many of the moves worked out beforehand between the men, it was a thrilling spectacle, and a huge element of danger remained as the horses thundered towards each other and the lances cracked and shattered.

Between bouts, the knights and squires displayed their skills at the quintain. There were wrestling matches and demonstrations of weapon-craft in front of the lodges, the blades flickering with the speed of summer lightning.

Her heart in her mouth, her hands clammy, Jeanette watched Thomas Holland gallop down the lists on his powerful black. The staccato snorts of the horse and the drum of hooves on the hard turf vibrated through her own body. He punched his opponent clean out of the saddle with a direct strike, and turned at the end of the tilt to canter back, dismount and assist the fallen man to his feet, making sure he was all right, and slapping his shoulder. The black warhorse stood as meekly as a lamb behind the men, but eventually shoved Thomas in the back with his nose, to laughter and applause from the stands. Thomas bowed to their audience, then tapped the stallion's shoulder to make him bend a foreleg and bow too. Then he leaped into the saddle and rode off to ecstatic cheers.

Jeanette's body rioted with overwhelming emotions she had no experience to name and she could not take her eyes from Thomas and his horse as they left the field.

He rode again several more times, taking two more opponents in clear victory and conceding a draw to Lady Katerine's husband William Montagu, Earl of Salisbury. The latter, in contrast to Thomas's light-hearted fluidity, sat solidly in the saddle, treating the joust as serious warfare rather than play. That Thomas emerged with a draw and unscathed was in itself a kind of victory, applauded in the lodges.

Thomas and his brother also demonstrated their sword skills to the spectators. The display, carefully choreographed, was still a dangerous dance, so fast that the blades were a silver blur. These were the elite young knights in the service of England's king. Highly trained, virile and ambitious, their talent was displayed not only as entertainment for the English court, but to show King Edward's Flemish allies how strong a contender he was for the French throne with men such as these in his entourage. Jeanette watched, enthralled. Thomas was elegant but powerful and as light on his feet as a swallow in flight.

When it came time for the Queen to present the prizes, William Montagu was awarded the accolade of supreme champion of the tourney, receiving a silver gilt aquamanile in the shape of a knight on horseback, and a bright plume of peacock feathers to adorn his helmet. His wife looked on, flushed with pride. Jeanette thought with partisan indignation that it was only because Montagu was an earl and the King's close friend that he had been awarded the prize. Thomas had been as good, if not better.

Nevertheless, the Holland brothers received a pair of engraved silver bowls for their sword skills. As they knelt to receive their reward, Jeanette noticed with a flash of excitement that Thomas had threaded her blue flower through a band on his sleeve. She watched him avidly for a look or a sign, but his attention was focused on the King and Queen, and then he and Otto bowed and moved on to make way for the next prize winner.

Jeanette would have rushed after him, but it was impossible, and anyway, she would not have known what to say. She felt giddy, as though she had been drinking effervescent wine, and once more received a sharp reprimand to sit still and behave, this time from Lady St Maur, her eyes narrow with disapproval.

Leaving the stands a short while later with the Queen's entourage, Jeanette walked across the frozen ground where Thomas had fought with Otto and felt a sudden sharpness under her shoe. Wincing in pain, she looked down and saw a small, shield-shaped belt pendant sticking out of the mud at a slanted angle. The piece was enamelled with the Holland blazon of a golden lion on an azure background. Her heart leaped, for it was a sign!

'What's that?' Joan asked her as she stooped to pick it up.

'It's a belt fitting,' Jeanette said. 'It must have fallen off during the fighting.' She closed her fist over it. 'I shall keep it for luck, and to remember this day.' And because it belonged to Thomas, but Joan didn't need to know that.

Holding hands with the little princesses, Joan on one side and Isabelle the other, Jeanette stepped with the household maidens in a round dance they had been practising for the pleasure of the King, the Queen and their guests. The knights had performed their part in parade and joust; now it was the turn of the court damsels to provide an entertainment.

Jeanette was a light and skilful dancer. She loved moving her body and adored music. No one called her to task, and her willowy grace commanded approving smiles. She wore her thick golden hair in an ornate braid decorated with a chaplet of evergreen and red berries. A red velvet gown clung to her lithe body. Her shoes were gilded green leather with lozenge-shaped cut-outs. Her white silk hose, fine as gossamer, were a gift from the Queen. The allowance she received from her mother did not run to such extravagance. Every now and again Jeanette flicked her gown to show a momentary peek of her ankle, embraced by the delicate strap of her shoe.

Dancing before the court, relishing the moment, she experienced a sensation of power. Thomas Holland was standing among a group of household knights and she tried to catch his eye. He looked up once, and smiled at her with impersonal courtesy, before tilting his head to listen to what a companion was saying.

The dance ended on a flourish of pipes, and the maidens swept curtseys and returned to their places on a wave of applause. Dishes of sugared fruit and nuts were handed round the tables, and a group of tumblers took their turn before the high table, juggling with balls, painted to look like golden apples. The young princesses were carried off to bed by their nurses, but the older maidens were permitted to stay a little longer. It was not just an indulgence of the season, but an opportunity for the royal family to display the young ladies – rare jewels in their wardship – as potential marriage partners for the right alliance.

Several women, including married ones, had gathered around the knights, eager to enjoy the presence of virile prowess. Jeanette watched Thomas laugh and flirt with the ladies every bit as much as they flirted with him. She fiercely willed him to look her way. At last he did, and, smiling, excused himself from the group and made his way across the room to her.

She inhaled the scent of rosemary and sandalwood from his clothes. His green household robe was different and newer, embellished with velvet. Pinned to his breast in a garland were several cloth-and-wire flowers that the ladies had cast earlier, including her own.

'Demoiselle,' he said, 'I hope you enjoyed today's sport?'

'Indeed, yes,' she replied. 'You are wearing my flower, the blue one – I made it myself.'

'Then I shall treasure it.' Gravely amused, he touched the little decoration. 'Which part of the tourney did you enjoy most?'

'Why, that you all survived, of course,' she answered pertly.

'Would you expect otherwise? The King has every faith in us.' His eyes sparkled. 'Do you think you could hold a seat as well?'

Jeanette put her nose in the air. 'I am a good enough rider, messire.'

'I am sure you are – in many circumstances.'

His words sent a delicious frisson down her spine, and an awareness of danger. For him, it was clearly a routine exchange of courtly flirtation, for she sensed his attention wandering and knew he was about to move on.

'You dropped this on the field.' She showed him the enamelled belt pendant.

He looked at the little shield on the palm of her hand, before folding her fingers over it. 'Keep it in exchange for a flower,' he said.

Jeanette clutched the pendant, the sensation of his touch tingling on her skin, and knew she was in possession of the greatest treasure in the world. 'I will always shout for you in the lists, messire.'

'And I shall be honoured to carry your favour, demoiselle.' He bowed, enjoying the moment. Another dance struck up, and although he had been about to make his farewells, he changed his mind and extended his hand. 'We should seal the bargain and dance.'

Her eyes opened wide, but she gave him her hand and let him lead her to join the other courtiers. To the music of drum, lute and pipe they moved side by side in a circle, sometimes hand in hand, and sometimes hand on hip. Thomas changed the step at one point, flicking her a conspiratorial glance as he crossed one foot over the other and back, nodding encouragement when she followed him. Then she surprised him into laughter by making a double step of her own that he had to follow. The circles surged forward into a tight knot like the centre of a daisy, and then back out again, becoming petals. As the dance ended on a shout and a clap, they were both alive in the joy of the moment.

Thomas bowed to her. 'Never have I stepped with a finer partner, demoiselle,' he said. 'Unless it be my brother Otto in the dance of the sword.'

Jeanette curtseyed, feeling hot. 'I know, sire, I saw.'

He lightly touched her elbow. 'I must attend to my duties now, but thank you for your company – I have enjoyed it beyond measure.'

She masked her disappointment by giving him a smile, both shy and mischievous, and made sure she was the first to turn away so that he would see her back and she would not see his. In truth, she could have danced with him for ever.

When she retired to prepare for bed, she threaded the little belt mount on to a blue silk ribbon and fastened it around her neck. The laughter and chatter of the other ladies sailed over her head. All she could think about was the dancing and the feel of Thomas's hand holding hers.

'Jeanette!'

She surfaced with a jolt to Lady Katerine's bark.

'Stop daydreaming, girl. The Queen commands you to comb her hair.'

She scrambled into her wits, and tucked the little shield down inside her chemise so that no one would see, before hurrying into the royal chamber where Queen Philippa was sitting on a chair, holding the freshly swaddled Lionel in her arms and lovingly fastening a little embroidered cap over his downy hair.

'Ah, Jeanette, come, tend my hair.' She kissed the baby's brow. 'Infants,' she said with a smile. 'They are so small for so short a time and then barely children for a moment before they are grown. I remember when you came to court with your brothers – such a tiny little girl with chubby legs, and those big eyes. Now look at you – taller than I am and a beautiful young woman.'

Jeanette looked down, feeling embarrassed.

'I want the best for all the damsels in my household.'

Philippa gestured for Lionel's nurse to take him and settle him in his crib and then pointed to her box of combs and unguents, indicating that Jeanette should begin her task.

Wondering if she was about to receive a lecture, Jeanette rose from her curtsey and came to stand behind the Queen. Philippa's hair was a blue-black mass of vigorous curls and she had to carefully work the comb through the waves, constantly dipping the tines in rose water and smoothing with a cloth to avoid ferocious tangles.

'The time is coming,' Philippa said, 'when you will marry, as I am sure you have been told by your mother and others. I hear you have bled every month for a year now.'

Jeanette swallowed. 'Yes, madam, but I am content in your service.'

'Of course you are.' The Queen looked round at her and smiled. 'And for now, I am content that you remain so. You danced beautifully for the court tonight, and your lessons are progressing well – other than your needlework.'

Jeanette chewed her lip, but Philippa's dark eyes were sparkling with humour. 'It is not given to everyone to possess that skill. You have many others for a husband to commend. You are quick to understand, you never panic, and you are always practical.'

She turned to the front again. 'It is true you are often heedless of consequences and far too headstrong, but you are young enough for that flaw to be adjusted before marriage.'

'Yes, madam.' So, this was a lecture after all. She had no doubt that Lady Katerine and Lady St Maur had found time to have words about her.

'Come, my dear, do not be glum,' Philippa said cheerfully. 'I have not summoned you to scold you, but to say that I recognise your talents and that your faults may be corrected with a little application. I was married when I was little older than you are now, and had the responsibility of a husband and a kingdom written on to the blank pages of my book. What will be written on yours and how you will embellish its worthiness remains to be seen. I want you to succeed, because then I shall have succeeded too, as will every woman in this chamber. You do this for others as well as yourself.'

The words entered Jeanette's being at a deeper level than Lady Katerine's scolding over trifles; she could not dismiss them in the same wise. They were an inspiration rather than fuel for defiance. Embroidery might be a lost cause, but she could work on other areas. She would do it for the Queen, not for her mother or Katerine of Salisbury. 'I do understand, madam,' she said. 'I shall try my best.'

'Good, then we have a pact.' Philippa turned again to give her a conspiratorial smile. 'You can come to me with anything, and I will listen, I promise.'

Jeanette curtseyed, her throat tight with emotion. She worked on until the Queen's hair lay in a thick plait, textured like brocade. Philippa thanked her and from a nearby basket produced two shining twists of teal-coloured silk ribbon. 'These arrived from a mercer today, and I think they will enhance the colour of your eyes.'

'Thank you, madam. They are beautiful and you are very kind.'

Philippa waved her hand. 'Not at all. Go now to your bed and sleep well, and we shall begin a new day in the morning.'

Jeanette curtseyed again and departed. Kicking off her shoes at her own bedside, she lay down on the coverlet. She now had two strands of thought to occupy her mind, twisting and shimmering like the ribbons. The one concerning Thomas Holland remained uppermost as she touched the pendant lying between her breasts, but as she closed her eyes she vowed that she would make a better effort to play her part in the household – providing they did not expect miracles of her sewing.

5

Monastery of St Bavo, Ghent, August 1339

Over the next several months Jeanette applied herself to her duties with diligence. The sewing was still a chore, but she improved sufficiently to set stitches in silk without ruining the work. She learned to bite her tongue and not to storm off in a temper, even if she had to clench her jaw and mentally pin herself to her seat while convinced of the idiocy of others.

She was still lively when dancing, and romped like a child herself when she played with the smaller children in the household – indeed it was a good excuse to run and release her pent-up feelings. To escape, she would walk the household's pet dogs with Hawise, and visit the mews as often as she was permitted to see Athena and train with her.

Lady Katerine still rebuked her for being too exuberant, and especially for being over-familiar with people beneath her rank, but her castigation became less frequent and Jeanette suspected the Queen's influence had something to do with it. Philippa often summoned Jeanette to tend her hair or rub her feet, and

rewarded her with little gifts and nuggets of praise. Three exquisite gold pins for her headdress. A new chemise of finest Cambrai
linen. A pair of red leather shoes stamped with little gold lions.
Jeanette adored them and twirled around the chamber, pointing
her feet, until she caught Lady Katerine's eye and immediately
assumed a demure pose, although she could not hide her smile.

The King was often absent about military and diplomatic
business. While the Queen held court and entertained their
Flemish allies with gracious audiences and discussions of coali-
tion over lavish meals, he was busy securing funds and
encouraging his supporters to stand firm against the French.
Jeanette would occasionally see Thomas Holland at court among
the knights, but after the Christmas tourney he had been busy
about his duties, and there had been few opportunities to speak
with him. The times he was in the household, their exchanges
were no more than swift words of formal greeting, pleasant
enough but distantly courteous. The lack of contact only served
to make Jeanette's feelings more febrile. When she caught a
glimpse of him her stomach would somersault and she would
stare without blinking, lest she miss a single moment.

Towards the end of a hot summer, the King assembled an
army of almost five thousand men and prepared to tackle the
French whose ships had been raiding English ports along the
southern seaboard and seizing English vessels. Queen Philippa,
pregnant again, spent much of her time in her chamber resting
with her feet on a stool, drinking restorative tisanes for her sickness.

One sweltering afternoon, she sent Jeanette, chaperoned by
Hawise, on an errand to fetch some flowers from the garden to
freshen the room. Jeanette begged spicy-sweet gillyflowers from
the senior gardener and softer-scented roses, marbled pink and
white, that she wrapped in a roll of damp napkin to avoid the
thorns. Some lavender too, for steeping. Jeanette waded among

the humming crowd of bees in the flowers without fear. She liked their industry and their furry striped cloaks.

She returned to the Queen's chamber by a meandering route to give herself a few last moments of freedom. Crossing a courtyard, she came by surprise upon a small group of household knights, among them Thomas Holland, polishing his sword and dagger. He had removed his green livery tunic and rolled back his shirt sleeves to reveal strong forearms, lightly dusted with dark hair. The sight sent a spark through her body and she had to pause and draw breath before walking forward, kicking out her skirt to show off her dainty red shoes.

Glancing up, he smiled. 'Demoiselle,' he said, 'what are you doing here, wandering with flowers? I take it they are not for us this time?' He gestured to his companions.

'The Queen sent me to pick some for her chamber,' Jeanette answered, feeling flustered but trying to project a superior air.

The other knights looked on, grinning.

'They are beautiful,' Thomas said courteously. 'I always imagine that heaven, should I ever step through its portals, will smell of such blooms. My mother is fond of them too.' He returned his attention to his sword where the steel already shone brighter than a mirror along the blade. She watched, fascinated, and he paused and looked at her. 'You should take your leave, demoiselle. This is no place for one of the Queen's wards – you do not want those flowers to lose their petals.'

'Then I shall bid you farewell,' Jeanette replied with a raised chin. 'And I shall keep you and your companions in my prayers, in hope of heaven.'

'That is kind of you; I am sure we shall all feel their benefit.'

Jeanette inclined her head, and turned away with a deliberate flash of her red shoes that also exposed a glimpse of ankle.

* * *

Thomas shook his head and grinned to himself as he resumed his polishing. The King's delectable young cousin was rapidly growing up. With the King intent on his campaign against the French, he was occupied daily with matters of organisation and quartermastering, and as often as not away from court. Preoccupied and busy, he had only noticed Jeanette occasionally from afar. His distant impression was that she had steadied as the women took her in hand, but obviously that streak of daring had not been quenched, rather it had gone underground. The way she had shown off her dainty shoes and flashed her ankle had amused him, but aroused a flicker of interest too – which he suspected was exactly what she had intended. However, he was no soft-bearded squire to dance attendance while she waited for her marriage to be arranged. Beautiful girls who dallied in the presence of soldiers on the cusp of war were playing a very dangerous game indeed.

The late summer evening still held the residual heat from the day. Jeanette had said her prayers and prepared for sleep, but she was not ready to put her head on the pillow and close her eyes. The other ladies were undressing, attending to their toilet and holding quiet conversations over hair-combing, sorting laundry, folding clothes, rubbing unguent into their hands. Clad in her chemise, Jeanette finished plaiting her hair and went to lean out of the open casement window to enjoy the air while her chaperones were distracted. People were still about, busy with their duties. With the army so close to leaving, there remained much to be done and servants and soldiers were constantly coming and going with supplies and messages. She watched the bustle, loving the energy of it all.

And then she saw Thomas Holland, walking in the late gloaming, with Blanchette, a white gazehound belonging to the

King. Usually, a kennel boy or one of the King's squires would have undertaken the duty, but this evening it was Thomas. He was absorbed in his own thoughts and had not seen her lingering at the window, where she should not have been lingering at all. Loath to lose a propitious opportunity, Jeanette called out to attract his attention.

He turned and looked up at her outlined above him, and took a couple of steps back. 'By my faith, young mistress!' he declared. 'Should you not be tucked up in bed by now?'

'What would you know of my bedtime, messire?' she replied pertly, pulling her chemise around her body and folding her arms.

'Very little, I admit. I would come and help you, my lady, but as you see, I have my lord's hound to walk.' His smile flashed.

'You need not concern yourself,' she said airily, brazening the moment out with more aplomb than she felt. 'I am well attended, I assure you.'

'Well, if that is indeed the case, I shall bid you good evening and may you sleep well.' He bowed. 'But I would close the window for your own safety.'

'What have I to fear with such loyal knights at my beck and call to guard me?'

'Not after tomorrow, demoiselle, for the King's beck and call are the command we all answer.'

'Is that why you are walking his dog?' she asked, half curious, half to bait him.

He shrugged. 'Sometimes a man needs fresh air to clear his thoughts, and what better way than this? The dog is exercised, and so am I. Once again, goodnight.' He walked on, the gaze-hound padding at his side.

Jeanette snatched the casement shut and pressed the palms of her hands to her hot face.

'Do not let Lady Katerine catch you talking out of windows to men at night,' Joan Bredon warned.

Jeanette puffed out her cheeks. 'I was only looking out for a moment and Messire Holland happened past with Blanchette.'

'Yes, but you called out to him – in your chemise, with your hair uncovered!'

'You are as bad as Lady Katerine!' Jeanette snapped. 'It is not fair that a man may walk alone with his dog at dusk, but if I did such a thing, I would be thrashed!' She was so annoyed at the thought of how unfair it was that she stamped her foot.

Joan looked hurt. 'I'm your friend – I don't want you to get into trouble and undo all your hard work. It may not be fair, but it is the way things are.'

'Well, it shouldn't be!' Jeanette retorted, but then went to Joan and hugged her fiercely before getting into bed.

'He is handsome though, isn't he?' she said after a moment.

'I suppose so,' Joan conceded, punching her pillow. 'But is he really worth all the trouble you'd be in?'

Jeanette let out an irritated sigh. 'Well, he will be gone tomorrow, so I won't know.'

The thought of not seeing Thomas again for months on end quenched her spirits like descending fog. Hanging out of the window for even that brief exchange had been worth every iota of the risk she had taken, and she didn't care.

6

Ghent, January 1340

On a sharp January morning, Jeanette stood with the rest of the court in Ghent's marketplace to witness King Edward being formally proclaimed King of France before a gathering of allies, burghers and nobles, both Flemish and English. Edward's new heraldry depicted the royal leopards of England quartered above the blue and gold lilies of France, the hierarchy designed to demonstrate the precedence of his claim through his mother's Capet line over the Valois French King Philip, who had occupied the French throne for ten years. Edward was determined to take that throne for himself, and this public display with his pregnant wife at his side was his proclamation of intent.

Jeanette had heard the rumours populating the court – that the King was in straitened financial circumstances, although it was hard to believe it from all this sumptuous array. She had been presented with new clothes for the event: an undergown of red silk hugged her new curves, topped by an open-sided gown of expensive blue velvet powdered with fleur de lys to match the new heraldry.

Edward, resplendent in his new livery, wore a fleur de lys crown upon his wavy golden hair. His household knights were all dressed in new garments and their polished armour glittered with starbursts of light. Jeanette sent a glance towards Thomas Holland; it was the first time she had set eyes on him since his return, and she felt she had grown up considerably during his absence on campaign. In her own estimation she was not only a princess, but a full woman of the court, and this ceremony served to cement that awareness. He, however, had not so much as looked in her direction or acknowledged that he was aware of her presence.

Following the proclamation of Edward's kingship, the citizens were provided with copious amounts of bread, meat and cheese, and the royal company retired to their own celebratory banquet. Queen Philippa had conceived the next royal offspring in the summer before her husband rode off to war, and processed beside the King, her well-rounded belly revealing to all the fecundity of her womb, and the powerful virility of her husband.

Jeanette enjoyed all the set rituals of the feast. The rose-scented water poured over her fingers from a jug shaped like a knight on horseback, with the water flowing out of the horse's mouth. The dainty morsels of fish and chicken, dabbed in delicious spicy sauces. Today was a momentous occasion to add to her collection of memories, like stringing bright jewels on a golden thread. Feasts were familiar territory, but not ones like this in such gorgeous array.

Between the various courses she took her leave with Joan and Hawise to visit the latrine. On their return to the room, Thomas Holland was talking to a duty guard, but paused to bow to the women.

'My ladies, may I say how fine you all look,' he said, and his gaze lingered on Jeanette as it had not earlier in the day when guarding the King. 'A man could easily lose his heart.'

Jeanette modestly lowered her eyes. 'I pray you do not, Sir Thomas,' she said, 'for I fear you would not find it again.'

'I think you may have the truth of it there, demoiselle. I shall have to be careful.'

'Indeed you shall, sire.'

'Will you ladies be joining the hunt tomorrow, or remaining with the Queen?' he asked. 'According to one of the huntsmen, a white hart has been seen, although the man might have been trying to please the King, knowing his interest in such tales.'

Jeanette's ears pricked up since she loved Arthurian stories too, with all their colour and drama. Several involved the presence of a mystical white stag. The one she had most recently read was that of Yvain, the Knight of the Lion, who chased one such beast to a magical fountain in the middle of the woods. It had not escaped her that Thomas's own blazon was that of a lion. 'Yes, we hope to hunt,' she said. 'Perhaps we shall be fortunate. Have you ever seen a white hart, messire?'

He shook his head. 'No, but it would be a sacred thing.'

She saw something in his eyes, deeper, more profound than superficial banter.

Otto Holland joined them, with Henry de la Haye at his side, and bowing to the women, he touched Thomas's arm. 'You are sought by Sir Walter,' he said. 'Orders from the King.'

'Ladies, my duty calls,' Thomas said. 'I must bid you adieu and wish you good rest tonight.' His lips twitched. 'Keep your windows shut against the night air and I shall see you in the morning at the hunt.' With a bow, he departed, and Jeanette followed him with hungry eyes.

'Dear God, Jeanette, you are playing with fire,' Joan warned in a whisper. 'Step away before you are burned!'

'Tush!' Jeanette snapped. 'I have done nothing wrong.'

Joan shook her head. 'I cannot stop you, but be careful.' She squeezed Jeanette's arm. 'Please.'

'Of course I will,' Jeanette replied, with barely concealed irritation. 'You are such a worry-wart, Jo. Nothing is going to happen, I promise.'

Joan still didn't look convinced, but some jugglers had just somersaulted into the room with a little dog wearing jester's bells, and Jeanette tugged her friend away to watch the entertainment, happy now that she had spoken to Thomas, and eagerly anticipating tomorrow's hunt.

Thomas eyed Walter Manny. 'England?' he said.

The knight leaned back on the bench and picked up his cup. He was Thomas's senior commander in the field and Thomas liked and respected him. Broad-chested and powerful with a sprinkling of early grey in his bronze curls, his eyes were shrewd and hard. 'Not for you and your men,' Manny said. 'The King is going to England to raise funds, gather supplies, and muster more troops for our campaign, but the Queen is staying here. She is close to her time for travail and must be protected. She will also stand surety to the Flemish for the King's swift return. Your task is to safeguard her and her household until further orders.'

Thomas dipped his head. He would have liked to return to England to see his mother and sister, but orders were orders and it was not a demotion by any means. Remaining to guard the Queen meant less jostling for position and an opportunity for his star to rise. Plus, the King's delectable cousin Jeanette would be among the Queen's ladies so at least there were some entertaining diversions in prospect.

Walter Manny smiled. 'The Queen likes your pretty face and your good manners in the hall, so you get the lap of luxury while we have to put up with living in tents and fighting over lodgings. Don't let looking after women dull your edge and turn you soft while we are gone.'

'Oh, I doubt for a moment he'll be soft!' someone quipped from the back of the gathering.

Thomas flushed but took the ribbing in good part; he would have trusted any of these men with his life. Manny's remark was ironically amusing too – in another life before promotion, he had been the Queen's squire and walker of her hounds.

'I will ensure the Queen is kept safe and untroubled during her confinement,' Thomas said, once the joshing had died down. 'My life is hers.'

'I know you will do a fine job,' Manny said. 'We have a few weeks yet, but you should begin preparations. The Queen is to spend her confinement in the convent of St Bavo, and you will need to organise the supplies, the guard rota, and liaise with the other captains. I leave it in your capable hands.'

The meeting broke up. Returning to the hall, Thomas found it empty. The revellers had gone and the fire had been covered. A few lamps still burned where people were bedding down for the night. He took an apple from a bowl on a table that was yet to be cleared, and eating it, sought his own bed.

In the clear early winter morning, the court prepared to hunt. Dogs circled the courtyard, panting, yodelling, yapping, tangling their leashes and tripping the less experienced handlers. Horseshoes rang on the cobbles and occasional sparks shot from striking hooves as the grooms fetched coursers and palfreys to their masters. Jeanette's black mare, Ebony, snorted and pawed, eager for the chase, silver bells ringing on her red leather breastband.

A young attendant waited to boost Jeanette into the saddle, but having observed Thomas Holland among the gathering, not yet mounted, she called to him. She had heard while dressing that he was not going to England with the King, but remaining to protect the Queen's household, and she was full of anticipation at the prospect of so many delicious opportunities ripening on the tree.

He walked over to her, the wind ruffling the pheasant feathers in his green felt cap. 'Demoiselle, how may I be of service?'

She sensed a degree of impatience in his delivery even though it was perfectly polite. 'I require your assistance to help me into the saddle,' she said imperiously. Turning her back, she lifted her foot to the stirrup. She was riding astride today, rather than using a formal chair seat.

'Of course, demoiselle,' he answered neutrally. 'Nothing would give me more pleasure.'

He cupped his hand beneath her shoe and she felt his strength as he boosted her up. Once she was mounted, she raised her skirt slightly. 'Is my foot secure? I would not want to take a fall.'

He shot her a look that she returned with fierce daring. He grasped her foot and the stirrup in his hands and stroked his thumb over her ankle. 'In my opinion, you are safe to ride as far – and as hard – as you desire.'

She stared down at him. Usually, he would be standing above her, and their reversed positions made her feel alluring and powerful. 'Thank you, sire, be assured I shall do so.' She gathered her reins, dug in her heels and flapped her skirt back into position over her foot so rapidly that he had to step back in haste. Thomas watched her ride off, and shaking his head, turned to his courser. His cheek stung where she had flicked him. He should take Otto's advice and leave well alone, for he knew he was licking honey off thorns. But when the honey was this tempting, it was difficult to resist.

He set his foot in the stirrup, mounted his iron-grey courser, Charbon, and trotted to join her. 'Be careful you are not unseated,' he said.

'Be assured that will not happen,' she replied with a flirtatious sidelong look. 'And if I was, I would trust you to help me. I can trust you, can I not, Messire Holland?'

'With your life – and mine should I need to protect and defend you, but that is not the sole part of trustworthiness,' Thomas said, his voice no longer smooth. 'Let me give you a word of advice. Those who tease sleeping lions are likely to be mauled.' He touched his hat feathers in salute, and rode off, judging that he had made reparations to his pride. Jeanette swallowed. A thrill ran through her body, part fear, and part response to his challenge. 'I will show you, my fine lord,' she said softly.

The falconers had brought the hawks from the mews on their cadges, including Jeanette's beloved Athena. Taking the bird on her gloved wrist, she gently stroked the mottled breast. The silver bells on her jesses jingled and her hood was plumed with blue jay feathers. Most of the nobles sported much larger birds. The King had a magnificent white gyrfalcon. Thomas's hunting bird was a strong female goshawk. Watching him gentle her and make soft kissing sounds, she imagined his fingers upon her in the same wise, and shivered.

They rode out into the countryside, and despite the sharp winter cold, everyone was exhilarated. Jeanette did not forget about Thomas, but her emotions became less febrile as she lost herself in the pleasure of the ride in the fresh air and the joy of flying Athena. She always imagined that she was airborne with her, and free to soar instead of being bound to the earth and convention.

The King was in fine spirits, especially when his gyrfalcon brought down a crane to loud acclaim, for while cranes were a common prey of the great birds, they were no victims and could kill in their own right with vicious stabs of their sword-like beaks. Athena, fierce and experienced, took two pigeons and made a creditable showing. She behaved impeccably on Jeanette's fist, unlike some that bated and shrieked, and one that flew off and refused to return to its owner's glove. Thomas Holland's goshawk made several kills, and then took time for a leisurely preen on her master's glove, alert but relaxed.

There was talk of the white stag that had been seen, but the King was not in a mood to chase deer, and the event was set aside for another time. Talk was one thing, locating the creature – if it existed – quite another.

They rode home in the late afternoon with dusk encroaching and a mist rising from the land in grey wraith-fingers. In the courtyard, a groom assisted Jeanette to dismount, for Thomas Holland had given his courser to his squire, his falcon to one of his staff, and was nowhere to be seen. Her mood dampened like the fog as she wondered if he had deliberately made himself scarce.

The Queen, burdened by her pregnancy, did not wish to eat in the great hall. Jeanette changed from her hunting attire into softer garments, and sat down in Philippa's apartments to dine with the other ladies. She was aware of the Queen observing her with thoughtful eyes, and as the attendants were clearing away, Philippa leaned towards her. 'My dear, the King wishes to speak with you, and I said I would send you to him once we had eaten.' She summoned one of her chamber attendants, Paen de Roet, and bade him to escort Jeanette to the King. 'Don't look so alarmed,' she added, smiling. 'You are not in trouble. Indeed, I think you will find what the King has to say very interesting.'

Jeanette curtseyed, eyelids lowered. Her contact with the King was of the passing variety. He would speak to her in the hall sometimes, and if he visited the Queen would include her in the ladies and make sociable remarks of small consequence. For him to summon her personally could only mean one thing, and she was not ready to hear it.

De Roet escorted her to the chamber where the King was busy with matters of administration. At the back of the room, his great bed bore a silk coverlet embroidered with the recent blazon quartering the arms of France and England. A few other nobles were attending him, including the earls of Warwick and Salisbury, and the usual scribes, messengers and envoys, among them a couple of Gascon lords.

Brought to Edward's chair by de Roet, Jeanette sank in a deep curtsey and bowed her head.

King Edward rose, lifted her to her feet, and kissed her cheeks. 'Cousin,' he said, 'come sit by me. Did you enjoy the hunt today?'

'Yes, sire, very much.' He settled back in his chair and she perched on a stool at his feet. 'I loved flying Athena, and what a sight to see your gyrfalcon bring down that crane.'

He beamed with pleasure. 'Indeed, it is not every day you see such a thing.' He crossed his long legs, encased in bright scarlet hose. 'And I noticed that little merlin of yours. You have some skill, cousin.'

'I have had her since I was a little girl, sire. The Queen gave her to me.'

'Well, your care for her shows.' He beckoned a servant to pour wine into two goblets of pale green glass decorated with smaller dots of blue. 'Now, then,' he said when they had each taken an obligatory sip, 'you may be wondering why I have asked to see you, but I think you may have an idea.'

Her throat was so tight she could barely speak. 'Yes, sire.'

Edward eyed her shrewdly. 'I have talked to the Queen, and we are both agreed on the matter of settling your future. If I am to have allies, I must secure the bonds of trust and friendship between us and I know you understand that necessity. That is why I have requested your presence and given you wine as a lady of the court, and not a child. I do not believe you think of yourself as a child, my dear. You are well grown and ready for marriage.'

Jeanette swallowed, feeling cornered. She had known this was coming, but her stomach still plummeted.

'I know you may be shocked, but you are the same age as the Queen was when we were wed, and you are just as courageous. I know your father would be proud of you.'

Jeanette took another sip of wine, and almost choked. 'Who am I to marry, sire?'

Edward glanced towards the two Gascon nobles. 'The seigneur Armand d'Albret, son of Bernard d'Albret. He is a fine young man of your own age. His father is an ally and keen for the match.'

Jeanette fought to keep the dismay from her expression. Gascony was somewhere she had often heard mentioned in conversation, but it was a distant place, far from the court, with a different culture and language. She might thrive on adventure and new experiences, but she had no desire to be an isolated, powerless bride to a youth she had never met. She would have no friends and little influence beyond that of a marriage contract. She might never see Thomas again – or her brother for that matter.

'I believe the match will suit you very well indeed,' Edward continued when she did not reply. 'We shall pursue the contract once I return and hopefully you shall be wed by the autumn.' He regarded her expectantly. 'I shall tell your mother as soon as I return to England.'

Jeanette gulped against the dreadful tightness closing her throat. 'Sire, I . . . I thank you,' she said hoarsely. 'I do not know what to say.'

He raised his brows. 'I see I have taken you by surprise. I am putting the negotiations in the hands of Sir Oliver Ingham, my steward in Gascony, for the time being, and until matters are settled beyond a doubt we shall not make a public announcement. However, I counsel you to prepare your trousseau, and make ready for your new role.'

Jeanette bowed her head, lost for a reply. She rose to her feet at his gesture. She could see others poised on their toes, ready for their turn to speak with him, and he was already moving on from their interview.

She knew she could not refuse; she was a sparrow tossed in a storm wind, wings over tail. She curtseyed, and took her leave, carrying herself with pride and grace until she was out of the door, but then grabbed her skirts in her fists and started to run despite Paen de Roet's shout. On and on, through corridors and cloisters, past the startled guards and into the raw January air, until her legs gave out and she buckled to her knees, a terrible stitch in her side. The enormity of what she had tried to outrun caught up with her like a gazehound on a hare, and she sucked breath after breath over her larynx, filled with a visceral revulsion so strong that it made her retch.

De Roet appeared, striding swiftly, and paused to lean against the wall and press his hand to his ribs. 'Young mistress, we should return to the other ladies,' he panted, and after a moment stooped to take her arm and draw her to her feet, clucking his tongue. 'This will not do, indeed it will not. What will the Queen say?'

Jeanette slowly straightened up and swallowed hard, still feeling that she might vomit at any moment, but trying to control herself, trying to think rationally. She would not wed this youth, whoever he was. If there was a way of preventing it, she would find it. Brides had to be suitable after all, and opening a nego- tiation was not the same as accomplishing the end result. 'Yes,' she said, and drawing a deep breath, looked into de Roet's anxious brown eyes. 'We should return to the Queen. And you are right that this will not do at all.'

By the time Jeanette returned to the women, she was composed, although she could do nothing about her blotchy face, or the soiled patches on her gown where she had fallen to her knees. The women looked at her askance and a few shook their heads in outright disapproval. Philippa dismissed everyone and commanded Jeanette to come and sit at her side.

'Well then,' she said. 'The King has told you the news.'

'Yes, madam.' Jeanette folded her hands in her lap.

'I see it has come as a shock, but it is a good match for you, and no reason to weep. Indeed, I should have thought to see you smiling.'

Jeanette's chin trembled. She could not have smiled if her life depended on it.

'You are of an age, and it is your duty, as well as one of the reasons you sailed with us to Flanders,' Philippa continued. 'It will be good for you to take responsibility for a husband and household, and you will be forming an alliance to benefit your cousin the King. You have it within you to be a fine consort and mother to strong children who will be a credit to your lineage.'

Jeanette almost shuddered. She didn't want to become a 'fine consort' in the mould they intended for her. What was fine about being sent to Gascony to wed someone she had never seen and be put to work bearing children and organising a household amid strangers? 'I do not want to leave you,' she said. 'The court is my home.'

'But you are ready to fly this nest and make one of your own,'

Philippa said. 'Come now, let us have smiles, not tears, and tomorrow we shall begin finding fine cloth and jewels for your trousseau. Won't that be delightful? This match means a great deal to the King, and it is your duty to please him and your family. You would do well to remember it.'

Jeanette retired to bed early and curled up in a ball, feeling miserable and trapped – and more determined than ever that she was not going to Gascony. There had to be a way out.

7

Monastery of St Bavo, Ghent, January 1340

In the morning, Jeanette's misery was compounded when, after mass, a falconer from the mews requested to see her. She recognised Thomas Holland's man, John de la Salle. He was in his mid-twenties with nut-brown hair and a close-cropped beard that glinted with red.

'My lady, forgive me for bringing you sad news, but your merlin . . . I found her on the floor this morning.' He held out a linen cloth folded in four, and drew aside one of the quarters to show her Athena's cold little body, perfect but lifeless. The chequered brown wings neatly folded, the legs furled, the fine skin closed over her once bright eyes. 'I am sorry,' he said gently. 'I know she was old, but I have also seen your love for her. She was a fierce, true huntress and she lived a good life. I have brought her to you, for it seemed wrong to just sweep her into the midden as though she was nothing.'

Jeanette's eyes filled with tears. She stroked Athena's soft breast feathers, and the top of her sleek head. 'Thank you for your kindness,' she said in a choked voice. 'I shall bury her in the garden.'

'My lady,' he answered, bowing. 'Again, I am sorry.'

Hawise saw him to the door and murmured something to him, and he answered softly in return, touched her arm, and was gone.

Jeanette fetched her cloak, and without begging leave of Lady Katerine, or the Queen, who was resting, went with Hawise to bury Athena in the small garden attached to the Queen's lodgings. She borrowed a trowel from a lay worker, took the linen bundle to a secluded soil bed where the earth was not iron hard, and dug a deep hole. She opened the cloth for a last look and watched the brown feathers stir in the breeze, never to fly again. She kissed Athena and covered her and placed her in the ground, feeling as though she was burying her own younger self; her hopes, her dreams. It seemed like a portent, coming as it did on the heels of the marriage arrangement. Tears rolled down her face as she filled in the hole and the soil covered her little merlin, who had once flown so clean and true, and was now weighted down and grounded.

When she returned to the ladies, the Queen had learned of Athena's death and extended genuine words of sympathy. 'We all understand what it is like to lose a beloved companion crea-ture, perhaps one we have trained ourselves, and that we have given our heart. I shall arrange for you to have a new bird from the mews. I know your merlin was especially dear to you and it will never replace what you have lost but you will need to hunt and it is time you move on, as in all things.'

'Thank you, madam,' Jeanette said numbly. The Queen was trying to encourage her to think positively about the proposed marriage, but her heart was so raw she did not think she would ever be happy again. Indeed, she felt as if she had buried that emotion with her beloved merlin.

* * *

A week later, on the Queen's insistence, Jeanette visited the mews for the first time since losing Athena. She was under instructions to choose another bird from those available, and although she was still heavy and sore from the loss, at least it was time away from the bower and all the sewing, gossiping and talk of marriage.

The slatted bars in the door and the window of the mews sent rays of diffused light into the hawk housing and the familiar scent of bird dung hit her, although it was not too pungent, for the mews was kept clean and the sand on the floor changed frequently. In the subdued light, birds sat on perches and blocks, the bells on their jesses tinkling. Some wore hoods and some did not, and perched keen-eyed, or preened their feathers. The falconer John de la Salle was present with a youth, clearly an apprentice. Thomas Holland stood with them, his goshawk Empress perched on his gauntlet, tearing into a gobbet of red meat held in his fist.

Looking up at her entrance, he smiled. 'The Queen mentioned you were coming to choose a new bird,' he said. 'I am sorry about your merlin – it is never easy to lose something you love.' Quietly, smoothly, he returned Empress to her perch and left her with her meal.

'I can never replace her,' Jeanette said with a pang, for this moment was another stage in being forced to let go.

'Nor should you, but if you wish to ride out to sport, then you must train a new one. I have some skill with birds, as does John here, and I think we may have one for you, but he is still young and he will take a little work. I suspect you are keen for a challenge though.' Their eyes met briefly before he turned to de la Salle and took a young male peregrine from him. 'Do you have your gauntlet?'

Jeanette nodded, and pulled out the thick suede glove folded over her belt. 'He is big for a male,' she said.

'Indeed, and well grown. He is coming up to a year old, so he will last you well, but he is still raw at the edges.'

Thomas placed the falcon on her wrist and the young bird danced and bated, wings flapping. Before she could take proper hold of his jesses, he broke free and flew across the mews, straps and bells jingling. Jeanette knew perfectly well how to handle birds of prey. Thomas was looking at her and she was hot with chagrin at her mistake.

'Bring him back,' she said. 'I will be ready next time.'

Thomas took a small, bloody piece of meat from his belt pouch and held it up in his fist. The young falcon launched himself, sailed to his glove, and attacked the meat, gulping it down, eyes fierce. Thomas transferred him to Jeanette, and she gripped the jesses firmly. Thomas gave her another morsel to offer the bird, and when the young peregrine had finished she gently covered his head with the hood Thomas handed to her. The falcon bated his wings, but not vigorously, and she held him and let him settle. As he calmed, something changed within her and settled too.

'You can have him back now,' she said to Thomas. 'I shall return to work with him every day for a little while so we may come to know each other.'

He raised one eyebrow, and she realised, mortified, that he might misconstrue her words as referring to more than just the falcon.

Smiling, he inclined his head. 'I have my duties – the more so when the King takes his leave – but Master de la Salle will be here if I am not and will assist you at need.'

He gently took the peregrine from her wrist, and although there was no physical contact between them because of the gauntlets, the hair still rose on her nape. They were standing in each other's space, and she inhaled the scent of his skin. He bowed to her and she gathered her cloak, nodded regally to him, and went outside, where she took a deep breath of cold air to clear her head before returning to the Queen.

Over the next few weeks Jeanette visited the mews every day to spend time with her new peregrine. She pored over books and treatises on training falcons and sought advice from all quarters, soaking up knowledge like moss soaking up rain water. The Queen, a keen handler of hunting birds herself, delighted in instructing her, even visiting the mews to see the new bird and commend her handling. She presented Jeanette with a gift of a supple white suede glove, decorated with a red silk tassel.

Sometimes Thomas was present and sometimes not. Jeanette lived for the moments when he was there. However, the flame of her infatuation, although still intense, was steadier and more grounded now, because they were both focusing on the birds and it was an area of mutual, serious interest and discussion.

'You are doing a fine job with him,' Thomas praised as the peregrine flew to her smoothly and settled without bating his wings.

She smiled, and fed the bird a morsel of meat. 'He is very fine. I am grateful to you and Master de la Salle for all your help and advice.'

'No, mistress, the work has mostly been yours.'

She flushed at the compliment. 'I am going to name him Frederick,' she said, 'for the emperor who wrote the treatise on falconry. I have been reading the Queen's copy.' She secured the falcon on his perch and stepped back to admire him.

'A fitting name, demoiselle. I was thinking that perhaps he is ready to be taken up on horseback and ridden out?'

Their eyes met in simple friendship. 'I would like that,' she said. 'Thank you.'

'At a time mutually agreeable then.'

The King's falconer arrived as they were leaving the mews, carrying his master's white gyrfalcon on his glove – a magnificent creature, fierce and proud with plumage gleaming like icy snow.

'Do you know the legend of Saint Bavo to whom this convent is dedicated?' Thomas asked.

Jeanette shook her head. 'No, sire, I do not.'

'He was accused of stealing a gyrfalcon and condemned to death, but on the day of his execution the missing bird appeared and flew down in front of his judges to prove his innocence; ever since, he has been the patron saint of falconers. It is said to have happened exactly where we are standing, and there has been a mews on the site ever since that time.'

Jeanette looked round, seeing their environment with new eyes. 'You have a veritable store of tales and legends,' she said.

'Everyone should. Stories stir men's minds, hearts and souls until they become part of it. And then they live in the tale and the tale lives in them – and both become immortal.'

His complexion brightened as he spoke, and Jeanette's heart flooded with warmth. She understood precisely what he was saying. 'Then let us have many tales of our lives,' she said, 'and let us be magical.'

He bowed to her again, and took his leave, and she watched him go with a new and tender feeling in her solar plexus. Hawise hurried to her side, for, while waiting, she had been talking to John de la Salle, and her own cheeks were pink.

Jeanette returned to the Queen with her mind in a dream. Her relationship with Thomas had changed as they worked together with the birds; she was no longer a silly girl ogling his looks and giggling with the other young women. They were well past that stage. He talked to her as he would to a grown woman of the court, and with the natural camaraderie of a mutual interest – as a friend. But it was more than that. It was like the tension in the air before a thunderstorm. Before the lightning struck the dry grass and set it ablaze.

That night when she prayed, she asked the Virgin and St Bavo to let her have Thomas instead of Armand d'Albret, and swore she would give anything to make it come true – absolutely anything.

'You know the King is planning his cousin's marriage to the son of Bernard d'Albret,' Otto said.

The brothers were sitting at a table in the guardroom after Thomas had returned from checking the men on duty and ensuring their diligence. Thomas's knight Henry de la Haye was with them.

Thomas poured a fresh cup of wine. 'Yes, of course. The messengers set out before he left. What of it?' He lifted the cup and drank. The King had departed for England three weeks ago, leaving the heavily pregnant Queen as surety for his return with arms and supplies.

'Tongues will start wagging if you keep on riding out with Jeanette of Kent.'

Thomas lowered the cup and gave Otto a hard look. 'I do not,' he said shortly. 'We have been out on horseback once a week at the most to accustom her new falcon to being carried thus. It's not ready to fly in a big hunt yet but they are doing well. And we always have an escort.' He gestured to Henry de la Haye.

'That is true.' The young knight lifted his own cup in toast. He was mildly drunk. 'I can say, hand on my heart – or any other part you wish – that nothing untoward has gone forth.'

'And you spend time in the mews too,' Otto said doggedly. 'People notice.'

'There is nothing to notice, and "people" should mind their own business,' Thomas snapped. Otto was treading on sensitive ground. What had begun as an amusing flirtation to while away the time had developed over the past weeks into something far more intimate and dangerous. He enjoyed her company, and looked forward to their rides together and the training sessions at the mews more than he should. He could not imagine her married to some boy in Gascony. The matter was not yet set in stone for the King baited many a hook to see what he could land, and would sometimes toss back the catch, but it was looking very likely.

Otto shrugged. 'I do mind my own business, brother, but I always tell you the truth as I see it.'

'Well, now you have.'

'I hear there's a new girl at the Gilders,' Henry spoke up. 'Yellow hair to her arse, and a grip inside like a wet velvet glove.'

Thomas refreshed his cup. 'By all means try her out then, but when talk flashes around about a new girl, she very quickly becomes not so new!'

'I'll take that chance.' Henry stood up and waggled his brows at Otto. 'Want to come, are you up for it?' he asked with deliberate innuendo.

Otto drained his cup. 'I'm always up for it! What about you, Tom?'

Thomas shook his head. 'I have duties to attend to,' he said, 'but you go and enjoy yourselves.'

'We will.' Otto slapped Thomas's shoulder. 'Don't get too staid and serious, brother. You need to keep your juices flowing, and better one of the girls at the Gilders than risking other kinds of damnation.'

Thomas rolled his eyes. 'Be gone. The only kind of damnation I have tonight is checking the stores to see what's needed and making sure the men on duty know exactly what that duty entails. You can tell me about the girl in the morning – if you remember!'

Otto made a rude gesture. 'At least I will have that option,' he said as a parting sally over his shoulder.

The compline bell was ringing out from the abbey, and as Thomas picked up his wine to finish it his yeoman, Duncalfe, arrived to announce that the Queen's labour pains had begun.

Her complexion red with effort, double-chinned, sweat rolling off her face, Philippa pushed and pushed again with guttural groans as she gripped the birthing ropes. It was the first occasion that Jeanette had been allowed to stay in the birth chamber itself, but with her marriage under discussion she was deemed old enough to do so and watch the process of birth. She was not disturbed, for she had seen a dairy maid at Donington bear a baby, and had witnessed the arrival of puppies, kittens and foals many times over. Her only fear was of this being her lot next year and every year after until her body was exhausted and she died.

The baby's head crowned between Philippa's parted legs and emerged like an enormous apple, and with the next few pushes the entire torso slipped free and into the midwife's waiting hands – bloody, pink and grey, covered in white grease. The midwife lifted the baby on high to drain his lungs and he sent out a loud wail of protest. 'A boy!' the woman cried in triumph. 'Madam, you have another son!'

A maid hurried forward with a warm towel to dry him, and the midwife snicked the cord with a small pair of shears. Philippa gasped and laughed as she released her grasp on the ropes, and briefly took the baby in her arms. 'Little man,' she said, making sure for herself that he was a boy and whole. She kissed his wet brow, then handed him to Lady St Maur to be washed. 'Send word to my lord immediately!' she commanded, her face shiny with tears of joy and exhaustion.

Jeanette stood by the hearth watching the baby having his first bath in a silver ewer of warm water. He had long limbs, a lick of gilt hair and a lusty cry. A pang went through her at the sight of the miracle of life, and this helpless little creature that needed protection.

Lady St Maur finished washing him and gently rubbed his gums with honey so that he would only ever know life's sweetness.

'May I hold him?' Jeanette ventured.

For a moment she thought Lady St Maur would refuse, but then, with a reserved smile, she gave him to Jeanette. 'Just for a moment,' she said.

Jeanette cradled the baby's warm weight in her arms and looked into his screwed-up little face. She touched his miniature clenched fists, then wordlessly returned him to Lady St Maur with tears in her eyes. The other ladies were looking at her knowingly and she turned away, for she could not bear it.

A midwife left the room with the afterbirth in a cloth-covered bowl. The Queen was brought to a fresh bed, and the infant given to her, clean from his bath. Philippa cooed at him with adoring satisfaction. The ladies gathered around, praising the baby and also Philippa for her strength and success in producing a third son for the English succession. A jug of sweet wine and pastries were sent round in celebration, and the messengers went out to proclaim the news far and wide.

Jeanette drank the wine to toast the baby, who was to be named John. Her brother's name, and her own too in male version. She rubbed the Queen's feet with rose unguents, and another lady played a lute softly in the background. A young girl rocked the baby's cradle and he soon fell asleep after his ordeal. The wet nurse sat by the fire, washing and warming her breasts, ready for when the princeling wished to feed, and Philippa's own breasts were bound up to stop the milk, and checks made to ensure the bleeding from her womb had eased.

Jeanette gazed round at the group of smiling women, relaxed and warm together, celebrating a new life. So much pride and joy. Then she thought of going to Gascony as a bride to this unknown boy Armand d'Albret. Having to live among strangers. Having to bed with someone she did not know and might even loathe. She would be expected to do her duty and bear him children in pain and blood and struggle, and was horrified. All these women thought she was tearful over a baby because she wanted one of her own, when it was no such thing.

Eventually the Queen slept, and Jeanette begged leave to go and check on her peregrine, knowing she would burst if she did not escape.

Lady St Maur rolled her eyes. 'You and that bird,' she said, but she was smiling. 'Very well, but do not be gone long. Take Joan with you.'

Jeanette needed no second bidding. With Hawise in tow as well, she grabbed her cloak and sped from the Queen's chamber. She wanted to run until she was breathless but could only step out briskly, kicking the hem of her gown.

'Slow down!' Joan gasped. 'What's the rush? Wait, wait! I have a stone in my shoe!'

Jeanette sighed in exasperation and danced on the spot while her friend unlatched her soft leather slipper and shook out a piece of grit.

'Did you see his little hands, and the way he looked at us?' Joan gushed as she pushed her foot back into the shoe. 'What a perfect little miracle!'

Jeanette forced a smile but it fell from her face almost immediately. 'I don't want that to be me in a year's time in Gascony,' she said. 'I don't care how miraculous or beautiful. I would rather be an outcast on the road than have that happen.'

Joan stared at her, open-mouthed. 'You do not mean it.'

'I have never meant anything more sincerely in my life,' Jeanette said grimly.

'How do you know it will be terrible? Your husband might be as handsome as the sun and you might adore him.'

'I doubt it. He'll be a boy, thinking that he can have anything he wants, and encouraged by his father to take it, and unable to do any wrong in the eyes of his mother.'

'It will only be terrible if you make it terrible,' Joan remonstrated. 'Look on the good side. You shall have fine weather and good wine. You shan't have Lady Salisbury breathing down your neck, and you will have the eternal gratitude of the King and Queen. Your husband's family will treat you well because you are the King's own cousin and they dare not do otherwise.'

Jeanette shook her head. 'You do not understand,' she said impatiently. 'You are not the one being sent to Gascony.'

Arriving at the mews, she put on her glove and went straight to Frederick's perch, persuading the young peregrine on to her wrist with a shred of meat.

John de la Salle appeared from the depths of the building and bowed to the young women. 'Great news so I hear, my ladies,' he said. 'A new prince has been safely delivered.'

'Yes,' Jeanette replied. 'We saw him born, and the Queen is well. Where is your lord?'

'Attending his duties,' John answered. 'Were you particularly seeking him?'

She shook her head and blushed. 'No – it was a passing enquiry.' She fussed Frederick for a little longer before going to

Thomas's goshawk where she perched on a stump. The bird regarded her with bright amber eyes before turning to preen her wings, at ease in Jeanette's presence.

She stayed a while longer, until the sun was starting to set, and Joan was fretting to return to the ladies, but then saw Thomas and Otto crossing the yard with Henry de la Haye and several other knights, and her heart kicked as it always did.

Evidently having caught sight of them too, Thomas approached and bowed. 'I would have thought you ladies would be with the Queen.'

'I came to visit Frederick,' Jeanette answered. 'We have the Queen's leave.'

'And I assume you are bound back to her chambers before the dark catches you outside?'

Jeanette saw the indulgent amusement on the faces of the men with him, and a devil took her tongue. 'Where else would we be going, Sir Thomas?' she asked. 'To the tavern?'

'That I do not know, but it is my duty to escort you to safety and protect you whatever your destination.'

'Then, thank you. In that case, I know I shall always be safe wherever I find myself.'

'Indeed, that is true,' he replied, and set out to walk her, Joan and Hawise back to the Queen's apartments with the other men.

At the doorway, Jeanette paused and turned to him. 'I shall be doling out alms tomorrow in thanks for the Queen's safe deliverance,' she said. 'Perhaps you might escort us there and assist us – unless of course you have other duties.'

He tilted his head. 'It may be possible. I make no promises, but we shall endeavour to join you. We bid you good evening, ladies.' He bowed, and walked off with his companions. He didn't look round but Henry de la Haye did, and winked roguishly.

Joan clucked her tongue at his impertinence. 'I cannot believe you suggested such a thing!'

'Why not?' Jeanette asked. 'It will be more fun to have their company, and safer too.'

'I am not so sure of that. What will the Queen say?'

'Why would she object?' Jeanette raised her brows. 'It will reflect well on the household if we are all involved. Sir Thomas and his brother are valiant knights and well thought of and Sir Henry is one of theirs. I am certain that Messire Hazelrigg can be persuaded to attend too.' Jeanette looked at her friend with her tongue in her cheek.

Joan shook her head, but blushed furiously, for she had her own soft spot for the northern English knight who was often in Thomas's company. 'What about the Countess of Salisbury?'

'What about her? It will be a public and religious duty, and the men will give it gravitas – even Henry de la Haye. She will have no cause for complaint and we won't be the only ladies present. You worry too much.'

Joan gave her a reproachful look. 'And you take too many risks.'

'Hah, then we shall meet in the middle,' Jeanette said incorrigibly.

The next day, Jeanette, Joan, Hawise and several other ladies from the Queen's chamber gathered to dole out alms to the poor at the monastery gates. Usually, the almoners and designated servants distributed the donations, but today, in thanksgiving, the Queen's ladies were involved in the task, and as well as the food, small amounts of money and items of clothing were handed out.

Jeanette played her part with a whole heart and a wide and ready smile. She was in charge of dispensing the bread, while

Joan ladled pottage into the bowls people had brought with them. Thomas and Otto arrived with their retinues to assist and stand guard, and the loaves of bread and jugs of beer were soon emptied, and all the money and clothing gone.

'Thank you,' Jeanette said, smiling at Thomas as she gathered up the empty baskets.

'It has been my pleasure, demoiselle.'

He had brought one of his old hoods and two thick blankets to give away and had provided a small purse of alms money. His manner towards the folk who had come to receive charity had been courteous and good-humoured. Jeanette had noted his common touch which did not detract from the authority he possessed to lead men and maintain his rank. He had tousled a small boy's hair, and jested with a toothless old woman who had cackled at him with lecherous appreciation, saying if she had been thirty years younger . . .

Once more, he escorted her and the ladies back to the royal apartments, and carried the baskets himself.

'You look like a housewife going to market,' she said, amused and very aware of his presence at her side. Their pace was a saunter, eking out the moment.

'Looks can be deceptive,' he replied. 'It is what lies beneath that matters.'

He leaned a little towards her, and Jeanette's breath shortened.

'Then I suppose that like all truth it is buried, and must be sought by diligent investigation,' she said pertly, giving as good as she got, and was rewarded by the flash of his grin.

'I have always found that to be the case, demoiselle,' he said, as they came to the Queen's door. 'And usually well rewarded.'

'Is that so?' she said with a provocative, sideways look, and gestured to Joan and Hawise to go ahead, each carrying some baskets. Taking the last two from him, she stepped so close that their outer garments brushed against each other. 'Shall we take the hawks out soon?'

'Do you not have the Queen to care for?'

'As long as I comb her hair properly and rub her feet, she will give me permission. Indeed, I do not know for how much longer I will be able to train him if I have to go to Gascony.'

He cleared his throat. 'Nothing will be decided until the King's return. You still have time.'

'No, I do not,' she said bitterly, her mood dampening. 'I don't want to go to Gascony, but who listens? If I refuse, I will be accused of shirking my duty and being ungrateful. Indeed, they will not let me refuse. Do you think it is ever possible to wed for love? To wed for choice?'

He looked taken aback. 'I suppose it must be, but it is easy to say and much less simple to do, and seldom for the likes of us, for we are bound by duty and family expectation.' He took a back-step. 'You should return to the Queen.'

She remained where she was, her eyes drinking him in. The last thing she wanted to do was be trapped in the bower again.

'Jeanette!' Joan hissed, coming back down the stairs. 'What are you doing? Make haste before you get us both into trouble!'

The spell broke and she tore her gaze from him, but as she started up the stairs, she looked over her shoulder and gave him another long look.

When she was gone, Thomas palmed his face. This beautiful, mercurial girl so knowing but so vulnerable was twisting him in knots and it was not good. He would find himself thinking about her at odd moments of the day and he looked forward to their training sessions with the hawks, with a hungry, hollow sensation of need in the pit of his belly.

She was so different from the other young women at court.

He loved her unaffected walk – no silly mincing steps like some of the damsels, but a proper long-legged stride. Her natural manner, her smile, her mischief that sparked his own. The scent of her, and the changing expressions in her eyes. Otto was entirely right to warn him against dallying with her, but he could not stay away. Last night he had taken himself off to the Gilders with Otto and Henry, and had relieved some of the pressure in his cods. The new girl had been exactly as his brother described, but it hadn't stopped him thinking about Jeanette. It was probably fortunate that she was going to this Gascon marriage soon, and that he too would be called away to his duties, because otherwise, rather than dancing around the fire, he would well and truly be in it.

8

Monastery of St Bavo, Ghent, March 1340

While the Queen recovered from John's birth, Jeanette continued to visit the mews to train Frederick. A few times she absconded the bower to watch the knights at their training when she knew Thomas would be there, and her body stirred as she watched him ride. The muscles of the stallion and the man, moving as one. The thrust of the destrier's powerful haunches. The push and pull of Thomas's hips between pommel and cantle, his hands light but firm on the reins. He was perfect in motion and her throat was dry and her pelvis heavy with a melting pain that was almost like flux cramps.

She watched him in the hall when everyone ate together. He would look back and it was like lightning. Feeling the power of her womanhood, she would push out her bosom and jut her hip to gain a reaction from him – teasing, excited by the danger.

There had been no news from Gascony concerning the marriage proposal. Her mother had written, saying she must obey the King in all things, but she had given no indication as to whether or not she approved. She had sent the gift of an embroidered chemise for her marriage chest which Jeanette had barely looked at, stuffing it away and slamming the lid. Her trousseau continued to grow. She had two new gowns, a set of linen bedsheets, a silk coverlet and pillow cloths, and each addition to the tally tilted her equilibrium ever further from a state of balance.

The Queen, although not yet churched, held gatherings in her chamber and often invited some of the favoured knights to lend their company to play at backgammon and chess with the ladies. Ten days after John's birth, the Queen decided on such a gathering, for the day was overcast, cold and wet. Looking forward to the event, which would enliven the afternoon, Jeanette bustled about the chamber, humming to herself, plumping cushions, playing tag with the children and dogs, until Katerine rebuked her for over-exciting them.

Dainty pastries arrived at the chamber door, together with trays of almond-stuffed dates and brightly coloured eggs – the hens were laying well again as the spring advanced. There were small squares of salty cheese, sugared fruits, raisins and nuts. Jeanette stole some of the latter from a silver dish, ate some herself, and divided the others between the Queen's daughters Isabelle and Joan – and was rebuked again by Katerine for lacking decorum. The scolding only made Jeanette rebellious and she poked out her tongue behind Lady Katerine's back, deliberately childish, and made the little princesses giggle.

She retired to her curtained-off bed space and with Hawise's assistance changed her gown ready to welcome the visitors. Her underdress was of deep blue velvet with a gold belt that hugged her hips, and the sleeveless overgown of silky golden damask shone with a filigree pattern of ferns and birds. Hawise coiled Jeanette's thick golden plaits over her ears and set a band of pearls at her brow. Propping up her little ivory hand mirror, Jeanette applied a dab of carmine to her lips and very lightly darkened her brows as a foil to enhance her eyes, and knew with sinful vanity that she looked utterly ravishing.

Satisfied, she returned to the Queen's inner chamber. Musicians were tuning their instruments and the Queen's ladies were putting the finishing touches to Philippa's headdress, fussing around her like bees.

Seven-year-old Princess Isabelle was crying and rubbing her eyes and Jeanette went to comfort her. 'What's the matter, *ma très chère*?' She touched the child's brow and it felt hot and clammy beneath her palm.

'My belly hurts,' Isabelle whimpered, and without warning vomited spectacularly over Jeanette's beautiful gown.

Isabelle's nurse rushed over and grabbed the child's hand. 'You've been giving her sweetmeats!' She glared at Jeanette. 'You know they do not agree with her, yet you persist!'

'Do not blame me!' Jeanette retorted. 'You are the one supposed to be watching her!' She stood up, wrinkling her nose at the stench. 'I scarcely think this is the result of a few dried fruits!'

The Queen intervened, sharply ordering the nurse to take Isabelle away and see to her. 'Your gown can be cleaned,' she told Jeanette briskly. 'Go and change quickly, everyone will soon be here.'

Grimacing, Jeanette retired. Isabelle's vomit had soaked the underdress too, and through to her chemise. The smell made her want to retch herself as she stripped off the stained clothing and washed herself in the bowl of tepid rose water that still stood on her coffer. She bundled the chemise away for the laundry women. The gown and underdress would have to be carefully sponged by the wardrobe mistress and then brushed. From the pole above her bed, she pulled down her spare chemise and her red silk gown. The garment had fitted perfectly well at the January parade, but two months later was so tight across her breasts she had to remove the clean chemise and wear the gown next to her skin. Requiring Hawise's assistance to secure the laces and button the sleeves from elbow to wrist, she moved from behind the curtain to call to her.

At that moment, Thomas arrived, bearing two backgammon boards and a soft cloth bag of gaming pieces. Jeanette gasped and froze, her laces unfastened either side of her waist, exposing a pale gleam of flesh, and her nipples clearly outlined where the dress strained across her breasts. One of her braids had come uncoiled when she had been pulling her chemise over her head, and hung down, adding to her dishevelment. Her gasp sent his gaze straight to her; his eyes widened and he dropped the bag, scattering the pieces all over the floor.

Jeanette knew she should turn her back and draw the curtain across, but she faced him and jutted her chin. His gaze dropped from her face to her body and her breathing quickened.

Two of the counters had rolled to her feet and she stooped to pick them up.

He stooped too. 'Dear God, mistress,' he muttered. 'What are you doing to me?'

'Do not blame me!' she hissed. 'Am I a seer to know you would arrive at this very moment?'

'I do not know, mistress, you tell me.'

She flashed him a furious look at his hint that she had done this on purpose, but excitement licked through her all the same.

'What is this?' The Queen's voice whipped the air. 'Jeanette!'

She leaped to her feet, and Thomas shot to his, his head almost colliding with hers.

'Madam, I dropped the gaming pieces,' he said, and then pressed his lips together.

'I was helping him to pick them up,' Jeanette added. 'I was summoning—'

'In a state of undress with your laces untied?' The Queen cut her off, her expression furious. 'Where is your decorum? Go at once and make yourself decent!'

Jeanette fled into her bed space and tore the curtain across, tears of rage blurring her vision at the unfairness and humiliation. On the other side of the curtain the Queen was remonstrating with Thomas.

'Pick up those pieces, put the boards on the table, and then you may retire,' she said icily. 'I thought better of you than this.'

Thomas replied in a tone Jeanette had never heard him use before, flat and tight. 'Madam, I swear to you it is not as it seemed. Indeed, I am your loyal servant and obedient to your will. My apologies if I have offended you and your ladies.'

After a short but pertinent silence, the Queen spoke again, stiffly. 'Yes, you have offended, but I accept your apology and I trust that it was indeed a mistake of timing and not something less honourable. It will be better if you leave.'

'Madam,' Thomas said.

Jeanette heard him walking away and then the closing of the door with deliberation. Moments later, the Queen parted the curtain and gave Jeanette a hard look. Behind her stood Katerine of Salisbury with pursed lips, but a thoughtful glint in her eyes.

'I did not know Messire Holland was there, I swear it!' Jeanette cried. 'I was summoning Hawise to help with my fastenings and he walked into the room – and then he dropped the pieces.'

'Well, that is unfortunate,' Philippa said, 'but you did not have to help him pick them up and expose yourself in that unseemly way. You should have retired on the instant. We cannot have any hint of scandal attaching to you while the Gascony match remains in play. I would have credited you with more sense and I am disappointed.'

'Yes, madam, I am sorry,' Jeanette said, contritely, but her heart had leaped as she realised she had a way out of the Gascon match.

'Good, then let that be the end of the matter. Make yourself presentable and we shall say no more.' Philippa withdrew, snatching the curtain across.

Exhaling, Jeanette closed her eyes, and dug her fingernails into her palms.

Hawise hurried in to help her lace her gown, and fasten her sleeves. 'Oh, my lady!' she said. 'It truly was not your fault!'

Jeanette shook her head. 'As the Queen says, it is over and done with.'

Except it wasn't over at all, and even as Hawise rewound her braid and pinned it back into place, Jeanette was remembering how Thomas had been unable to take his eyes from her breasts.

In the stables, two days later, Thomas dismissed his groom and set about attending to his stallion Noir himself. The action of currying the horse's coat, stripping out the winter hair, helped to steady him. He was avoiding people as much as possible, and when he had to interact was curt and taciturn, not lingering to talk but concerning himself with duty. He had stayed away from the mews, although John de la Salle informed him that Jeanette had visited several times to tend her falcon, and had asked for him. He had avoided the hall too, and when obliged to be there had held himself aloof. In the evenings he played dice with his men in the guardroom and tavern, but with only half a mind, and had lost more often than he had won. Angry with himself, he had taken it out on others and Otto had had to drag him out of a brawl last night before the daggers came out. Even a visit to the Gilders had not improved his mood. No matter how accomplished the woman, his need had not been assuaged beyond a numb release that had done nothing for his desire.

He kept thinking about Jeanette standing before him looking like a wanton woman in the midst of being tumbled by her lover, the scent of her body, her breasts, the nipples studding beneath the tight ruby silk, the clear, aquamarine eyes and full, red lips. It was too much.

Was it deliberate? He had no idea. Instinctive perhaps. And part of it was his own spring fever, for she could not have known he would walk in as she was summoning her maid. Then again, she had faced him, brazening it out rather than turning away.

Grimly, he swept the comb along Noir's rump, dragging out swatches of winter hair and dander. The stallion stamped a hoof and Thomas spoke to reassure him, and then, sensing a presence, turned, thoroughly prepared to snap at the groom; but it wasn't a servant, it was Jeanette, and unchaperoned. Her eyes were wide, her pupils dark against the clear sea-blue.

'Mistress, you should not be here,' he said curtly. 'Where is your maid?'

'With your falconer,' she replied. 'I went to visit Frederick, and Master John said you were here. I left Hawise with him to give them an opportunity to talk for a little while. You must know they are courting.'

'That is no reason for you to come here alone.'

'Well, if you would speak to me in the hall instead of ignoring me, I would not have to resort to doing so!'

Throwing down the curry comb, he moved away from the stallion and went to pick up his tunic from the hay pile at the far side of the stall.

'Just what game are you playing with me?' he demanded.

'I am not playing games!'

'Then what is it you want of me, mistress? Let us have done with this charade once and for all.'

She came and stood before him, as close as she had done after the alms-giving. 'They want to send me away to Gascony to marry, and I do not wish to go. It is not right that I should make my vows and pledge my faith to someone I have never seen and do not know. What am I to do?'

'Your duty, as we all must,' Thomas said curtly. 'It has ever been thus.'

'But it shouldn't be. It is neither right nor fair. I won't let them; I swear I will not. I would rather die!' She closed the last fraction of space between them and put her arms around his neck. 'I know what I want!'

He knew he should push her away, but their bodies were pressed so close. He could feel the line of thigh and waist, her breasts round and firm, and he knew she must be very aware of his own response to such stimulation. 'In God's name . . .'

'Would you marry me, Thomas?' she asked. 'Would you give me your name?' She raised her face to his.

He gave up the unequal struggle and ceased to think. He did not know if this was part of her game, or for real, but the use of his name, the look on her face, her question, tipped him over the edge, and he kissed her. She made a small kitten sound in her throat and pushed up against him.

The pile of hay in the corner where he had tossed his tunic and cloak now became a place to lie down with her, prickly soft and fragrantly scented. A time-honoured bed for tumbling. Her arms gripped him fiercely, and when he lay over her she moaned and arched her spine. She was innocent, but she was knowing, and made no effort to stop him when he pushed up her skirts. Her legs were long and shapely, and the soft space between her thighs was thatched with crisp gold. He closed his

eyes and started to draw back, but she urged him on fiercely.
Digging her fingers into his arms. He was desperate, straining, and
she was desperate too, her hips making small, needy undulations.

'Oh God,' she whispered. 'Don't stop.'

Gasping, he freed himself and pushed into her in a single
thrust as if he was meeting an opponent on the tourney field.
She wriggled and cried out, but he was beyond anything but
the feel of being inside her. It was like charging down the tilt,
fully committed. So close, so close. Within seconds he was
finished, and the sensation was so swift, so strong, that it was
an instinct more than a pleasure, but such a blessed relief that
he could only gasp like a landed fish as the sensations continued
to flicker, and eventually fade.

Beneath him, she made small, distressed sounds, and as he came
to himself he was shocked and ashamed. But even as he diminished within her, he still wanted her. Slowly he eased from her
body and covered himself. She sat up and folded her arms
around her waist, her head bent, and his feelings of guilt
increased fourfold.

'I do not know what to say,' he said, 'except that this should
never have happened, and I am sorry.'

She shook her head and finally looked at him. 'I wanted this,
and I should thank you,' she said. 'Now I know what to expect
when I go to a husband. It is not so bad, for at least it is swiftly
done.'

His guilt thickened, and he even, appallingly, felt an edge of
anger towards her because she had pushed him first. 'You were
as eager as I was – I believed you were with me.'

She gave him a baffled, wary look. 'I was with you,' she
replied, 'but you had forgotten me. I did not expect . . . I did
not know it would be so . . .' She swallowed and swiped at her
eyes, before scrambling to her feet. 'I must go. Hawise will come

looking for me, and if anyone finds out, they will kill you.' Her voice was breathless with the effort of holding back tears.

He dragged on his tunic and stood up. 'I have despoiled you,' he said, and drew her back into his arms. 'We cannot leave it like this. We need to talk; we need to decide what to do. The King entrusted me to protect you, and I have done the opposite, and I am sorry.'

'Well, I am not,' she said fiercely. 'I am glad it happened. If you are not, there is nothing more to say. You said yesterday that it was what lay underneath that mattered – and you were right!' Wrenching away from him, she ran out of the stable towards the mews.

Thomas groaned and palmed his face and acknowledged to himself that it had happened because she had wanted it to happen more than he had wanted to stop, and he was the more culpable because he had the experience to know better and be accountable. But done was done and now he must deal with it, even if it meant his death. He was already dishonoured.

Having made sure the stallion was secure, he left at a brisk walk for the mews, not knowing what he was going to say to her. But he was too late. Jeanette and her maid had gone.

Jeanette drew the curtain across her bed space, sat down on her mattress and hugged herself, overwhelmed. Her virginity was gone and she was sore between her legs. She had thought she knew what to expect, but it wasn't this. The experience had been as swift as a stallion with a mare in the breeding pen. When she had gone to him, she had intended that it might happen and that it would be a lever if necessary to cast doubt on her proposed marriage to Armand d'Albret. She had imagined too how it might be in the moment if she gave free rein to all the lovely, melting feelings inside her when she thought of Thomas in bed at night. But imagining was not the same as encountering the visceral reality.

With shaking fingers, she removed her gown and chemise, the latter smeared with tell-tale blood-stains. She was pulling on a clean chemise when Hawise returned from hanging up their cloaks.

The maid's eyes widened and she put her hand over her mouth.

Jeanette handed her the stained chemise. 'Do something with this. No one must know.'

'Indeed not!' Hawise was swift to understand the situation through her shock. 'I shall scrub this myself in cold water and salt.' She set the bundle to one side and quickly helped Jeanette into clean garments and tidied her hair. 'Mistress, what happened? Did he force you? I thought you were upset when you came to the mews.'

Jeanette shook her head. 'I knew exactly what I was doing – indeed I pushed him into it . . . but now . . .' Her chin wobbled.

'Now you wish you had not,' Hawise said.

Jeanette flashed her an angry look, but then her face crumpled. 'I wish it had been different,' she said tearily. 'Now I have even less reason to go to Gascony if this is what it is . . .' She looked at Hawise. 'Have you and the falconer . . .'

Hawise reddened. 'No,' she said. 'But almost . . .'

'I did not realise; I did not understand . . . I still don't.' She wiped her eyes on the back of her hand. 'Whatever happens, I am not going to Gascony,' she said vehemently. 'I swear it on my soul.'

Hawise looked alarmed. 'My lady, you should not say—'

Jeanette laughed bitterly. 'Oh, I have gone far beyond "should not"!'

At a loss, Hawise picked up the chemise. 'I shall go and deal with this, my lady.'

Jeanette nodded, and Hawise left, a little tight-lipped.

Jeanette went out to join the other ladies and picked up some sewing, keeping her head down, not looking at anyone, feeling sick.

Thomas was absent for the next two days, busy with essential military matters, but he dined in the Queen's hall on the third day at noon. Jeanette had no opportunity to speak with him, for he was in a different part of the hall with the soldiers. Their eyes met several times though, assessing, cautious. After the meal, the Queen summoned Jeanette to rub her feet, and then to read to her, but at last she managed to gain permission to visit her hawk.

'Do not be too long,' Philippa said. 'Be back before sunset.'

'Yes, madam.' Jeanette curtseyed and was out of the door in an instant, fastening her cloak as she flew, Hawise hurrying in her wake.

In the mews, John de la Salle was busy with his apprentice, but there was no sign of Thomas. 'He has gone to his lodgings to reckon with some accounts,' John said.

Jeanette turned to Hawise. 'I have to see Thomas alone,' she said. 'Stay here with John. He won't say anything – no one will know.'

'My lady, you should not do this.' Hawise shook her head in alarm. 'It is too dangerous! What if someone does find out?'

'They won't,' Jeanette said stubbornly. 'Quick, give me your cloak and take mine, and wait in the mews.'

Hawise reluctantly did as Jeanette asked, persuaded by the opportunity to spend time with John, and not in a position of power to refuse. Jeanette swung Hawise's plain woollen cloak round her shoulders and pulled up the collar to form a shallow hood.

'I shan't be long.'

'Be sooner than that, my lady,' Hawise replied anxiously.

Jeanette hurried to Thomas's lodging in the compound, her stomach churning, but her step determined. His sturdy manservant Duncalfe opened the door to her knock, and frowned at her.

'I am here to see your master on a personal matter,' she said.

Duncalfe's gaze darted and she stood firm, ready to argue, but Thomas came to the door. 'Leave us,' he told his manservant. 'But stay on guard and give me good warning of any approach.'

'Sir,' Duncalfe said, phlegmatically, and without looking at Jeanette, stepped outside, easing his way past her.

Thomas stood aside and Jeanette entered the chamber. Parchments were piled on a trestle table near the window. Thomas's cloak lay across the end of his bed, which was neatly made and smooth.

'Do not tell me I should not be here,' she said before he could speak. 'I know what I am risking, and that it involves your life too. You said we should talk, so talk we shall. I hope your manservant is trustworthy.'

'He is,' Thomas said shortly. 'Unto death.' He barred the door, went to the wine jug on the table and poured a measure into his cup. 'We shall have to share.'

Jeanette sat on his bed, removed her own cloak and put it on top of his. 'I shall happily set my lips to the same place as yours – after all, we have already shared so much more.'

He handed her the cup and regarded her with troubled eyes. 'I have taken from you what can never be returned, and for that I am deeply sorry and ashamed, for it is a stain on my honour that has dishonoured you also.'

'I told you, I am not sorry.' She lifted her chin, defiant because she was scared. 'Done is done, and better you than a Gascon boy. You have been my first, paid for in blood, and that can never be changed.'

He tensed at her fierceness. 'But it was still dishonourable, and I would not have wished it to happen like that.'

She drank, and returned him the cup. 'Neither would I, and I have wondered if it is all there is. Is that what binds men and women and fires up priests to write of damnation, and poets of pleasure? If so, I am baffled. I do not know why the Queen smiles when the King has visited her bed. Why does she sleep so long and then stretch like a cat in the morning?'

He turned his head away for a moment. Studying his lean profile, the curl of his hair around his ear, her heart flooded with a raw, painful emotion. If this was love, it was bloody.

'Jeanette,' he said, and shook his head, clearly at a loss.

'I want you to show me,' she said. 'I want to be with you until I can no longer be with you; even if it is only for an hour, it will be for the rest of my life.'

He took a shuddering breath. 'And if I say we should draw back now and not take a single step further for both our sakes?'

'Then I shall answer that I have seen you joust and you did not hesitate to dare and that your aim was true. I shall say that what happened between us is only half begun and it cannot be finished when we have only run one course. Shall I call you a coward?'

His gaze brightened with indignation and sparked to match her own. 'No man would say that to me and survive.'

'But I am not a man, as well you have discovered. Thomas, you owe me this. You are in my debt and I intend to claim it, one way or another.'

In the silence that followed, Jeanette felt the tension pulling between them like wild horses straining at either end of a taut rope. She left the bed and came to put her arms around his neck as she had done before. 'I mean it,' she said. 'With every part of my being. Now mean it with every part of yours – or else cry quarter and leave the field. Which is it to be? Nothing, or for ever?'

'God help me,' he muttered, and kissed her.

And when their kisses led them to his bed, it was different. She could feel the rapid thud of his heart and hear his shaking breath, but this time he held back. He removed her clothes and she helped him to remove his in a sensual dance until they were as naked as Adam and Eve. She pulled out her hair pins and let her hair tumble down in a skein of heavy gold, and gloried in his soft oath of appreciation. He was at her mercy just as much as she was at his. Even if this was wrong, she had never felt a moment so right, so whole. If they were to joust, then she would meet him full tilt in the lists.

She arched against him, and this time when he entered her it was a smooth glide. He moved against her with taut control and she saw the tension in his throat and jaw and the effort he was making to rein himself in. Filled with power, she rested her hands on his buttocks to feel the movement and watched over her shoulder, head raised to see and to remember.

His movements became more ragged and she strained against him, pulling him closer still, and suddenly she was caught up in a wild surge of delicious sensation that made her cry aloud. He gave a final thrust, and with a sob, hastily withdrew himself and spilled against her thigh, before collapsing, gasping her name into her shoulder.

She lay for a moment, one arm bent across her eyes, and then slowly lowered it and smiled. She reached out and pushed her fingers through his raven-wing hair. 'Now I understand a little more,' she said, and licked her lips, still tasting his kisses, savouring the experience.

He gave a shaken laugh. 'It was a close-run thing. I could not have lasted much longer.'

When he had recovered a little, he left the bed and fetched a cloth to wipe them both. She shivered, for the early spring afternoon was cold. He gestured for her to get into bed, then poured some more wine and joined her, pulling up the coverlet. 'Only for a moment, to get warm,' he said. 'If they find you gone, there will be hell to pay.'

She wanted to toss her head and say she did not care, but Thomas would suffer the consequences too, as would Hawise. 'My maid is waiting for me at the mews,' she said. 'I cannot stay long anyway.'

They drank the wine, sharing the cup. She playfully dripped some on to his chest and then licked it off on the tip of her tongue. He reciprocated, and she shivered; the feel of him tracing lazy patterns on her skin was delectable, and she turned to him when the wine was finished and they indulged in a second bout, where once again he withdrew at the final moment.

Afterwards, he helped her to dress and tidy her hair, his touch delicate. 'I shall escort you and your maid back to the hall,' he said, sweeping on his own cloak. 'There shall be no questions.'

When they left his lodgings, the sky was gilded with the flame colours of sunset, and arriving at the mews they found Hawise hopping from foot to foot in agitation.

'I am in time,' Jeanette said as they exchanged cloaks. 'I told you I would be back, and Messire Holland will escort us.'

'It is my duty and my pleasure,' he said. He and Jeanette exchanged swift, conspiratorial glances and hidden smiles.

Their return was smooth. The guards saluted Thomas and the women without a second look, for they were accustomed to Jeanette's visits to the mews, and Thomas was a commander, they saw nothing untoward.

On the threshold, bidding farewell, Jeanette turned to him. 'I think I need to ride out with Frederick, to further his training,' she said. 'Shall I see you on the morrow?'

'Do you feel fit to ride, mistress?' he replied with a gleam in his eyes.

'Just as far as I desire,' she answered with a mischievous smile and a tilt of her chin. 'Is that not what you told me?'

9

Monastery of St Bavo, Ghent, April 1340

Jeanette lay back on her cloak on the grassy bank starred with yellow celandine and early sunbursts of dandelion. April was returning warmth to the land and clothing the trees in delicate new leaves of spring green. A scent of damp grass fragranced the air as the two horses grazed, bridles jingling, and a busy clamour of birdsong marked the urgency of the season. Her own emotions were brimming with a blend of happiness, effervescent excitement, and relish at kicking over the traces and behaving as though she had all the freedom in the world to do as she desired – and the rest she chose to bury.

She and Thomas had met many times over the past few weeks, not just to take carnal pleasure in each other's bodies, but to talk and banter and be together. Sometimes she would sneak away to his chamber, disguised in her maid's dark cloak and hood, and the clandestine escapade was an intoxication in itself. They were careful to avoid discovery, but there was still a piquant thrill in knowing they might be caught.

Thomas would come to the Queen's chamber with a message and they would meet on the stairs and share a swift kiss. Then there were the quick touches of hands in the hall, a look, a smile. Secretly brushing his groin as they passed in a corridor. The mews and the stables had become their sanctuaries and they would lie together at the back of Noir's stall, making love, whispering, touching. And today in the woods on this grassy bank. She refused to think of tomorrow, or even to the end of the day, but to live in the moment, for it was all they had.

'I suppose we should return,' Thomas said reluctantly. 'The women will be looking for you, and I have my duties.' He was stretched out on the grass beside her, arms bent behind his head.

Jeanette puffed out her cheeks in a sigh. 'Back to embroidery,' she said. 'I hate it. I don't know what I would do without these moments.' She leaned over to kiss him, knowing she would never grow tired of doing this. She traced his eyebrows with her fingertips. 'I wish there was only us in the world.'

'Like Adam and Eve?' he asked, grinning. 'I would enjoy seeing you clad in nothing but your hair every day.'

She hit him playfully. 'You know what I mean.'

Catching her wrist, he turned it over and kissed the delicate blue veins on the inside. 'Ah, but the purgatory of embroidery and attending to duty only sweetens the stolen moments.'

They rose and brushed themselves down. Hawise and John had been waiting a short but discreet distance away with the birds and horses. It was a bittersweet pleasure for Jeanette to watch her chamber lady and Thomas's falconer conducting their own courtship openly, without having to be secret.

Several days later, while Hawise was helping her to dress in the morning, Jeanette caught her breath as the maid tightened the side laces of her undergown, for her breasts were full and tender. She had overslept and felt nauseous and still tired.

Hawise said quietly, 'Mistress, it is perhaps not my place to say, but the laundress has not washed your flux cloths in the last month. Is all well with you?'

'Of course it is!' Jeanette snapped. 'And you are right, it is not your place to say!'

Hawise curtseyed and moved away, her eyes downcast.

Jeanette sat down on the bed and, fiddling with her plait, counted back over the past weeks. She had lain with Thomas on numerous occasions, but he had always been careful not to spill his seed inside her, even if it was a sin to – except for that very first time in the stables. She knew the theory that a woman could not conceive unless she released her own seed – signalled by pelvic shivers of pleasure – and it had not happened then, but perhaps that particular science was wrong.

Hawise returned with a selection of hair ribbons for her plait, and Jeanette sighed. 'I am sorry,' she said. 'But there is no cause for worry. I am certain my flux will come any day.'

'Indeed, my lady,' Hawise agreed, but her expression did not match the tone of her voice. 'A midwife told my mother that if any woman should find that her womb is congested so that her flux fails, she should bathe in water as hot as she can abide and partake of vigorous walks and riding.' Her cheeks reddened. 'If she has a husband, she should indulge in energetic love-sport, for it will also assist in the matter. If it is more than that, then it is in God's hands.'

Jeanette raised a thoughtful brow at the information, especially the latter advice, and thanked her maid. 'That is useful to know,' she said, 'but I am sure the situation will resolve itself soon.'

She lost no time in following the directions, and Thomas, as the recipient, was delighted and wide-eyed at her increased wildness, especially when she straddled him in a manner that the Church considered utterly sinful. She felt so powerful watching the look on his face as she moved above him, glorying in her own sinuous carnality, even while praying that all this determined activity would bring about the desired result.

After a week of strenuous effort and several baths, there was still no flow of blood. Her breasts had grown more tender, and she had started to feel nauseous on waking in the morning. The remedies had failed, and this was more than a congestion. She studied her body as she prepared to dress. Her waist was still narrow, her belly flat. But what would happen when it started to swell? The latest style of overgown was loose and full, and she would be able to hide her condition for several months, but there would come a moment of reckoning. What then would the Queen and her ladies say – and do? How would her mother respond? They would all want to know who the father was, and if they discovered that it would be the end for Thomas. Even if the Gascon marriage did happen, it was already too late to claim the child as that of her bridegroom.

She left the matter for another three days in fading hope that her flux would come, and then decided to approach Thomas and tell him. While attending the Queen to comb her hair, she sought permission to visit her hawk.

Philippa smiled at her. 'If that bird was your husband, you would be the most attentive wife in the land.'

Jeanette flushed and looked down.

'I know it is difficult when you are awaiting news from Gascony,' Philippa said with sympathy. 'Do not fret; it will arrive in its own good time.'

Jeanette felt sick. 'Yes, madam.'

Philippa called for one of her jewel boxes, riffled among the contents, and presented Jeanette with a little sapphire and pearl brooch. The Queen's response to anyone who was down in the mouth was to either stuff the person with sweetmeats or bestow small fripperies upon them. 'Now,' she said, 'be of good cheer, and go and visit that bird of yours.'

Jeanette took the trinket, curtseyed and hurried from the room, then had to stop and lean against the wall to combat a wave of nausea.

Hawise touched her arm. 'Your cloak, my lady,' she said.

Jeanette straightened and swallowed hard. Hawise draped the garment around her shoulders and made a show of fastening the Queen's pin to the collar until Jeanette was able to continue.

Once they arrived at the mews, Jeanette sent John de la Salle with a message for Thomas to come, and that it was urgent. Then she sat down on a bench outside to wait for him. She dared not go inside to the falcons. They would sense her tension and bate their wings, and the smell of their excrement might overwhelm her delicate stomach.

When she saw Thomas pacing towards her, tall and graceful, his hand on his sword hilt, her heart kicked in her chest with love, anxiety and fear.

He took one look at her face and sat down at her side. 'What is wrong?'

Now that it came to telling him, her throat was blocked and she could only shake her head.

'Has something happened with the Queen? Is there news from Gascony?'

'No.' She twisted her hands in her lap. 'I . . . I believe I am with child.' She forced out the words. 'I do not know what I am going to do.'

He drew back sharply to look at her, first in the eyes, and then down at her body. 'With child,' he said.

She nodded, and her chin wobbled. 'I think that first time . . .'

'Dear God.' He rubbed his palm over his jaw stubble and after a hesitation, sighed. 'Do not worry, I will make it right, I promise.'

'How will you do that?' she demanded on a rising tide of panic. 'What about the King and Queen? What about my family? What will they do to us? Look at what happened to your father, and to mine!' She burst into tears.

'Hush now, hush.' He drew her against him, and she tightly gripped his worn leather jerkin in her fists. 'Look, we are in a bind, I admit, but there is a way to make it right. I shall marry you, as you once asked. It will cause a scandal and it will not be easy, but if you have my ring on your finger, and we speak the proper vows, then it is no dishonour.'

'It will mean death for you, and disgrace for me,' she said.

'What alternative is there? Even if we have done wrong, it is a wrong we can right, especially for the child you carry. It shall not be a bastard, but born within lawful wedlock.'

She looked at him through tear-blurred eyes. He would not be allowed to live for dishonouring her and ruining the King's dynastic plans. She would be hidden away until the child was born and everything would be kept secret. 'It will mean your life,' she said. 'Do you not understand?'

He grimaced. 'I am ready to pay that price.'

'And what will be the use in that? How will that make it right if you leave me to deal with this on my own?'

'Look, I shall think of something. We need not announce it to the world yet, but we should wed immediately. Come to me here on the morrow afternoon and we shall make our vows before witnesses. Hawise and John will stand as two, and Otto and Henry de la Haye. Once we are husband and wife, we can decide what to do next.'

Jeanette swallowed at the enormity of what he was saying. She was being swept away on a rising tide, with only straws to grasp.

'Are you willing?' He held her shoulders and looked into her eyes.

Dear Holy Virgin . . . 'Yes,' she whispered. She still could not see a way out of the dilemma, but there had to be an opening further along, there just had! And she was the one who had first asked if he would marry her. 'Yes, I am willing.'

He dried her tears on the cuff of his shirt. 'Then we shall do this, and be brave. Know that I love you, and my life is yours.' He touched her damp cheek. 'Go now. Behave as usual before others, and I will see to the rest, and meet you tomorrow. All will be well, I promise – trust me.'

Jeanette nodded. In the midst of this terrible flood, trusting him was the only branch she had.

That evening, Thomas invited Otto to eat with him in his chamber. The brothers often met to catch up on their lives, discuss orders, and sometimes to play chess and dice away from the tavern. Thomas had little appetite for the cold spiced fowl and bread, but tried to make a show of eating, while Otto devoured the meal with gusto.

At length, Thomas wiped his hands on his napkin and refreshed his cup. 'I have something to ask you,' he said.

Otto held out his own cup for a refill and pushed aside his dish, empty save for well-picked bones. 'What is it, brother?'

Thomas dug one hand through his hair. 'I trust you to keep this secret – at least for now, until I can see my way clear.'

'You can trust me with your life – although I hope it will never come to that.'

'It may indeed come to that, but I have no one else who I would have stand in your stead.'

Otto raised his brows, but opened his hands. 'Then don't tarry, tell me what it is.'

'I am asking you to be a witness to my marriage.'

Otto stared, then laughed in disbelief and shook his head. 'Well, that is not what I was expecting to hear. Who is the fortunate lady, and why the secrecy?'

'It's Jeanette of Kent, the King's cousin.'

'Jeanette?' Otto's jaw dropped.

'Yes.'

'Dear God, Tom, how did this come about? Do the King and Queen know?'

'Nobody knows beyond you, John de la Salle and Jeanette's maid. We are to wed tomorrow and say our vows before a Franciscan friar.'

Otto shook his head.

'It has to be marriage,' Thomas said grimly. 'We have lain together and she is with child.'

Otto regarded Thomas in shocked silence. What an utter disaster for their attempts to rehabilitate their family. They were on probation, and this would scupper them. He might even lose his brother. 'And once the deed is done, what then?' he demanded when he could speak. 'When are you going to tell the King and Queen?'

Thomas's face twisted. 'I do not know. We have a few weeks' grace before anything need be said and I shall think of something. A marriage will make the situation more honourable than it is just now. I shall endow her with my worldly goods and we shall manage. I put my faith in God and I shall do penance for my sin, but I must see it through.'

'I warned you,' Otto said furiously. 'Numerous times.'

'I know you did, but that doesn't help now,' Thomas snapped. 'I am to blame. I take it entirely upon myself. If you wish to distance yourself, then do so and I will understand.'

'Do you love her?' It was almost an accusation.

Thomas palmed his face. 'Yes,' he said simply. 'More than my life.'

'Well, that much is certainly obvious, because you might well die.' Otto curled his lip. 'At least we know you're not throwing it away purely because you've been led by your cock.'

'Yes, rub it in. As far into the wounds as you can, for I deserve every grain of salt and more.'

Otto picked up his cup then thumped it down again with an expletive. He started for the door, set his hand to the latch, then turned around and exhaled hard. 'I think you are God's greatest fool, but no matter how much salt I grind into your cuts at your behest, it does not alter our kinship. I will stand at your side even to the gates of hell, as I know you would stand at mine if the tables were turned. Let fate do its worst and let it be what it will be and Heaven help us.'

Thomas strode over to Otto and embraced him in a heartfelt clasp. 'Thank you,' he said hoarsely. 'I am forever indebted to you.'

Otto snorted and pushed him away. 'Indeed you are, you fool!'

At a knock on the door the brothers swiftly drew apart. Otto opened it and found John de la Salle standing outside, revolving his hat in his hands.

'What is it?' A jolt shot through Thomas. He had asked John earlier if he would stand witness on the morrow, and wondered if there was a problem.

John entered the room, and shuffled his feet, his expression awkward. 'Sire,' he said, 'I was thinking about tomorrow . . .'

'What of it?' Thomas demanded, fearing that the falconer was about to renege on his word.

'I was wondering . . . would it be presumptuous to ask that the priest also marry myself and Mistress Hawise? We wish to be wed, and if we served as witnesses to your joining with the lady Jeanette, then you might witness ours also.' His hat-turning grew more rapid. 'It means too that if anyone comes across a wedding, we can say without a word of a lie that I am marrying Mistress Hawise.' He flicked an anxious glance at Thomas and Otto. 'Forgive me if I have spoken out of turn.'

Thomas clapped his shoulder, his blow heavy with relief. 'Not in the least!' This was the perfect cover. 'Indeed, I congratulate you heartily. It is a fine plan, and an excuse for a celebration afterwards. I am delighted for you and the lady, of course, but this could not be better!' He poured wine and gave it to de la Salle. 'A toast,' he said. 'To marriage – may we all wed our true loves and stay the course, whatever the future holds.'

10

Monastery of St Bavo, Ghent, April 1340

Jeanette and Thomas were married in the room from which the alms were handed out to the citizens of Ghent. They made their vows before Father Geoffrey, a recently ordained Franciscan friar with whom Thomas had spoken on several occasions, and with four witnesses in attendance – John de la Salle, Hawise, Otto and Henry de la Haye.

'Are you certain of this?' the friar asked, looking between Thomas and Jeanette, his expression serious. 'Once you agree to be bound before witnesses, there is no going back and your union will stand in the sight of God until death you do part.'

Jeanette nodded firmly. 'Yes,' she said. 'I agree to wed this man until death do us part.' She looked at Thomas. He was dressed in his green livery, the best velvet set, brushed and clean, and her heart was melting.

'As do I agree the same with this woman,' Thomas declared with the same determination. 'To have and to hold until death do us part, and with all my worldly goods I do endow her. With my body I will honour her, and I shall love and cherish her all of my days. Amen.'

'Then, as you stand before me now, and before God and these witnesses, let you be man and wife.'

Thomas took Jeanette's hand and slipped his own gold seal ring on her heart finger in token of their vows. And then, Hawise and John de la Salle swore their own vows, and all was witnessed and the hastily drawn-up contracts attested and sealed.

Thomas kissed her softly. 'Now our child shall be born in wedlock,' he said. 'And let no one call him or her a bastard, or frame this as a false union. We shall travel this path, and we shall prevail, even if we cannot yet see around the corner.'

Jeanette returned his kiss and silently prayed he was right, and that they had not brought calamity down upon themselves. She turned to embrace Hawise and John, and congratulate them on their own nuptials. At least under the pretext of celebrating her maid's wedding, she and Thomas could have their moment.

'I am sorry this is not the grand wedding you should be enjoying,' Thomas said as they shared a meal of bread and beef stew in a nearby ale house, 'but I swear I will cherish you for the rest of our lives.'

They could neither hold hands nor kiss in a public place. That was all for John and Hawise, who drew the cheers and attention, but they did manage to squeeze fingers and touch legs beneath the trestle.

'It is a finer wedding than any other I might have had,' she said. 'We may be marrying out of necessity, but we are also marrying for love, and how many married people at court can say the same?'

Later, when Hawise and John had retired to John's lodging by the mews to spend their wedding night, Thomas returned Jeanette to the Queen's apartments, but paused in the shadow of the wall to draw her against him for a long kiss. Holding her close, he stroked her face. 'We will find a way to bring this into the open, I swear,' he said. 'We have been wed before witnesses and that is what matters.'

'I know, I trust you.' Again, she thought of the branch in the flood.

They kissed once more with lingering hunger, before he escorted her to the door of the Queen's domicile and told the guard they had been celebrating the marriage of his falconer and Jeanette's maid. Having seen her safely inside, Thomas returned to his own quarters and leaned against the door, taking a moment to collect himself. His wife, his pregnant wife. He was still trying to come to terms with what he had done, and the future consequences for himself, his family and his beautiful Jeanette. He had said he would find a way. But he did not know what it was or even how to begin.

In the morning, after mass, Thomas was giving orders to the guards when a squire summoned him to the presence of his senior commander, Maurice of Berkeley.

Thomas's stomach jinked, his first thought being that the marriage had been discovered, but the squire's face wore no particular expression and he seemed to think the matter was routine. He followed the youth to Maurice's lodgings and found the banneret seated at a table, a satchel of messages at his elbow. An inky-fingered scribe toiled at a lectern by the open window.

'Ah, Tom!' Maurice beckoned to him, poured a cup of wine, and shoved a platter of bread and sausage in his direction. 'Orders from the King.' He extended a strip of parchment. 'Your services are required in England. Get your men together and find a ship.'

Thomas picked up the parchment and looked numbly at the orders.

'It's good news for you,' Maurice said. 'Better than kicking your heels here day and night attending on women. It's an opportunity to climb another rung of the ladder since the King wants you in person.' He gave a teasing grin. 'You are a marked man!'

In more ways than one, Thomas thought, swallowing.

Maurice raised one eyebrow. 'I can see your good fortune has numbed your delight.'

'It is unexpected,' Thomas said blankly.

'Not really.' Maurice cut some sausage from the platter he had offered to Thomas. 'The King is preparing to return to Ghent but needs aid garnering supplies, and you have a particular skill for it. You will not be gone for long.'

Thomas poured and drank some wine, but ignored the food, his mind racing with the implications.

'There's a ship leaving on tonight's tide – be on it.'

Thomas nodded stiffly. 'Of course.'

He took his leave. Maurice pursed his lips and looked at the door and wondered about certain rumours he had heard. Then he shook his head and returned to work. Sometimes it was best not to become embroiled.

Thomas found Otto and Henry at sword practice with the squires. Wiping his brow, Otto gestured for the lads and Henry to continue with their sparring, and stepped aside. 'What is it?'

'Orders to return to England immediately.' Thomas showed him the parchment.

Otto read what was written and shrugged. 'Nothing for it then if it's a royal order. I'll take the lads off their training and begin seeing to it. Duncalfe can go to the docks and talk to the ship's master.' He looked at Thomas, an unspoken question in his eyes.

'It could not have come at a worse time. I cannot leave her – dare not.'

Otto snorted. 'Don't talk like a fool. We have no choice. If we disobey a royal summons, we shall be obligated for far more than just a secret marriage. Look what happened to our father when he ignored a call to arms. We are finished if we do not go, and I personally want to keep my head on my shoulders.'

Thomas knew Otto was right – the solid dog in the kennel who never deviated – and he would always speak truth to him, no matter how disagreeable. 'Get it organised,' he said with a brusque nod. 'I shall talk to Jeanette.'

Jeanette gazed at the baby lying against his wet nurse's arm. Little John of Ghent had his father's golden-gilt hair, his mother's smile, and he was beautiful. She still could not equate this baby before her with the idea that there was probably another such growing inside her own womb. The act of mating began in such a small way with the meeting of seed, and it was almost impossible to believe that it led eventually to this outcome. The secret of yesterday's marriage was like that too. A seed that would grow and grow, and yet how was it to be told without the world falling apart?

The Queen summoned her to attend on her, together with Katerine of Salisbury and Lady St Maur. Leaving the wet nurse and the baby, Jeanette wondered if the Queen wanted her to rub her feet or comb her hair, but she had not sent the maid to bring her toiletry box and had dismissed the other women, so that no one else was within hearing.

Philippa's expression was pursed and taut. 'Messages have arrived from the King this morning,' she said, and indicated a piece of parchment set to one side. 'Jeanette, it seems that Bernard d'Albret has chosen not to pursue the proposed betrothal between you and his son and has informed the King that while he is not averse to negotiating a bride for his boy, he considers you unsuitable.'

Experiencing a rush of relief, Jeanette lowered her gaze, concealing her delight.

'The King is disappointed that the match has not come to fruition, but will seek a different heiress for our ally. We have no desire to see the family negotiate for a French bride.'

Jeanette wondered why the Queen looked so disgruntled. It was a set-back, but not worth the dark expression on Philippa's face. Lady Katerine on the other hand had perked up, even if her lips were set in a straight line.

The Queen took a deep breath. 'One of the reasons Bernard d'Albret decided against the match was that he had heard reports of your conduct at court, and he feels his son will be better settled with a bride more likely to attend to her embroidery and her household affairs rather than spending her time flying hawks and being too familiar with servants and soldiers.'

Heat seared Jeanette's face. 'Madam, I—'

Philippa raised her hand. 'I do not wish to hear excuses or reasons, and I must take part of the blame. We have all been too trusting and lax with you while I have been in confinement, but that will change immediately. You shall remain at my side and devote yourself to duties in the chamber. If you wish to visit your falcon, you shall go once a week with one of my squires and a senior lady, rather than just your maid for company. There are others who can attend to your bird. The groom will exercise your horse and others shall run errands for the moment. Once the King returns, we shall decide what is to be done to secure you a fresh match.'

A feeling of sick panic rose inside Jeanette. She would suffocate in such a caged existence. She needed to see Thomas; she had to get word to him. Bowing her head, she feigned a contrition she was far from feeling.

Philippa waved her hand. 'I do not know what else to say. You have such potential, yet you squander it. It is time you took responsibility for your position at court. Do I make myself clear? As has been said to you before, you are a woman now, not a spoiled child.'

'Yes, madam, and I beg your forgiveness.' The words emerged by rote, while Jeanette's mind raced.

'Good. Then we shall say no more. You shall remain in this chamber under strict supervision as of now.' She gave Jeanette a hard stare. 'I suspect it will also assist matters that certain household knights are under orders to leave immediately for England to assist with mustering the fleet.'

Jeanette drew a sharp, involuntary breath, and her chest constricted. She dared not ask the names of the knights, but she already knew.

'You shall eat here today in my chamber, not in the hall,' Philippa continued, gently relentless. 'Now, go and join the other ladies and we shall speak no more on the matter.'

Jeanette curtseyed, and feeling as though she was dragging a lump of lead behind her, went to the other women. She had to talk to Thomas.

Katerine of Salisbury sat down beside her and picked up her embroidery. 'It is for your own good, my dear, as you will come to realise in time,' she said, her blue eyes sharp. 'I am sorry the Gascony marriage is not to be, but another match will be forthcoming soon enough. I shall write to your mother straight away.'

Katerine's smug expression worried Jeanette: the Countess of Salisbury was a schemer with her claws in many a cloth.

She tried to busy herself with her sewing, but pricked her finger on her needle. The sight of the welling crimson bead of blood made her stomach writhe, and she had to bolt for the latrine, where, leaning over the shaft, she was violently sick.

Katerine, like a hound on a scent, followed her and gave her doubled-over body a thoughtful look. 'Clearly you have eaten something that has not agreed with you,' she said. 'Too many sweetmeats, I suspect. That would explain your recent behaviour. Your humours have become badly unbalanced by a surfeit of rich food and excitement. Go and lie down. You can finish your sewing later. I shall prepare you a tisane to set matters right.'

Jeanette was immediately suspicious of Katerine's kindness, but was glad to go and curl up on her bed. What a bind she was in, and Thomas too. If he was suspected of more than flirting, the King would have him put to death, whether she was wearing a wedding ring or not.

Hawise arrived, bearing a cup of spring water.

'I have to get word to Thomas,' she whispered, gripping the maid's hand.

'They won't let me go either,' Hawise whispered back, 'not even to see John, but Hannekyn can take a message.' She gestured at one of the young chamber attendants who always blushed when Jeanette spoke to him.

Jeanette nodded. 'Send him with a message for John asking him to care for Frederick until I can fly him again, and that I shall count each moment until that time. John will know what it means.'

Hawise curtseyed and went about her usual business, but approached Hannekyn after a while, murmured to him and pressed a coin into his hand. Moments later, the youth collected his cloak and left on his errand.

Jeanette slept briefly but was woken by Hannekyn's return.

The young man hung up his cloak and murmured to Hawise, who then came to Jeanette's bedside, her eyes bright with sympathetic tears.

'Messire Thomas and his brother have already sailed for England,' Hawise said. 'John is staying to care for the falcons and he said to give you this.' She pressed a falcon's hood into Jeanette's hand decorated with a soft tuft of pheasant feathers. 'He says to look inside.'

Horrified that Thomas was gone, Jeanette shook her head from side to side. 'No,' she said. 'No!'

'I am sorry, my lady, but it is so.'

Jeanette bit back a howl of anguish, knowing she dared not react. After a moment, she looked at the little hood in her hand, and put two fingers into the soft leather where she felt a small, round, hard object pressed up against the end seam that proved to be a tightly rolled ribbon of parchment. Unwinding it, she read the words, cramped, smudged and written in haste. Thomas exhorted her to be brave and staunch, and said that with God's help he would be with her again soon, but he had no choice except to obey the King's order in the immediate moment.

After what the Queen had said, she felt sick with terror for Thomas's life. This scrap of a note might be the last thing she ever had of him apart from the child growing in her womb, for which she would be disgraced. 'What will become of us?' she whispered, feeling overwhelmed by the welter of recent events and how alone she suddenly was. They were doomed. She pleated the parchment back into the falcon hood and put it in her jewel casket with her rings and brooches. Then she curled up again on her bed and drew out the ribbon on which Thomas's belt pendant was threaded, and beside it, his gold seal ring – her wedding ring. She gripped both in her hand, imprinting their shapes into her flesh.

Katerine arrived, bearing a cup filled with a steaming tisane. 'Come,' she said briskly, 'I have prepared this to balance your humours.'

Jeanette turned her head away, and Katerine's voice became stern.

'You must drink it while it is hot. I promised your mother I would care for you as if you were my own daughter. I am sorry to say I have lapsed at times, but I intend to make up for it now.'

Jeanette just wanted to curl up and be alone, but perhaps if she drank the tisane, Katerine would let her be. She sat up and sipped the brew, grimacing. Katerine watched her. 'All of it,' she insisted. 'Even the dregs, for they are the part that work best. You must drink another cup of this after dark, and when you wake in the morning, all will be well.'

Shuddering, Jeanette finished the tisane. The gritty dregs in the bottom made her retch, but Katerine gripped her shoulder. 'None of that now. You must keep it down or it will not work.' She gave her a box of sweetmeats and made her eat a small piece of sugared ginger. 'Rest now, and I shall return later.' She touched Jeanette's cheek with her fingertips. 'A word of advice. You may dislike me, but you will discover for yourself as you grow what it is to be a woman in this world, and that we must deal according to our resources, and turn them to our advantage.' Rising from the bedside, she took the cup and departed in a whisper of silk.

Feeling heavy and lethargic, Jeanette closed her eyes and slept. Katerine returned soon after dusk with a second dose of the tisane and Jeanette was so groggy that she could barely sit up to drink it and soon fell into a deep, drugged slumber. Towards dawn, she awoke to griping pain in her lower abdomen. Staggering from the bed, she managed to reach the latrine, and as she sat over the hole, her bowels voided themselves in a sudden, agonising plummet. Pain expanded through her lower back and became a griping, constricting agony. And then red, sticky heat between her legs. She lifted her chemise above her waist, looked down and screamed.

Hawise appeared at her side with a candle, her eyes enormous.

'Help me,' Jeanette whimpered. 'Dear God, Hawise, help me! What is happening?'

Hawise stared. 'My lady, your flux has come!'

Countess Katerine arrived and her nostrils flared at the stench of faeces and blood. 'Go and fetch Mistress St Maur,' she commanded Hawise. 'Quickly and quietly now.'

Hawise hurried away and Katerine gripped Jeanette's arms. 'Come now,' she said. 'In order to balance your humours, you first have to purge out the bad ones until nothing remains.'

Consumed by fiery pain, Jeanette was beyond responding. Lady St Maur arrived and, clucking her tongue, took charge.

'Not a word of this beyond this space,' Katerine said to the woman as they exchanged glances, and Lady St Maur nodded her head in complicit agreement.

'Come, come, Jeanette,' Lady St Maur soothed. 'I know it is bad now, but it will ease soon.' She turned to Hawise. 'Have a bowl of warm water ready and your lady's flux cloths, and more to spare.' She examined Jeanette again. 'There now, the worst is over. You will bleed for some days but your womb will settle down, and you will be better.'

Jeanette moaned and shook her head, certain that she wouldn't.

Between them the women helped Jeanette to a freshly made bed, and dressed her in a clean chemise, with a wad of flux cloths placed between her legs to absorb the blood. She felt weak and sore and empty.

'Sleep now,' Katerine murmured, stroking Jeanette's brow.

'We shall watch over you, and as I promised you, all will be well.'

Jeanette wanted to pull away in disgust from Katerine's cool, long-fingered touch, but she lacked the strength. 'No, it won't,' she whispered. She knew she had lost the child. That her dilemma was solved should have filled her with relief, but there was only shock and misery and pain. She turned her face to the wall and closed her eyes, and let the tears come as the blood trickled slowly into the flux cloths.

11

Hertford, Hertfordshire, May 1340

In England, King Edward was assembling a fleet to return to Ghent, bearing troops, money and supplies for his campaign against France. Thomas had spent the last three weeks recruiting and acquiring men and provisions. His particular skill for logistics had been tested to the limit, but he had enjoyed the challenge, and risen to it. He realised how much he had been stagnating in the smaller pool of guarding the Queen and her household. He was also aware that had he been able to stretch himself, he might not have failed the test of temptation with Jeanette that had led them into a scrape that would probably sink his ambitions and perhaps end his life.

Summoned to the King's presence soon after morning mass, Thomas was as tense as a primed bowstring. He dared not speak of marrying Jeanette just now, while the business was all about their return to Ghent. The matter had to be approached delicately at the right moment. Edward had recently received bad news that his close friend William Montagu, Earl of Salisbury, had been captured by the French during a reconnaissance manoeuvre and was being held for ransom, and his mood was dour.

Thomas arrived to find the King seated at a table with a jug of wine and a loaf of bread. 'Sire,' he said, kneeling and doffing his hat.

Edward gestured for him to rise but did not invite him to sit. 'You have done well,' he said. 'I am pleased with your work and how swiftly you have accomplished your tasks. It is rare to find a fighting man who can think like a clerk, a staller and a ship master all in the same parcel.'

'Thank you, sire,' Thomas said, pleased that his skills had been noted.

'I have more work for you before we embark, but you may see my officials for my requirements. If I have summoned you, it is to give praise where praise is due. I always pay such debts to those who serve me well. However, there is another matter that greatly concerns me.'

'Sire?' Thomas hoped he did not look as guilty as he felt.

'Disturbing rumours have come to my ears regarding your familiarity with my young cousin Jeanette of Kent. It is neither seemly nor suitable for you to take an interest in the young lady. She is a valuable asset to me when it comes to making alliances. Reports of untoward behaviour have been regarded with dismay by certain interested parties. Your duty is to protect the women in the Queen's care, not take advantage and compromise their integrity, no matter how delectable they are, and no matter how much they tease you. My cousin is not innocent in this I suspect, and wilful enough to create a reputation for herself in order to escape a match of which she does not herself approve. My order to you is to distance yourself forthwith, so neither she nor your career are compromised – nor your family name.' He gave

Thomas a fierce stare. 'I know you understand perfectly well what I mean.'

Thomas's stomach knotted as he wondered how much the King actually knew. If he spoke up, without a doubt he would be thrown into the sea in a sealed barrel and it would do nothing to aid Jeanette's position. He returned Edward a wide-eyed look that he hoped passed for innocence, and swallowed hard. But he did not protest the accusation.

Edward nodded curtly. 'There are plenty of ladies at court who are not out of bounds and who I am sure will accommodate you. All men have to sow their wild oats, but they must do so appropriately, and let that be all I need to say.'

'Yes, sire,' Thomas said. How on earth was he going to broach the subject of his marriage now? Dear Christ.

Edward waved in dismissal. 'I leave you to your duties, and I shall hear your report in due course.'

Thomas bowed from the royal presence, cold sweat clamming his armpits, and for a man so decisive in battle and organised in logistics, he had no idea what to do.

Three days later, Thomas and Otto arrived at Castle Acre to collect a contingent of serjeants and archers who were being provided for the King's enterprise by John, Earl de Warenne. For the past year de Warenne had been conducting an affair with Otto and Thomas's sister Isabel while striving to have his loveless, long-term marriage annulled so he could offer Isabel honourable wedlock.

The brothers had known de Warenne all their lives – he had always been a family friend, even in the difficult times surrounding their father's death. Learning of his affair with their sister had been a shock, but Thomas could hardly throw stones given his own circumstances. Their mother had accepted the matter with her usual pragmatism. Isabel had always known her own mind, and if de Warenne could persuade the papal court to annul his marriage, then she stood to become a countess to one of the wealthiest men in England as well as one of the most illustrious.

Isabel was waiting to greet their arrival, and the moment the grooms had taken the horses, she ran into Thomas's arms with a glad cry and a hug, and then the same for Otto. She was tall and slim, with the same black hair and dark eyes as Thomas. Only a year separated them – she was the older, and always made certain he knew it.

John de Warenne arrived from the direction of the stables, beating dust and straw from his tunic. He was a limber man in late middle age, with a head of thick silver hair and intelligent light-brown eyes. He greeted the brothers with genuine pleasure, and not a shred of awkwardness despite his arrangement with Isabel. She was lady of the castle, even if not by official title, and when she summoned refreshments, she was obeyed with alacrity.

'So,' the Earl said as they relaxed with wine and cinnamon wafers, 'you are bound back to Flanders in the next few days. The French will attempt a blockade and try to capture or sink our ships. We have had the devil of a time with their attacks on English ports. Your opponent is formidable and has a large fleet.'

'That is why the King wants experienced fighting men aboard every one of our vessels,' Thomas replied. 'He knows what we face.'

'Does he?' John looked dubious.

'Two hundred ships to our hundred and fifty, most of them bigger, with at least ten thousand fighting men – more than three times our numbers.'

Isabel made a small sound, and Otto touched her shoulder.

John folded his arms and looked wry. 'You speak as if it is of no consequence. I am assuming you have more to protect yourself than the false immortality of youth.'

'I would be a fool to rely on that, sire,' Thomas said. 'The French may have strength of numbers, but we have our archers, and their bows will compensate for that discrepancy. Our soldiers are more experienced, and the King is a fine strategist. The rest lies with God. If I thought we were about to sail into disaster, I would not be relaxing in your good company but trying to do something about it. Yes, we shall have to fight, but that is our task.'

John called for more wine.

'Shall you visit our mother?' Isabel enquired.

Thomas shook his head. 'We are under orders to sail any day and what time I have left will be spent supplying the ships. I shall write to her and hope to see her before long.' He took a drink and looked at de Warenne. Of anyone in the world, he could confide in this man about his marriage. After all, the Earl and his sister were a couple outside polite society. 'I have some news for you both, but it is of a personal nature and I must swear you to silence. It cannot go beyond this room.'

De Warenne looked surprised, but waved his hand. 'Of course, my boy. Whatever you say shall go no further, my oath on it.' He gestured for the servants to retire.

Thomas had to force himself to begin speaking, but then the words began to flow, and he quickened his pace, the sooner to be finished. De Warenne's face remained impassive throughout. 'I have done a terrible thing,' Thomas concluded. 'I know I have sinned, that I should have avoided temptation, but it is done, and now I am caught in a bind, as is Jeanette, for what should we do now? I need advice, and you are the best person to give it.'

De Warenne raked his fingers through his thatch of hair, and exhaled hard. 'I am not sure I can tell you what to do. You have woven a tangled web with this girl, and she the King's own cousin – and very young to be certain of her own mind. You are wise to keep it to yourself for now, but it will only be a matter of time before the entire situation becomes known to all. You are certain that the King is unaware?'

'He thinks it no more than a flirtation that must be cooled, and has warned me to keep my distance.' Thomas grimaced. 'But how can I do that when Jeanette is lawfully my wife and will bear our child before winter's end? She cannot keep that hidden under her skirts for long, and she will be disgraced, even with a wedding ring. I have to own up to my responsibility. If I die for it, then so be it, but she must be protected. Of course, I would rather live out my life with her and our children.' He looked at Isabel, who was staring at him in shock, her hand over her mouth.

'Indeed, I understand very well,' de Warenne said. 'Admitting your folly does not solve your dilemma.' He folded his arms. 'Of course I shall do everything in my power to support you and your family when the news becomes known. I shall protect you as much as I can and intercede with the King on your behalf. For now, I counsel you to hold your arrow, for once it is shot, you cannot loose it again, and something might yet turn up that none of us has considered.'

Thomas sighed bleakly. 'If I prove myself in battle and make myself indispensable in the King's service, it might soften his wrath when he finds out.'

'That is one way,' John agreed.

'But you might be killed!' Isabel said with dismay. She had been silent while he told his tale, but with growing agitation.

'Perhaps that might not be so bad a thing,' he said with a

shrug. 'I am not in a state of honour or grace – and I might die anyway for what I have done.'

She was scornful. 'Dying will solve nothing, and will be even harder on those you leave behind – but I suppose you had not thought of that.'

'In truth I have, and it burdens me,' he said, giving her a sharp look, 'but you were ever the voice of my conscience, sister.'

She clenched her fists. 'I cannot believe you have done this. That girl has played with you and seduced you because she did not wish to make that other marriage – she chose you as her way out.' Her eyes flashed with indignation.

'It was not like that,' he retorted, caught on the raw, for Isabel's assessment had at times been part of his own thinking.

'Then what was it like? Tell me.'

De Warenne quickly stepped between them. 'My love, I know you would defend Thomas with your life against all comers,' he said with a flattening motion of his palm, 'but you should reserve your judgement, as I am sure your mother would advise you to do. You might want to allow in the thought that love has a part to play in all of this. Your brother is a grown man and experienced soldier, not a child, and knows his own mind – as you know yours. It is not your choice, but his. Look at us and those who judge us. Would you make yourself one of them?'

Isabel bit her lip. 'Of course not,' she said. 'I should not judge – but I do because Thomas is my brother!' She moved around him to Thomas and gave him a fierce hug. 'I am sorry for what I said – of course we will both help you all we can.'

Thomas knew that even if she was sorry, it was what she thought, but he did not hold it against her. 'We are always friends,' he said ruefully, 'even when we fight and disagree.'

'Do not do anything rash, promise me.'

'I shall try to keep body and soul together for at least a while longer,' he answered, feeling burdened and unsettled even while he tried to smile, and kissed her cheek, continuing to restore the balance between them. If they saw matters differently, it was always from a perspective of family love.

'Do not worry, sister,' Otto said, patting her back. 'I shall look out for him.'

'Well, do not get yourself killed either! Sometimes I wish I had never had brothers at all, only sisters.' She looked at them severely. 'You swore me to silence, but our mother has a right to know.'

'Tell her if you will,' Thomas said. 'But let it go no further than that.'

12

At sea off the Flemish coast, June 1340

Standing beside the King on the deck of the *Thomas* facing the might of the French fleet, Thomas flexed his shoulders and opened and closed his hands, preparing for battle. Some men were fidgeting and jittery with excitement and fear. Some prayed on their knees and said their rosaries. Others busied themselves with their equipment or made boastful jests. And some kept their thoughts sealed in silence.

Despite moving to loosen his muscles, Thomas was calm and focused. There was going to be a battle, a hard one they could not afford to lose. Many said the odds were stacked against them, but Thomas only saw challenges to overcome. His own response before and during combat was one of heightened clarity and awareness and was a reason for his position as an elite knight of the royal household. When his mind was this focused, there was no room to pick at the sore spot of his clandestine marriage to Jeanette. Everything but now could wait.

Beside him, Otto too was still and absorbed. They had fought side by side for so many years that there was nothing to say and nothing to polish for it had all been perfected on the practice field.

The English banners rippled in the wind, the lilies of France quartered with the lions of England, streaming out. The sun was behind them, bright and high in the summer sky and to their advantage, since the hordes of crossbowmen lining the decks of the French ships would be squinting into the light when they shot at the English.

The sky was as clear as fine blue cloth. Gentle whitecaps scudded the waves driven by a good breeze from the north-west, which was exactly what the English needed for their approach. The King looked up at the sun and the moment of waiting strung out like a thin silver wire. Lined up in three rows, the French ships barred the entrance to the harbour of Sluys with the foremost row comprised of the largest galleys and cogs with extra planks nailed to the sides to increase the height and prevent easy boarding. The ships were chained together to form a floating barrier to prevent the English from breaking through and looked formidable. Edward's former flagship the *Christopher*, which had been captured in a raid by the French some months ago, had pride of place in the front ranks. Edward regarded the sight as an incentive, a challenge, and an insult.

'Well,' he said to Thomas, 'what say you, Master Holland?'

Thomas smiled. 'I say, sire, that they are like a shoal of fish and that we shall soon for the expenditure of a little effort have netted a very fine catch.'

Edward's lips twitched. 'I believe that is a clear assessment. Let every man do his best and look to his post. Master Crabbe.'

The King signalled to his ship's master. John Crabbe was a

redoubtable, leather-faced warrior in his mid-sixties but still hale and vigorous. He had a long life of piracy behind him and had fought with the Scots against the King in the past, but Edward had persuaded him to change his allegiance, and Crabbe, intent on a secure future for himself, had entered Edward's service.

A broad-chested yeoman raised an ivory oliphant to his lips and blew the approach. The sound of the horn blared out across the waves and was taken up by the other ships. The anchors rose dripping from the sea, and the English ships sailed in majesty out of the sun towards the might of the much larger French navy.

As their formation neared the French lines, Thomas drew his sword in a silver shiver. The royal vessel was equipped with fighting men and archers in the castles atop prow and stern. Either side they were flanked by ships composed mostly of bowmen, supplied with vast quantities of arrows. The French favoured the use of the crossbow – an instrument to be feared, but the numerical advantage of missiles and range was with the swifter English bows. Thomas had often watched his own Northamptonshire archers at their training – had even joined them at practice. English bows could loose ten arrows in the time it took to load and shoot two from a crossbow. And the French arbalesters would be shooting sun-blind.

The breeze was steady but gentle, and Crabbe and the other ship masters constantly shouted orders to adjust position. The great square sails came up and down along the line, and sometimes anchors were deployed to keep the English ships in formation. As the distance closed between the two sides, Thomas could hear the French trumpets and horns blaring out, not so much to accompany attack as to signal their own positioning.

The chained ships at the front of the line were fouling each other's advance, and the high seaboards made them unwieldy and slow to manoeuvre.

At a signal from the King, their own trumpets blared the attack, and the soldiers roared threats and battle cries, adding to the cacophony.

'The French are mad,' Otto said. 'Why didn't they make for open water and then carve in among us? They have twice our number, but they have hamstrung themselves.'

'They have an experienced commander but I suspect they've overruled him because he is Genoese, not French. Good advantage for us though.' Thomas grinned wolfishly.

Steadily, surely, the French sailed within range of the English longbows. Thomas signalled to the archers clustered in their wooden fighting castles fore and aft to string their bows, and strung his own of Spanish yew, as did Otto, the King and other knights, for every arrow at this opening stage before the ships closed together would count. Samson, one of Thomas's archers from the Holland manor at Broughton, gave him a gap-toothed smile as he handed over a sheaf of twenty arrows, bodkin-pointed and fletched with goose feathers.

As the ships closed across the water, the shout went up to nock the arrows in the bowstring. Then, 'Draw!'

Thomas pulled back until his arm was level with his right ear and his vambraced left arm extended straight. All along the English front line of vessels, throngs of archers performed the same task. Closer . . . closer, the summer sea ploughed by a hundred and fifty keels.

'Loose!'

Thomas released all the pent-up tension from his arm into the blazing midsummer sky and was already setting the next arrow to the nock as thousands of razored tips sped in a vicious hornet-storm towards the leading French ships. Nock, draw, loose; nock, draw, loose. The arrows plummeted in a brutal hail upon the tightly packed French who had no chance of manoeuvring out of the way. So thick was the arrow storm, so close the ships, that the missiles diving from the sky could not miss. The built-up sides of the French vessels were no defence, and neither were the crossbowmen, hampered in their shooting by the sun's glare and the deadly hail. Some of the bigger French vessels possessed stone throwers, but they had to be operated by crews who were taking cover, and their aim was inaccurate.

Thomas rapidly shot his twenty arrows, and then another twenty. As they drew closer to the French ships the archers began directing their aim at specific soldiers rather than shooting high. However, they were wary themselves now, because they were within range of the crossbows, and not every French archer had fallen. Yet still their assault continued until they were within thirty yards of the French front line. Then it was time to discard the longbow, draw weapons and prepare the grapnels for boarding.

The reinforced strakes of the former English ship the *Saint George* reared up before them as the spiked ropes snaked out and drew her breast to breast with the *Thomas*. In the crow's nests, the English archers were ready to pick off or pin down anyone trying to hack the boarding ropes.

Thomas and Otto were first on deck, climbing swiftly up the nets attached to the grapnels and over the top. Thomas ducked a blow aimed at his torso and downed his man. An English marksman brought down another before he could cleave Thomas's head, and then Otto was beside him, and the deadly dance began.

Thomas ploughed into the thick of the brawl, and as the

battle grew harder and ever more desperate, the steelier and steadier he became. The alchemy of sword and long dagger in tandem. The kick, the punch, the smooth twist and the pivot. He knew every move, every permutation. He could finely judge what each opponent would do, and linked to that judgement was pure, swift instinct. Yet, despite his pinpoint focus, he did not lose the wider perspective, and knew what was happening around him. He was aware of the King fighting to his left with household knights Walter Manny and William Burgesh either side.

Edward missed his parry and took a slash to his leg, and then another to his arm, but Manny reached him and cut the French soldier down. Thomas had disengaged and backed to protect the King, but Edward waved his sword. 'I am all right!' he panted, breathing hard, teeth bared. 'Go on, go on!'

Thomas and Otto plunged back into the fray until no French were left aboard the ship, at least none that breathed. Henry de la Haye, his surcoat blood-soaked, handed Thomas the English flag, and Thomas cast the fabric over his shoulder and scaled the rigging to the crow's nest, where he tore down the French Oriflamme banner and let the quartered English lions snap out in the wind, to a resounding cheer from the deck.

The battle raged on throughout the long summer afternoon. As the sun slipped in the sky and the colours of dusk smudged the horizon, the English continued to press forward with relentless determination. The ships of the French front line had either been seized or had fled, and Edward ordered crews from his own second row to take the captured French vessels and push forward to demolish the next French line. One by one English banners flapped in the breeze as ship after ship succumbed, and the Flemish, watching from the shore, put to sea in their own craft and turned on the French like vultures at a lion's kill.

By sunset, the French third line had broken and scattered, and Edward's smaller fleet had recaptured many more English ships including the *Christopher*. The decks of the great galley were awash with blood and arrows. From the forecastle, Thomas directed his archer Samson and two of his companions to gather up the shafts and drop them in an empty barrel to be sorted for reuse. A detail of men at arms was picking up the French dead, stripping them of valuables, and casting them over the side. Thomas gazed into the heavy green water, no longer blue as the sun declined in the sky. He could not see any bodies, but knew many would float in the coming days and that thousands were now sinking down in the fathoms under the ship's keels.

'The fish will all speak French, the feast we have given them,' Otto said, joining him. The vambrace on his left arm was cut almost through. 'And then if we catch the fish and eat them, shall we have devoured our enemy, do you think?'

Thomas snorted. 'You have some strange fancies at times, and not ones I want to consider when eating my dinner!' He gestured to the vambrace. 'Are you hurt?'

Otto shook his head. 'One of the bastards had a good try, but this was the only casualty. You?'

'Not a scratch,' Thomas said, although he knew he would have a few bruises when it came to the accounting. 'The King took that cut to the thigh though. If we failed in anything, it was in protecting him.' But then Edward was not a child to be constantly watched and coddled. He knew his own mind and the risks involved, and the injury had not looked severe.

He slapped his hand down on the top of the wooden castle hoarding and gazed at the sea of English banners waving against the blood-red sky. 'We have destroyed the French king's fleet and the army he was assembling to invade England.' He shook his head in wonder at the sheer enormity of their achievement. There would be booty and glory for all.

'God was with us,' Otto said, 'as He was not with the French.'

'And with our archers,' Thomas replied, remembering the death rain of arrows whistling over the sea as he watched the soldiers at their work on the deck, where the fallen shafts lay as thick as floor-straw in places. He stooped and picked one up, barred with trimmed goose feathers and a sharp bodkin head. 'This is what won the battle,' he said. 'These kept them pinned down – and their own folly. Had they sailed out to meet us, we would now be the ones at the bottom of the sea.' It was a sobering thought. How so many small moments and decisions could amalgamate into a force strong enough to turn the wheel of fate.

Edward spent the night on the *Christopher*. The tally of the dead amounted to five hundred English and over ten thousand French, with a hundred and sixty-six French ships captured – more than the total English fleet – and twenty-four sunk. It had been a triumph and a rout.

Despite his injuries, the King was in good spirits. His chirurgeon had cleaned and stitched his thigh wound, and smeared it with honey. Edward sat with his leg propped on a stool to aid healing while his scribes toiled around him, writing news of the victory; a messenger had already set out to the Queen to inform her of their success.

Thomas and Otto made their report and returned to the *Thomas*. Now in dock, they could hear the roistering in the drinking houses on shore. Men capered and caroused on the decks of the captured ships, drunk on wine and the exhilaration of being alive to celebrate, and with the promise of booty to come.

The brothers sat down either side of an upturned tub to consume roast capon and a clear French wine purloined from the *Saint George*.

'Are you going to tell the King about your marriage?' Otto asked. 'You could do it now while he is in a good mood about the victory.'

Thomas shook his head. 'I need to speak with Jeanette first, and he has other matters on his mind as well as contending with his wound. Let it wait a better time.' He was procrastinating – he knew the King would not respond well whenever he broached the matter. 'I shall tell him when the time is right,' he said, to assuage his conscience, 'but if you want to go ashore and celebrate, do not let me stop you.'

'Without you?'

Thomas shrugged ruefully. 'I have to count how many arrows we have salvaged, and what equipment needs replacement or repair. Henry will go with you of a certainty.'

'You could do that tomorrow in daylight – it would be far easier.' Otto pushed aside his dish and stood up.

'Perhaps, but I know how easy it would be to get drunk and wake up lying across some harlot with a thousand demons banging hammers inside my skull. Besides, I have a reputation to uphold now that must stand me in good stead with the King.'

'As you please,' Otto said. 'At least you know what you'll be missing.'

Standing among the Queen's ladies, Jeanette watched King Edward return to Ghent in triumph amid a fanfare of silver trumpets and horn blasts. News of the miraculous victory at

Sluys had spread far and wide, and the city was decked out to greet the returning heroes.

The glossy coats of the horses shone with starbursts of sunlight, and the armour of the knights and attendants twinkled and flashed, dazzling the eyes. Harnesses jingled, and horseshoes struck blue sparks on the cobbles. The supply carts rumbled behind, piled with booty from hundreds of French ships.

Positioned in the middle of the women, Jeanette stood with Katerine of Salisbury, who was watching her closely for any signs of infraction. The Countess's mood was pensive and irritable for her husband was still a prisoner of the French with his ransom to be arranged.

Jeanette sought Thomas in the throng. They had heard at court of the King's injury and that he had been resting while the captured ships were unloaded and the victory consolidated, but he had sent messages daily, informing the Queen of his progress. Jeanette was glad for the victory, and that Thomas was alive – news would have come to them in the daily dispatches if he wasn't – but she was deflated and afraid of the news she had for him.

She saw him riding not far from the King with Otto at his side, the brothers clad in the green and scarlet livery of the household knights. He leaned in to reply to a comment made by one of the men, but then raised his head, searching the crowd, and like an arrow finding its mark, unerringly caught her gaze. Jeanette hastily looked down, unsure of how to respond. They no longer needed to be married. He could ride away without commitment. The only people who knew were their servants and the young friar, and they were all sworn to secrecy. But she didn't want it to be an ending.

Katerine of Salisbury had stuck to her like a limpet to a rock ever since making her drink that tisane and nursing her in the time afterwards. A week ago, her monthly bleed had come as usual, and Katerine had pronounced with satisfaction that all was now functioning as it should. Jeanette had barely left the Queen's apartment during the last six weeks, and when she did, was so closely chaperoned that there had been no opportunity to send word to Thomas. Her life had become a prison.

13

Monastery of St Bavo, Ghent, July 1340

For the next week, Katerine kept Jeanette under close scrutiny. The Queen was too preoccupied with her husband's return to concern herself with her ladies, but Katerine remained strict and watchful, ensuring Jeanette had no opportunity to approach any of the knights.

Letters arrived from Jeanette's mother, exhorting her to continue with her lessons, to comport herself with dignity and not bring disgrace on her family. Feeling resentful and ashamed, Jeanette tore them up, and cried to herself. It was like being stuck in quicksand and sucked ever further down.

The times she did see Thomas among company, she was afraid, and when their eyes did meet she saw the growing bafflement and anger in his. He sent messages via John de la Salle and Hawise to meet him in the mews, but Katerine wouldn't let her out of her sight and Jeanette was too heartsick to make the effort to abscond.

At the start of the following week, the Queen sent Jeanette

and Hawise to the alms building with a basket of bread and cheese to hand out at the gate. Katerine was suffering from one of the bad headaches that came upon her sometimes, and had been forced to lie down with a sick bowl at her side, her vigilance abandoned.

Jeanette gave the basket to the almoner, but as she turned to leave, Thomas arrived, and a white-hot bolt of panic shot through her. Thomas nodded to Hawise. 'Give us a moment, mistress,' he said, in such a way that Hawise curtseyed and left, with a worried look over her shoulder at her mistress.

'Why have you been avoiding me?' he demanded.

Feeling sick, Jeanette placed her hands on her belly like a shield. 'I haven't. The Countess of Salisbury watches me and gives me no opportunity. She is unwell today, and I am only here on a quick errand. I must go, or they will come looking.'

'No,' he said firmly. 'Stay, and tell me why you will not look at me and why you shun my company. You were busy enough before, yet you managed to find moments for us to be alone. What has changed? And do not take me for a fool!'

Jeanette crumpled inside at the expression on his face. She didn't know what to say or do. 'I do not have the courage to tell you.'

'Tell me what?' His gaze sharpened. 'Have you forsaken me so soon while I have been in danger for my life? Have I been no more than an excuse to get you out of the Gascon marriage, and a plaything to while away your time?'

'No, never that!'

'Then why avoid me as you have been doing?' he asked grimly. 'What is it, then? Tell me – after all, we are husband and wife. You should share whatever is bothering you, and I will take the burden too.'

She shook her head again. 'I . . . Oh dear God, Thomas.

The Countess of Salisbury gave me a drink to balance my humours, and it brought on my flux. There is no child.' She flushed with guilt, remembering the advice she had used at first that had not worked. 'The Countess said the tisane would make me better because I was being sick all the time. You were gone the day after our wedding, perhaps never to return, and they wouldn't let me leave the Queen's apartments. I had no help, no succour, no protection.'

'You mean, the moment I was gone, you lost faith,' he said with bitter accusation.

'It wasn't like that. You were not there,' she repeated. 'They knew we had been meeting. I was so afraid – and so alone.'

'And now you will not come near me or speak to me?'

'If I do, how long do you think you will live?' she answered, with a flash of spirit. 'Do you think they will not punish us both for this? Lady Katerine knew we had been lying together, I am certain. If she has not spoken of it to anyone else, it is because it would cause too great a scandal in the Queen's household, and diminish her own influence. The Queen just thinks there has been an inappropriate flirtation, but if she were to learn the truth . . .' She broke off and shook her head. 'She would not be lenient.'

'So where do we stand?' he demanded. 'Do you now deny your marriage vows? Are you still my wife?'

'Of course I am!'

'But you will not talk with me, and you turn your gaze, and the child is no more.'

She shook her head. 'I fear for your life if they find out – and I want you in the world.'

'Then how shall we ever live our lives as man and wife?' he asked with impatient exasperation. 'When shall it be known? You want me in the world, but you will not speak to me. What kind of a marriage is that?'

She swallowed, and dropped her gaze.

'Look at me. At least afford me that courtesy.'

Scared, upset and ashamed, she raised her head and jutted her chin. 'I thought you were going to speak to the King when you went to England, but clearly you did not.'

A red flush crawled up his own neck. 'He warned me off before I could say anything. I know we must be careful, but when you turn your shoulder and behave as if I am nothing to you, what am I to do?'

'I hear you have performed great deeds – the King will look on you with favour if you speak.'

'And will you look on me with favour too, or am I chasing my tail?'

'I love you, Thomas.' It was simple. It should be a joyful cause for celebration, but the moment they shared their marriage with the world, they would become doomed lovers instead of secret ones. 'But how shall we be husband and wife unless we let it be known? And if we let it be known, what will then happen to us?'

From nearby they heard the sound of two youths in conversation, and she realised the danger in which they stood, just for so small a thing.

He let out a hard sigh. 'Return to the Queen, and stay with her ladies,' he said. 'We are setting out to war again within a few days. Perhaps there will be time for even greater deeds than at Sluys.' Taking her right hand, he placed a large, rough-cut ruby in her palm, scratched and opaque on the outside but with a glowing red centre. 'This stands for my heart,' he said. 'Take it and keep it safe. It came from a treasure chest on a French ship, and it is part of my claim on the booty given to me by the King. I was going to have it made into a pendant for you to wear around your neck. We shall talk again when I return from campaign, should I be fortunate to survive, and then we shall see where we stand, and I shall speak my case to the King. We are married in the eyes of God, and that is a holy sacrament. I shall not give you up.'

He bowed stiffly and walked away. She watched the graceful motion of his body, and her heart almost broke. The rough edges of the stone were sharp as she closed her fist over it before stowing it in the alms purse at her belt and going outside to Hawise.

'They will wonder what has taken you so long,' Hawise said.

'I shall say I have been at prayer. In truth I do not care whether they wonder or not. I have told him about the child. We are saying nothing of our marriage until he returns from the next campaign – there is no urgency now, is there?' She walked off briskly, making it clear she did not wish to say anything else for she was hollow inside.

Their return was greeted with a few sharp queries from Katerine's maid about the length of their absence, but Katerine herself was sleeping, and Jeanette murmured in a subdued voice that she had remained at prayer, because she had felt the need, and the moment of danger passed.

Thomas sat down at the trestle table in his lodging and sent his squire to fetch bread and cheese.

Otto, who had been checking their equipment, joined him at the board. 'Have you seen her?'

'Yes.' Thomas rubbed his face. 'She has lost the child,' he said. 'The Countess of Salisbury gave her a tisane to "balance her humours", and she miscarried.'

'Ah Tom, I am sorry . . .' Otto reached out to clasp his arm. 'So the Countess of Salisbury knows?'

Thomas grimaced. 'About Jeanette being with child – yes, but not about the marriage. The King and Queen are still unaware beyond what they consider an ill-advised flirtation between us.'

'Do you think the Countess will tell the King and Queen about the child?'

'I doubt it. She was Jeanette's chaperone and it will reflect badly on her if they find out. But the fact that she knows is a threat. She has the Queen's ear and also the King's because of her husband's close friendship with him – not to mention her own.' There were certain rumours concerning the King and Lady Salisbury that travelled like thin wisps of vapour in some corners of the court.

The squire returned with the food and a brimming jug. Thomas thanked and dismissed him.

Otto poured wine for both of them and reached for the bread. 'What are you going to do?'

Thomas frowned. 'That Jeanette was with child at all is the result of my own sin and dishonour – Jeanette's too, but she is less to blame than I am. I knew what I was doing and I yielded to temptation instead of walking away. We both know we dare not reveal our marriage to the King and Queen at this point without damaging consequences.'

'So, you are both going to pretend nothing happened?' Otto chewed and swallowed. 'That will have its consequences too, brother.'

'Yes, but for now it is the wisest course to take. I shall be absent on campaign for at least another month, so nothing can be done before then, and perhaps it should be longer than that.' He took some bread himself but made no attempt to eat it.

Otto raised a questioning brow.

Thomas sighed. 'She is too young for the burdens that have been set on her. Even without what happened she would have been no wife for Armand d'Albret. She is like a young hawk that has been forced to fly before it has fully fledged. We are away on campaign with the King and after that he will release us from our contract until he needs us again.' He broke the bread in half and gazed at the scattered crumbs as though they might tell the future. 'I have a mind to take the cross and go to Bavaria. I shall use my profession in God's service to atone for my sins for a year and a day. Should God grant me the grace to return from that undertaking, then perhaps He will also show me the road ahead. And in the meantime, Jeanette will have had time to grow her wings.'

Otto shook his head. 'That is an undertaking,' he said doubtfully, 'and a great risk.'

'I have been thinking upon it for a while. I cannot continue without a clean start, and Jeanette needs time. We dare not expose our marriage for now, so I must make other plans. I know your own plans may be different. I do not expect you to accompany me.'

Otto shrugged. 'I may not have the same burdens to carry and atonements to make as you, but every man should pay his dues to God in his life. Of course I shall ride at your side. What else would I do?'

'Then thank you, with all my heart.' Now it was Thomas's turn to reach out for a hand clasp.

'If nothing else, it will keep you away from the temptations at court for a while,' Otto said with an attempt at humour.

'I think I have been cured of that for life,' Thomas replied wryly, 'but what about you?'

'Oh, a soldier's life for me.' Otto raised his cup in a toast. 'Roll the dice and lie with a woman for tuppence, rather than the price of my life.' The smile fell from his face. 'You are doing the right thing.'

'I hope so,' Thomas replied, 'I truly do, but God help me, and God help Jeanette.'

14

At sea between Flanders and England, August 1340

Jeanette stood outside the deck shelter watching the Flemish coastline slowly diminish from sight. The breeze behind their ship freshened and the square sail bellied out. Gulls teemed above the rigging, and the banners rippled, flying the leopards and lilies of England.

Arms folded beneath her cloak, she hugged herself for comfort, thinking of the voyage to Flanders a little over two years ago – how she had been brimming with excitement at the prospect of adventure. When she had set her eyes on Thomas, it had been like a pillar of golden light shooting through her body. Now, on the return voyage, all that excitement had vanished as though it had been poured into a dirty hole in the ground and stamped over. She was flat, deflated by the things she had learned and experienced. She had arrived a light-footed girl, and returned burdened with invisible weights and a bitter knowledge of what the world could do.

Part of her was glad to be leaving Flanders, but each surge

of the ship took her further away from Thomas and the life they might have had in another time and place. She thought of their last whispered meeting in a corridor. He had taken her hands and told her he was leaving in the morning for Tournai and then going to serve God on crusade for a year and a day.

'I will return for you,' he had said, 'and I shall put my case before the King concerning our marriage, I swear, but first I must atone for my sins and make my peace with God. All I ask is that you wait for me and make your own peace with Him too, for then we shall have a clean start.'

She had felt as though he was pushing her off the edge of a cliff. He was going into grave danger; she might never see him again. It had been difficult enough when he went to England, and now he wanted to travel even further away. How was that love? 'You will be gone longer than I have known you,' she had said, her voice quivering with accusation and dismay.

Still holding her hands, he had knelt to her. 'I vow that when I return, I shall claim you before the King and Queen, and all will know.' Then he had risen to his feet and kissed her, and she had put her arms around him and held him tightly, clinging to him with desperate love and furious anger.

She shivered, and folded her arms more tightly inside her cloak. He had promised to return, but how could anyone make a promise like that with certainty? What if he was going to his death? Everything that had been true and bright now was tarnished. She had a wedding ring, a pendant, a ruby and a marriage contract, and every single item had to be hidden from sight, like the marriage itself. All she had to show to the world were secrets – too many of them. Why should either of them have to atone for love?

Thomas had been gone a week when she had been told to pack her baggage for a return to England. The King and Queen had arranged to send the younger children home for safety while they remained in Flanders. The two little princesses, Isabelle and Joan, and the infant boys Lionel and John were all to leave with their nurses. Lady Salisbury was accompanying them, and Jeanette too. Hawise was attending her, but John de la Salle had gone with Thomas. Thomas's hawk was being returned to England, to his mother's household, to be cared for. Frederick had remained in the royal mews, to be shipped over later in the year with the Queen's hawks.

The wind freshened and the sail flapped. Clouds scudded across the sky, fast as wolves, and a rain squall approached in a sweep from the west. Sighing, Jeanette returned to the deck shelter and found Lady Katerine, green at the gills, her lips pressed tightly together. Jeanette experienced a glimmer of superiority, since her own stomach was sturdy when sailing, and she even smiled a little as she handed Katerine a brass basin and commented how hungry she was, and how she could just eat a big wedge of pigeon pie swimming in cream sauce.

Katerine gave up the unequal struggle, seized the bowl and retched into it.

A few weeks later, Jeanette stood watching a group of youths at weapons practice on the green at the Tower of London. She had escaped the confines of the ladies' chamber by offering to walk with the little princesses Joan and Isabelle, and their lap dogs. Her own Grippe ran with them, sniffing and busy.

The King's heir, the lord Edward, was among the squires, tall for his years, his dark hair glinted with bronze. Her brother John was with him, and flaxen-haired William Montagu, Lady Katerine's son. Edward was besting his opponents with accomplished natural talent, although John and Montagu were doing their best not to let him win. Jeanette, however, was unimpressed.

Having watched Thomas and Otto at their own deadly play, these were mere boys in comparison, albeit with developing skills. Edward was easily the most talented, and had the advantage of longer legs and reach too. John was the least enthusiastic, but dutiful and committed.

'Edward is the best.' Eight-year-old Isabelle delivered her opinion with partisan authority, her delicate nose tilted in the air.

'Yes, he is,' Jeanette answered with a smile. Perhaps she should praise her brother, but it would not be the truth, and she had no intention of appending any good qualities to William Montagu. In earlier childhood gatherings they had never been friends. The times he wasn't ignoring her, he treated her as inferior because of her sex. When she had been ten and he eight, he had punched her in the stomach and she had tipped a bucket of discarded fish heads over him in retaliation. It had not ended well. She had never understood why Edward and John were his friends, but had decided that it was a matter of masculine solidarity.

Edward glanced up, saw her with his little sisters, and waved. Isabelle and Joan set off at a run and Jeanette followed, with the dogs straining their leashes. Edward grinned, his dark hazel eyes sparkling with good humour.

'We stopped to watch our protectors honing their skills,' Jeanette said, smiling. 'I am certain we shall never be in any danger with such stalwart assistance.'

Edward swept a courteous bow. John was pink in the face at being observed by his sister and the young princesses. William looked down his nose. 'Should you not be with the ladies in the bower?' he asked, mainly addressing Jeanette.

'Even ladies are permitted to walk their dogs, and we had permission,' she retorted with irritation, and was aware of

Edward looking amused. 'Perhaps our presence will spur you on to greater effort than you are making now.'

William snorted with contempt, but a spark kindled in Edward's eyes. 'Indeed, you are right!' he declared. 'Come, the best of three!'

With less alacrity than the Prince, the other two returned to their sparring.

Edward made a few missteps because he was watching her and his sisters from the side of his eye, but swiftly recovered his concentration and disarmed William. Red-faced, the youth scowled at Jeanette, as if it was all her fault. She smiled sweetly in return, and his flush darkened. Edward swiftly divested John of his sword too, his superior skill obvious. Magnanimous in defeat, he clapped the others on the shoulder, declaring it had been a good bout. His eyes met Jeanette's, seeking approval, but they were filled with mischief too, and she had to smile, while his sisters danced and clapped.

Following dinner, eaten in the royal chambers, Edward lightly touched Jeanette's arm. 'Come,' he said, 'I have something to show you.' She looked at the other women who were taking out their sewing and preparing to settle down to an afternoon of gossip and stitchery, but Edward was insistent. 'Leave them. They won't gainsay me. You won't get into trouble – hah, and I don't suppose you would care if you did!' His eyes sparkled with laughter and daring.

Excitement bubbled up inside her and turned into a surge of the joy she thought she had lost. She took Edward's outstretched hand, and they sped from the hall, down the steps and across the grass. His grip was firm and she had to hold up her skirts with her other hand and lengthen her stride to keep up with him, laughing out loud.

He led her to the stables where the pungent smell of hay and dust, dung and urine filled her nostrils, but in a familiar way. She wondered why he had brought her here – surely not to go riding because a whole entourage would have had to be organised. Remembering Thomas and the stables at St Bavo, she hung back, so that Edward gave her a quizzical look.

'What's wrong?'

'Nothing.' She hid her feelings behind a bright smile. 'What do you want to show me?'

Edward took her to a stall where a small horse stood champing hay – a compact dappled grey, sturdily built with pricked ears and wide-set intelligent dark eyes.

'This is Courage,' he announced proudly.

Jeanette made herself focus. Edward was her friend and she didn't want to let him down. 'What a beauty!' Courage couldn't compare to the magnificence of Thomas's Noir, but she appreciated his quality.

'My father gave him to me for my year day. I'm going to train for the tourney with him.'

She made suitably impressed noises, and patted the horse's warm grey neck.

Edward took her hand again. 'I have something else to show you too.' He led her to the harness room, and showed her a long beam along which was spread a swathe of horse barding embroidered with the royal arms of England in crusted gold. Jeanette's jaw dropped. Edward watched her with his hands on his hips and an ear-to-ear smile on his face. 'My father gave me this on my year day too. It's for parades and special occasions, of course.' He sounded a little put out about that, as if he would like to ride in it every day.

Jeanette tentatively stroked the rich cloth. 'I can just imagine.'

'Do you want to sit on it?'

Jeanette saw the devilry sparking in his eyes, and felt an answering frisson of her own. 'Why not?'

Edward climbed up on to the bar and sat across the barding. He put his hand down to her and pulled her up behind him, but astride, not side-seat. She tucked in her skirts and he began to make the back-and-forth motion of riding, and she moved with him, putting her arms around his waist and leaning her cheek in to his ribcage.

'Does your horse not go any faster than this?' she asked with mock disdain.

'Oh yes, faster than the wind! As fast as you want to go, but you must hold on tightly!'

His words reminded her of Thomas's with such a sharp jolt that she stopped smiling. She loved Edward dearly, but he was just one of her brother's friends, and a boy. They shared a sense of humour and adventure and she hoped they always would, but he was the heir to the throne – a future king. Their bond was as strong as rawhide and as fragile as glass. She held on tightly, feeling the discomfort of the wooden bar under her legs, feeling Edward's lean young body under her hands and the swift movement of his ribcage. So very tightly indeed.

'Do you remember when your mother told you off for riding your hobby horse astride?' Edward asked, laughter in his voice. 'And you shouted for all to hear that it was a stupid rule and it wasn't fair?'

'Yes, and I was taken away and beaten for it, and all the boys just carried on playing,' she said indignantly. 'I still say it's a stupid rule and not fair.'

'Do you then wish you'd been born a boy?'

'Frequently,' she replied, and he looked round at her, almost taken aback.

Voices intruded on the moment, and they heard a groom

saying to someone that he had seen neither the lord Edward nor the lady Jeanette.

Edward stopped, and Jeanette loosened her arms from around his waist. He jumped off the bar and lifted her down, and she hastily straightened her gown, her heart thumping. Going to the door, Edward opened it on the senior groom and one of the chamber stewards.

'Were you seeking us?' he enquired. 'I was showing my cousin the new barding for my horse.' His manner had changed from that of smiling youth to imperious prince, but Jeanette squirmed, for by explaining himself he had made the moment seem suspect. She would receive the blame yet again for being unseemly. Things were still unfair.

The steward dropped his gaze and said neutrally, 'Sire, you are both sought. The Dowager Countess of Kent is here.'

Jeanette's stomach knotted at the news of her mother's arrival. Edward shot her a sidelong glance. 'Then we shall come.' He held out his arm to her. 'Cousin,' he said, 'we should not keep your lady mother waiting.'

Jeanette laid her hand along his sleeve. 'Indeed not,' she replied, thinking the opposite, thinking that her mother could wait for ever.

On her return to the great chamber on Edward's arm, she saw her mother sitting in a window seat, waiting, hands folded tightly in her lap, watching everyone who entered the hall. On seeing Jeanette, Margaret rose to her feet.

Edward walked over to her and bowed deeply, and Margaret curtseyed.

'My lady mother,' Jeanette said formally, and curtseyed too.

'I beg your indulgence, madam,' Edward said, 'it is my fault Jeanette was not here to greet you. I pray you will forgive me.'

'Of course, sire,' Margaret replied, her own smile strained.

Edward excused himself, abandoning Jeanette to her fate, giving her arm a surreptitious squeeze as he departed.

Jeanette discovered that she was looking down at her mother instead of being eye to eye as before and was now a full head taller. Two years had wrought so many changes, her height the least of them.

Margaret stood on tip-toe to kiss her daughter on either cheek with her customary cool peck. Then she stepped back, her gaze wandering to the stalks of straw clinging to the hem of Jeanette's gown.

'The lord Edward invited me to see his new horse and the barding for it,' Jeanette said, heat sweeping into her cheeks. 'It would have been unseemly to refuse.'

'And the moment you see an open door, you are straight out of it,' her mother said, brows knitted. 'That has not changed. Come, we shall talk.'

She drew Jeanette to the window seat and sat down, decorously arranging her skirts. Jeanette swept the straw from hers, and, belatedly noticing some dung on her shoes, tucked her feet under the shelter of her hem.

Margaret asked her how she had fared in Flanders – how far her education as a highborn lady of the Queen's chamber had progressed, and what she had learned. Jeanette answered in a voice devoid of colour, giving her mother the hard, small fruits, and none of the harvest. What could she say that would not bring opprobrium down on her head? Let her ask Katerine of Salisbury if she wanted to know more, although for certain Katerine would say nothing since her own reputation lay at stake. The same for Lady St Maur.

Her mother's expression grew more set with each monosyllabic reply, and Jeanette's stomach tightened until she thought it must surely touch her spine. They had so little in common; it was like talking through a narrow gap in a wall, each of them speaking but not hearing what the other said – not wanting to hear.

'I am glad to see you and I understand you are doing well,' Margaret said, 'but I was disturbed to learn that the Gascon marriage the King was planning for you had failed because of your skittish behaviour. Considering the state of your gown, you do not appear to have moderated it in the time since.'

Jeanette flashed her mother a resentful look. 'The Gascon marriage failed because the lords in question were not sufficiently committed. They were flirting with the French too, and it did not suit their purpose.'

Her mother eyed her narrowly. 'That may be the case, although from what I have heard from the Countess of Salisbury, you were certainly to blame in part, because it did not suit your purpose either. Now you are home, it is time to pay attention to that improvement of decorum. You will learn to behave as befits your womanhood.'

Jeanette let the words wash over her like water off wax.

'I have your best interests at heart,' her mother said. 'Believe me.'

Jeanette said nothing. The interests of her mother's heart were locked into the prestige and status of the family and there was nothing left for love – indeed, perhaps love was the enemy, for love was belief, not reason.

As soon as she could, Jeanette escaped to play at tables and hazard with the other young courtiers, Edward among them, and swiftly engaged herself in their company. When she did cast a side glance in her mother's direction, she saw that Katerine of Salisbury had joined her, and also Katerine's elderly but still robust mother-in-law, Elizabeth de Montfort. The women were talking together in a huddle like witches over a cauldron, and she saw them look at her.

'That's plotting if ever I saw it,' Edward said with amusement as he prepared to cast his dice.

Jeanette sniffed and turned a little on her stool so that her back was to the women. 'They are probably just numbering my faults between them and deciding how to put me in a cage.'

'They'll have a hard task doing that.' He threw his dice, cursed at his score, and handed the horn shaker to Jeanette.

'Yes, I'd rather die,' she said.

'Hah, rather them in the attempt!' he replied, and grinned at her.

15

Reading, Berkshire, December 1340

Jeanette swirled amid the dancers at the Christmas court, gold stars shining on her dark blue velvet gown. More stars gleamed in her braided hair, and powdered her shoes. Prince Edward took her by the waist and lifted her, swinging her round and placing her down, his arms strong with developing muscle. Their eyes met in a moment of shared exhilaration and she experienced a pang in her stomach, of affection and physical attraction, although only a small fire compared to the all-consuming blaze she felt for Thomas.

There had been no word from him, but she prayed for his safe return every night before she climbed into bed, and tried to keep her faith, hoping he had not abandoned his of her. She had settled once again into daily life with the royal children, functioning as an extra pair of hands, part nursemaid, part royal ward. Ever since the King and the court had returned from Flanders in late November, she had been kept very busy.

The dance finished; Edward bowed and Jeanette curtseyed to

him, and they smiled at each other. Katerine of Salisbury arrived, her gown of ash-pink velvet shimmering with crystals and gold bezants. Her husband had been released by the French in a hostage exchange in late September and had returned to court with the King, and all was well in their world.

Katerine made her obeisance to the young Prince, who inclined his head but did not bow, and then she turned to Jeanette. 'The Queen wishes to speak with you in her chamber,' she said.

Jeanette looked at her in surprise. 'What about?' She had often attended on the Queen since November to rub her feet or comb her hair, but Philippa was pregnant again and had retired from the festivities to rest and Jeanette was not expecting a summons.

'She will tell you,' Katerine said briskly. 'Make haste, do not keep her waiting.'

Bemused, Jeanette followed Katerine and an usher to the Queen's chamber. As she left the hall, she looked over her shoulder at Edward, but he shrugged and opened his hands to say he was at a loss. She shivered, for away from the hearth and the press of celebrating people the air was icy and she did not have her cloak.

At the Queen's door, the usher knocked and craved admittance and a steward bade them enter. The air was immediately warmer here, heated by a glowing hearth and strategically positioned braziers. A blaze of beeswax candles gave off a cumulative honey scent, and added more warmth and ambience. Philippa lay on her bed, swathed in furs and silk, comfortably propped up by a mound of silk pillows. Her pet squirrel Poppet sat on a velvet cushion near her head, manipulating a walnut in his dextrous little paws.

'Ah, my dear.' Philippa beckoned Jeanette to her side, rings shining on every finger. 'You look beautiful. Are you enjoying the entertainments?'

'Yes, madam, very much.'

'I am glad to hear it, and I know how well you dance.'

At a gesture, a lady came forward with an exquisite small wine glass and a platter of pastries. Jeanette sipped the sweet, almost sticky wine and ate a pastry. Powdered Venetian sugar tingled on her tongue.

Philippa settled against her cushions. 'I have asked you to come to me because the King and I have been reconsidering the matter of your future.'

Jeanette almost choked on her last bite of pastry, and had to take a hasty swallow of her wine.

'It is unfortunate that the Gascon marriage was not to be, and let the reasons why remain in the past. We expected too much of you then.' Philippa gave her a sympathetic smile. 'Now you are older and wiser and it is seemly that you should marry and have a husband to care for. Your mother's brother has approached us on behalf of your family and the groom's family has also signalled their intent for their son.' Philippa's eyes twinkled. 'I believe this time the young man will be a perfect match for you, and you know him well.'

Jeanette was still swallowing convulsively and struggling to breathe. Dear Holy Virgin, was she going to speak of Thomas and allow them to wed?

'Come, have a guess at his identity,' Philippa teased.

'Madam, I cannot think,' Jeanette replied in a strangled voice.

'Your uncle and your mother are delighted, I can tell you.'

The sudden flash of hope in Jeanette's breast vanished as quickly as it had arrived. Not Thomas then.

Philippa tilted her head. 'I see I have overwhelmed you. I know you will be pleased, for he is a handsome young man with a promising future, and an earldom to inherit in time. Come now, not even the smallest notion?'

Jeanette looked down at her hands and shook her head. 'No, madam.'

'Oh, I do not believe that – you are not a fool. Take another drink, my dear, and steady yourself. When you have dwelt as a maiden for so long, it is a daunting thing to become a wife, but you have nothing to fear. You will be a married woman, with your own household, and dare I say it, as many dogs and hawks as you wish – and children in the fullness of time, of course.'

Jeanette took another sip of the wine, and shuddered.

Philippa straightened against her pillows and clucked her tongue in a show of impatience. 'You are to wed William Montagu at Langley before Lent and we shall hold a fine wedding at court. What do you say?'

Jeanette almost retched. She could not marry when she was already a wife, but she dared say nothing to the Queen because of the consequences, especially not with Katerine of Salisbury standing smiling beside her, knowing what she knew. She needed time to think. 'I do not know what to say, madam,' she whispered.

Philippa's eyes narrowed. 'Come now, are you not just a little bit pleased?'

Jeanette gulped. 'Yes, madam,' she said numbly. Dear God, this was the end of the world!

Philippa's expression lost its smiling generosity. 'I must tell you that the King is looking forward to your delight in this match after all the trouble over the last proposal. I know your mother is hoping for great things, as is the Countess of Salisbury. We shall announce the betrothal tomorrow, by which time I hope you will have thought upon your great good fortune. In due course you shall be the Countess of Salisbury yourself and hold an exalted position at court. For now, you may go.' With a wave of her hand, she dismissed Jeanette, clearly irritated and out of sorts.

Katerine took her arm as they curtseyed out of the Queen's presence. 'For once in your spoiled life, do as you are bidden with good grace,' she hissed. 'We both know what lies in your past and you would not wish it brought to light for your sake and that of others. You are being given a second chance and you shall not throw it away.'

Jeanette wrenched free of Katerine's grip. 'It is no second chance,' she retorted. 'Indeed, I never had a first one!'

Katerine pressed her lips together and escorted her not back to the festivities but to her own chamber, and instructed her women to watch Jeanette. 'I fear she is overwrought and may exhibit signs of hysteria,' she said. 'If she does, then give her one of my tisanes.'

Jeanette sat down numbly on her bed, clenching her emotion tightly inside. The last thing she wanted was to be forced to drink one of Katerine's horrible potions.

Hawise arrived to tend to her, and as she removed the pins from Jeanette's hair, Jeanette said flatly, 'The King and Queen have arranged my marriage. I am to wed William Montagu within the month.'

Hawise stared. 'How can you when you are already wed to Sir Thomas?' she whispered, glancing round.

Jeanette shook her head. 'He is not here to support my claim, and how can I stand on my own in his absence?' She seized the pillow off the bed and pressed it to her body. 'Even if I send a message to Thomas, it won't reach him for months, if ever. I do not know where he is. If I consent to this marriage, it is a mortal sin and I am going against my vows and against God. Whichever way I turn I am trapped!' She shuddered. 'William

Montagu is a vile brat. I would not wed him in a hundred years even if I was free to do so!' She rocked back and forth, over the pillow. 'What am I to do? They are announcing the betrothal tomorrow.'

'A betrothal can be annulled,' Hawise said, 'as can a marriage. You have a copy of the contract in your coffer. You have me as a witness.'

'Yes, but the other witnesses are scattered. John is with Thomas, as are Otto and Henry. If you spoke up without Thomas here, who would believe you? Indeed, you would endanger yourself. Father Geoffrey is possibly still in Ghent, but it would take weeks to find him. And to whom should I show the contract?'

Hawise sat down and folded an arm around Jeanette's shoulders in hopeless reassurance. 'There is nothing you can do tonight, my lady, but we shall think of something.'

Words intended to comfort, but bearing no structure or certainty. She could run away, but they would find her and punish her. Part of her wished she had never met Thomas, and she was angry with him that yet again he had left her to deal with trouble alone, but even if their affair had never happened, she would still be confronted by the unpalatable fact that they were expecting her to marry a boy she loathed – to live as his wife and bear his children. The thought of having to lie with him sickened her.

The only glimmer of hope was that her marriage to Thomas meant that if they forced her into this match with Montagu, it would be invalid. It wouldn't be the truth ever, and that gave her the smallest spark of bleak and desolate relief.

In the morning Jeanette was presented to the King and Queen after mass to make the betrothal with both families bearing witness. Her mother was smiling with satisfaction – indeed everyone seemed inordinately pleased. Jeanette's brother John was present, her mother's brother, Thomas Wake, and Prince Edward too. William Montagu stood tall and proud with a smile on his lips, and eyed Jeanette like a cat that had caught a mouse and was about to play with it.

Jeanette was required to take William's hand, but there was nothing for either of them to say at this stage, and their guardians spoke for them, agreeing that the marriage would take place five weeks hence at the Royal Palace of Langley.

William squeezed her hand, but not in a kind way, and she responded by digging in her nails, leaving deep half-moon imprints in his skin.

The matter was briskly concluded as just another item of business. Jeanette rejoined the Queen's ladies and William departed to his tutors, but before he did he leaned in close to murmur in her ear: 'When we are wed, you will know your place, for I shall teach you to honour me.'

'Never!' she hissed, and he sneered at her.

Jeanette bit the inside of her mouth. Surely God would never permit this travesty to happen . . . but then who knew what the will of God truly was.

Many miles away, Thomas watched Raoul de Brienne, a French knight, cast the four ivory dice across the gaming board with a flick of his long fingers and yet again turn up a winning score. Thomas had never known a man so fortunate at games of chance. He himself had won perhaps twice in the ten evenings they had shared supper and companionship while on the road through the forests of Bavaria. Since they were travelling on a holy campaign, fighting for God and seeking remission of their sins, no money was involved, only spills of wood. Had they been playing for coin, Thomas would have been destitute by now.

Puffing out his cheeks in irritation, he tossed the last of his spills to de Brienne. 'I swear, if I did not know those dice were genuine, I would accuse you of loading them. How do you do it?'

De Brienne's grin lit up his bright brown eyes. 'Dame Fortune loves me,' he said, gathering the spills and returning them to their little box, 'or at least at the moment she does.'

Thomas and Otto had become good friends with de Brienne during the campaign. On home ground, as a Frenchman, de Brienne would be their enemy, but here in Prussia they were allies, sharing camaraderie round the fire. They had borrowed each other's equipment at need, watched each other's back on the march and in battle, and spent companionable evenings mending harnesses, telling stories and gambling together. When they returned home, they would be on opposite sides, but for now they were friends.

De Brienne glanced towards the flapping sides of the campaign tent. 'The wind's getting up,' he said. Leaving the table, he fetched a bag of spare tent pegs from a chest by his bed. 'We should make all secure. I don't want my shelter to go flying off in the middle of the night – nor yours – I can feel that it's going to rain too.'

Together the men set to work to add extra security to de Brienne's tent, and then did the same for Thomas's, working companionably side by side with their men and checking that everything was well pinned down. Otto arrived, fastening up his braies, while the laundry woman who had been occupying his camp bed hurried off to her own domicile.

Thomas rolled his eyes, and de Brienne chuckled. Otto picked up a mallet to bang in a peg and swung it with no sign of diminished strength. 'I'll go to confession in the morning,' he said.

'Doubtless you will have plenty to confess,' Thomas said drily.

'Hah, no more than the usual – and she was worth it!'

'Let's hope she thought the same about you!'

'I've not had any complaints so far.'

De Brienne hammered in another peg and stood up. 'What will you and your brother do when our time here is done?' he asked.

Thomas shrugged. 'Return to our king suitably shriven and hope to advance ourselves in his service.' He had said nothing about Jeanette to de Brienne – that remained a secret held close to his chest – but he often thought about his beloved bride waiting for him at court. He missed that gut-jolt sensation of being with her – her beauty, her sensuality, her mischief and sharp intelligence – and was often beset by a disturbing sensation that it was all a dream or a story told round an evening fire that would be ashes in the morning.

'It is not so good that Dame Fortune has made enemies of us at home,' Raoul said as he put his mallet aside. 'But I wish you well all the same, and if ever we can be of service to each other as men of honour, I hope we shall remember each other well.'

'It is more than a hope,' Thomas answered with grace, 'it is a certainty.'

As the first heavy spots of rain started to fall, the men clasped hands before hastening to take shelter under their now firmly secured canvas.

Jeanette entered her mother's chamber, dread welling inside her. Following the marriage agreement, her mother had gone to the family house at Westminster with Jeanette's uncle, Lord Wake, and the rest of the Kent entourage. Jeanette had been sent from court to stay with her family for the final fortnight before the wedding, and with time running out, her hopes of stopping the marriage were burning down to a stub.

Margaret rose from her chair, greeted Jeanette with a dry kiss, and gave her an exasperated look. 'The Queen has written to say you are moping about this marriage and that the faces you have been making would curdle milk. Enough is enough, daughter. You will not disgrace your blood, and you will wed William Montagu.'

'He is a puffed-up boy, and the thought of having him for a husband makes me sick,' Jeanette said, her lip curling.

'Hold, my dear.' Margaret gripped Jeanette's hand. 'It matters not what you think. You will comply with what is right for the family – for both our families.'

Jeanette struggled free of her mother's bony grip. 'You are forcing me into this for the supposed sake of the family? What has all your striving brought you, mother?'

Margaret's face whitened. 'An ungrateful, disobedient daughter, that is what.'

Jeanette drew a deep breath. 'I shall never marry William Montagu. Even if you force me to the altar, it will be no true marriage – for I am already wedded and bedded.'

Her mother's gaze shot wide in astonishment. And then she laughed. 'You expect me to believe you? This is just another of your silly tales. You do not fool me. You shall do as you are told.'

'But it is true!' Jeanette stamped the floor so hard that the sole of her foot rang with pain. 'I am married!'

'If that is the case, then where is this supposed husband of yours?' Margaret scoffed.

'He is away fighting, but he is going to return for me.'

'I see. So, he is not here to protect you or claim his right? How very convenient. If you think you can escape from a marriage lawfully contracted by your guardians with such tales, you are mistaken, and I shall hear no more of your nonsense.'

Jeanette stood her ground. 'I have a contract, and I have witnesses,' she retorted. 'I can prove my marriage before man and God.'

Margaret narrowed her eyes. 'Then tell me who you think you have married and we shall see.' Her mouth twisted in revulsion. 'In God's name, do not tell me you have disgraced yourself with some peasant and given yourself in return for a ring of plaited rushes and a false promise.'

Trembling, Jeanette delved beneath her neckline and produced her wedding ring on its silk ribbon. 'No, mother. I have a ring, a contract and witnesses, as I have said – and I will stand before God and proclaim it to all!'

Her mother made motions with her jaw as if attempting to chew on nails. 'You are lying,' she said icily. 'The Countess of Salisbury has had your care for two years and she would know if such a thing were true, and would certainly not be involving her son if it were.'

'She wants my dowry and a closer connection with the King,' Jeanette retorted.

'A gold ring proves nothing, and you have many in your coffer. You shall consent to this marriage.'

'I shall not,' Jeanette said fiercely, her will to fight thoroughly aroused and caution thrown to the wind.

'Show me this contract of yours,' Margaret said. 'If it exists.'

Jeanette marched away to fetch it with sparks in her heels, snatching the parchment from the bottom of her jewel coffer, her anger incandescent. She marched back to her mother and thrust the document under her nose. 'Here,' she said. 'Thomas, Lord Holland and I were wed on the Feast of Saint George before he sailed for England to assist with the King's fleet. I am no virgin and we have lain together as man and wife on many occasions – and my wedding ring bears his seal!'

Margaret snatched the contract, stared at it, then looked at Jeanette, her complexion white. 'You have disgraced yourself and you have disgraced your family,' she spat, her rage so full and tight that there was no room for it to burst. 'This man is a nothing. The son of a traitor, and you of royal blood. I have no doubt he tricked you into the match in order to despoil your body. No daughter of mine shall wear such shame. I call the marriage dishonourable and false.' She jerked to her feet, stalked to the brazier and thrust the parchment into the coals, grabbing the poker to push it down and let it burn.

Jeanette gasped and lunged, intent on recovering the smouldering piece of parchment, but Margaret held her off with the poker, a glint in her eye just as fierce as Jeanette's.

'You will not put a stop to this!' Jeanette shouted. 'I am married in the sight of God, and there is nothing you can do! There are other copies, there are witnesses!'

Margaret brandished the poker. 'I will not see the sacrifices I have made for you and your brother be brought to nothing! Your reckless father died and left me to fight for your inheritance and try to prevent it from being swallowed up by ruthless men who would pick our family to its very bones. Your marriage to William Montagu will secure our dynasty and bring lustre to theirs. You shall wed William Montagu and no tawdry, worthless contract of lust will stop it from happening.'

Jeanette barely recognised her mother. Before, even if there had been impatience, even if there had been irritation and distance, there had still existed a spark of connection, but this flame was from an entirely different kindling.

'No,' she said, immovable herself. 'I will not. You will never make me!'

'We shall see what your uncle says on the matter.' The poker still in her hand, Margaret swept from the chamber, and seconds later the key turned in the lock.

'No!' Jeanette ran to the door and tugged on the ring, but it did not yield. She banged her fists on the wood and kicked it, stubbing her toe, to no avail, and still she continued to thump and kick and scream until she exhausted her energy, and finally slumped, leaning against the door and sobbing, feeling desperate and abandoned. Thomas was far away, and she had no one to help her. She had been so determined not to be a pawn, but had become one anyway. The thought of marriage to William Montagu made her flesh crawl, and she rubbed her arms.

The daylight through the open shutters faded and a deep winter dusk darkened the room. The candles burned low on their prickets and the fire in the hearth turned to hot ash, and still she sat, head down, tears drying on her face. She wanted to run away, but where would she go? Finding Thomas would be an impossible task. She could continue to refuse the marriage, but what might they do to Thomas when he returned? They would get rid of him by either arranging his death or buying him off. Her fear – as great within her as her fear for his life – was that he might agree to take their money, because it had more value than his vows to her.

At last, in the near dark, the key grated in the lock, and she sprang to her feet and faced the door, shivering.

'Now then,' said her uncle Thomas, entering the room, closing the door behind him and squinting at her through the gloom. He was tall and thin, the seams of life on his face like worn, carved leather. 'Niece, what is all this nonsense? I have just been confronted by your mother in a terrible state.' His eyes were serious and grave, devoid of their usual twinkle.

Jeanette's chin wobbled. He had stood in lieu of her father

as head of the family since she was a tiny child, and she had always had a certain fondness for him. He was less strict than her mother, albeit from a distance. He opened his arms, and she stepped into them for a hug, inhaling the scent of the wool oils in his thick tunic and responding to his comforting gesture with a suppressed sob.

'Come, child, I am certain we can mend this misunderstanding.' He patted her back before drawing away and made her sit down near the brazier while he mended it with fresh coals, and revitalised the candles. Eventually he sat down opposite her, lapping his cloak over his bony knees. 'This marriage proposal may have surprised you, but it was bound to happen sooner or later, and there are many far less suitable candidates with whom you could have been matched, believe me. Montagu's a handsome lad, and his family has high influence.'

'Uncle, it is not a misunderstanding,' Jeanette said. 'Certainly not on my part. I cannot wed William Montagu for I am already married to Sir Thomas Holland, as I am sure my mother has told you.'

'Yes,' he said neutrally. 'And she mentioned the contract.'

'Which she threw into the fire,' Jeanette said angrily. 'How could she do that to her own daughter? It matters not – there are copies.' She had little hope that he would listen. He would endorse her mother, and do what profited the family, no matter her wishes. 'I am married to Thomas Holland,' she repeated. 'We were wed at Saint Bavo's before witnesses on the feast of Saint George.'

'And you have evidence of this, beyond that scrap of parchment you showed to your mother?' He leaned towards her, his gaze intent, searching her face.

Jeanette tossed her head. 'It was far more than a "scrap of parchment". It had Thomas's seal pressed in the wax from his own signet ring with which we were wed. Of course I have evidence! The marriage was witnessed by Sir Otto Holland, by Henry de la Haye, by Thomas's falconer John de la Salle, and by my chamber lady Hawise. She married de la Salle at the same time and Thomas and I stood in mutual witness of their marriage – and all this was before a Franciscan friar.'

'I see.' Her uncle clasped his hands and pressed his thumbs together and there was a long silence, punctuated by the tick of the new coals settling in the brazier. 'This is all hearsay though,' he said at length. 'Your "husband" – if such he is – is away fighting, rather than remaining to protect you. Surely he could have stayed and stood by his oath if it meant that much to him.'

'He has gone in order to do penance for his soul and to make a clean breast of his sins.' Jeanette was dismayed at her uncle's argument, which set ablaze the doubt in her own mind. Her throat had tightened with panic and her voice was emerging as a quiver. 'He will return for me. He promised.'

'Ah, young men and their promises.' Her uncle shook his head sadly. 'It is unfortunate that the other male witnesses are with him in the service of God. One might think it a lucky escape for him, from consequences and responsibility.'

'No, it is not that!' Her voice was heated in Thomas's defence. 'And it still leaves my maid Hawise, and the friar who officiated!'

'So it does.' Her uncle rubbed his jaw. 'Well then, we shall have to see, but from what your mother says, it would appear that this so-called marriage of yours would not stand up in any court of law in this land. Your "husband" has thought better of his sins and has disappeared to cleanse himself in the holy wars. You would do best for everyone's sake to stay quiet and do as your mother bids you.'

She stared at him, aghast. 'You do not believe me! You would rather believe my mother? I swear to you on my soul that I am married, and furthermore that the marriage was consummated many times over. I am no virgin.'

Her uncle's complexion turned dusky and he looked at her with a curl of disgust. 'If such is the case, it only confirms it was a union to facilitate base lust. I know exactly what these young bucks at court are like. You will put this behind you and do as you are bidden for the good of all, especially yourself.'

Jeanette's stomach churned. 'It was not like that. We were truly married in love and honour. Will you go against God's law?'

'I shall go with the law of honour and common sense,' he said tautly. 'I do not believe that this marriage you claim was any more than an excuse for licentiousness. Friars are renowned for their complicity in such matters in return for the right fee. I doubt the man was even ordained.'

'It *was* a true marriage!' Jeanette's voice rose and cracked. 'Would you send your own niece into the lion's den because it is easier than hearing the truth? You have no right, and I will not come to the altar. I refuse to be a part of your schemes!'

Tight-faced, her uncle stood up. 'Your mother spoke the truth – there is no sense in you. You are defying her authority and mine, and we are your guardians. You shall remain here and think upon your behaviour, and when I return I hope you will have a different reply for me. Your mother says you have been over-indulged at court and that too much rich food and luxury has affected you, and I am inclined to agree. A diet of gruel and water shall sustain you for now.'

'That shall suit me very well, uncle, and I shall not change my answer,' Jeanette retorted. 'I am lawfully married to Thomas Holland, and when he returns, he shall claim me.'

'I doubt that very much,' he said grimly, and banged from the room exactly as her mother had done. Again, she heard the key grate in the lock.

Several hours passed and no one came. Jeanette paced the room back and forth like a caged lioness. Perhaps they intended to weaken her by thirst and starvation. Let them. She would never give in.

Eventually the door was unlocked, and Agnes, her mother's chamber lady, entered the room. She was an older woman with a whiskery chin and a severe attitude. The tray she carried held a bowl of gruel and a stone jug of water, exactly as her uncle had promised. Outside, a serjeant stood guard, making it clear she had no chance of escape.

'Where is my own lady?' Jeanette demanded. 'What have you done with Hawise?'

Agnes set down the tray on the trestle. 'Your mother has taken her into her own charge,' she said. 'I am to serve you for now, and the Countess of Salisbury shall assign you new ladies once you are wed.'

Jeanette stared at her, horrified, feeling as if she had been punched in the stomach. 'I want Hawise!'

'That is not possible.' Agnes gave her a narrow look. 'Your mother will come to you shortly to take you to pray.' The maid performed a perfunctory curtsey and departed.

Jeanette glared at the tray, her fear sharpening. Hawise had been her companion and attendant since they were small girls. Even given their difference in rank, Hawise being a yeoman's daughter, in many ways they were as close as sisters. Not having her to confide in and lean upon was like having a hole in her side. Without her there was no one to understand and help ease her situation. And Hawise too might be in danger for what she knew.

Ignoring the gruel and water, Jeanette went to the thin window slit, inhaled the bitter winter air, and felt that same chill in her soul.

A week later, Jeanette was still locked in her room on the same diet. She had taken to eating what they gave her, in order to have the strength to resist. The only time she was permitted to leave the chamber was to attend church with her mother under close guard. Kneeling to pray, she pleaded with God to bring Thomas home on the next ship. In the desolate hours of solitary confinement, she even started to blame him for leaving her and forcing her to deal with this situation on her own.

Her mother had provided her with a pile of sewing, but she had thrown it in a corner and refused to look at it. She cried for her dog and her horse, and for Frederick, and her anger festered and grew.

Four days before the wedding, on the eve of travelling to Langley, her mother visited outside the usual prayer times. She held a piece of parchment in her hand and her expression was almost triumphant. She sat down at the small table opposite Jeanette. 'I am not here today to force you into something you do not wish, or even to reason with you,' she announced. 'I know such a thing is beyond our abilities, so I must leave it to God and his angels.'

'Then why are you here?' Jeanette asked. 'To torment me?'

Margaret sighed wearily. 'You may believe your uncle and I are monsters, but truly we are not. We want the best for everyone.'

Jeanette looked away, steeling herself for the next onslaught.

'You continue to maintain that you were married to Thomas Holland, but young girls are so easily duped. I will not argue with you, for that ground will yield no harvest. What I have come to say is that the point is moot, for Thomas Holland has been killed in battle – God rest his soul. Even if you were married, which I doubt, the union no longer stands, for you are a widow.'

Jeanette shot her focus back to her mother as the words slowly penetrated. 'No! You are lying. I would know if Thomas was dead!'

'And how would you know?' Margaret demanded. 'Have you heard from him? I think not. You were always a means to an end for that young man, and now he is no more.'

Numb with shock, Jeanette stared at her. 'I do not believe you. He cannot be dead, for I would have felt it in here.' She thumped her breast.

Margaret gave her a pitying look. 'The news has come from reports sent to the King. Believe them, not me. This unfortunate interlude of yours will be forgotten. You shall be made ready for your marriage to William Montagu and you shall do your duty.'

'Never!' Jeanette bared her teeth.

Her mother sighed again. 'You must accept that he is dead. I have had to deal with such news myself twice over and move on from it. How easy it would have been to stamp and scream that it wasn't fair, and that the world should move as I wished, but when your father died I had a baby in my womb, and you and your brother to care for. I had duties and responsibilities to others that I could not forsake by throwing a childish fit. Now it is your turn. I did not make all the sacrifices in my life to watch my spoiled daughter wreck them with her selfish unseemliness. You will do your duty, or spend the rest of your life as a nun, and that is my last word.' She rose and went to the door.

Jeanette clenched her fists. 'I want Hawise back,' she said. 'I don't want Agnes.'

Her mother turned. 'If you cooperate and agree to this match you can have many things, daughter. Your maid, as many dogs and horses and clothes as you wish. In time you shall be the Countess of Salisbury with estates to govern and heirs to raise. Weigh that in the balance of your mind and change your face before next I see you.'

After her mother had gone, Jeanette crumpled to the floor, clutched her stomach, and curled up in a tight ball of misery. 'You're not dead, you're not, you're not!' she wailed. 'You can't be, for I would have felt it!' But a worm of doubt crept in, and she wondered if it was true. Had she been deluding herself all along? Why wasn't Thomas here to help her? Why did he have to go on his stupid crusade? Emotion tore through her like a storm tide. Rage and grief and despair. She sobbed until she was ragged and deflated, her heart wrung out of all the fullness it had once held for life, for love, for Thomas. It was all as nothing.

16

A campaign tent somewhere in Prussia, February 1341

The pain was excruciating. Thomas writhed on his pallet, sweat-soaked, raging with fever. Dreams of demons and angels fighting over his soul had accosted him throughout the night and now he stood on the edge of hell's pit, so close he could feel the flames searing his skin and biting at his injured eye socket. He thrashed, trying to escape the fiery, sulphurous stink of the shark-mouth and dripping yellow teeth.

Voices resonated inside his skull like shouts in a cavern. Someone was holding him down, telling him not to fight, that all was well, but he knew it wasn't.

'Help him, in the name of sweet Christ, do something!' He recognised Otto's voice, breaking with tears.

'My son, it is in God's hands now,' came the answer, wearily patient.

If it was in God's hands, then Thomas knew his transgressions were weights at his ankles, dragging him into the pit. He had seen enough Dooms in church paintings to know the fate of sinners.

Someone set a cup to his lips and dribbled cold liquid into his mouth. He choked and tried to fend them off, but his arms wouldn't work. A cold compress covered his brows and eyes and his vision brightened with vivid colours while pain seared through him in ropes of lightning. He heard Jeanette screaming out to someone that he was not dead and saw her curled in a ball, inconsolable with grief.

'I am not dead!' he shouted. 'I will come to you, through hell if I must.'

He fought to leave the bed, but hands held him fast like shackles and he had no strength to break free.

'Do not dare die, you selfish whoreson,' he heard Otto croak, and felt himself being grasped and shaken. 'I refuse to bring home your horse with an empty saddle and tell our mother you're never returning. I don't want to face everyone who loves you with a box in my hands holding your embalmed heart. Have you not done enough to us already, you bastard?'

The demons pierced him with their claws, and his soul teetered on the edge. Otto was sobbing while Henry de la Haye murmured consoling platitudes. Thomas gathered every part of himself and made a final tremendous effort, throwing himself forward, screaming that he repented of everything and rejected Satan and all his works. He struck out, and suddenly there was a white sword in his hand and the devils drew back from him. The light returned, burning through his skull, and he reached into it. The left side was black and swirling with red heat and he could see nothing, but on the right, through stinging sweat, he made out a room with a fire, and people gathered around him. Other wounded men lay on pallets on the floor and he could hear their groans. Was this his deathbed? Perhaps they were waiting for their souls to be harvested – an unholy convoy. While he was trying to puzzle out his surroundings, oblivion descended on him in a snuffing black cloak.

He woke again to throbbing pain on the left side of his face, but the fire and the hallucinations had gone. Winter daylight cast the room in stark tints of blue and grey. Looking round, he could see nothing out of his left eye, but his right took in Otto, sitting at his bedside, head drooped in slumber, sandy hair lank and surcoat grimy. He tried to speak but all that emerged was a corvid croak.

Otto shot awake at the sound and leaned over him. 'Thomas? Thank Christ!'

Thomas struggled to speak, feeling as though his throat was full of dust and feathers, and Otto roared for help. Moments later a priest arrived with Henry and John de la Salle on his heels.

The priest poured water and lifted Thomas's head to drink. He was so weak he could barely swallow, but he still managed to drain the cup, and when the priest refilled it, he drank that too.

'Thank God to see you return to the land of the living,' Otto said, sleeving away tears. 'I feared for your life. I was despairing of what I would say to mother of your demise.'

'I heard you,' Thomas said huskily. 'You were standing with me at the gates of hell and I thought for sure that was where I was bound.'

'We thought you were going to die. You have been sick with wound fever for five days.'

'Wound fever?' Thomas slowly put his thoughts together. To have wound fever he would have to be badly injured, and the only place he was aware of pain was his face. Raising his hand, he touched bandages on the left side, and a fleeting memory came to him of a moment of impact and a white-hot streak of sensation.

'Scatter from a slingshot,' Otto said. 'You took off your helmet for a moment and down you went. Raoul de Brienne got the bastard, but you were off your guard.'

Thomas touched the bandage again. 'How bad?'

Otto looked away for a moment and then back at Thomas. 'We do not know yet, but likely you have lost the sight in your left eye.'

The water he had just drunk threatened to come back up. 'So, I am half blind.'

'Probably, but your limbs are still sound, and you have the sight of the other eye. You will still be able to do a soldier's job with a little adjustment.' He cleared his throat. 'Do not think too hard on it now. Rest and get better first.'

Thomas's eye socket throbbed to the pounding of his heart, signalling that he was indeed alive, but very changed. Perhaps Jeanette would not want him now that he was not whole, and perhaps it was the price that God was exacting from him for his sins. He was lethargic with exhaustion even though he had only been awake long enough to take a drink, and he felt utterly wretched.

'Sleep now,' said the priest. 'I will return shortly and dress your wound and see if you will take some broth and bread.'

When he had gone, Otto plumped Thomas's pillow. 'I am glad you are still here,' he said.

Thomas was not sure he felt the same way. It might be better for all if he had died. They would grieve and then they would move on and he would have a hero's memory in their thoughts. Jeanette would be free to wed again, and everything would return to the stream as if there had never been a flood. But if God had willed him to live, it must be for a purpose – or because he had more punishment to fulfil.

Sleep swept over him and this time it was dreamless and only lasted from noon to compline. When he woke again, he was lucid and hungry, and death's shadow had left the room.

Jeanette went to her wedding in a state of numb shock, silently screaming for help but with none to be had. She had been convinced each morning that something would happen to prevent it. God would stop it somehow, but God was not listening – at least not to her.

Her mother and her uncle had kept her closely guarded, giving her no opportunity to speak out about her first marriage. Thomas might be dead, but potential for bringing scandal to the family remained, and she had been warned that if she said anything at all she would be severely punished and sent to a convent. From now on, her behaviour must be impeccable. They had taken her ring away by force, although she had managed to conceal the ruby and the little belt pendant from them.

She hated her wedding robes. Her undergown of pale gold silk was topped by an overgown of blue and gold brocade, heavy as a hauberk with a trailing hem that took four maids to hold when she walked. She was just the support to wear it and exhibit the wealth and importance of her family – a princess. The headdress was secured tightly to her scalp and her hair had been braided and coiled either side of her temples. Already her head ached from the tug against the pins. She thought of the simple elegance of her first wedding gown, worn from a choice of her daily clothes, and her hair loosely plaited, with barely a pin in sight. She remembered Thomas's hands in her hair and the melting sensations as they kissed, and lay together. The thought of having to do that with William Montagu made her want to vomit.

Her mother's and Katerine's ladies primped and fussed,

tweaking and arranging. Queen Philippa had sent her a magnificent pearl brooch, and as she watched Hawise stab the pin into the fabric, it felt like a dagger in her flesh, even though her skin lay beneath miles of heavy cloth. She and Hawise exchanged a knowing look. So much enforced silence adding to the oppressive weight of the burden she carried.

Her mother, wearing a severe but splendid gown of embroidered dark blue velvet, looked her up and down, and brushed an imaginary speck from Jeanette's shoulder. 'Remember what I have told you,' she said. 'Remember our bargain. Your life can be comfortable, or not, and the same goes for those of your household who are attending you in service.' She cast a withering glance at Hawise, who looked down and withdrew a pace.

'Yes, mother, I remember our bargain with every breath I take,' Jeanette said, filled with pain that it should come to this with no going back. The bridge was well and truly burning.

Her uncle Thomas, robed in velvet and furs, a gold chain around his neck, arrived to escort her to church. 'It is time.' He held out his arm. 'You know what you must do. It is not about you this day, but about your duty to your lineage, and its future success.'

Still Jeanette hung back, trying to delay the inevitable.

'I know you are afraid and that you do not want to do this,' her uncle said, 'but many young women feel exactly as you do at the outset. The boy is nothing to be afraid of, and if you are a good wife, you will do well together. It will be of great benefit to you to have a settled home and a family away from the court, and one day you shall be a countess, just like your mother.'

Jeanette swallowed bile. Her uncle was a hypocrite. He had married his own wife, Blanche of Lancaster, for love when he was eighteen and without royal consent. Indeed, he had been heavily fined for it, even if the bride's father had approved. However, he appeared to have conveniently forgotten the circumstances of his own match in his determination to push hers through. His wife, her aunt Blanche, was kind and sympathetic, but neutral, and she could tell everyone thought she was making a fuss over nothing.

Waiting at the church door was Lord Montagu, Earl of Salisbury, with his household, everyone robed in rich winter furs and heavy fabrics. Her husband-to-be, golden-haired and handsome, stood beside his father. At thirteen years old, his features were still cherubic and boyish, but with a glint of hair on his upper lip. The thought of sharing a bed with him repulsed her. She prayed she would not have to consummate the marriage, but knew it would probably happen, for an unconsummated marriage was one that could be dissolved and they would want to secure her dowry and the tie of bloodline. She had nowhere to turn and nowhere to run. The King and Queen were present as witnesses, and both were smiling with benign delight.

The Bishop of London, Ralph Stratford, was present to marry them, adorned in his full robes of office. Closer and closer drew the moment until it was upon her, and the weight of the burden increased until she felt as though she was being crushed. She mumbled her responses without raising her eyes, and refused to look at William Montagu as he pushed the thick gold wedding ring on to her finger. Unable to bear what was taking place, she shut herself away, and it was an emotionless shell that made its way through the ceremony. It was not happening to her, but to someone else who stood in her place.

Following the wedding mass, the party processed to a banquet in the great hall and Jeanette had to rest her hand along her new husband's arm. His manner was supercilious, and she wanted to kick him. She told herself that soon he would return to Prince Edward's household to continue his military training, while she would live at court and they would only meet in formal circumstances. Just a few more hours and it would all be over.

The wedding feast involved numerous courses and entertainments to celebrate the marriage and while away the long winter afternoon. Dancers, jugglers and tumblers performed by the light of torch and candle and fire. Beef in rich sauce glistened in the dishes. There was wheat frumenty with spices and dried fruits. White bread, sweet raisin wines and almond sugar-paste, which the pregnant Queen consumed in large quantities.

When it came time for the bedding ceremony, Jeanette retreated further into the shadow-life and let the shell take her place.

A sumptuous chamber had been prepared for the event with braziers burning to keep the cold at bay and the bed piled with covers and furs.

The Queen kissed Jeanette warmly on the cheek, and taking her hand, placed it on her own pregnant belly. 'May fortune favour you tonight,' she said. 'I shall pray that you conceive an heir for your lord.'

Jeanette almost gagged. She swallowed hard, and Philippa pinched her cheek. 'Do not be shy now,' she said with a soft laugh. 'All will be well; it is a natural thing.'

But it wouldn't be well, it would never be, however anyone tried to cloak it. And it didn't seem a natural thing at all.

The Queen stepped back and the King took Jeanette's hand and patted it. 'You must put the past behind you,' he said, his expression benign, but warning in his voice. 'It is time to settle

down and find fulfilment in becoming a good and dutiful wife.'
He chucked her chin and looked into her face. 'Courage, my
dear. You were always a wilful child, but now you have it within
you to become a strong woman, and one day a great matriarch.
Listen and learn, and you will do very well.' He kissed her cheek,
released his grip, and took his leave.

'Remember what I have taught you,' her mother said when
her turn came. 'Do not disgrace your family.'

'I do not think my family could carry any more disgrace than
has already been heaped upon it at this moment,' Jeanette replied
in a low voice.

Her mother narrowed her eyes. 'You are a wife now,' she said
curtly. 'Do your duty.'

'As well as you have done yours, mother,' Jeanette answered,
adding yet another row of stones in the wall between them.

The guests undressed the newlyweds to their undergarments
of chemise and shirt, and placed them side by side in the great
bed together. The Bishop intoned a blessing with a sprinkling
of holy water, and then everyone departed, the priest the last
to leave, closing the door behind him – although Jeanette knew
someone would be listening outside with an ear flattened against
the wood.

She looked at William Montagu with distaste even though he
was handsome and well made. 'You shall not touch me,' she
warned. Flinging herself from the bed, she went to stand in a
corner of the room with her back against the wall.

He gazed at her in astonishment, then rose and came straight
after her. 'You are my wife now. You have to do as I say, and if
you defy me, I have the right to beat you.' He raised a clenched
fist to emphasise his point.

'Oh, such bravery.' She curled her lip. 'Do you truly think
that will work? If you beat me, I will fight back, and how will

that look when you emerge tomorrow morning covered in bites and scratches? How do you think others will respond when they see my bruises? Some might smile and say it is what I deserve, but remember, I am the King's cousin. My father was a prince, and my grandfather a king.'

His gaze flickered. 'But you have sworn in church to obey me and do your duty, and do it you will, because it is God's holy law and you are required to pay the debt.'

Nausea roiled in her belly. He was still a boy, even if he stood on the cusp of manhood. Was he even capable? She cast a quick look in the direction of his groin, but there was nothing to see. With a shrug, she flounced past him to the flagon and cups set out on the trestle. She poured wine and drank it down like a soldier about to go into battle, and then again, before going to lie on the bed. Putting her knees up, she opened her legs. 'Well then,' she said with weary scorn, 'let us have it over and done with – if you must.'

He eyed her like a startled hare, and his face flushed scarlet. But then he rallied to her challenge. He too poured himself a drink and gulped it down, and then leaped on her, crushing her flat, and dragging up her chemise. 'You will not taunt me!' His voice broke with an adolescent crackle.

'I am not taunting you; I am doing my duty as you have said I must. I am not stopping you!'

He fumbled between his own legs and she felt heat against her thigh and realised he was indeed capable and erect, and suddenly she wished she had not challenged him. He pushed at her and she gave a strangled yelp, for his jab was sore, but then he gasped and she felt him spill against her thigh, too over-wrought to follow through. After a moment he rolled off her, his chest heaving, and turned his back. Jeanette sat up and with a grimace wiped herself on her chemise. She said nothing to taunt him further but he turned to look at her, his face filled with fury and shame.

'Don't you dare say a word of this outside this room, or you will be sorry.'

Jeanette shrugged. 'Why would I? You have done your duty, and I have done mine. It is no one else's business. Neither of us need say anything at all.'

He glowered at her and got back into bed and turned his back. She heard him sniff and wondered if he was crying. She got into bed too and lay on the edge, with the cold, sticky patch clamming her chemise.

She remembered lying with Thomas. The melting, glorious feelings and the moments of intimacy when they could not get enough of each other and were one creature, limbs entwined, fitting together, sword and sheath. Even in anger there had been a full and burning passion with both of them committed full tilt. Tears prickled her eyes and she bit her lip and despaired to think that this might be how it was for the rest of her life.

In the morning the women came to take the sheet to wash it, and Lady Katerine contrived to smear some blood-stains over the linen from a phial concealed in her hand, and then disposed of, as proof of the consummation. Jeanette's contempt for Katerine and her mother increased. William distanced himself from the women and made a swift exit, complicit with Jeanette in mutual antipathy. He had no desire to bed with her and face further humiliation, and she equally had no desire to bed with him.

Two days later, he departed with Prince Edward and Jeanette's brother, John, for Edward's household at Berkeley. For her part, Jeanette remained at Langley for Queen Philippa's lying in, as did Katerine and Katerine's mother-in-law, Elizabeth de

Montfort, a stout, overbearing woman who had come to dwell in the Salisbury household to help educate – and manage – the new bride.

As Jeanette's mother prepared to return to her estates at Donington, Jeanette asked her pointedly for her casket of jewels now that she was a wife in her own right.

Margaret fastened her cloak and turned towards the waiting cart. 'When you have proven yourself a responsible wife, you may have them,' she said.

'But they are mine!'

'And you shall have them – when you show me you are worthy.'

Jeanette pressed her lips together. There was no point in protesting since her mother did not have them with her, but she knew the time would never be right. Her uncle Thomas kissed her cheek and she bore it stoically, but as far as she was concerned, he had colluded in this betrayal and that particular bridge was burned too.

A few weeks after Jeanette's marriage, John de Warenne, Earl of Surrey came to Langley, bringing with him his young mistress, Isabel Holland. Thomas had often mentioned his sister with affection and had explained to Jeanette the circumstances of her relationship with de Warenne.

A pang of loss and longing tore through Jeanette as she watched Isabel curtsey to the Queen, for the young woman so resembled her brother, with the same dark eyes and hair. Isabel was graceful like Thomas as she rose from her curtsey, and Philippa gestured for Jeanette to bring Isabel a drink.

'We were so sorry to learn of your brother's death,' Philippa said. 'He was a promising knight of the household and a good companion. We deeply mourn his loss.'

Isabel blinked in surprise. 'Madam, I do not know where you heard such news, but Thomas is certainly not dead. He was wounded in the face, and has lost the sight of an eye, but Otto wrote to say he is making a good recovery.'

Jeanette gasped, and the world spun. Someone took her arm and helped her to a bench. Someone else hurried to burn feathers under her nose in case her womb had gone wandering around her body.

'Jeanette is a new bride,' Katerine said with gentle concern as Jeanette coughed and spluttered. 'It would be best if she went to lie down for a while.' Her words held a certain intimation for those who might want to jump to conclusions given the recent marriage and wedding night.

'Of course,' Philippa said, also looking concerned.

Isabel Holland gazed at Jeanette with narrowed eyes and set lips.

Jeanette batted away the woman holding the bunch of singed feathers. 'Let me be, I am all right!' she said crossly, but Katerine would hear none of it, and hurried her from the room.

'My mother lied to me!' Jeanette rounded on the older woman. 'She told me Thomas was dead, when he was not. And if he is not dead, then I am still wed to him and my marriage to your son is invalid!'

Katerine seized Jeanette's arm in an iron grip. 'Hold your tongue! I will brook no more of your foolish behaviour. Your mother has told me all about your ridiculous claim to be married to the man, and for a certainty, your head is in the clouds if you think it ever meant anything to him. This news is still only hearsay, and Thomas Holland is not here to prove with his body that he still lives. Your marriage vows were made and witnessed before the King and Queen with the approval of the entire court. Whatever you think happened in Ghent is nothing but a figment of your imagination and the duping of a silly girl by a grown man who took advantage, to your shame and his disgrace.'

'It was real,' Jeanette said in a wobbling voice, 'and I was not duped. If Thomas is alive, then I am still his wife.'

'And if you know what is good for you, you will keep your mouth closed,' Katerine retorted. 'Who is going to take your part? Certainly no one here. Who is going to believe a girl's silly prattling? Do you truly believe that, if Thomas Holland is indeed alive and returns, he will still want to claim you for his wife when you have married another in his absence? Mark my words, he will not ruin his life for you. Even supposing he might have considered it once, if his fighting skills have been damaged by his injury, he will be useless to the King. As a younger son with nothing to his name to live on, he will have no livelihood to support you. What then? Will you be content to live in poverty on a dung heap? Give up this foolishness now, for everyone's sake including your own.'

Katerine's words sank into her like a lead anchor, dragging her down. She was determined not to give in, but tears rolled down her face.

'In the name of God, see sense. It is pointless to long after an illusion.'

'I want to speak with Isabel Holland,' Jeanette said, swiping at her tears.

'That would be unwise. The woman is a common adulteress. I do not wish you to be more disturbed than you already are.' She took Jeanette by the shoulders and turned her face to face. 'A man may die very easily, especially if he is already weakened by a battle injury. Think on that, my girl, when considering what you say in front of others who have power that you do not.'

Jeanette wanted to spit that she was not intimidated by threats, but Katerine was right. She was indeed powerless. Katerine and her own mother were thoroughly capable of arranging Thomas's death.

'Do I make myself clear?' Katerine fixed her with a hard stare.

'Yes, my lady,' Jeanette replied, still defiant, but subdued into caution. It was horrible to be pinned down, but she vowed it would not be for ever.

The opportunity to speak with Isabel Holland arrived when Jeanette went to pray with the rest of the family the next morning. Katerine had kept Jeanette close to her side, but there was a moment outside the church after mass when Isabel was standing alone pulling on her fur-lined gloves, and Jeanette joined her.

Isabel's gaze was unfriendly. Clearly, she knew Jeanette's identity. 'While he was in England with the King, my brother told me about your marriage to him in Flanders,' she said starkly, without preamble. 'And now you have turned your back and bigamously married Salisbury's heir.'

'I did not know,' Jeanette said in a faltering voice. 'I swear I did not. They told me Thomas was dead. Is he truly still alive?'

Isabel nodded curtly.

'Oh, thank Christ – but you said he had been wounded?'

'Yes, and we do not know how badly, even though Otto says he is recovering.' Her eyes flashed with accusation. 'He would not have gone were it not for you.'

'I had no choice.' Tears filled Jeanette's eyes, but part of it was anger that Isabel Holland was blaming her, when she herself had a sullied reputation. So many lies, so much hypocrisy from other women. 'Think as you will, but you should ask yourself why it is easier to set the fault at my door than it is at your brother's.'

Isabel stood tall. 'Are you accusing Thomas?'

'I am saying you do not know the circumstances, yet you judge me and not him.'

Isabel's face turned pink. 'I know my brother.'

'Do you? I think not. And you certainly do not know me.'

'I know enough from what I have seen,' Isabel retorted.

'And do you always do that? From what you have seen? You did not see what happened in Flanders, and yet you sit in judgement – how dare you!'

Isabel said nothing, and Jeanette swallowed her anger for she had no time and did not want to make an enemy of Isabel, even if the signs were not auspicious. She was aware of Katerine and Lady Elizabeth descending on them.

'Tell Thomas to be careful,' she said quickly. 'Please, if you have any regard for the truth, tell him that this match is not of my choosing, but my family's, and they told me he was dead. I know you do not think well of me – but please, I beg you.'

Isabel arched her brows, but gave a slight nod and turned away, inclining her head to Katerine and Elizabeth, who pointedly ignored her.

'Now we see why we cannot trust you for a moment,' Katerine scolded. 'You should know not to keep such company.'

'It is all the same to me,' Jeanette said. 'I see no difference from other company I am forced to keep.'

Lady Elizabeth's florid features reddened. 'You are insolent.'

'I am truthful,' Jeanette retorted.

'You are deluded,' Katerine snapped. 'Even if by a miracle Thomas Holland has survived his wounds, it does not alter the fact that your union with him was no marriage, but the duping of a foolish girl. He won't be able to prove it, and I doubt he will want to, for it will be his downfall. His family know this too and you will find no succour there. Nor from the King, for why should he listen to the words of a maimed man for whom he will have no use?'

Despite a prickle of terror that they were speaking the truth, Jeanette raised her chin in defiance. She would rather die than yield, and while she could not speak for Thomas, she knew her own mind.

17

Royal Palace of Langley, Hertfordshire, June 1341

Thomas drew rein as he approached the palace at Langley where the Queen was recuperating, following the birth of a fourth living son, Edmund. The heat of the late morning sun blazed across his shoulders and spine. His blind eye itched and ached behind the leather patch, and he dearly wanted to rub the area, but was striving not to inflame the healing scar.

He was growing accustomed to having sight in only one eye but he still made mistakes and misjudgements, especially of distance, and would grow frustrated and angry to the point of rage, and then be ashamed and mortified at his loss of control. He had to be able to fight and earn his wages and had redoubled his efforts. He had always been the best, and if he had to strive ten times harder than before to achieve it, he would do whatever it took.

They had been on the road home for many weeks, but at least the weather and the sea crossings had been kind. He had continued to heal and regain his strength and had declined to return to court until he deemed himself fit to kneel before the King.

While waiting to take ship from Flanders, he had received a crumpled, travel-stained letter from his sister Isabel, informing him that Jeanette had married William Montagu, heir to the earldom of Salisbury, at Langley in February, before the entire court, and that whatever marriage she had contracted with Thomas had been deemed null and void by her guardians, who had furthermore spread false news of his death. Reading that letter had been like being served a dish of maggots. Jeanette must have been complicit, and it had made him physically sick.

He bit the inside of his cheek. He had ridden to Ghent before embarking for England to seek the friar who had married them in St Bavo, only to discover that the young man had died of a fever in the early winter while at his ministry. Had he been of a superstitious mindset, Thomas might have taken it as an omen, but it only put iron in his soul.

A vast array of tents and pavilions had been set up near the waterside to house the servants, officials and knights of the court. Thomas rode past them, a pang of familiarity clenching his stomach like nauseous hunger. This was the life to which he should be returning, yet he was unsure of his welcome, or even if he wanted it. A hero home from the wars – perhaps – or else a one-eyed soldier, wasted before his time and of no further use to anyone, including himself and the girl who had brought him down. How much was publicly known? How much was hidden in the shadows or locked out of sight and denied? The moment he rode through those gates he might already be a marked man.

'Tom?' Otto glanced at him with concern. 'You need not announce yourself today if you would rather stay and pitch our tents, or ride on.'

'No, I shall face this now.' Thomas set his jaw. 'Tomorrow

will not make matters any different – it will only postpone the inevitable.'

They rode on to the castle and were admitted through the gates by the guards who directed them to a place where they could pitch their tents and deposit their baggage. John de la Salle and a couple of attendants took the horses to the stable block to be watered and tended. Thomas's throat was parched and he gulped from his flask and tasted the tannic flavour of leather. He dared not drink wine for it would only give him false courage and a stumbling tongue.

Once the tent was pitched, and the Holland flag planted, with its rampant golden lion on a blue ground, Thomas washed away the dust of the road and took his green and scarlet court tunic from his baggage, smoothing the creases as best he could. He combed his hair and recently trimmed beard. Now the moment had arrived, he was reluctant to go to the hall, but knew procrastination would only exacerbate his discomfort.

'Good luck, sire,' said Henry de la Haye, who was staying to guard the tents and finish unpacking their kit.

Thomas adjusted his belt, brushed his hands down his sleeves and, having given Henry a curt nod, stepped outside. Otto was waiting for him, also suitably garbed, his sandy-gold hair standing up in tufts that defied all grooming.

'Ready?' Otto said.

'As much as I shall ever be.' The turbulent energy churning inside him was almost overwhelming, and he welcomed Otto's solid presence at his side.

'The King will be pleased to see us.'

'You think so?'

Otto shrugged. 'Why should he not? We've gained experience and prestige and not at his expense. He will be planning new campaigns where our skills will be needed.'

Thomas grimaced, still unsure.

The hall was packed with members of the royal household dining at scrubbed wooden trestles, or at grander tables covered in white napery. Conversation was a steady rumble of voices, punctuated by the scraping of spoons on wooden dishes, and the dull chime of knives against earthenware. An usher found Thomas and Otto places by squeezing them on to the end of a board between two visiting knights. The brothers bowed to the dais where the King and Queen were dining, but with the meal already in full flow, their presence went unnoticed.

As dishes of spiced wheat grains and salmon in green herbs were brought to the board, Thomas gazed around and saw Jeanette sitting at one of the wings of the high table with Katerine of Salisbury to one side of her, and Lady Elizabeth de Montfort on the other. A plain wimple of white linen tightly framed her face, giving her the appearance of a nun. The veil part had fallen forward, covering her cheek, and her head was down. Her gown was simple too and of a grey-blue shade that drained her complexion. As she picked up her spoon, a plain gold ring gleamed on her wedding finger, and it was not his.

Thomas swallowed down his nausea. Being told in a letter by his sister that Jeanette had entered into a marriage with William Montagu was one thing, but seeing her sitting with the family was another. There was no sign of the youth she was supposed to have married and Thomas felt that he might kill him with one blow if he was here.

He took some of the frumenty and salmon, struggling for normality, but all he wanted to do was pick up the table and overturn it. Otto watched him with concern. Thomas tried to eat but almost choked on the first mouthful. He forced it down with a difficult swallow, but could not manage another morsel, and pushed to his feet.

'No, stay,' he said as Otto started to rise too. 'I need to be on my own.'

He strode rapidly from the hall and immediately vomited, clammy with cold sweat. He cursed himself for the world's greatest fool that he could face anyone in battle yet not find the wherewithal to sit and dine in the royal hall, as he had done unthinkingly so many times before his wounding and before Jeanette.

Straightening up, ignoring the curious regard of the soldiers on duty, he made his way to the stable block where he rinsed his mouth and swilled his face at the trough, steadying himself with the actions of routine. Having dismissed John de la Salle, who was seeing to Noir, he gripped his fingers in the stallion's rippled black mane and pressed his face into the warm neck.

Jeanette had looked up from her meal when she heard a commotion at one of the benches and started when she saw Otto sitting there and Thomas leaving. Katerine had not noticed, being deep in conversation with one of the other diners. Jeanette caught Otto's eye, and he gave a swift shake of the head and looked down.

Jeanette wiped her lips on her napkin and murmured to Katerine that she had to visit the latrine.

Katerine looked heavenwards. 'Can it not wait?'

Jeanette shook her head and clutched her stomach. 'I fear not, my lady mother.'

'Well, make haste,' Katerine said irritably. 'It is not seemly, but I do not know what else I should expect.'

Jeanette curtseyed to her mother-in-law and fled the table. Otto raised his brows at her but she ignored him and hurried out.

There was no sign of Thomas, but she saw John de la Salle

and, blank-faced, he directed her to the stables where she came upon him standing with Noir, his head pressed into the stallion's neck, his body shuddering.

'Thomas?'

He spun round, and she gasped at the sight of his eye patch and the scar running into it.

'Go away,' he snarled. 'Have you not done enough to me?'

'It is not what it seems,' she whispered. Her heart flooding with love and pain, she held out an imploring hand.

'Is it not when you wear another man's ring?'

'I swear so, on my life! I had no choice. You weren't here, although I prayed and prayed for you to come. I tried to stop the marriage. I told my mother and my uncle that we were already wed, but they wouldn't listen. Everyone said it was no solid marriage, but a foolish lust – that I had been duped and seduced out of my maidenhead. My mother ripped up my contract and burned it in front of my face, and she took my ring.' Her eyes blazed with tears. 'They showed me a letter that said you were dead and told me if I did not wed William Montagu they would put me in a convent. What was I to do? The King is close friends with Lord and Lady Montagu and would not have listened. Everyone was determined the wedding should happen. I fought it until I could fight no more. You must believe me.'

Deep creases engraved his cheeks, and he turned his head away.

'Why don't you look at me?' she asked with hurt bewilderment.

After a long pause he did turn round, but his expression was inscrutable. 'I do not know what to believe.'

'I am telling you the truth, Thomas. I was forced into this marriage that is no marriage at all. I am still wedded to you. I shall live my life in a place of nothing because I do not have you.' She grasped his arm and felt its rigidity. 'Help me out of this bind, I beg you.'

'Why do you think I am more able than you to do so?' he demanded bitterly. 'Who will listen? And if they do listen, what do you think will happen? You had better go – your husband will be wondering where you are.'

Her anger rose, and her frustration at his obtuseness. 'He is not here, and he is no more my husband than is a sheep in a field. You are my true husband in God's eyes, and in mine – and I shall love you until the end of my life, I swear it on my soul.'

He looked at her, a muscle flickering on one cheek.

'When they said you were dead, I believed them – everyone did. I only discovered you were still alive after my marriage to William Montagu – your sister told me, and she likes me not.'

She reached up to stroke the damaged side of his face with a feather-touch, and he drew back, but not all the way, and she continued her tracery. He closed his good eye and his throat worked.

Jeanette took away her hand, opened her alms pouch, and brought out the rough-cut ruby. 'You gave me this in token of your heart, and I kept it, and it became mine. Now I return it to you as a changed thing – as my own heart.' She placed it in the centre of his palm. 'Do with it as you choose, for it is yours and always will be. I ask you to help me annul this marriage. I have two lives and I am living the wrong one – and I do not believe either of us can bear it.'

She turned and walked away from him, not knowing how she managed to put one foot in front of the other but making the steps anyway in the certainty that she had to do it before they were discovered, and before the enormity of the moment went beyond bearing.

Back in the great hall, her mother-in-law was waiting to pounce, her eyes sharp. 'You were gone a long time.'

'I am not well, madam,' Jeanette answered. 'I beg leave to retire.'

Katerine eyed her narrowly, but gestured for her servant, Mary, to accompany her with Hawise.

Once in her chamber, Jeanette sat down on her bed and stared at the wall. She did not know if Thomas would fight for their marriage or let it go. If he broached the subject to the King and Queen, he would be putting himself in terrible danger. With the Montagus so high in royal favour, he could do nothing. That was the depressing reality.

'Thomas is back,' she told Hawise, 'and so is John. Go and find him – seek your own joy.'

'My lady . . .' Hawise's face lit with a mingling of pleasure and doubt.

'I do not know how long they will be here. Go.' Jeanette waved her hand. 'Make haste.'

Hawise took her cloak, curtseyed to Jeanette, and sped from the room on light feet.

Jeanette folded over, her face in her hands, feeling utterly wretched.

In the stables, Thomas shuddered, then drew a deep breath. He knew Jeanette was not lying. She had asked him to get her out of the marriage, and he had felt a treacherous glimmer of hope that there might be a way forward, but he would have to wade through so much mire to do so, and against such odds. Was it worth it? Why not just burn his own marriage contracts, swear the witnesses to silence, and ride away? The priest was dead, and he knew Otto would be relieved.

He gazed at the ruby she had returned to him, glinting like a dull red coal in his hand. And then he put it in his pouch and turned to harnessing the stallion.

Otto arrived as he was adjusting the girths. 'Where are you going? The King will be asking for you.'

Thomas shook his head. 'I cannot go and I cannot stay,' he said. 'I am caught in limbo.'

'Shall I come with you?'

Thomas regarded his brother's earnest, troubled face and shook his head. 'No. I am in sore need of my own company for a while.'

'I take it you have spoken with Jeanette?'

Thomas strapped his travelling pack to the back of the saddle with his spare cloak and bed roll. 'They told her I was dead. She says she was forced into the match with William Montagu and has asked me to help her.'

Otto lifted his brows. 'That is a tall and dangerous order.'

Thomas set his foot in the stirrup. 'Since when has that ever been a hindrance?'

'Never, so far, but you keep on raising the stakes.'

Thomas swung into the saddle and gathered the reins. 'The higher the stakes, the greater the prize – so they say.'

'But the greater the loss if the gamble fails,' Otto warned.

Thomas puffed out his breath. 'I need to think and I cannot do that with Jeanette a breath away from my body. If anyone enquires after me, including the King, say you do not know where I am, but you are certain I shall return soon.'

Otto rumpled his hair, making it stick up more than ever. 'Well, make sure you do not make a lie of my certainty,' he said, to which Thomas raised his hand in a gesture of acknowledgement before turning his rein to the gate.

Leaving Langley, Thomas rode along the river bank for several miles. Eventually, at dusk, he pitched his makeshift canvas shelter under an oak tree, and hobbled the stallion to graze. Gazing up at the stars, his arms pillowing his head, he wondered what everything was about. All of this small petty striving set against God's great firmament.

Did he want to fight for Jeanette, or did he want to leave it all behind and pretend it had never happened? But he had never been any good at pretending. Jeanette was his wife – that was the heart of the matter, encapsulated in an imperfect red jewel. She had beseeched him to help her. God alone knew what pressure she had been put under to agree to the marriage, and she had thought him dead.

If he made his claim before the King now, he would not succeed for there was too great a boulder blocking his road. He needed to find a way forward or around. He had to find allies at court, and someone he could trust to give him an honest opinion and support while remaining pragmatic. Not Otto, who might be loyal and stalwart but barely hid the notion that while he supported Thomas, he thought him mad and that he should move on to pastures new. His consideration landed on John de Warenne, his sister's lover. John would have the understanding, and the legal knowledge, because of his own enduring marriage dispute. He would know who to approach, and what to do.

Eventually, he fell asleep, wrapped in his cloak, while the stars wheeled above him, and the world turned. When he woke in the grey pre-dawn light, the dew was glistening on the grass, and as he broke his fast on stale bread and a lump of cheese, he knew his road, even if the boulder still remained.

The King greeted Thomas cordially later that morning as the trestles were being set up for dinner, remarking that he was glad to see him returned, and sorry that he had been wounded. Nothing in his demeanour suggested disapproval or knowledge of the clandestine marriage. Everything seemed to have been swept into a neat pile and disposed of by others. The King was relaxed and intent on military matters.

'It has not affected my ability in the field, sire,' Thomas said, keen to dispel any notion that he was now infirm. 'I am eager to serve you in any way you wish.'

'I am glad to hear it,' Edward replied, 'for I shall have need of your services, and even if you cannot fight, you are invaluable to me as a quartermaster.'

'Sire, I assure you I can fight,' Thomas said vehemently. 'My injury has only increased my will to prove myself. You will not find me lacking in any part – indeed the opposite.'

Edward raised his brows at Thomas's intensity. 'Well, we shall see. I am glad to have you back, as is the Queen, and I shall send you to her now.' He waved to an usher and gave him the order. 'I'll need you for organising the campaign in Brittany at summer's end.'

'Sire.' Thomas bowed. 'May I then request your leave to visit my mother in the meantime?'

'As you wish, but be back within a month.' The King waved his dismissal and Thomas bowed once more and followed the servant out.

The Queen's chamber was occupied by a multitude of seamstresses busily creating and embellishing the lavish wardrobe demanded by a royal lady. Italian silks and velvets in opulent tints and shades of violet, crimson and emerald green were spread across trestle tables. Bags of gemstones far-travelled from the mines in India and Ceylon, pearls and gold and silver wire. Linens, soft, clean and white in contrast, decorated with delicate German smocking. The spaces between the industrious seamstresses were occupied by maids and nursemaids, servants and clerks, dogs and scribes. The Queen was busy with one of the latter, but looked up at Thomas's arrival, and a smile lit her face. 'Ah, Thomas!' She beckoned to him, then set her hand over her rounded belly. She was not currently pregnant, but the constant bearing of children had taken its toll on her figure, as had the box of sweetmeats always at her side. Poppet, her squirrel, perched on her shoulder, eating almonds.

A concerned look crossed her face. 'We were all so sorry to hear of your injury. Indeed, we were told that you had died, and I am deeply glad that our mourning was premature.'

'As you can see, madam, I am well, and not greatly discommoded,' Thomas replied, sweeping Philippa a deep bow. He could feel Katerine of Salisbury's gimlet stare upon him. Jeanette sat in the background robed in plain colours, that horrible tight wimple framing her face.

'I thank God for it, but still you have been sorely wounded,' the Queen said.

'Yes, madam, sadly I lost the sight of an eye, but I hope I have gained wisdom and experience in exchange.' He smiled ruefully. 'I assure you I can still tourney and compete with any knight in the land.'

'I do not doubt it,' Philippa answered with compassion, and Thomas realised that to be taken seriously again he would have to prove himself beyond words. The awareness was unpleasant, but further whetted his determination.

'I understand you and the King are to be congratulated on the birth of a new prince.'

Philippa's face lit up with a smile. She signalled, and the new addition to the royal family, wrapped in swaddling, was presented by his nurse. 'This is Edmund,' she said. 'Born almost three weeks ago.'

Thomas looked dutifully at the parcelled child that resembled any other small baby to his masculine eye. He made suitably admiring remarks and enquired after the health of the others. Edward, the heir, was absent at Berkeley, but his brothers Lionel and John were summoned from their play, and Thomas commented on how much they had grown – busy infant boys of two and a half and fifteen months. Isabelle and Joan greeted him with smiles and silent but curious regard for his eye patch.

When it was time to take his leave, the Queen gave him a green jewel for his hat from her famous trinket box and said she hoped to speak to him again later. Thomas thanked her with courteous enthusiasm and turned to go.

While he had been speaking with Philippa and engaging with the royal offspring, Jeanette had positioned herself near the door, and the flash of her gaze as she lifted it to his opened up a cavern of memories and longing within him – indelible and visceral. He wanted to seize her in his arms and ride off with her, away from all this falsehood and incarceration. The irony was that he had every right to do so, yet was unable to act.

He drew a deep breath and strode from the room before he betrayed either of them, and, returning to his tent, slumped on his camp stool and groaned.

Otto shouldered through the tent flaps and looked at him. 'Where did you go last night?'

Thomas raised his head. 'I slept under the stars in no man's land. Just me and my horse and my ghosts and God.'

'And did all of you come to a decision?' Otto went to the wine jug.

'Not immediately, but yes, we did.'

'And?'

Thomas fingered the green hat jewel, wondering how much it was worth if he sold it. 'I still love her. I still want her with all my being, and she is my lawful wife. She married William Montagu under coercion, believing me dead. Yet I cannot claim her because we are in the same quandary as before. No one will believe us if we speak, and everyone except me and Jeanette is delighted with a match that unites their interests. I am just a damaged household knight with a traitor for a father.'

'That sounds rather like you have decided to give up,' Otto said.

Thomas shook his head. 'I considered it, but I think of Jeanette and know I cannot. I have to find the funds to challenge the match and employ an attorney to speak for me. I shall discuss the matter with John de Warenne – he has long acquaintance with such dealings and will advise me well.'

Otto raised his cup. 'De Warenne has not had much success though, has he? He's still married despite decades of trying to obtain an annulment. I hold out little hope that our sister will ever stand at the church door with him.'

'Even so, he has the experience to advise me.'

Otto conceded the point with a shrug. 'Will you make it public knowledge?'

'It would be pointless. I need to be on solid ground with the funds to carry it through the Church courts if I am to stand any chance of success. If I do it now, I will be dismissed out of hand, endanger my own life and destroy my family's reputation. That is why I need to speak to de Warenne. He will not steer me false.' He grimaced in frustration. 'I must bide my time, and it is beyond hard when I want it to be now.'

'You would not consider giving her up?' Otto ventured, stepping into the lion's den. 'Would it not be better for all concerned?'

'No,' Thomas said vehemently. 'We made our vows before God. I cannot make that go away. Jeanette was coerced into this match by her family, and she does not wish to remain wed to William Montagu. It is a matter of sacred vows and honour as well as love. I thought about it all of last night and I am still thinking now, but I still come to the same conclusion. I cannot and will not give her up.'

Otto grunted. 'I am glad I am a younger son and a simple man. I earn a wage, I tumble a woman for a coin and put no fetters on myself.'

'There is certainly wisdom in that approach,' Thomas said with weary amusement.

Otto pressed a light hand on Thomas's shoulder. 'I won't say all will be well – I am not sure it can be – but I will pray for the best outcome, and you have my loyalty whatever happens.'

'Thank you,' Thomas said, deeply touched and even a little guilty. 'I owe you more than I can ever repay.'

'Call it quits,' Otto said with a grin. 'I will remind you next time I need to pay my gambling debts.'

18

Royal Palace of Langley, Hertfordshire, June 1341

Over the next couple of days, Jeanette tried to find ways to escape and meet Thomas, but as soon as they realised Thomas had returned, Katerine and Elizabeth kept her secluded in the women's quarters.

On the third morning, Katerine told Jeanette to pack her things. 'I have sought the Queen's permission for you and my mother to retire to our manor at Bisham for the rest of the summer,' she said. 'I think it best if you are gone from court for a while and the Queen agrees it will suit your humours. If you are to have children with my son, your womb needs to settle down.' Jeanette glared at her in dismay and resentment, but Katerine was unmoved. 'Sulk as much as you wish, it changes nothing. You shall leave after dinner today.' She began issuing orders for Jeanette's baggage chests to be packed.

Jeanette knew she was being removed from any opportunity to speak with Thomas or members of his retinue. A part of her thought she might as well be dead, even while another part glinted with steely defiance.

When she emerged into the strong June sunlight, escorted by Katerine and Elizabeth and carrying Grippe in her arms, for his hind legs were not good these days, a covered baggage cart stood ready, with an escort of Montagu retainers. Frederick had been taken from the Queen's mews, hooded, and placed in his travelling crate.

'Come, make haste,' Katerine said testily. 'You are keeping everyone waiting.'

Jeanette immediately made a deliberate show of sauntering just to annoy Katerine, and looked around, hoping against hope that her prayers would be answered, but the courtyard remained empty save for servants going about their business. With a heavy heart she clambered into the cart and settled herself against the cushions, her hairline itchy with sweat in the summer heat. Lady Elizabeth joined her and plumped down opposite her on the interior bench, her weight making the cart lurch. The look she gave Jeanette warned without words what would happen if there was any kind of rebellion or upset.

Jeanette looked away through the arched opening and saw a troop of horsemen trotting into the yard. And there was Thomas, dismounting from a sweating palfrey. She drew a short breath and feasted her gaze on him. His linen shirt was open at the throat, his tunic slung across the saddle, and the sight of the long, lean frame that she had known so intimately, both clothed and naked, sent a pang of desolate longing through her.

He looked up and across at the cart, and their eyes met and held. Raising his right hand to his lips, he kissed his clenched fist and then opened out his palm in her direction. Jeanette had a brief moment to return the gesture before Elizabeth made an angry sound, and levered herself up from her bench to unhook the covering curtain and snatch it over the entrance.

'Enough of that, my girl,' she snapped.

Jeanette gave her a contemptuous look and then smiled, knowing how much it would infuriate the old woman.

As the cart rolled out of the compound, she concentrated on the vision of Thomas as she had just seen him, and her determination solidified.

When Thomas and Otto arrived at the family manor of Thorpe, Maude, Lady Holland, was in the yard with the poultry maid, watching the latest batch of pullets. Thomas smiled, watching her shade her eyes and point while the poultry woman nodded in agreement. His mother kept a close eye on the estate finances, and ensured she received good value for every penny she spent.

Hearing the horses, his mother turned, and her face lit up. With a welcoming cry, she hurried over to the sweat-lathered horses and embraced Otto, the first to dismount, calling him her bright-haired, dependable boy. And then she turned to Thomas. Her gaze fixed on the scarring disappearing into his eye patch, and she made a soft sound of distress. 'Oh, my son! I am glad to have you home and alive, but what have you done – your face!'

'I didn't move fast enough, Mama,' he replied with a shrug, and kissed her cheek before sweeping her into an enormous hug. 'Fear not, I have healed well and it hasn't slowed me down.' Releasing her, he raised his head and, gazing around, let out a deep breath. 'Ah, it is so good to be home.'

'And it is so good to see you,' she said. 'I would keep you both here all the time if I could!'

Taking his arm, with Otto walking at her other side, she drew them towards the manor.

'You wouldn't want that,' Otto said. 'We'd be far too much trouble.'

'Hah, do I not know it, but at least I would keep you from harm.'

Once they had washed away the dust of travel and changed into lighter indoor garb, they sat down in her chamber with a jug of wine and a dish of nutmeg custard tarts.

Maude turned to Thomas again. 'Now,' she said briskly, 'what is all this I hear about you being married to Jeanette of Kent?'

Thomas paused, a tart halfway to his mouth. 'I do not know what you have heard, Mama,' he said warily.

'Your sister told me.' She gave him a steady, sorrowful look. 'I wish you had found the grace and courage to tell me, your own mother, yourself.'

Thomas looked abashed. 'I was going to, but circumstances moved ahead of me. I was hoping I could resolve the matter and present Jeanette to you in all honour as my wife, but the situation has grown more complicated than that.'

His mother gave an exasperated sigh. 'What were you thinking to become involved with the King's own cousin – a royal lady?'

'I wasn't thinking,' Thomas said wryly. 'I expect Isabel has had her full say.'

'Indeed she has, but I have learned to reserve my judgement, especially where siblings are concerned. Isabel has your best interests at heart, but you do not always agree on what those interests are.'

Thomas said nothing and busied himself eating his tart. He knew his sister only too well.

His mother eyed him sternly. 'Tell me your version,' she said. 'And I want the truth.'

Heat seeped into his face as he was reminded of the many times she had reprimanded him for boyhood misdemeanours.

But he had to admit that this was more than a simple prank. Clearing his throat, he said, 'We came to know each other while I was guarding the Queen and Jeanette was one of her damsels. Her hawk died and I helped her to train her new one . . . and it developed from there – from the time we spent together.'

'And what was it about this girl that you had to go behind the King's back?' she asked, to the point. 'What led you to such a rash action?'

Thomas hesitated. He did not know what to say to his mother, but he owed her a truthful answer. 'We had lain together,' he said, 'and she was with child.'

She put her hand to her mouth. 'Oh, Thomas!'

'It was not just lust,' he said defensively. 'I love her, and she is my life.'

'And the child?'

His expression twisted. He didn't want to think about it. 'She lost it before it quickened – the Countess of Salisbury gave her a tisane to "balance her humours". She was supposed to be chaperoning Jeanette; perhaps she feared recrimination, or perhaps her plans went deeper. Whatever happened, Jeanette lost the child. I had to leave to attend the King, and then I took the cross to atone for my sins. When I returned to make a clean breast of everything, I discovered Jeanette had been coerced into a bigamous marriage with William Montagu. They had told her I was dead – and that is how things now stand.'

Maude regarded him with a gaze that was half compassionate and half reproachful. 'This is indeed a tangled web – a dangerous one too. What will you do?'

'I scarcely know, except that we made our vows in the sight of God, and she no more desires her match with William Montagu than I do.'

'Does the King know? Does the Queen?'

'Not that I am aware. I have not approached them, for the time has not been right and the matter of the Montagu marriage will not be easy to resolve.'

His mother reached for her wine and took a fortifying swallow. 'You will find it difficult to undo this coil without angering powerful people. Your life – our lives – are in their hands and we have neither the money nor the influence to fight them on their terms.' She looked at him directly. 'I do not know how I am going to help you with this. You may have to accept the blot on your soul and take another wife, or else live your life in silence.'

Thomas drew back abruptly. 'I will not do that, mother. I will find a way and nothing shall stop me. I mean it.'

'Yes, I do not doubt it.' Her chin wobbled, but she rallied, and Thomas remembered her saying to him as a small boy watching his father ride off to war that when men set out to do battle, it did not help to see the anguish in the eyes of those who loved them. 'I can see you are set on your course,' she said with resignation, 'but you are wise to be cautious and not make any sudden moves given the stakes involved for everyone.'

'I have thought long and hard about it,' he said. 'I know I have caused great difficulty and upset, but I have learned some hard lessons. Nothing will come of this until I am ready to move. I will not put you or any of my family at risk.'

She raised her brows. 'I doubt it will be your choice. The moment you do move, you will endanger us all, whatever you say. Nevertheless, I will do what I can to help you. You are my son, my flesh and blood.'

Thomas dipped his head, acknowledging her offer, filled with feelings of guilt and unworthiness.

'Be very careful,' she said. 'You as well, Otto.'

Otto spread his hands and gave her his usual innocent, wide-eyed look. 'I have tried to turn him from this course to no avail, but since he is set upon it, I shall do my best to keep him out of trouble – not that I always succeed.' He nudged Thomas's arm and Thomas nudged him back, hard, letting the gesture serve for acknowledgement and affection.

'I have orders for Brittany and I can do nothing before then,' Thomas said. 'I need to gather sworn witness documents and consult with lawyers versed in such matters. And before I can do that, I must accumulate funds to pay for their services, which means acquiring booty and taking ransoms on campaign. I also need to speak with John de Warenne, for he has the legal knowledge to guide me.' He rubbed his face at the side of the eye patch. 'I do not foresee an easy resolution – the Montagu family is too deeply invested not to fight, and Jeanette's mother the same – but even so I must take up the challenge.'

His mother shook her head. 'I will say nothing more. I know your tenacity when fixed on a desire. But, my son, be sure it is truly what you want.'

'Yes, Mama, it is,' he replied, setting his jaw.

19

Manor of Bisham, Berkshire, December 1343

Jeanette drew rein and waited for the falconer to join her, so that she could place Frederick on his glove. It had been a productive morning's hunt and two pigeons and four mallards hung at the man's saddle. The dogs were panting and ready to turn for home, but Jeanette wasn't. Riding out on a day like this was as close to freedom as she could come and it kept her from going utterly mad. The December day was crisp and sunny even if the air was bitter. The fresh air, the frosty scent of winter and the movement of the horse beneath her soothed her raw, hurting soul. It was a great pity that her unwanted boy-husband was riding with her, but she was ignoring him, and pretending he wasn't there.

She tried to avoid him as much as possible and he spent most of his time in reciprocation. He was mostly absent, dwelling in Prince Edward's household, but was visiting Bisham for a couple of weeks, and to Jeanette, every hour seemed to stretch for a year. One of the reasons for his visit was the necessity of begetting an heir to secure the family dynasty, even though he had a brother. His parents desired the connection to royal blood and she and William had been married for nearly three years with no sign of offspring.

He had come to her chamber a few times, but she had lain as limp as a corpse and dissuaded him in every way possible, knowing he too had little taste for the deed, and it was only the insistence of his mother and grandmother that pushed him. The old lady kept giving Jeanette fertility tisanes that Jeanette contrived either to spit out, or swallow then visit the latrine and stick her fingers down her throat.

She had heard nothing from Thomas, but then she was stuck at Bisham, and from the little she had been able to glean he had been absent on campaign, fighting in Brittany, in Gascony and in Spain, even under the command of William's father the Earl of Salisbury at times. Wherever there was war he had been a part of it. She was hoping he might broach the subject of their marriage with William's father, but she had heard nothing and it was becoming increasingly difficult to believe they would ever be together. Since the only alternative was despair, she clung grimly to her hope, but it didn't make her happy. She did not know where he was now, whether still on campaign or at home.

Tears would fill her eyes when she thought of hawking and hunting with Thomas in Flanders. The joyful companionship, and the breathless, exquisite moments by the riverside or in the woods. In her mind's eye it was perfect. To be out on similar pursuits with William Montagu made her feel as if those moments were being sullied by a tarnished overlay of discontent.

Unable to bear the thought of returning to the manor and the gimlet scrutiny of Lady Elizabeth, she gathered the reins and dug in her heels. The mare took off with a startled snort, and Jeanette urged her on with voice, hands and heels to a swift gallop. As the ground rushed beneath the mare's hooves, and the wind streamed past Jeanette's face and rippled her headdress, the tight knot inside her started to unwind and she shouted with exhilaration, wishing the mare would race faster still.

Hard, fast hoofbeats thundered behind her and she knew without looking round that William was in pursuit and gaining. She urged the mare on, determined not to give in, but his horse was faster, and he drew alongside, reaching out, seizing her rein and heading her to a rearing stop so that she had to hold on hard to prevent herself from falling off.

'Where do you think you are going?' he demanded angrily. 'Off to your imaginary husband, I suppose!'

'I would if I could!' Jeanette retorted. 'And he is not imaginary. You are the one who does not exist!'

He raised his whip to strike her and she did not flinch. 'Hurt me all you want, but it will never change the truth.'

He pulled the blow, his blue eyes glittering. 'You keep up this pretence beyond reason. If Thomas Holland was your sworn husband he would have come for you by now, but he hasn't, has he? Hah, he ignored you at court when he returned and said nothing to the King. It never happened!'

'You will see,' she said with a toss of her head. 'And you will remember this time and all the other times I told you it was true.'

He made an exasperated sound. 'You are foolish.'

'If I am then you should help me, for who would want such a wife in the first place?'

Returning to the manor in hostile silence, they found it in a state of upheaval. A messenger had arrived from court, and

William's grandmother was chivvying the servants and lashing out with her fearsome ebony walking stick to assert her authority. 'We are summoned to Windsor for the Christmas season,' she said irritably, as if it was their fault. 'Who knows if this weather will hold, and the cart needs a new wheel.'

'To Windsor, madam?' Jeanette strove to flatten her joy lest it further antagonise her husband's grandmother. 'Has the King summoned us?'

'Who else?' Lady Elizabeth snapped. 'I need not tell you that any nonsense from you will not be tolerated. Do I make myself clear?'

'Yes, madam.'

Jeanette dropped her gaze while inside she was dancing with excitement. Thomas might be there, and even if he wasn't she could still find out what had been happening. They wouldn't be able to keep her shut away all of the time.

Arriving in Windsor, Jeanette felt as though she had been pitched into the middle of a storm. The town and the castle were bursting at the seams with knights and soldiers and hangers-on. There were armourers and harness makers, traders selling belts and spurs and daggers. Gaudy jewellery, pilgrim badges, fertility badges, hot wafers drizzled with spiced honey, eel pies, gingerbread, purses and pins, false hair, candles, pigs and poultry, and whores, cut-purses and masters of the loaded dice seeking gullible victims. Bemused by the mad cacophony, Jeanette wondered if her reaction was caused by the bucolic existence she had been living. It all seemed so noisy and sprawling, garish, with fierce colours and exotic aromas. She looked out for Thomas, but it was like seeking a particular pebble on a beach full of pebbles.

Entering the castle grounds, she was amazed to see a great

circular construction in the upper ward, surrounded by scaffolding. The sound of hammering rang out and workmen toiled, red-cheeked in the winter afternoon, working on the roof shingles. The knight who was escorting them to their quarters grinned at their astonishment and puffed out his chest to share his knowledge that the King had ordered the building of a great dwelling he was calling the Round Table in which he intended to hold feasts and entertainments where deeds of prowess would be performed, reminiscent of the court of King Arthur.

'Forty thousand oak roof tiles,' he announced, gesturing to the men hard at work. 'A grand tournament is to be held with twenty-four of the King's best knights against all comers!'

William's eyes sparkled. Jeanette wondered as to the identity of the knights, suspecting that Thomas and Otto might be among them, and her breathing shortened with anxious anticipation while Lady Elizabeth looked around with the superior air of someone pretending to have seen it all before.

Their lodgings, as usual when attending such events, were a couple of large tents, lined with rich silk and luxuriously furnished. They had been set up in the outer bailey in the lee of a wall. Lady Elizabeth wallowed out of the cart and grimaced as she landed on her bad hip, then proceeded to scold the attendants as if it was all their fault. Jeanette gave the men a sympathetic look. At least she wasn't lashing about with her notorious stick, because she was using it as a support.

Their horses were led away to the stables beside the smithy, and the party took refreshment and exchanged their dusty garments for fresh clothes appropriate to the court. Elizabeth, her stout figure encased in dark-red wool, ordered Jeanette to wear her plainest wimple and conceal her hair. 'Have you painted your lips and cheeks?' she demanded suspiciously.

'They're just cold-reddened, my lady,' Jeanette replied. It wasn't exactly true; a touch of the rouge pot might have been involved. If she had to wear a head covering that made her look like a nun, then she would be an exotic nun – a fallen one. The notion made her lips curl with a bitter smile.

One of Queen Philippa's squires arrived to escort them to her lodgings in the upper bailey and William formally offered Jeanette his arm. She declined to take it, but did walk at his side.

The Queen's lodging stood against the north wall of the upper bailey, incorporating the nursery, her private chamber, and her own hall for receiving guests and supplicants. Today the latter was full of people drinking wine, talking in groups, and being presented.

Resplendent in purple velvet embroidered with golden squirrels, Philippa sat on a gilded chair at the far end of the chamber. The royal children attended on either side. Prince Edward and his sisters Isabelle and Joan, now twelve and ten. Five-year-old Lionel was present and three-year-old John. Edmund, aged two, were in the company of their nurses while Philippa's ladies stood in attendance nearby, including Katerine of Salisbury.

Jeanette curtseyed to the Queen, who gestured for her to rise, and smiled warmly. 'It is good to see you,' she said. 'How are you faring, my dear?'

'I am well, madam,' Jeanette replied, aware that Katerine and Elizabeth were watching her closely for any infraction.

Philippa leaned forward to pinch Jeanette's cheek. 'You look a little downcast, my dear. We shall have to feed you up and put a glow back in your complexion if you are going to bloom for your husband and give him some little ones!' She cast a twinkling look at William, who blushed and dropped his gaze.

219

Jeanette pressed her lips together for want of a suitable answer and curtseyed again.

Philippa beamed, but her shrewd eyes missed nothing.

Katerine hurried Jeanette away as soon as possible while the Queen was receiving other supplicants. 'If there is a single moment of nonsense while we are here,' she said against Jeanette's ear, 'you shall be sent straight back to Bisham.'

Jeanette looked daggers at Katerine. 'Do not worry, I shall do exactly as you expect of me.'

The words, decidedly ambiguous, made Katerine frown.

Prince Edward joined them, and Katerine had to curtsey. He acknowledged everyone's deference, and grinned at William. 'I hope you'll be returning to Berkeley after Christmas, but I'll understand if you do not!' he said, winking at him, then turned to Jeanette. 'I am so glad to see you here, cousin. If you need cheering up as my mother says, I promise you masques and dances and tourneys. There will be no time to be glum, not at this great "Round Table".'

Jeanette smiled, because this was Edward and his humour and friendship always lifted her spirits, even if it was more of a candle flicker than a steady flame. 'I am glad to see you too, sire,' she murmured.

Her brother John had been standing behind Edward, and now came forward to kiss her. 'Sister,' he said. 'How is it with you?'

Jeanette gave him a look. What did he know? He was three years younger. His close friends were Edward and William, and he truly had no notion of the reality for her. 'I am glad to be back at court,' she said, and meant it, but with a horrible churning in her stomach when she thought of the false life she was leading. But confiding in anyone would only see her forced back into house arrest.

As they returned in a group to their tents in the lower ward, a party of knights arrived from the training ground, jesting together after their exertions, exuberant, red-faced, breath smoking the air. Jeanette's gaze lit on Otto, and then Thomas at his side, and she inhaled sharply. So he *was* back then! He was deep in conversation with another knight but looked up, and for a fleeting moment their eyes met with an intensity like fire. And then the groups passed each other and the moment moved on, but she was shaken, and desperate to escape somehow and speak to him.

In the late winter afternoon, the court had gathered in the King's Great Hall in the lower bailey to feast on small dainties and be entertained by minstrels, tumblers and tale tellers. The building had been transformed into the court of King Arthur for the duration of the winter festivities. Hangings of painted canvas draped the walls, festooned with swatches of evergreen. Embroidered hassocks covered the tiered benches and white napery cloths gleamed on the tables. Glass goblets and dishes of silver-gilt adorned the high table itself.

King Edward presided over the packed hall, not just playing at but becoming King Arthur, with Queen Philippa beside him as his Guinevere. He wore red velvet, embroidered with golden lions, and Philippa the same. Poppet had a collar stitched with gold crowns and acorns from which dangled a leash of golden leather.

Jeanette had been presented with a crimson velvet gown trimmed with ermine, and a gem-set gold circlet for her hair, engraved with running deer. She had been given the part of a court damsel and been presented with an obligatory basket of artificial petals to throw at the knights and performers as they entertained the crowd with feats and tumbling skills.

Thomas stood among the knights gathered around the King and Queen, resplendent in his royal livery of forest-green and scarlet velvet. Jeanette watched him, pouring all her love, longing and frustration into her stare. He avoided looking at her, keeping his focus firmly on the King and Queen.

For the next entertainment, a group of knights disguised in costumes of green rags and dyed red feathers leaped into the centre of the room, twirling and dancing before their audience as 'wild men of the woods' brandishing crude wooden clubs. Jeanette saw Thomas unobtrusively leave the room. She started to follow him but her wrist was immediately grasped by her mother-in-law. 'Stay with me,' Katerine commanded. 'I know your propensity for wandering off and there are too many young knights here with their eye on a chance.'

Jeanette set her jaw and looked at Katerine with loathing.

The wild woodmen cavorted and danced in their ragged costumes, uttering halloos, striking their wooden batons against each other, click-clack. A core of them performed an intricate percussion in the middle of the room to the lustful wail of bagpipes, while those at the edges ran at the young women, leaping and leering, wagging their backsides, their behaviour straddling a delicious line between outrage and stomach-clenching mirth, making their victims scream.

When they eventually capered from the chamber, uttering loud wails and unearthly shrieks, the squires and naperers came around the tables and boards with dishes of nuts and sweetmeats, and replenished the jugs. To a fanfare of trumpets at the end of the hall, the doors swung open and Thomas Holland rode into the room on Noir. The stallion's mane was combed over to one side in a rippling black waterfall twined with red artificial flowers and his harness and breast pieces were spangled with gold stars. Thomas wore a royal livery robe, but of a different style with fancy dagging at the hem and sleeve ends, each point stitched with a golden crotal bell.

He made Noir rear and paw the air, and when he dropped to all fours, Thomas leaped up on to the saddle and stood with his hands on his hips, smiling broadly. He performed a back-flip over Noir's rump and then made the horse lie down, stretch out its neck and pretend to be dead. He selected a young page from the audience to come and cup his hand over the horse's ear and whisper the magic words of revival. Noir snorted, pushed to his feet and shook himself, to great laughter and applause.

Thomas commanded him to paw the ground with his hooves to count out how many children the King and Queen had, right leg for the boys and left leg for the girls. And finally, at a touch, Noir bowed his head and foreleg before the diners at the high table. Philippa clapped, enchanted, and threw Thomas a soft velvet purse of coins. The King's son John offered Noir an apple, which the stallion took with precise delicacy before loudly crunching it up. Man and horse bowed once more. Thomas leaped back into the saddle and rode out. On the way, Noir snatched a hat off someone's head to raucous applause, and Thomas retrieved it and set it on his own.

Jeanette's hands stung with clapping and her heart brimmed with pride. She remembered how he had always been teaching Noir such tricks when they were in Flanders. Some people had frowned on it, but Thomas said that a fully trained horse was a partnership you could trust in battle.

Katerine's lips were tightly pursed, but her husband was cuffing tears of mirth from his eyes – until Katerine spoke to him in a low voice that did not carry but which wiped the humour from his face and replaced it with irritation.

When Thomas returned to the feast, to loud acclaim and

whoops of delight, Katerine grabbed Jeanette's arm. 'Make one move towards that man and you shall be on the cart back to Bisham tomorrow morning, I swear,' she warned, and drew her away into a tight group of ladies, which only increased Jeanette's determination to find a way to speak with Thomas – even if it was to bid farewell.

Katerine personally escorted Jeanette back to the Salisbury tents and soon afterwards the Earl arrived, still looking annoyed. He sat down on a chair in the main tent and punched the fleece-stuffed back cushion. Then he regarded Jeanette, his brows drawn into a heavy frown.

'I have heard arrant nonsense about this supposed marriage between you and Thomas Holland for almost three years now and I have held my tongue and left my wife to deal with the matter,' he said. 'But it seems I must step in. I well know these young bucks at court and their ways, especially those Holland boys. Without them the Flanders brothels would not have turned so great a profit while we were there. Do you really think a match between you and the younger son of a disgraced knight will stand up to scrutiny? You were married in church to our son and the match has been consummated. We have clear evidence and reliable witnesses, which is more than you have for your tawdry claim to be wed to Thomas Holland.' He leaned forward, fixing her with his stare. 'We were on campaign together for nine months and not once in that time did Holland broach the subject to me. Nor has he made any approach since we have returned. Why is that, do you think? Perhaps because it was never real? Perhaps because it was a foolish flirtation best forgotten by all?'

Jeanette swallowed a choking sensation of fear. What if he was right? 'He is my husband, sworn before a friar and witnesses at the Abbey of Saint Bavo, and although my own mother took my ring and tore up one contract, there are others. There is plenty of evidence.'

The Earl raised a scornful brow. 'So much evidence that Holland hasn't seen fit to come forward to put his case?'

'Because he has no funds to do so. God knows the truth.'

'There was no first marriage,' Katerine said coldly. 'You would have needed the consent of your mother and the King, and since neither were forthcoming, it renders the matter null and void. The burden of proof may not fall on us, but such falsehood certainly falls upon our reputation. We shall not allow our honour to be sullied by your pernicious lies and silly delusions, and you shall certainly not be permitted to spread them abroad.'

'They are not lies and delusions!' Jeanette cried in distraught frustration. 'I am telling the truth!'

'I have heard enough,' the Earl growled, and he looked at his wife and mother. 'I see what you are up against. Take her from my sight and confine her until she learns that silence is a virtue. I shall speak to Holland myself, and see what can be done.'

Jeanette stood her ground, ready to fight, but a flick of the Earl's fingers brought his squires from the side of the room, and they took her by the arms and dragged her away to a separate tent and set a guard. Lady Elizabeth followed and, leaning on her stick, regarded Jeanette with angry contempt. 'I will tie you to the tent post if I must,' she said.

Jeanette knew Elizabeth would do exactly as she threatened, and beat her too. She sat down on the bed, folded her arms and turned her head away, determined she would find a way to contact Thomas. If he believed the marriage was not real, then let him tell her himself.

* * *

Thomas was sitting on his bed polishing his tourney armour, and Otto was resting on his own pallet, arms behind his head, when a squire put his head through the tent flap to announce that the Earl of Salisbury desired to have words.

Otto stood up and donned his cloak. 'I'll be over at Walter Manny's tent if you need me,' he said with a knowing look, and departed, holding the tent flap open on the way out for the Earl.

'This is an unlooked-for pleasure, sire.' Thomas set his armour aside. 'Shall I send my squire for wine?' He wondered what Montagu wanted – it must either be concerned with the forthcoming tourney where they were both taking part as royal champions, or something to do with Jeanette. On so many occasions during their campaign in Granada last year he had almost spoken to him but at the last moment held back, knowing there was nothing to be done at that point, and indeed that such engagement might endanger his life even if the Earl was an honourable soldier.

Montagu grunted irritably. 'It is no pleasure, and I am not here to drink with you,' he said curtly. 'I have come on a serious matter pertaining to my family's honour and I want to clear up certain matters between us.'

Thomas's gaze sharpened. There were no doubts now. 'What certain matters would they be, my lord?'

The Earl curled his lip. 'Do not act the innocent with me, Holland, you know very well what I mean.' He folded his arms and scowled at Thomas. 'My son's wife is making preposterous claims that you and she were married at Saint Bavo while you were a household knight protecting the Queen. I can understand how an impressionable young girl might attach herself to a handsome young chevalier, but this fantasy of hers has gone too far and is threatening my family's honour.'

'It is no fantasy, sire,' Thomas replied. 'I can summon my brother and he will tell you precisely what happened, for he was a witness to the event, as was my man John de la Salle, my knight Henry de la Haye, also my wife's chamber lady Hawise. And in the presence of a Franciscan friar.'

The Earl's face brightened with anger and the veins bulged in his neck. Thomas surreptitiously glanced around for his sword in case he needed to defend himself.

'I have no doubt that you employed some kind of trickery to win a vulnerable young woman's affections – trickery that, whatever you say, would not stand up in any English ecclesiastical court.'

'I did no such thing, my lord,' Thomas said with quiet vehemence. 'Jeanette is my beloved wife – in every way.'

The Earl's complexion darkened further. 'If I were you, I would not cast such words abroad. I can assure you that the King will not want to hear any of this and it will be your downfall if you go to him with your preposterous claim.'

'Are you so sure of that? I have the proof and witnesses.'

'I am very sure,' Montagu ground out. 'Look, this is ridiculous. Let us stop this nonsense now. How much do you want to walk away? How much will it take for you to leave us alone, including that poor, deluded young woman?'

Thomas rubbed his chin as if considering, but in truth he had been pole-axed by astonishment. Clearly the Earl thought him the kind of man who could be bought off with a bribe. The kind of man who would resort to bribery in the first place. Someone dishonourable. And by making such an approach, Salisbury was smirching his own honour.

After a moment he pulled himself together. He had no intention of letting this go, but he had to ponder how to cast his own dice. 'You are generous indeed to think of bartering funds for my silence, but you are mistaken if you believe I would sell my mortal soul for coin or privilege. If I did agree to your suggestion – and I am sure your terms would be most generous – I would be endangering my eternal soul. In God's eyes I am a married man, my lord, and it is your son who has wed the lady under false pretences.' He paused to steady his voice. 'I have it on good authority that the lady was persuaded into the match because her mother told her I was dead, and that the marriage was conducted under misapprehension and not truly of the lady's free will, for she was not in her right mind at the time.'

Montagu unfolded his arms. Thomas could see his heart beating hard in his throat and the Earl's eyes were glassy with rage. He was not accustomed to being gainsaid. 'You could lose everything over this,' he snarled. 'You have no money to fight your case and the King will not listen, for it is not in his inter-ests to do so. Take stock of what I have said and reconsider. There is nothing in this for you.'

'There is nothing for you either,' Thomas retorted. 'How secure do you think your heirs will be with a claim of bastardy hanging over them because their parents' marriage was invalid?'

'You would not dare!' Montagu spluttered. 'I will see you dead first.'

'Is that why you sent everyone away? So you could threaten me?' Thomas curled his lip. 'Do you think if I die, that Jeanette will hold her peace? Do you think Otto will, or the other witnesses? Yes, I lack the funds to pursue this through the English courts, but I will find the wherewithal – whatever it takes.'

'You are as deluded as she is.'

'Well then, we are matched in our convictions, and we clearly deserve each other,' Thomas retorted.

Montagu straightened and puffed out his chest. 'I have tried to be reasonable with you, but I warn you now: take this further, and your career will perish and your family will suffer – I will make sure of it. If you have any sense, you will accept my offer and walk away. There are plenty of other heiresses in the world without stealing what belongs to my son. It is up to you.' Turning on his heel, he shouldered his way out of the tent like a thunderstorm.

Thomas exhaled on a hard sigh. The cool ice that sustained him in battle situations retreated and he only held himself together by keeping every muscle tight, and bunching his fists.

Otto slipped back into the tent a moment later. 'What was that about?' he asked.

Thomas shuddered and rubbed the back of his neck. 'He offered me money and advantages to walk away from my marriage with Jeanette and pretend it never happened – and threatened to make it difficult if I did not.'

'Judging by the look on his face when he came out, you refused him.'

'I did – and in no uncertain terms.'

'Perhaps he has a point, for how are you going to prove this against such opposition, even with witnesses? You say you will not give her up, but you do not have her now. How will Jeanette fight when they have her as their hostage? And how will you when you cannot and will not be heard?'

'So you think I should accept his offer and walk away, instead of striving to regain my right?' Thomas glared at his brother, feeling as if he had been kicked in the teeth twice.

Otto opened his hands. 'You should consider it. I know you probably won't, but if not, then you know what you are setting on yourself. I will support you whatever you do because we are flesh and blood, but if you ask my advice, I would say you should look at the practicalities.'

'I have looked at them, and believe me, I have considered walking away, but in the end I cannot. I admit Montagu's offer might be tempting, depending on what he puts on the table, but Jeanette trusts me to get her out of this sham of a marriage, and I have sworn I will do so. You know me, Otto. If I go into battle, I mean it.'

'Yes, I do know, and I also know the cost.' Otto grimaced. 'The only way forward is to increase your reputation as a battle captain and become indispensable to the King, and by taking rich ransoms. You will have to put yourself in the thick of the fight.'

Thomas met his brother's candid gaze. 'If I forfeit my life, then it will be honourably, and if I succeed, I shall have the resources to claim Jeanette. I cannot trust the English Church – they will support the King and the Montagus. I will take my claim to the papal court at Avignon – eventually. It doesn't matter what trials are set before me, I will accomplish them or die in the attempt.' He gave Otto a twisted smile. 'Is that not what it means to be a true knight of the Round Table?'

Jeanette arrived at the tourney ground in the great courtyard to the south of the royal lodgings. The Salisbury matriarchs were keeping her under close domestic guard and had warned her that a single word out of place would result in dire consequences for everyone, including Thomas Holland. The onus was on her to discourage him if she did not want to see him come to harm.

Jugs of hot spiced wine were being served to the spectators to keep them warm. Jeanette's gown and cloak were lined with fur, and the obligatory thick wimple covered her tightly coiled hair. The tension was giving her a headache and she rubbed her temples.

Thomas and Otto had positions as two of the twenty-four knights of the Round Table – Sir Gareth and Sir Gawain – as they prepared, with their fellow chevaliers, to take on all challengers. The Earl of Salisbury in the role of Sir Bors was puffing about, filled with self-importance, his bluster exacerbated by his bad mood. There were mummers, tumblers, folk in fantastical disguises. A dancing bear muzzled and chained.

Jeanette had to look at Thomas. It was like a sailor's sunstone, seeking its true path across the ocean. He caught her eye and kissed his hand as he had done before. She copied his gesture in a brief flare of defiance, but she was anxious about him in the lists. He would be at a disadvantage, having the sight of only one eye and with the possible threat from the Salisbury faction. Crossing herself, she prayed to God and St Michael, patron of soldiers, to protect him.

The tourney commenced with a series of demonstrations from the squires and aspiring knights. Prince Edward displayed his skills at the tilting ring, riding his new destrier – not the one he had shown Jeanette three years ago, which he had outgrown, but another grey named Wilfrid, taller and stronger with a black mane and tail. Despite her worries, Jeanette was able to laugh and cheer him on as he slid every single garlanded ring on to his lance from the target with smooth skill, and he did look magnificent on his new horse – well made, lithe and beautiful. Glowing with pride, the Queen stood up to applaud his prowess. Edward saluted the stands, made his mount half rear, and cantered off with a flourish.

William Montagu performed the same deed and acquitted himself almost as well as Edward, to great acclaim. Jeanette watched, recognising his skill but feeling dull inside. She knew she should give praise where it was due, but sat with her hands in her lap, frozen.

After the smaller contests and some jousts and tilts run by the young knights to prove their valour came the main event while the winter light was at its zenith, and the knights chosen to represent the King's Round Table paraded out to take on all comers.

Thomas was riding Noir and the stallion's black coat was winter-plush where it showed between the blue and gold barding of the Holland heraldry. Noir's nostrils were wide, his ears pricked as he high-stepped and tossed his head. Jeanette's heart was so full of pride and fear she was certain it would burst. She had seen Thomas joust before many times in Flanders – could still remember that first time – but the sensations now were magnified to the point of pain.

The knights took turns to ride against challengers who had come to be tried in the arena. It was a way of recruiting young-sters with ability, and an opportunity for the King and his seasoned captains to see who might be worthy of sponsorship and promotion.

Jeanette tightly clasped her hands as she watched Thomas ride against Sir Reginald de Cobham, who was superbly skilled. Both men struck true and rocked each other in the saddle, but neither unhorsed the other, nor did they in the next two passes, and rode off the field together in camaraderie. Otto took on Robert Dalton and unhorsed him, and then was himself unhorsed by an eager Flemish knight, but emerged unharmed and bowed to the crowd.

The bouts and jousts continued. Jeanette tensed whenever Thomas rode, but relaxed and took pleasure in the sport when he was not on the field. He certainly seemed to be enjoying himself and showed no lessening in skill despite his compromised vision, which made her appreciate the fierceness of his will and determination.

The glimpses she caught of him on the side-lines showed him comfortable in the company of other knights, talking easily, slapping shoulders, and she experienced a flicker of envy that he was free to do this in his natural surroundings, while she was trapped with these two women, who were biding their time until they could pack her off to Bisham again, or one of the Salisbury manors in Dorset, away from contact with the court.

The sun travelled low in the sky, slanting ruddy-gold light over the tourney field as the last bouts of the day were run through the mud. Jeanette folded her arms against the encroaching cold and watched Thomas ride off on Jet, his second-string stallion, followed by his squires with Noir on a lead rein. He dismounted at the corner of the lists, to stay and watch the final exchanges. His helmet removed, he glanced in her direction and gave her their hand kiss signal, which she returned. Neither Katerine nor Elizabeth noticed, for their attention was riveted on the field where the Earl of Salisbury was fretting his bay and facing his final challenger, a powerful Flemish knight by the name of Costen de Roos. The men had worked out a dramatic move to please the crowds and had been practising for several days.

At the herald's signal, the men unleashed their destriers towards each other at thunderous speed; their lances cracked on their shields and shattered in a spray of splinters. The crowd roared, urging them on to a second run. Montagu turned the big bay, but as he spurred down the lists again, the stallion skidded on the muddy ground, pitched forward and fell, tossing Montagu over the saddle and slamming him on the ground. The horse rolled to gain momentum, scrambled to its feet and galloped off, reins trailing. Katerine screamed, her hands pressed to her mouth, and people went running to the fallen man, including Thomas, while others sped to catch the horse.

The Flemish lord was out of the saddle and kneeling by Salisbury's head. Jeanette saw Thomas tear off his scarf and hand it to one of the others bent over the Earl, who bound it around his arm in a tourniquet. Two attendants ran on to the field carrying a board and lifted the Earl on to it. The King's surgeon arrived to walk at Montagu's side as he was carried away to his tent.

Katerine stood up, her face white. Lady Elizabeth was gasping like a landed trout, and clutching her breast. 'My son!' she wheezed. 'My son!' Jeanette knew she should feel sorry for her, but that wasn't the dark feeling in her heart.

Once within his tent, the Earl was laid upon his bed. Katerine and Elizabeth pushed their way through the press of folk surrounding him while Jeanette stood outside, peering in. She could hear the Earl groaning, so he wasn't dead, but the sounds were of agonising injury.

Thomas came out of the tent and, seeing her, shook his head. 'He fell on a lance splinter,' he said, 'and the horse has crushed his body.' Blood from the Earl's wound had spattered Thomas's armour and his leg greaves were mud-caked. 'He will die without a miracle.' He looked round. 'I won't linger, but we must talk. Meet me in the garden by the long stable tomorrow morning after mass.' He took her hand, gave it a quick squeeze, and departed, calling to his squires.

Jeanette watched him walk away and took his words inside her like a golden light, before steeling herself to enter the tent.

The Earl was conscious but clearly in severe pain, with cold sweat clamming his face and his pupils wide, dark holes. William arrived, and stared in glassy shock at his father. A wave of unbidden compassion surged through Jeanette, and she briefly touched his arm, but he ignored her, his attention entirely on his father.

From what she was seeing, and from what Thomas had said, Jeanette suspected that he would not recover. William would become a ward of court under the King's guidance and the earldom would be subject to administration until he came of age, which wouldn't be for several years. What it meant for her own situation she did not know, but it would certainly change the future landscape.

The Earl was borne from his tent and taken to a room in the royal lodgings with a bed and brazier. The surgeon had managed to stem the bleeding in his arm and had stitched the wound. He had been dosed with poppy syrup to ease the pain but had several broken ribs, heavy bruising from the fall and crushing injuries down one side of his body.

The King came to visit him, and gazed at his friend, propped against the pillows, his face grey. 'I am sorry,' Edward said. 'Rest and get better. I would not have had this happen to you in ten thousand years.'

The Earl mumbled a vague reply, barely opening his eyes.

The King turned from the bed to Katerine. 'Kate . . . if I had known, I would never have held this tournament. If there is anything I can do . . . I will help you in any way I can, you know that.'

A long look passed between them. 'Thank you, sire,' Katerine said. 'I have sore need of your wisdom and guidance.'

Observing the way their eyes met, Jeanette was jolted into sudden awareness. That look was entirely familiar, for she recognised it from her own situation with Thomas. Well, well.

The King lifted his hands as if not knowing what to do, then awkwardly patted Katerine's shoulder. 'I will return tomorrow and see how he fares. He has the services of my physician, and I shall pray for him and beg God's mercy.'

He took his leave. Jeanette curtseyed, kept her eyes lowered and busied herself folding and tidying, making herself useful and unobtrusive, while pondering the implications of what she had just seen.

20

Windsor Castle, Berkshire, January 1344

In the morning the Earl was still in great pain and feverish, but able to drink some spring water from a silver cup and to sip the broth that Katerine spooned into his mouth. While all the attention was on the patient, Jeanette collected her cloak and quietly left the room.

Outside, a brightness in the grey overcast of cloud suggested that the sun might eventually break through. The gardens lay through a small postern gate beside the sumpter horse stables. Otto stood near the postern, talking to Henry de la Haye as if in casual conversation. He glanced her way and nodded his head. She returned his greeting and slipped into the garden as stealthily as a cat.

Thomas was sitting on a bench at the far end, gazing at the hoar frost silvering the grass, his stillness a surprise, when usually even if at rest he was busy with his fingers, mending harness, cleaning his armour or whittling wood.

He looked up and a tide of love and longing swept through

her. She spoke his name, saw her own name form on his lips, and then he sprang to his feet and in a dozen strides reached her and pulled her into his arms. She dug her hands into his hair and they kissed, wildly, moltenly, with utter desperation, then pulled apart, panting, and stared at each other.

'We have to make this right,' he said, vehemently. 'All I think about is you. Nothing in my life makes any sense but wanting you.'

She folded her arms inside her cloak. The grass, hung with droplets of melting frost, struck cold through her thin indoor shoes. 'I cannot stand this pretence of a marriage,' she said with a shudder. 'You are my true husband. I have waited and I am still waiting – sometimes I wonder if it is all in vain.'

'No, never that! I swear I will unbind you whatever it takes!'

'And how long will "whatever it takes" be?' she asked in desperation.

'I wish I could say tomorrow, but I cannot, even though I swear I will do it and we shall be together.' He took her hand and squeezed it. 'How is the Earl?'

'A little better. He is awake and aware, but in great pain.'

Thomas's expression clouded. 'Before the tourney he offered me money and lands to walk away from my claim to our marriage and warned me that the King would not listen if I told my tale, and that he would personally ensure that my career foundered if I took matters further. At best I would be dismissed from service, and at worst, punished in darker ways. So now I must keep my distance, lest the details emerge and people think I had a hand in his death.'

She put her hand to her mouth. 'Dear God.'

'I doubt God has anything to do with any of this,' he said grimly. 'If the Earl dies, your husband will become a royal ward of whoever the King chooses to bestow custody – although it will probably be his mother. She will not want to give you up, but even so, her power has limitations.'

'I do not know,' Jeanette said, and told him about the moment she had observed between Katerine and the King. 'Even if nothing more, they have deep affection for each other and she will use it to her advantage, and the Earl of Salisbury is his close friend. The King will be persuaded by his own needs, not mine or yours.'

Thomas frowned in thought. 'There will still be opportunities to make a name for myself and to raise my status – if I become invaluable to the King in battle and acquire some wealthy ransoms.'

Jeanette said nothing, for his strategy depended on his success in war – always a great risk – and the Salisburys, even if the Earl died, already had royal support and patronage.

'I am going to take our case to the papal court.'

'The papal court?' She looked at him in surprise.

'The English Church will not listen unless they receive orders from the Pope. They are in the pay of the King and we would not receive a fair hearing. But it requires a deep purse to reach the Pope.' He set his jaw. 'We shall win in the end, whatever it takes.'

They embraced again, with tender desperation, but when they parted Jeanette looked over her shoulder. 'We should go before people miss us. I don't want to, but we must – for both our sakes.'

'I promise you,' he reiterated. 'I swear on my oath as a knight that we shall be together as lawful husband and wife.'

She nodded, wanting to believe, but it was such a high mountain to climb and they were still in the foothills. She stood on tip-toe to kiss him again, then broke from him and hurried away, trying not to think on how long a promise might take to accomplish, or how easily it could be broken.

Otto and Henry were still outside, but now talking to Prince Edward, who looked at her askance and raised his brows. Heat flooded Jeanette's cheeks as she performed a swift curtsey.

'How is the Earl this morning?' he enquired, to the point.

'He is not well, but he has taken a little wine and some broth,' she answered, breathlessly. 'I must go to him; you will excuse me.'

He looked after her thoughtfully, frowned at Otto and Henry, and with sudden decision, entered the garden.

Thomas, who had been giving Jeanette time to leave so they would not be seen together, regarded the approach of the young heir to the throne with sinking dismay. Edward's expression was neutral, but his eyes were cynical and knowing.

'A cold morning for a tryst,' Edward said, 'especially with William Montagu's wife, and your lookouts posted. You should be careful; people might easily misconstrue what they see.'

Thomas heard censure in Edward's tone, but no outright hostility. The young man's voice had but recently broken, but was going to be deep and strong once developed. He was whippet-thin, all arms and legs as he grew into manhood, but he had a mature outlook for his years. Thomas had undertaken some of his training before the tourney and had been impressed with his abilities. Now he had to decide whether he could trust him.

'Sire, I confess that this was a prearranged meeting with the lady Jeanette, away from prying eyes, but it was not dishonourable even if it was in secret.'

'Indeed? Then I think you must disclose the reason for that secret to me, for William Montagu is my friend and Jeanette is my father's cousin. My father is considering lending you to my household and it will depend on my response. I can put in a word, or say nothing. From where I am standing, your actions are less than honourable.'

Thomas clenched his fists, caught on the horns of a dilemma. Transferring to the Prince's household held great appeal to him, for this young scion was the future.

The Prince wrapped his hands around his belt. 'Jeanette and I were childhood playmates and friends as well as kin. I would never want any harm to come to her, and if anyone attempted to do so, I would defend her like a lion.'

'Then we share the same goals, sire,' Thomas replied.

'Will once told me that Jeanette believes in some fanciful way that she is married to you. He says it is untrue and the result of a girlish fantasy, but now I come upon you making a tryst with her in the garden. You tell me that such a meeting is not dishonourable, and it leads me to ask if you and Jeanette are truly wed?'

'Yes, sire, at Saint Bavo before witnesses almost four years ago.'

'But in secret?' His tone was censorious. 'You told no one?'

Thomas flushed. 'No,' he said, and hesitated.

'Go on,' Edward said, frowning.

'We had lain together and I wanted to be honourable, so I made it right. But then I was summoned to England by your father.' He did not mention the child, for it was not a necessary part of the narrative and Edward did not need to know. 'I left my will at Saint Bavo in Ghent with instructions that my worldly goods were to go to Jeanette in the event of my death, and I had it witnessed, the same day as my marriage.'

Edward's gaze widened.

'But then Jeanette was sent home and a match arranged for her with William Montagu while I was absent. They told her I was dead.' Thomas touched his scarred face. 'I am not proud of what happened. Indeed, I am sorry that it did, and I admit my dishonour in lying with Jeanette, but it does not alter our love for each other, or that we were married in the sight of God. Her family and her marital family deny such a marriage ever took place, that it was false and dishonourable, but such a stance is the very reverse of the truth we know. When Jeanette has tried to speak out, she has been silenced with threats and disbelief.'

'Some would say you married Jeanette in order to further your own career,' Edward said curtly.

Thomas snorted. 'How far has it got me if that is the case? I would have to be mad to think it would benefit me! I married her to try and make a dishonourable thing more honourable – and because I do truly love her. I took the cross to atone for my sins and to make a fresh start. When I returned, I was going to confess to your father, but by the time I set foot in England, matters had progressed far beyond that.'

'I take it you have sure proof of the marriage?'

'Yes, I do, and I have talked to John de Warenne on the matter since he has much knowledge of the law. To have any chance of winning Jeanette, I will have to take my case to Avignon, and that means to the order of Saint Silver and Saint Gold.'

'And you would not walk away? That too might be deemed honourable in some quarters, and a matter of common sense.'

Thomas shook his head. 'Jeanette has asked me to rescue her and I promised I would do all in my power. Besides, how would I walk away from a holy vow? If she had told me to let her be and to go, I would have done so, even while damning my soul. But she desires to remain my wife.'

'It is certainly a dilemma,' Edward said with knitted brows. 'I will talk to Jeanette and see what she says. I cannot take your part or hers for William Montagu is my good friend, but I will

keep my own counsel and say nothing of this to others. I advise
you to do the same and not to approach my father for now. To
bring this affair into the open would sully Jeanette's reputation,
and I care more for her than I do you.' He cast a meaningful
glance around the garden. 'Your meeting with her today was
foolish. What if others had discovered you?'

'Her family has deliberately kept us apart – this was the only
opportunity we had,' Thomas answered defensively.

'Even so, you should be more prudent for it seems to me you
have already been many times careless thus far.'

Thomas reddened, feeling the sting of the words, and also
the truth in them, and coming from a youth of just fifteen years.
'I heed you, sire.'

'Then we are done.' Edward nodded brusquely. 'I counsel
you again to tread cautiously and to do nothing unless you are
certain of your outcome.'

On the fourth morning after his accident, the Earl of Salisbury,
who had been rallying, suddenly took a turn for the worse. The
royal physician bled him several times to no avail, and the Earl
became confused, incoherent, and then insensible. Jeanette stood
at the foot of the bed, forced to be present in her role of daughter-
in-law. The entire family had gathered at his bedside, listening to
his breath rattle in his throat with longer and longer gaps between
each one. Jeanette counted her own breaths, and wondered if his
dying would be yet another lock securing her cage.

Katerine sat by her husband, blank-faced, lips moving in silent
prayer. William stood behind her, rigidly upright, his jaw with
its fledgling fluff of beard set so tightly that small tremors shuddered his rigidity. Behind him the windows were open to the
chill January air, ready to receive the Earl's soul, and despite
the braziers, the room was icy.

The rasping breath stopped for a dozen heartbeats, then started again, ragged, stertorous, and the chaplain folded the Earl's hands over a decorated cross.

A sudden flurry at the door heralded the King's arrival, and Prince Edward with him. Brushing aside the bows and curtseys of obeisance, the King strode directly to the bedside. His glance cut across the dying man to Katerine. She averted her gaze but a soft flush crept from her throat into her face.

The Earl's breath ceased again for the count of five slow heartbeats, then ten, and the silence extended, as those gathered all held their own living breath. A cold, rain-laden breeze stirred the bed hangings, and the priest leaned over the Earl.

'His soul has gone to God,' he said, signing his breast.

Lady Elizabeth uttered a wail and flung herself over the body, embracing her son and tearing off her headdress to expose her wiry grey braids. Katerine's blank mask folded and she put her face into her hands. William stood frozen, and white-faced. Edward gripped his shoulder and murmured in his ear. Jeanette knew she should go to him, but she couldn't, and instead pushed her way from the room.

Her father-in-law had been such a powerful, vital man, an accomplished courtier, a warrior of repute, a statesman, and it was all gone in a moment, in the single slip of a horse's hoof on muddy ground. That was all it took for anyone to die. Now the women would truly take over the household, which was a sobering, frightening thought.

The Earl's body was washed and then dressed in his finest garments and armour, ready to be borne away to the priory at Bisham for burial. Windsor chapel was crowded for the funeral mass, and Jeanette saw Thomas standing with the other household knights praying for the Earl's soul. His head was bent, and she could tell he was genuinely at prayer, not just paying lip service. She dropped her own gaze, feeling humbled and a little ashamed. She could not pray though. Where dislike and anger had resided, there was now a blank area stretched over a hollow, like the skin over a drum, waiting to be struck, but as yet without a beat. She could not mourn the death, but the shock had left her wondering on each person's lot in life, and how fleeting it was. She wanted to seize the day, but her way was barred, and there was nothing she could do about it except endure.

As the funeral cortege collected in the courtyard to travel the ten miles to the Salisburys' manor at Bisham, Prince Edward found a moment to take Jeanette aside.

'What is this about you and Thomas Holland?' he asked in a quiet voice as he drew on his gloves.

Jeanette looked into his face. A new, adult shrewdness had sharpened his hazel eyes, and although they were friends, she did not know if she could trust him. 'What have you heard?'

'He seems to think you are married to him, and the only reason he is not pressing his case is that he lacks the funds and expertise to take the matter through the courts. And perhaps too he fears for his career and his life – I know I would.' He tilted his head. 'Is it true?'

Jeanette hesitated, then raised her chin. 'Yes,' she said. 'We spoke our vows before witnesses, and he did not force me to it. At the outset I was the one who pursued him.' She saw the frown between his swift brows. 'No one will listen because their interests lie elsewhere. We have no one to speak for us, and your father will pay no heed for certain.'

Edward said nothing, and she knew he must be conflicted. What could he do? His father had been close friends with the Earl of Salisbury and the same with Katerine from what she had seen. He would not want a scandal of this magnitude on top of the Earl's death. Edward and William had been companions since boyhood. Probably Edward was thinking like everyone else that she should never have become embroiled with Thomas.

'I am sorry,' he said. 'I do not think there is anything I can do. I would help to resolve matters if I could.'

Jeanette nodded, but wondered what form that resolving would take – in her favour, or in William's? Edward might be her friend, but he was also heir to the throne and he was governed by political expedience even if he had sympathy for her. She touched his arm. 'Just keep me in your prayers,' she said, 'as I keep you in mine.'

'Of course, you do not need to ask.' He looked relieved before he turned away.

Jeanette went to the cart and climbed in beside Katerine and Elizabeth. The two women were silent. Elizabeth's doughy features were pale and blurred with grief for her son, and Katerine was tight-lipped with shadows smudging her eye sockets. Whatever was between her and the King, her husband's death had still left its mark on her, and she had clearly cared for him.

Jeanette's new terrier pup Nosewyse, Grippe's replacement, came to lie across her lap and she stroked his soft tan coat, taking comfort in the motion of her palm over his fur.

That evening, Edward sat down with his mother to play a game of chess and talk privately. 'Thomas Holland and my cousin Jeanette tell me an interesting thing,' he said casually. 'I wonder if you have heard any rumours yourself.'

His mother eyed him warily. 'What have they said?'

'They seem to think they are man and wife, and that it happened at Saint Bavo before witnesses, but I do not know whether Thomas is exaggerating his case, and it might not be true in the legal sense. If it gets further spread abroad it could destroy Jeanette's reputation – I know there has been trouble about that before.' He toyed with a chess piece, turning it end over end in his fingers. 'I am fond of her, and Will Montagu,' he said, 'and I would hate to see that happen.'

His mother frowned. 'Indeed, I have heard such rumours, and I have discouraged them. Keep this matter to yourself, for it will cause more harm than good, and as you say, it will tarnish Jeanette's reputation. Better not to stoke a fire that may well sputter out of its own accord.'

'And if it continues to burn?'

'We decide what to do if that happens. Wait and see, and decide accordingly. That is my advice, and I hope you will take it.'

'I intend to,' Edward said, relieved that his mother's thoughts concurred with his own. Even so, he felt a little sordid, as if sweeping dirt behind the tapestry instead of cleaning it out, and that somehow his decision was letting Jeanette down. 'Do you really think it is true?' he asked. 'You were there at Saint Bavo after all.'

His mother refused to meet his gaze. 'It is not my task to keep an eye on the young ladies of my chamber every moment of every day – others have that duty. Much of the time I was with child and had other concerns. The Earl and Countess of Salisbury would not have contracted the match if they believed there was a prior agreement.'

'No, but do you think there is a possibility nonetheless?'

Philippa considered. 'Something may have happened between them,' she said, 'but a full marriage behind everyone's backs? That seems preposterous.' She raised a forefinger in warning. 'It is best not to meddle. Let it run its course without interference.'

'Yes, mother, I agree. It would be for the best – but will you keep an eye on Jeanette? Invite her to court when you can.'

His mother eyed him thoughtfully. 'I shall, but she shall have no favour beyond that which she earns. Her duty now, especially since her father by marriage has died, is to provide her husband with offspring to further the dynasty. She is no longer an innocent damsel.'

Edward set the piece back on the board. 'But her marriage to Montagu might still have to be proven. If there is doubt, the legitimacy of those offspring might be questioned.'

'Let it be,' Philippa said firmly. 'Now is not the time. Should the marriage be called into question, there is always recourse to the law.'

Edward nodded and, with a sigh mostly of relief, dropped the matter as his mother suggested, for what she said was true, and his conscience was clear. He had done his best. Jeanette might change her mind about her willingness to be wed to William Montagu, and if later a dispensation was required, it could be obtained. Thomas Holland had no funds to pursue his case, and might give up and seek elsewhere for a wife, and in the meantime, he had his career to pursue.

For now, even if the dogs were not yet sleeping, let them lie.

21

Manor of Bisham, Berkshire, May 1346

Jeanette rolled over in the bed, awakened by the sound of William washing his face in the ewer. He was naked, and the early morning light picked out the lines of muscle and sinew and tendon. Strong thighs, widening shoulders, taut, flat belly, the base thatched with curly, coarse blond hair and sizeable genitals. His fair hair gleamed. Watching him, she was unmoved by his looks and physique, and silently hoped he would leave the room and summon his attendants to his wardrobe chamber so she could have this space to herself.

He dried his face and looked over at the bed. 'I know you are awake,' he said. 'Do not pretend to slumber.'

Jeanette sat up, clutching the sheet around her breasts. 'Why? Is it better that I am awake?'

'I am going away to war this morning – I might not return. I know you would not care if that happened, but I thought you might have a shred of honour and decency to at least bid me farewell in a manner fitting to your station – and mine.'

Jeanette felt the guilt like an irritation of grit in a shoe. 'Do not worry,' she said haughtily, 'I will bid you a fitting farewell when you leave and no one shall fault my manners. But if you want me to beg you not to go with tears on my lashes, you will wait for ever. Do as you must and acquit yourself well. I will pray for you.'

He curled his lip. 'To do what – die?' The bright morning light revealed the anger and misery in his face, and she knew those same emotions must be reflected in her own.

'Never that,' she replied. 'I would not do that.'

'Would you not?' He stalked from the room, leaving her alone, calling for his servants.

Jeanette flapped back the covers and went to sit on the latrine. He had been at Bisham for three days and was preparing to ride to Yarmouth – to war. The King was mustering for a great battle campaign in France and had been ordering ships and supplies for most of the year. Now, in May, he was making ready to sail. William was serving in Prince Edward's contingent, as was her brother, under the keen eye of the earls of Warwick and Northumberland, although the division was ostensibly under Edward's command. The youths were going to be knighted once they had made landfall in Normandy and would receive their first proper taste of warfare, rather than in the chivalrous arena of the tourney field. William had talked of little else, regarding it as a great adventure.

Jeanette had briefly visited the court at Easter, but had gleaned little information. Like many of the other women, she only knew that the men were going away to fight and that all the decisions for running the estates at home would devolve on the shoulders of wives, mothers and deputies. Thomas had been absent from court, busy garnering supplies for the campaign. She worried that despite his sworn intention of winning her back, he was

letting matters ride, and that she would be stuck with William
Montagu for the rest of her days – in which case, those days
would be numbered.

Everywhere men were flocking to the muster. Archers both
mounted and on foot. Soldiers and spearmen, labourers, cart
drivers, carpenters, grooms, cooks, younger sons seeking adventure and fortune. Men with everything to gain. Men with nothing
to lose.

These recent three days at Bisham had been particularly
difficult because William had detoured specifically to visit her,
with the express command from his family to leave behind an
heir to the earldom before he went to war. Elizabeth had been
forcing all manner of potions down Jeanette's throat to aid
conception, and making sure she had no opportunity to make
herself sick. Jeanette had succeeded on at least two occasions
to avoid the full act with him, but last night was not one of
them. He had threatened to bring in his men to hold her
down, and she had yielded to him, and now she had to wait
in trepidation.

The cavalcade prepared to leave Bisham and take the road to
Portsmouth. The wains and wagons were laden with armour
and supplies including sheaf upon sheaf of arrows. She watched
William mount his palfrey and bit her lip. If he did lose his life
to a Genoese crossbow or a French sword, she knew that guilt
would weigh her down. She wanted to be free of him, but she
did not wish him dead. She had a terrible notion that if she did
wish such a thing on him, it might reverse itself and Thomas
might die instead.

She brought the stirrup cup to his saddle and presented it to
him. 'God speed your journey,' she said, 'and may God keep
you safe.'

He raised his brows.

'I truly mean it.' Heat rose in her face. 'I would not wish harm on you.'

He gave her a hard, but slightly puzzled, stare.

'You are going to war,' she said quietly, so that only he could hear. 'I would call a truce for now.'

He lifted the cup and drank. 'A truce,' he said with a grimace. 'Very well then. And may I return to good news.' He glanced pointedly at her waistline.

Jeanette took back the cup and performed a modest curtsey. 'I shall pray for good news every day,' she said. Let him take that as he chose.

He gathered the reins and the cavalcade rode out of the gate with a flourish of drums and trumpets. Jeanette stood and watched until the dust had settled in their wake and the poultry returned to pecking in the yard.

The late July sun hammered down like a fist, adding heat to the fires roaring up from the burning buildings amid a battle stench of smoke and blood. The screams and shouts of men fighting for survival on both sides mingled with the devouring crackle of the flames. Thomas felt the fiery heat on his face as he, Otto and their contingent surged through the city of Caen on a red apocalyptic wave of English soldiers, their senses on edge with the horrible exhilaration of destruction.

The troops were wild with blood lust and the scent of success, putting Thomas in mind of hounds at a kill. He could feel that energy surging through himself – a primeval drive to rend and tear with the barriers between life and death all ragged and bleeding into each other.

The King had issued a ban on looting, pillage and rape, but in the heat of battle it was like trying to control a wildfire. Yet

Thomas, as a commander, had to be a river to cleave and quench that fire. He had to bring his men under discipline through his own force of will, and control them, even while slackening their leashes.

The English army had landed at St Vaast twelve days ago, seizing and burning eight French warships as they sailed into port. Having disembarked, organised the chain of supply and rested the horses after their sea voyage, they had set out along the French coast, heading east, burning and plundering as they went, and taking down any resistance they encountered until they came to Caen.

Their own division under Prince Edward's banner had attacked the town from the Porte aux Dammes and forced open the Western gate. Together with Lord Talbot's men, the Earl of Warwick's troops and archers had poured through the gap on to the bridge between the old town and the new, and the morass of heavy hand-to-hand fighting had resembled a shoal of live fish flashing and writhing in a net.

The King had ordered a retreat in an effort to maintain discipline, but it was impossible amid the press. Whipping frenzied hounds off a kill was never an easy task and for the moment the English were forging forward, intent on taking the main obstacle in their path – the tower of the Pont St-Pierre.

The English forced the French back across the bridge to the very gates of the tower where some French knights in a fury of heavy fighting gained that safety. Others strove to make their escape into the citadel in the newer part of the city, and were cut down.

Breathing hard, blinking stinging sweat from his good eye, Thomas paused in a moment's lull to study the tower. The door might hold, but not for long – the seething mass of

English foot soldiers hammering at it would soon break through. Gouts of smoke gusted over the bridge from the burning ships on the river, and the water was full of men struggling and drowning.

A window high up in the tower suddenly popped open, and someone thrust out a banner on a pole, heavily tasselled, glinting with embroidery, and beside it, flapping limply on a spear, a stained white shirt. Thomas squinted up through his smarting vision.

'Hah, they want to surrender!' Otto said.

Others had seen the banners, and baying jeers rose from the clot of English soldiers on the bridge – and the attack on the doors increased.

Thomas stared, thinking quickly. 'That's Raoul de Brienne's banner!' He had not seen de Brienne since the Prussian campaign, but they had made a lasting bond during the many convivial evenings they had spent together at the camp fire. He was also the Comte d'Eu and a superb ransom prize – if he wasn't slaughtered first by the bloodthirsty mob.

The banners withdrew into the tower and a head emerged, wearing a pot helm that exposed the face. 'Thomas!' de Brienne bellowed. 'Thomas Holland! In God's name, man, as you love me, get me out of here, and give me – us – shelter!'

Thomas looked round. He was the only commander in the vicinity, and in this moment, if he succeeded, here was his miracle – his promise of enough wealth to take his case forward to Avignon and win Jeanette back. He raised his hand and waved to Raoul to acknowledge him, then spurred Noir forward. At first no one paid him any heed for they were too caught up in the intensity of their own desires. Thomas drew breath and gave out the cry that called his own men to rally around his banner, a loud 'Hoo!' sound drawn from the chest and the base of the throat. Otto took it up, then de la Haye and de la Salle, and the rest of the squires and knights of his immediate retinue, and it resonated, gaining power. 'Hoo, Hoo, Hoo!'

'Make way!' roared Otto. 'Make way in the name of King Edward!'

Gradually the soldiers fell back, although some had to be clubbed and struck with whips; but the majority came to heel.

Thomas rose in the saddle. 'I have orders to take alive an important hostage for the King!' he roared. 'Let no man stand in my way on pain of his own death!'

He rode up to the doors, dismounted, and banged upon the nail-studded oak with his sword hilt. 'Open up by order of King Edward, King of France and England!' he bellowed.

There was a taut silence from behind the door. At Thomas's back, Otto organised their own men and archers into a defensive seam to hold back the tide. Then they heard the rough scrabble of the draw bar, and the door yielded a crack to reveal the sweaty face of one of de Brienne's adjutants.

'Bring down your lord,' Thomas said brusquely. 'We offer him safe passage if he comes now, but I cannot guarantee his life beyond these moments. You see how it is. Those who would live, do it now and swiftly while you can.'

The door closed again.

'This is dangerous,' Otto muttered.

'When are our lives not bounded by danger?' Thomas replied with a mordant smile. 'How else do we know we're alive save when we are facing what we might lose and what we might gain?'

Otto grimaced at him. 'I prefer your reflections over a cup of wine after the fight, not on the battlefield.'

The door opened fully to reveal Raoul de Brienne and his

knights and squires, battered, bruised, one of them sporting a blood-soaked arrow wound below his collar bone.

De Brienne bowed to Thomas and presented him with his scabbarded sword. 'My lord, I yield myself and my men into your care and cry surrender.'

'And I accept your surrender in the name of King Edward of France and England,' Thomas declared loudly, accepting the blade. 'You are now under his protection and you will not be harmed. I give you my oath, even as you give me your surrender. Now come, and let us have you to safety.'

Leaving the tower, Thomas felt the hair prickling on the back of his neck for the atmosphere was as taut as a bowstring and the common soldiers resonated with tension, holding in the fragile moment between action and deed. A horse was found and de Brienne scrambled into the saddle, although the others had to go on foot, surrounded by Thomas's men.

'I owe you my life,' Raoul said as Thomas and his contingent pushed a path through the combatants, with Otto and Henry bellowing 'Make way, make way!' and the Holland lion banners wafting conspicuously.

'Indeed you do,' Thomas replied, although he tinged the words with sympathy. 'And more than that, you owe me a ransom.'

'I did not think you rescued me for love and chivalry alone,' the Frenchman said wryly.

'We are both men of the world who know how to deal in practicalities.'

Their conversation ceased as Thomas concentrated on taking his prize out of danger, and sent him on to the baggage camp under Otto's escort with several knights.

Once he was certain that his prize was clear and away, he returned to the fray with renewed vigour and determination, feeling rather like a blacksmith faced with hammering a molten piece of iron into a useable tool.

Thomas took a cup of wine from his squire in the hall of the Abbaye aux Dames where his men had laid claim to a sleeping area. He had removed his armour, washed and changed his clothes, but his nostrils were still full of the smell of blood and battle, of sweat and dust, smoke and ordure. He excelled in that arena, indeed took joy in the play of weapons and strategy, but today he had had a surfeit of carnage. The streets of Caen were littered with the gore of death – mostly French, both soldiers and civilians.

He had taken oaths of ransom and saved many from slaughter, putting them under the protection of his banner on promise of payment, but he could not save everyone and he had had to take a pragmatic approach. Save the wealthiest; save those who could help themselves and send the weak to the wall. That was how it had to be.

He took a drink to clear his throat and approached his most important catch of the day – Raoul de Brienne, Comte d'Eu, who was sitting on a straw mattress on the floor. His armour had been taken away, and also his shoes – a precaution given that the battle was not long won and that Raoul might attempt escape, although he would be mad to do so given the volatile mood of the soldiers and the difficulty of returning to his own side.

Thomas handed Raoul a cup of wine and hooked up a camp stool to sit on.

'I cannot thank you enough for saving my life,' Raoul said. 'Anything you want, my family will see you receive it.'

Thomas drank and did not answer immediately. In the way of things, he would not be collecting Raoul's ransom in person, but would sell it on to either the lord Edward or the King himself for an agreed sum. How much was negotiable, but Raoul was worth a tidy sum that would enable him to hire a good lawyer and begin his campaign at the papal court.

'I hear there are many dead,' Raoul said.

'That is so – but it is the nature of war. You could not have held us off whatever you did. Do not take yourself to task.'

'I know . . .' Raoul rubbed his face. 'I realise you must speak to the King about my ransom, but will you get word to my family that I am safe?'

'Of course.' Thomas refilled their cups. 'I shall require your formal pledge, but you will not find your captivity too onerous I hope.'

Raoul set down his cup and slid a signet ring from his finger, the centre set with an engraved Roman sardonyx. 'This I swear by my own privy seal,' he said. 'On my oath and on my soul and the souls of all my forefathers, I pledge myself to your keeping until the ransom shall be paid.'

Thomas slipped the ring on to his own finger. 'I accept your pledge in good faith and I will see that you are well treated.' He beckoned to John de la Salle. 'You will attend to the needs of the Comte d'Eu while he is in our charge. See that his armour is cleaned, and find him some soft shoes to wear.'

'Sir.' De la Salle bowed and set about his task.

'You will find John quick-witted and competent,' Thomas said. 'I will appoint others to care for your needs in due course, but it can wait until later.'

Raoul finished the second cup of wine and a flush mounted his cheeks. 'You know you cannot win. Your king has just had good fortune with him so far.'

Thomas smiled tolerantly. 'Everyone said that we would be destroyed at Sluys,' he replied. 'The French fleet was many times larger than ours. Yes, we had the luck of the wind and tide, but we made our own luck too and our king is skilled at spinning it from whatever fleece the fates give him, while yours doesn't always know what to do with his distaff.'

Raoul gave a snort of disagreement and waved his hand, but good-naturedly.

John de la Salle returned with a pair of soft-soled shoes from the spare baggage that were a reasonable fit once Raoul had laced them up.

'But beyond fortune, we have this,' Thomas said, and taking Raoul outside led him to the archers' tents set up under the Holland banner, where his and Otto's men were stirring a cauldron of stew and tending to their equipment.

'Samson, Godwin, bring your men,' Thomas commanded. 'I want you to show the Comte d'Eu how you earn your pay. Bring as many arrows as you can shoot to a count of sixty. I'll pay you a penny for each one.'

The men gathered their bows and strings and followed Thomas to the abbey gardens where one of them set up a series of markers.

Raoul looked sidelong at Thomas. 'Archers?' he said dubiously.

'Watch.' Thomas nodded to Samson, the group's leader. 'And pray for France.'

The archers had strung their bows, and Samson ordered them to nock their arrows, draw and loose. The barbed shafts hissed overhead and plummeted over the marker line. Thomas steadily recited the paternoster and the archers continued to shoot, emptying their arrow bags until Thomas cried 'Amen' and sent Joss, sixteen, the youngest of the group, to run and gather up the loosed arrows and bade him count them.

'Seven times seventeen, in the time it took me to say a paternoster,' Thomas said. 'Now tell me how many bolts one of your Genoese can shoot with his arbalest in the same time.'

'About six,' Raoul said, looking wry, 'but they have great accuracy and power.'

'Indeed, and are rightly to be respected.'

Thomas instructed Samson to set out the targets of cloth-stuffed straw at the range the men had been shooting, and had each archer take his turn at the target. No one missed, and all were near the centre.

'Now,' Thomas said, 'imagine you are charging into a rain like that on the back of a horse, and imagine that there are not seven men, but seven thousand. The best, like mine, will shoot seventeen arrows in the time it takes to say a swift paternoster, and even the worst will shoot twice as fast as your crossbowmen, and straight into your horses. They cannot miss. And in front of the archers, ranked up, will be the spearmen in a forest of blades. And the knights behind them are fresh and have yet to bloody their swords and lances.'

He thanked and dismissed the archers with a wave, telling Samson to come to him for payment in a while, and bidding them enjoy their dinner. Then he returned to his lodging with a subdued Raoul at his side.

'Now do you see?' he said. 'They are like good hounds, and they take great pride in their pack, but when it comes to battle, they become wolves – wolves that know how to stand hard. You cannot win against such pride and skill.'

Raoul rubbed his beard and said nothing. He returned to his pallet and sat down, his expression sombre. Thomas gave him more wine.

'One city does not a victory make,' Raoul said after a moment, but his tone was dull and heavy.

'No, but how do you think the rest of the campaign is going to go?'

Raoul swallowed and shook his head.

Thomas gripped his shoulder. 'We both know what can be won and lost. For now, be my valued and valuable guest.' Indeed, more valuable than Raoul de Brienne could imagine.

The English army rested for a few days, recuperating from wounds, amassing supplies and plunder, burying the few dead from their own ranks, mainly foot soldiers, and allowing the survivors of Caen to bury theirs.

On the other side of the city stood the great Abbey of St Stephen that housed the tomb of the King's ancestor, William, Duke of Normandy, called the Bastard and the Conqueror. Thomas took a moment to visit the tomb. As a child he had been told the grisly but fascinating tale of how King William's corpulent, decomposing corpse had burst as the mourners tried to place it in a stone coffin too small for the body, and how the overwhelming stench had almost felled the congregation.

Today, the unfortunate drama and indignity of that long ago interment lay beneath an engraved slab lacking an effigy, or any of the embellishments required of tombs these days. Austere, hard, like the reputation of the man whom Thomas's ancestors had followed across the Narrow Sea in search of fortune.

'Eight generations,' Prince Edward said, sauntering over to stand beside him. 'I wonder what he would have thought of me.'

'That you were a worthy scion, sire,' Thomas said diplomatically, but meant it too.

Edward gave a lop-sided smile. 'I hope so. My father has one of his rings, but he has to wind thread around it. Our ancestor had big hands – and now he is dust, but he lives on in me.' He looked at Thomas. 'That was well done yesterday to contain the soldiers and take Raoul de Brienne for ransom.'

'Yes, sire,' Thomas said. 'And that is a matter that needs to be arranged. I hear that Thomas Daniel took Robert de Tancarville, and that you have agreed to go surety for the ransom.'

'Indeed he did.' Edward studied his ancestor's tomb. 'I will speak to my father concerning de Brienne's ransom. I think he may decide to take it on for himself.'

Thomas had been considering asking the Prince to go surety, but he had already pledged for the seneschal, and his being a close friend of William Montagu added an extra layer of delicacy since Thomas would be using the ransom money to fund his petition in Avignon.

'Sire,' he said neutrally.

'It will be dealt with in due course.' The finality in the Prince's tone made it plain that he was not going to pursue the subject here and now.

Thomas was thoughtful after Edward had gone. Leaving the church, he returned to the camp. The English troops were besieging the castle, where the defenders were still holding out. Realistically he did not think their troops would take it, and they could not afford to be bogged down in a siege. The booty from the sacking of the town itself was being transferred to English ships and most of the hostages were being taken to England, but Thomas was keeping Raoul with him for the time being until he had secured the ransom deal.

Four days later the English army left Caen. The castle remained untaken, but the city had been stripped to the bone. Raoul rode under guard among Thomas's men on a plodding bay gelding.

As Thomas walked through the camp to his horse, he noticed a group of youths lounging together and laughing as if they were at a court picnic rather than preparing to ride out in the train of the English army. He tightened his lips as he noticed

William Montagu among them. He had done his utmost to be professional and pragmatic around these friends and companions of the Prince, and to treat them as he would any other young knights in an entourage, but sometimes he was hard-pressed to be civil.

On first landing, the King had knighted the youths before all the company, girding on their swords and giving them the blow of knighthood with his clenched fist. Most of them were incapable of growing beards, but deemed ready for their first taste of battle. In truth they had been nowhere near the fighting and always well protected, but nevertheless their banners had shimmied there, proclaiming their rank to all. He had been little different himself at their age – perhaps a little more driven – but their presence was a constant thorn in his side, especially Montagu. When he imagined him with Jeanette, his stomach curdled.

The youths were sniggering as he walked past, swapping ribald tales about women. One boy had just ended his story, and rocked back with folded arms, laughing. 'I swear her eyes nearly popped out of their sockets when she saw the size of it!'

'Women,' William Montagu boasted, not to be outdone. 'You have to show them who is master and bring them to heel. It's exactly like owning a dog. Jeanette might snarl at me but she soon answers to the leash when I'm on top of her.'

The words were like the sting of a lash to Thomas, and whipping round, he strode over to them. 'As I recall, you took your oath of knighthood when you landed on these shores,' he snapped. 'You will not disrespect women – indeed women of your own family. You should be about your duties, not gossiping as though you're in a drinking house. Go, all of you! Mount up and make ready.'

As they moved off, red-faced and resentful, he stepped in front of William and faced him eye to eye. 'If you ever speak that way again within my hearing, you will be cleaning armour for a week. Understood?'

The young Earl of Salisbury jutted his chin, resentment in his eyes.

'I said, is that understood?' Thomas clenched his fists, pushing down to restrain himself from striking the youth.

'Yes, sire,' William said stiffly. His gaze flicked to his friends.

'Get out of my sight,' Thomas said, his voice curdling with disgust. 'Do not think that privilege will protect you, for even if your father was the Earl of Salisbury, I think you will find that in matters of military discipline, the King will heed me, not you.'

William stalked off, and Thomas tried to choke down his antipathy. Young Montagu was a typical privileged youth on the cusp of manhood, bragging in front of his friends on his first battle campaign where bravado and bawdy talk were ways of dealing with the experience. He had tried not to single him out because of his tie with Jeanette, but some things were intolerable. It made him even more determined to establish Raoul's ransom, begin court proceedings and detach Jeanette from her travesty of a marriage to this callow boy.

Jeanette crouched inside the gardener's shed with five-year-old Prince Edmund. She inhaled the earthen smell of well-used tools and netting in the semi-darkness. Outside they could hear the shouts of the other children and nurses engaged in a game of hide and seek in the sultry August afternoon.

'They won't find us!' Edmund piped, and then giggled.

'They will unless we stay very quiet.'

'Shush, shush!' Edmund put his hands over his mouth.

The children had come outside to play with their nurses and

attendants, and Jeanette had leaped at the chance to be away from the Queen's stuffy confinement chamber. Philippa, following the birth of Mary last year, had recently been brought to bed of another little girl, baptised Margaret, in part after the patron saint of women in childbirth. Philippa had requested Jeanette's presence at Windsor during her confinement to assist the nurses in caring for the boisterous crowd of royal offspring. The Salisbury women had had no option but to comply with the summons.

Outside the shed door, paws scratched and a dog whined, then uttered a short, sharp bark. 'Nosewyse, go away!' Jeanette hissed to her small, tawny terrier who had an unfailing ability to sniff her out. Hearing her voice, Nosewyse merely increased the volume and persistence of his yapping.

An instant later the door was tugged open. 'Found you!' sang seven-year-old Lionel, capering in triumph. 'Found you, I found you!'

Nosewyse launched himself at Jeanette, frantically wagging his tail, tongue licking at the same speed, and she lost her balance, tumbling backwards into a pile of netting. Edmund sprang nimbly out of the way, while Jeanette shrieked and giggled, and finally, breathless, prised the dog off, regained her feet, and batted at her now dust-smeared skirt. One of her plaits had come adrift again. Her mother-in-law would call her a hoyden, but she didn't care.

'Now it's your turn to hunt!' Lionel cried, but an ominous rumble of thunder curtailed their intent. While Edmund and Jeanette had been hiding, the sky had rapidly darkened, and sudden spots of rain as large as groats sent them scurrying for the Queen's hall. By the time they arrived, the rain was sheeting down amid jagged blinks of lightning.

Laughing, half drowned, they tumbled into the Queen's

chamber. The children were taken by their nurses, and Jeanette hurried to change her sodden garments, and saw from a side glance Lady Katerine's purse-lipped disapproval. Hawise quickly helped Jeanette into a dry undergown of grey silk, laced the sides and buttoned the sleeves with nimble fingers, then moved on to Jeanette's hair, tidying the plaits and coiling them beneath a fresh veil.

While the royal children had been romping in the garden, the other ladies of the Queen's chamber had been busy preparing for Philippa's churching. Gowns and rich fabrics were spread across the bed in a sumptuous array. Boxes of pearls, jewels and spangles twinkled, waiting to be stitched on to the garments after the final fitting. Two extra seamstresses had been employed to see to the task. Philippa's squirrel had to be firmly dissuaded from trying to bury a nut amid a bundle of furs.

Jeanette went to the window to watch the lightning flash against the boiling clouds. She loved the excitement, the elemental power. Even getting wet had been exhilarating.

A messenger had arrived with the storm on his heels, and the Queen had taken him aside to receive his news, but now she returned to the centre of the room and clapped her hands for attention. Her face was pink and her brown eyes luminous.

'The King sends news of a great victory!' Philippa shouted above the rumble of thunder. 'The French army has been routed in the field with very light losses to our side, but complete devastation to theirs!'

A hubbub of excited congratulation ensued, and Philippa raised her hand for silence. 'The King wishes me to join him – once I am churched, we shall make preparations to cross the sea. For now, we shall celebrate his victory!' She sent servants to broach a keg of the best sweet wine.

Jeanette's heart danced as she thought of seeing Thomas

again. She had heard nothing so far, for Katerine and Elizabeth were vigilant in keeping her away from news, and she could only glean small grains of information when rubbing the Queen's feet or listening behind curtains. She knew there had been a victory at Caen where a great deal of booty and prisoners had been taken, and this new triumph presumably meant more of the same, but other than that she was ignorant. She knew William was safe because he had written to his mother. She could only assume that Thomas was too; he was a senior battle captain and mention would have been made had he fallen. For now, she had to ride the waves, but it felt like being alone in a small, oarless rowing boat.

22

Calais, Normandy, October 1346

The October evening carried a distinct smell of autumn in the air. In his tent outside the besieged walls of Calais, Thomas rolled his dice, and then snorted in disgust. He was playing with Otto and Raoul de Brienne, and Raoul was winning again. It amazed Thomas that his prisoner should be so fortunate with the dice, and yet deserted of luck at Caen – although perhaps the very fact that he had survived the slaughter was fortune enough. They were bidding for a fur-embellished cloak that was part of the campaign spoils. Black sable adorned the outer red wool, and glinted in the light of the lantern swinging from the tent roof.

Taking his turn, Raoul rattled the dice in the cup and threw a score that resoundingly beat both Otto and Thomas's efforts. With a triumphant shout, he fisted the air.

Thomas shook his head. 'You always were a mean dice player, Raoul, but I shouldn't begrudge you. That cloak will come in useful during the winter!'

'Hah!' Raoul rose and swept the cloak around his shoulders, fastening the red silk cords from which two tassels hung down.

'Very fine,' Thomas said. 'You wear it well.'

'You are right that I find myself in reduced circumstances,' Raoul admitted, 'but you are accommodating.' He looked at the brothers and folded his arms inside the garment. 'Let me tell you this though: you will not take Calais easily – perhaps never. It is going to be a long winter for all.'

'A good thing you won the cloak then.' Otto rose and rumpled his hair. 'I'm for my bed.' Bidding them goodnight, he departed to his own tent where Thomas knew a rather delectable laundry maid was waiting for him.

Raoul removed the cloak and said, 'I heard that Robert de Tancarville is to have his ransom set at six hundred marks. It is only a verbal agreement, but progress has been made.'

'Six hundred?' Thomas raised his brows as he returned the dice to their ivory box.

'Do you not think that a fair sum?' Raoul sat down and crossed his legs. 'How much do you expect to get for me?' He smiled sourly. 'Am I worth more or less?'

'It is not as simple as that,' Thomas said, a cloud of frustration settling its weight on him. Every time he broached the matter of Raoul's ransom he had been deflected by officials and told the King was too busy to see him, and that the matter would be resolved in due course. He must be patient and they would discuss the sum at a later date. Nearly three months had passed since Caen, and still Thomas was no further along his path.

He knew why. Matters had been looking optimistic and he had been promised a review, but then Queen Philippa had arrived with her women, including the widowed Countess of Salisbury, and suddenly an audience with the King had become impossible to obtain. Jeanette had arrived with the ladies, but was so closely guarded by Katerine and Elizabeth that he could not get near her. Even in the Queen's presence, there was no opportunity for contact beyond glances. He had managed to pay a troubadour to pass a message saying he had hopes of resolving the situation, but he had no means of knowing if she had received it.

'"Not as simple" – why?' Raoul asked. 'Are you requesting too much? Can the King not afford to pay you?'

Thomas shook his head. 'That is a part of it, but there are other elements at work – factions, you might say.'

'Anything you want to tell me, since it affects me too?' Raoul asked.

'There is nothing you can do, and telling you will make no difference to the outcome.' Thomas rose and went to wash his face and hands, ready to say his evening prayers. 'I shall continue to work on the delay and ask God's help.'

'Then I shall pray too,' Raoul said. 'Much as I have grown fond of you, my place is with my own king.'

'Yes, I know,' Thomas said quietly, and disappeared behind the curtain that partitioned his bed from the main part of the tent.

He didn't want to talk any longer. The evening's convivial conversation and dice playing were superficial pleasures that had swiftly dissipated, and he felt heavy and dejected. Tomorrow, he had orders to escort the Queen from Calais to Flanders under the Earl of Warwick's command, as part of a diplomatic mission. Making enquiries, he had discovered that Jeanette was remaining behind with the Salisbury household, including her cuckoo husband. Thinking about her with him sickened him, but he could do nothing until he had the ransom money to fund his legal campaign.

Kneeling at his bedside, he prayed for God to help him. God had brought him through fire and battle, and he had survived when so many times he might have died. Surely there was a moment of grace in all this striving.

After Caen they had moved along the coast, taking towns, plundering supplies, burning a swathe through the Norman countryside. King Philip of France had moved to intercept them and the two armies had clashed a month later in a field close to the small town of Crécy.

A stiff breeze billowed the outer skin of his tent, and in his mind's eye and memory it became first a storm wind and then the hissing of arrows darkening the sky across the battlefield. It became the thunder of bombards, roaring fire and smoke, sending iron bolts and balls of stone hurtling into the opposition. The screams of terrified, wounded horses and men, the smell of blood and entrails. He could feel the vibration of desperate battle. Behind his closed lids he saw again the French advancing at a pounding gallop, and the charge breaking up beneath the death storm of ten thousand arrows.

He had been on the right of the battlefield near the front with the Prince, watching from behind the massed lines of archers and men at arms. He would never forget the whistling thrum of the arrows flying from the bows, and the thud as they plummeted into horses and men. Nor those screams of the wounded and the dying, some of them in their own line as bolts from the Genoese crossbows found their mark.

At one stage a French charge had reached their lines and powered forward. The Prince's standard had gone down for an instant, immediately snatched up again, and Thomas and Otto had fought like furies to protect their young lord, and forced back the opposition. In the mass of the melee, side by side, they had faced death, looked into the eyes of the reaper, and beaten him aside. He would come for them eventually, and for their prince, but not this day.

The final effort for the French had been a charge led by Jean of Luxembourg, King of Bohemia. Ancient and almost blind, but brimming with ferocity and courage, he had had his men tie their horses together with him at their centre and ride forward all as one. Inevitably they had been brought down and killed, right in front of the Prince's line. Thomas suspected that Jean of Luxembourg had chosen his moment to die gloriously rather than crippled and sightless in his bed, and he had achieved his goal.

By the time the Earl of Warwick arrived with more troops to bolster the Prince's position, the danger had receded, depositing a flotsam of bloody corpses in its wake.

The English victory had been overwhelming. Philip of France had abandoned the field with the tattered remnants of an army that a short time since had been proud and shining and brave. When Thomas had returned to the battlefield next day to help the heralds to identify the dead, the French lords who had fallen were in excess of fifteen hundred, and thousands more ordinary men would never return to their mills and fields and towns. The fine horse flesh too. He had brought three horses to his own camp from the battlefield, two destriers with superficial wounds and another powerful bay, untouched, whose lord was numbered among the dead. Walking the field with Otto, seeing all the carnage without the battle-ice in his veins, had been a sombre experience and their conversation had diminished as they progressed, until they had spoken only to identify the dead. Finding Jean of Luxembourg had taken them to a deep silence as they viewed his body so close to their battle line, in a fallen chain of his household knights, the ostrich plumes on his helm blood-soaked and trampled.

Soldiers had arrived and wrapped his body in linen and borne him away for washing and burial. For others there would be a mass grave, and only the broken soil to mark their lying. Men who had been alive the day before with wives and children and families were now so much corpse-flesh, like meat in a butcher's shambles. Raoul, who had accompanied them and helped to identify several of his fellow countrymen, had fallen to his knees in the bloody mire and wept, berating himself for not being there, and Thomas had squeezed his shoulder and said nothing, because there was nothing to say and no comfort to be had.

On his return from this task, Thomas had sought solitude by visiting the horses his groom had brought off the battlefield, and had taken comfort from their strong bodies and their big hearts. They had always been his refuge from small boyhood. The first thing he had done when learning of his father's murder was run to the stables and seek comfort with his father's Lombard destrier.

He had been with Noir when Samson, captain of his archers, had arrived to check his own pack horse, with his companions a little behind. Thomas had already commended the men's bravery and skill the previous day, and seen that they had extra rations and six pence each. Having just witnessed the dreadful carnage wrought by their arrows, he had extra respect for and even unease at the collective abilities of these extraordinary yet ordinary men. They too had been skirting the battlefield, plundering the corpses of the lesser soldiers for food, weapons and anything that might come in useful.

Samson gazed at Noir with an admiring eye.

'Maybe you will have a horse like this one day,' Thomas said with a smile.

Samson scratched a louse from his beard and cracked it between his fingernails. 'I doubt it, my lord.'

Thomas stroked Noir's sleek black neck. 'You fought well. I am minded to give you a colt from my stud herd that you can raise for yourself when we return to England. If you wish, you shall remain in my personal service. I value good men.'

The archer regarded him with a cunning eye. Thomas was amused rather than offended: these men had a certain assurance that transcended their birth station, and the way they saw themselves was what made them so deadly in battle. He enjoyed their banter and their cocksure attitude, but he was still the lord who paid their wages and gave them orders. There was a strict line that neither would cross, even if they stood with their toes against it.

'Do you think all three of us will fit on such a horse's back, sire?' Samson asked craftily.

'Do not push it,' Thomas replied with good humour. 'Only one colt, but all of you shall be rewarded, that is my bond to you. If I succeed, then you succeed, and the same the other way around.'

'It was worth a try, my lord,' Samson replied with a grin.

'And I do not blame you for trying. That offer of employment holds fast for all of you. I leave you to talk it through.'

As Thomas had sent Samson and his companions on their way, he had felt a little restoration of normality. Life went on in its own fashion even in the midst of death.

A shouted exchange between two passing soldiers from outside the tent caused Thomas to jerk awake. He had fallen asleep on his knees, which were now as stiff as stone. Grimacing, he eased to his feet and, rubbing his legs, went to lie on his mattress. The slumber that had overtaken him at his prayers and filled his mind with dreaming memories of battle proved elusive to regain, and he lay on his back, staring into darkness, listening to the flap of the canvas in the wind and the sounds of the camp. His body ached with longing, and he thought of Otto making love in his own tent with his willing laundress. It would be easy to find a woman to assuage his own physical need, but it would be nothing – a moment of release without satisfaction beyond the spark of voiding his seed. It was Jeanette he wanted, and Jeanette he could not have.

23

Calais, Normandy, February 1347

Jeanette lay beside her unwanted husband in a bed in the house that the Salisbury family had taken on the outskirts of Calais, feeling like a caged hen. Thomas had left for Ghent yesterday, escorting the Queen, and she had been unable to speak with him before he went. Lady Katerine had remained in Calais, claiming an ague, although in truth there was nothing wrong with her. She just wanted to be near the King.

William rolled over and put his hand on her shoulder to turn her towards him, and she sat up, tossing her hair over her shoulder. 'There is no point in us lying together,' she said. 'I will not conceive whatever you do. I would have done so by now, the number of potions your mother and grandmother have forced down my throat – and yours come to that. And do not even begin upon the anointing of other parts!'

He flushed and looked away.

'Yes,' she said, 'I know all about those, but it hasn't made any difference.'

'But it might. What if I just want to lie with you because you are my wife and I have the right to claim that debt?'

Nosewyse leaped on to the bed between them and gave William a whiskery lick. He pushed the dog away, but not roughly.

'But I am not your wife, and it is a sin,' Jeanette said with a side glance at her treacherous dog who had quite taken to William. 'How many times must we return to this? If you must, then you must, but do not expect my joy or God's approval. There are plenty of women in the camp if you have a need. Go and visit one of them.'

For a moment she thought he might indeed force her, but then he made a sound of disgust and raised his hands in capitulation.

'You know your mother wants for nothing because she has the King's ear,' Jeanette said. 'Why do you think she is still here when the Queen has gone to Ghent?'

'Because she has an ague,' he answered defensively. 'She and my father have long been friends with the King – since well before I was born.'

'It has become much more than friendship,' Jeanette said. 'I have seen her standing beside him with her hand below his belt, and he did not push her away. She persuades him to do as she wills. How do you think our own marriage was brokered?'

His blue eyes filled with fury. 'Do not say such things about my mother!'

'I am only telling you what everyone knows,' she said. 'It's becoming increasingly obvious.'

He glared at her. 'If you say anything like that again, I will beat you – I mean it. I have the right, and no one would blame me.'

She looked him in the face. 'But I am not your wife, and you do not have the right.'

'That is not true—'

'You know it!' She thumped her fist on the bedclothes, and Nosewyse jumped on to the floor. 'Dear God, we both know it! Even if by some terrible miscarriage of justice we are forced to remain together, there will always be that question hanging over your heir – should you manage to beget one. I am poison for you, William; do you not understand? Accept it, and help us both. Let the marriage be annulled; find yourself a compliant wife who does not have a history – or reputation – like mine. I mean it.'

He shook his head, his expression crumpling into misery. 'I cannot.'

'Why not? Of what benefit am I to you?'

'It is about loyalty,' he said. 'I owe my allegiance to my family. What allegiance have you ever shown me?'

'You were pushed into this as much as I was,' she said with scornful impatience. 'Do not speak of loyalty. What do we owe either of our families between us? If you were free, you could wed again, to someone more suitable. You wouldn't keep being pushed into a room with me and told to make an heir. Be a man in a way that matters.'

He glared at her, gathered up his clothes, and slammed from the room.

Jeanette stared at the vibrating door and bit her lip, aware that she might have goaded him too far. He had been forced into her chamber by his mother and grandmother, in the hope that he would get her with child, but the sowing had been hers and he clearly disliked what she had planted. Whether he would think on it was another matter. She suspected he would just lock it away behind yet another slammed door.

Although she had not managed to speak with Thomas, she knew he had gained a potentially large ransom to fund his court case, but first he had to obtain official recognition of that ransom and an offer from the King, and while Katerine of Salisbury was busy in the royal bed, there was small chance of that.

Nosewyse looked at her and whined. 'Oh, be silent,' she said crossly, and folded her arms around her upraised knees.

'Will you not come and play dice with us?'

Sitting by himself in a window seat in Edward's private chamber, William looked up as Edward joined him. 'I am out of sorts,' he said. 'Go on without me.' He didn't want to socialise after the verbal bruising he had just received from Jeanette. Why couldn't she be reasonable? He tried his best and she spurned him at every turn.

Edward sat down beside him and stretched out his long legs, crossing them at the ankle. 'I thought you'd retired early to be with Jeanette.'

William shook his head. 'No,' he said dully. 'Or at least I did, but then we quarrelled. We always quarrel.'

'Jeanette can be difficult,' Edward said almost ruefully, 'but she can be warm and fun, and she is shrewd and perceptive. She reads me like a book at least! I am sorry you and she are at odds.'

William palmed his face. He didn't want to hear that she was shrewd and perceptive, especially after what she had said about his mother.

Edward leaned towards him, his eyes bright with concern. 'What is it? You know you can tell me anything and it will not go further, I promise on my word of honour as a knight.'

William sighed deeply. 'My mother and grandmother brought Jeanette to Calais explicitly for us to beget an heir. They say it is past time and they want her with child by Christmas, but I think it unlikely.'

'If you are not on good terms, it must be difficult.'

William puffed out his cheeks. 'My mother does not understand – refuses to understand. In truth I would rather spend the night on sentry duty in the snow than perform my other duty in the marriage bed.'

Heat burned into his face at admitting his vulnerability. He could not even get a cockstand these days to do the deed no matter how many potions and unguents he was given. He was eighteen years old and it should come as easily as pissing, but with Jeanette, he was as flaccid as a gouty old man. He wasn't going to admit that to Edward, whether he trusted him or not.

'She has sworn ever since we were wed that her true husband is Thomas Holland and that they made some kind of binding pact when they were in Flanders. My family has always refused to believe it, and even Jeanette's own mother says it is an untruth and a silly girl's whim – but what if it isn't?' He gave Edward a pleading look. 'I have seen the way she and Thomas Holland look at each other. Not once in our marriage has she ever given me such a glance. I am at a loss. Even if I do get Jeanette with child, what if she cries abroad that she is someone else's wife? What of my heirs then? They will be deemed bastards.' He picked up his drink and drained it to the lees.

Edward cleared his throat and said nothing.

'You know about this, don't you?' William accused, feeling sick with betrayal.

Edward winced. 'Yes, but I have said nothing, for the sake of your reputation and Jeanette's, for I do not know if it is true, or if it would stand up to scrutiny if brought before an ecclesiastical court. I thought it might die down without the need to say anything . . .'

William looked glum. 'If the marriage with Thomas Holland

is true, then her union with me will never be right while God disagrees.'

Edward frowned, wondering how he could help to resolve the situation without doing more harm and without compromising himself with Jeanette, with William, or indeed with Thomas Holland, whose services were invaluable. 'I am sure something can be done.'

'Then you are more certain than I am.' William rubbed his face again. 'I am still your father's ward and he has put me in my mother's care until I come of age, and she will never agree to dissolve the marriage. It would cost too much pride and money. She says it will all go away and that Holland does not have a case.'

'Do you truly wish your union with Jeanette to be dissolved?'

William grimaced. 'I wish it had never come about, but my loyalty to my family remains, and your father would never consent to such a thing.'

Edward narrowed his eyes thoughtfully. 'Leave this with me,' he said. 'I can think of at least one lever, and if nothing happens, you are still no worse off than you are now. If it does work, perhaps I can spring you and Jeanette from this coil.'

The glimmer of hope that sparked in William's breast died in the same moment. Edward was his lord and a dear friend, but he could not imagine what he could do about it. However, he nodded. 'If you wish,' he said.

'I believe my mother may be able to help unravel this coil. I shall speak with her when she returns from Ghent. She will give good advice on the matter at the least, and she will have a vested interest, I have no doubt.'

William flushed, thinking of what Jeanette had told him about his own mother and the King.

He met Edward's gaze, and Edward nodded, so there could

be no mistaking what they both knew but would not say. 'You are my friend,' Edward said. 'You always will be. Now, will you come and play dice and forget your worries? You can do nothing for now. A game of hazard and a cup of wine among friends will do you better than brooding on your sorrows like a laden donkey.'

William shrugged, found a smile from somewhere and, rising to his feet, followed Edward to the convivial arena of the gaming board.

Almost a month later, Edward sat with his mother in his chamber on the outskirts of Calais. A bitter late winter wind whistled at the shutters and they were both wrapped in fur-lined cloaks and eating small balls of stuffed marchpane at the fireside. He had invited her to his dwelling to play tables with him. A few members of her private household were present too, including Thomas Holland, who had been seconded to her employment for the past several weeks. He had been restored to her favour now that he possessed more maturity and had proven his exceptional military abilities.

Taking a respite from the game, Philippa leaned back and drank from her glass goblet. 'You wrote to me about William Montagu's marriage to Jeanette,' she said.

'I did,' Edward replied. 'We spoke of it before and you said we should leave it and see what happens, but it has gone neither forward nor back, and it needs to be made right. William doesn't want to be wed to Jeanette any more than she wishes to be wed to him, but he will do his duty by his family and will not actively seek to end the match. They are both miserable. I don't think I've ever seen him so out of sorts.'

'And you think that I can do something about it?' Philippa raised one eyebrow. 'Or that I should even want to do something about it? Is there a reason for me to rock that particular boat – a good reason? Many marriages are not made in heaven, but they are still successful. I thought Jeanette and William would be a good match, I still do, or I would never have endorsed it.' Her tone was defensive as she popped another marchpane ball into her mouth.

Edward contemplated the wine, shining golden-green through the goblet glass. 'Jeanette insists she was married within law to Holland at Saint Bavo, and he has told me the same tale. If true, it will damage the legitimacy of any heirs William does have with her, and if we turn a blind eye, are we not ignoring God's will?'

'That is something to consider,' she conceded, 'but more proof is needed than hearsay.'

'I want to help all of them. The Church will decide, I know, but the Church is open to other influences – including words from kings and queens.'

'Sometimes,' Philippa said. 'It does not always hold true.'

'My father gave Jeanette's marriage to the Salisbury family as a personal favour – the Countess pursued the matter strongly at one time, as did Jeanette's mother.' He saw his mother's lips purse. 'Perhaps you might think it fitting to take an interest, and voice your concern over the validity of the second marriage, given Jeanette and Thomas's insistence that they were wed in the eyes of God.'

Philippa said nothing, but did not stop him.

'Moreover, the Hollands have proved their exceptional worth on campaign. Thomas especially could rise to be much more. He understands not just battle, but logistics, and he knows how to get the best from men. It would be no mismatch or disgrace for Jeanette to be his wife. Perhaps it is time to show the dowager countesses of Salisbury and Kent where the influence of women truly lies.'

Philippa gave him a sharp look. 'Do not over-salt your dish,' she warned.

'Holland needs funds to pursue his case, and a good lawyer who knows his way around the Avignon court,' Edward continued. 'He needs letters of recommendation to the Pope – I thought you could write one. Holland has yet to be paid for the capture of Raoul de Brienne, and still hasn't been granted an audience to discuss it. If he could secure that ransom, he would have a fighting chance. It would be your right to intervene, and would be asserting your authority as Queen. If the directive comes from you, my father will not be able to put it aside. Lady Salisbury might have a certain power, but compared to yours, it is nothing.'

'You have thought this through indeed,' she said.

He shrugged, affecting nonchalance, but was secretly pleased. 'It addresses many concerns. Thomas shall have his ransom money, sufficient that his case is given a fair hearing. Whatever happens will be God's decision and our consciences will be clear for we shall have done our best and, in so doing, fulfilled our duty and made things right.'

His mother stroked her sleeve, changing the velvet from violet to midnight purple as her finger swept over the pile. 'What kind of sum did you have in mind?'

'I thought you might have a notion, mother. How much do you think Master Holland should be awarded for his capture of Raoul de Brienne?'

She gave him a considering look. 'He will need to pay a good lawyer, and have funds for the papal court. And money to live on beyond a soldier's wage should the court find in his favour and he has to support a royal wife. I shall think on the matter.'

Edward took her hand and kissed it. 'Thank you, Mama.'

She smiled at him fondly but shrewdly. 'I think we must both thank each other,' she said. 'When the time comes, you shall be a worthy king.'

Three nights later, Philippa dined privately with her husband. They had enjoyed roast venison in piquant sauce, mopped up with good white bread, and were now picking at nuts and fruit and sipping sweet wine. She had been deliberating her approach to him on the matter of Raoul de Brienne's ransom and had even wondered, despite her discussion with Edward, whether she should do this at all, because once embarked upon, there was no going back. However, she was not going to have Katerine of Salisbury dictating policy, and her eldest son seemed to think that none of the three people involved in the marriage were happy with their current lot.

Her husband would expect to lie with her tonight – that was why they were eating in private. He would be appreciative of their bond and considerate, and would send her jewels and gifts in the morning as tokens of his esteem. She loved him with all her heart. A powerful soldier, a player in the great game, and she was his consort, mother of his children, ruler of his domestic household and a diplomat behind the scenes. But like so many men, especially the active, virile ones, he could be a complete fool sometimes with other women. The pressure to release his superfluity of seed when she was not nearby sometimes regrettably caused him to stray.

'You are quiet, my dear.' He gave her a speculative look. 'Is something troubling you?'

She looked at his long fingers playing with the stem of his cup, hands that knew the most intimate parts of her body – hands that had wandered elsewhere of late. 'Yes,' she said. 'Something is troubling me deeply.' She left the table, returning with a small gold brooch in the shape of a heart set with sapphires, and placed it on the table between them. 'Do you recognise this?'

He looked at the ornament and gave a slight shake of his head. 'Where did you happen by it?'

Philippa picked up the jewel and tossed it at him. 'You know full well whose it is, since she constantly wears it on her head-band and her husband had it engraved with their initials entwined when they wed. How do you explain its presence amid your bedclothes? A laundress found it and brought it to me, although she might just as easily have turned the other way and let you or Katerine bribe her to silence.'

He stared at the brooch, his cheeks sucked in.

'I suppose you were offering her comfort and succour because her husband died.' The cold anger with which Philippa had started warmed to a simmer. 'Your sworn duty is to your queen, and not only to your queen, but to me, your wife, the mother of your heirs. Without me you would not have heirs, and yet you have taken up with your best friend's widow, who, for all that she is a countess, is no better than a common harlot in this matter. You are both shamed. William Montagu must be turning in his grave!'

'It is not what you think . . .'

'Then what is it?' she demanded. 'You both lacked the control? You only intended to comfort her? Are you going to throw feeble excuses in my face? Am I not worth more than that?'

He swallowed. 'Philippa, I am sorry . . . I did not . . .'

'Expect to be found out? How could you! How many do you think are laughing at us behind their hands? The great chivalrous king who is no more faithful than a rutting dog! Your eldest son knows full well. The Archbishop knows. Everyone from common soldier to earl of the realm is a party to my humiliation!' She did not have to feign the tears in her eyes. 'It is not the first time, and I know beyond a shred of doubt it will not be the last!'

Edward sat immobile for a moment, then pushed through the horror and guilty shock and, taking her hands, knelt at her feet. 'I am truly sorry,' he said. 'I love and revere you above all women, I swear, but I am a weak fool and I do not always resist temptation when you are not here. I know I should contain myself, and I beg your forgiveness for my lapse.'

'You speak fair words, but I do not trust you.' Her voice wobbled. 'Why, for the sake of your children, can you not save yourself for me? Why do you have to seek other pastures? Especially William Montagu's widow. How could you!'

'She was only a means to a release – she is nothing compared with you . . . I never meant it to happen.'

Philippa was not ready to yield her grievance. 'I have loved you since I first saw you and you cannot imagine what it does to me to see you dallying with other women and breaking your vows while I have remained true and faithful to mine. If you did not mean it to happen, then you should have ensured that it did not!'

'I know, I know. Don't weep. I hate to see you weep. I shall shrive myself and swear to cleave only to you if you will forgive me.'

Philippa sniffed, and eventually dried her tears, allowing him to cajole her as part of the mending process, and she could not resist the hangdog look in his eyes. He would stray again, led by that unruly instrument between his legs; nevertheless, he had a conscience and she had brought him back to his duty. For the moment, his pattern would be one of guilty, intense attention and lavish gifts. At this stage she could have whatever she wanted of him and he would be clay in her hands.

They went to bed and made love with passion, abandon and tenderness. Edward's chagrin made him thorough and eager to please, and Philippa wrapped herself around him, crying out, taking extra satisfaction in having him back in her bed and she with the upper hand.

In the early morning, before they went about their daily duties, they lay in each other's arms, having made love again with leisurely affection. Edward gently stroked Philippa's wide belly with its silvery striations, tracking the evidence of the ten children she had carried in her womb. She watched the slow movement of his hand, and returned the compliment, gently tugging on the stripe of hair that ran down his navel into the bush at his groin.

'I have been meaning to talk to you about something else,' she said.

'Oh yes?' Edward's tone was warily amused. They both knew the game, and the penances involved.

'About many things,' Philippa said, 'but one in particular because it worries my conscience.'

'And what would that be?'

'The matter of Jeanette of Kent's marriage to William Montagu.'

'Oh that,' he said, and the amusement left his voice, like the sun vanishing behind a cloud.

'Yes, that. Your son says that William is not content with the match, and Jeanette is insisting she was married to Thomas Holland, and forced by her mother and the Montagus into a marriage with young William. She won't reconcile herself to her circumstances. In hindsight, we should never have promoted the match, even if it seemed a good opportunity to do a friend a favour, and even if we knew nothing about Thomas Holland's claim then. Indeed, we do not officially know even now. It has all been hearsay and gossip behind curtains and tapestries – but it exists nonetheless.'

She felt the tension creeping into his body. 'I do not see what we can do about it.'

'Do you not? I can tell you a way, and it is one you may have been avoiding – perhaps as a result of pillow persuasion?'

'I am not sure I know what you mean,' Edward said stiffly.

Philippa gave a swift tug on the hair stripe running to his groin, but then moved her hand to soothe and venture lower. 'You need to speak with Thomas Holland,' she said. 'You have Raoul de Brienne's ransom to agree. Our son tells me you have been promising to do so, but avoiding the matter. We owe the Holland brothers a debt for their skills on this campaign, be it in battle or ensuring supplies and command. It will be some time before William Montagu will be of service to you, but you could be using Holland now by raising his status. Give him sufficient funds to at least have his case heard. That would be fair and just.'

Edward made a dubious sound.

'Look at the weights in the scales,' Philippa persisted. 'William is still in wardship. You need not abandon him, but we should set this thing to rights and make it certain, whichever way it is adjudged.'

'That girl has caused so much trouble,' Edward said irritably. 'If she and Holland had not overstepped the boundaries in Flanders, none of this would have happened.'

'If they overstepped the boundaries, then what of the Countess of Salisbury?' Philippa retorted. 'Her exploitation of your weakness notwithstanding, she was responsible for Jeanette in Flanders and her lack of care permitted that relationship to flourish. Thomas Holland was led by his loins like so many men, but both he and Jeanette have been steadfast in their intent. Who are we to stand in their way?'

Edward looked away for a moment, his face flushing with chagrin and exasperation. He turned back to her. 'How much do you think Thomas Holland should be given for this ransom?'

'We can talk about that tonight,' Philippa said, 'and you should send Katerine from court. There is no reason for her to be here. Her son has able servants to run his own household. I do not want her among my waiting women, and I am sure she has business to conduct in England now she is a widow.' Her voice was steely. 'That is what I want, more than gifts and promises.'

'Then you shall have it,' Edward replied. 'For I had no wish to hurt you, and I want us to be as we were.'

'So do I,' Philippa said.

They kissed again, and she smiled against his mouth.

24

Calais, Normandy, March 1347

Stiff with tension, Thomas knelt before the King in his private chamber. Edward was richly garbed in crimson velvet and gold. A hat of jewelled black velvet sat at an angle on his head. His right hand, adorned with several jewelled rings, drummed lightly on the arm of his carved chair. He commanded Thomas to rise and directed him to a small padded seat at his side.

Thomas swallowed. He had been waiting since well before Christmas for this summons. The Prince had been optimistic that it would happen, but Thomas had barely seen Jeanette, who continued to be closely chaperoned by the Salisbury women. When he did catch a glimpse of her, she was wan and pale, dressed in heavy garments that dragged her down, and so closely guarded that he had not managed to speak to her. Now the moment was in his hands like a set of reins, but with the sensation that they were slipping through his fingers and this was his last opportunity to seize and hold on. He had decided with advice from the Prince that the way to approach the King was to make the matter a general plea and not mention the marriage.

'Sire, thank you for granting me this audience,' he said.

'Indeed,' Edward replied, and his eyes were calculating, and held no warmth. 'Decisions have to be made, and I admit I have neglected this piece of business while dealing with other matters. I know you have been waiting for some time, but you shall wait no longer.'

Thomas straightened his shoulders. 'Thank you, sire. I ask you to facilitate the ransom of Raoul de Brienne, who has been in my personal custody since he surrendered himself to me at Caen. I have served you with loyalty throughout this campaign. Although I have incurred considerable expenses, I have only kept enough booty to support myself and pay my men. I have taken no liberties, but turned over the bulk to your household. However, I find myself beset by requirements beyond the reach of my purse.'

The King's fingers continued to beat on the chair, but he nodded. 'Go on.'

Thomas drew a deep breath. 'Therefore, I call upon your generosity, your fairness and renowned wisdom to make a ransom agreement with me in the matter of Raoul de Brienne, according not only to prowess, but to need, and pray you might see your way to helping me with that need.' Bowing his head, he set his right hand to his heart.

'A graceful and impassioned speech, as I would expect from you,' Edward said with a glint of amusement through the ice. He shifted in his chair and his fingers ceased their drumming. 'I acknowledge your value to me, and I have noted your loyalty. My son commends you, and endorses your pleas, as does the Queen in her heartfelt mercy, and I must take their sound advice into consideration. I would not wish to see you in penury and they have persuaded me to look on your request with favour.'

'Thank you, sire.' Thomas swallowed against the lump constricting his throat. How much, though? *How much?*

Edward hesitated and almost grimaced. Then drew a deep breath. 'I have fixed the sum for Raoul de Brienne's ransom at eighty thousand florins, to be paid in three instalments. The documentation is being drawn up.'

Thomas's jaw dropped in astonishment. He wondered if he had misheard. The seneschal Robert de Tancarville's ransom was only fixed at six hundred marks, and this sum outstripped it beyond belief. He could only stammer unintelligible words of gratitude, and Edward gestured impatiently.

'Take yourself in hand, man,' he said curtly. 'I expect your unquestioning service and loyalty to me, my queen and our heirs for the rest of your life. I hope it solves your dilemma to do as you must.' He leaned back in the chair. 'And while you are valuable to me, expect no further favours concerning your personal life.'

'Sire, yes, I understand.'

'I hope you do.' Edward nodded brusquely and dismissed him.

Thomas bowed from the room, unsure that his legs would hold him up. He was sick with relief and amazement verging on disbelief at the sum stated. And very aware that despite the stunning generosity, the King was not best pleased. Returning to his lodging, he slumped on his mattress, shaking, as he had never done on the battlefield.

Otto and Raoul de Brienne had been playing dice while they waited, and both regarded him in consternation.

'What's happened?' Otto demanded. 'Did it not go well?'

Thomas raised his head and laughed hoarsely. 'You have no idea.'

Otto poured him a drink, while Raoul eyed him in trepidation. 'The King refused you again?' he asked.

Thomas shook his head and gulped down the wine. 'On the contrary, the King agreed to set your ransom – but you are not going to like it. He's named the sum at eighty thousand florins.'

Raoul gazed at him, stunned. 'You must be mistaken – that is madness! It is the ransom someone would demand for a king or a prince! Where are my family to find that kind of money?'

'It was the last thing I was expecting,' Thomas said. 'I thought today he would either deny me, or offer a paltry sum. I am sorry, I would not have put this on you, but it means I can go forward now – indeed we both can, for at least we have a decision.'

'It is impossible,' Raoul said.

'If it is paid in instalments, doubtless some will be commuted at a later date.'

Raoul slumped, shaking his head.

Otto looked between them. 'Well,' he said, 'one man's success is often another's downfall, but as Thomas says, the King is bound to commute or defer some of the payment. I wonder why he fixed such a sum in the first place.'

In the top room of the Salisburys' lodging house, Jeanette was ignoring her needlework. She loathed sewing, and the more Katerine and Elizabeth pressed her to it, the more she baulked. This morning she had finished the sixth day since her flux and the cloth was clean of blood. Yet again she was not pregnant. William, when prodded to lie with her like a boar in the pen, was as reluctant as she was and these days did not bother to attempt the act. He would come to her chamber and share her bed, but they would stay firmly on their own halves with their backs to each other.

Of late they had begun talking in a stilted fashion about the difficulties of their marriage and their mutual hatred of being bound together. William still refused to do anything about it and openly defy his mother and grandmother. The latter continued to force vile fertility potions down Jeanette's throat, and kept leaving charms and spells under her pillow, which Jeanette would throw out of the window or cast into the fire. Elizabeth also dosed her with potions to put her in a daze and keep her compliant. Jeanette continued her attempts to avoid them, sometimes by pretending to swallow and then spitting them out, or making herself sick in the latrine. But sometimes she was outwitted and would move through the world in a fog. When she was summoned into company, the women would say she was unwell and would hurry her away within a short time of arriving. Today, however, was a good day. She had seen no one and had avoided the poisoned cup, although God alone knew what was waiting for her under the mattress or inside her pillow cover.

A sudden flurry at the door heralded Prince Edward's arrival, unaccompanied apart from a squire. The women rose and curtseyed, surprised to see him. Smiling, he bade them rise. 'I beg your indulgence, ladies,' he said. 'I ask you to lend me Jeanette's company for a brief while. My hound bitch has recently whelped, and I'd value her advice.'

'Can you not ask the kennel man, sire?' Elizabeth asked, nostrils flaring. 'I hardly think Jeanette is qualified in that area.' Her tone was curt with disapproval, her position as an ageing but hale matriarch giving her leeway to use a peremptory voice to the heir to the throne.

Edward turned to her with a charming smile and a steely eye. 'Jeanette knows a lot more than you think,' he replied. 'I desire to give one of the pups as a gift to a certain lady, and I want Jeanette's advice on which would be the best. Jeanette shall come to no harm in my company, I promise on my honour.'

The women had no recourse but to accept his word, but Jeanette noticed with pleasure that their cheeks were hollow and their lips pursed, as though they were having to swallow vinegar. In silence she collected her cloak, summoned Hawise, and made a hasty exit before they could raise further objections.

Stepping out from the lodging, Jeanette felt as though she had been released from fetters. 'A "certain lady"?' she asked. Everyone knew about Edward's mistress Edith and their baby son, born in November and named Edward after his father and grand-father. 'Will she not want to choose the pup herself?'

'I am sure she will,' he said. 'It was just an excuse to get you away from those women – there is someone who wants to talk to you very much, but has been finding it impossible, and I believe he has some news for you.'

Jeanette's heart started to pound in hard, swift strokes. 'Thomas,' she said, feeling dizzy. 'You are taking me to Thomas?'

Edward smiled broadly, and without another word brought her and Hawise to the lodging where his mistress dwelt with their infant son.

Edith was tall like Jeanette, with a sheaf of golden hair woven in two heavy plaits. With her wide-set cornflower-blue eyes and red lips, she could have been Jeanette's cousin or even a sister. Edward kissed her lips, then went to the cradle and tickled the baby under the chin with his forefinger. Jeanette swallowed, feeling faint. Edward was obviously delighted with himself, his expression sparkling with mischief.

Edith's maid brought refreshments – crisp little marrow tarts warm from a pastry-seller's oven. Clearly everything had been pre-planned, but Jeanette was too anxious to eat. Edward, however, devoured two in a moment and brushed crumbs from his recently fledged whiskers.

His squire opened the door to a sharp knock.

'Sire, you wanted to see . . .' Thomas's last word trailed to silence, and he stared at Jeanette as though poleaxed. She stared back, unable to move or speak.

'Not really,' Edward said, 'but someone else does. I have to return my cousin to the Countess of Salisbury before she sends out a search party and for the sake of propriety you only have a few moments, but better than nothing.' He inclined his head to them, and he and Edith retired to an inner chamber with the baby and servants.

Hawise curtseyed to Thomas and Jeanette. 'I shall be outside the door if you have need of me, my lady,' she said, and left the room, deftly taking with her a small stool to sit on and purloining two marrow tarts.

As the door closed, Thomas and Jeanette gazed at each other with longing and disbelief. And then Thomas took a pace forward and pulled her into his arms and they kissed until the only breath they had belonged to the other. Eventually they parted, gasping, laughing, crying. Jeanette's tears of joy turned to deep, heart-wrenching sobs. Thomas held and soothed her, rubbing her back, and eventually drew her to the bench near the brazier, gently putting aside the cushion cover on which Edith had been working.

'Listen,' he said, 'the King has fixed Raoul de Brienne's ransom at eighty thousand florins which means I have enough to take our lawsuit to Avignon. I have written to my mother asking her to accompany me, and I have received permission to go. The Queen has furnished me with the name of an attorney to represent my case, and I shall leave before Easter.'

Jeanette shook her head, overwhelmed.

'Come,' he said, 'what is wrong? Is it not good news?'

'Yes, of course it is!' She tried to swallow her emotion, only half succeeding. It was almost too painful to believe that matters were moving forward at last. She had been hanging on by her fingertips for ever and it was difficult to reach out and make the transition. 'Is it really true? I thought . . . I thought you might decide it would be more worthwhile to take a different woman to wife and use the ransom to settle down with her – that you might not want me any more.'

'I will always want you, to the end of my days. I have fought my way to this moment, and I will fight on to the next and the next until we are united – unless, of course, you do not want me?'

Aghast, she shook her head. 'I cannot bear to think of the future if we have to be apart. I have waited and waited, and there is nothing I can do, and I hate it!' She clenched her fists. 'What if the Pope does not find in our favour? What then?'

'I will not think like that. I have not come this far in order to fail. All I ask is that you keep faith. You say there is nothing you can do, but that is untrue. You can stay strong and resist with all you have. You will be called upon to testify that you were a willing party to the marriage and it will be pivotal to our claim.'

Jeanette jutted her chin. 'I can withstand anything they throw at me,' she said. 'Day upon day while you have been fighting your battles I have been fighting mine. My "husband" will put up little resistance. His attorney might stand against us in Avignon before the Pope, but his mother and grandmother are the ones blocking our way. It brings royalty into their bloodline should I bear a son, and they do not want to lose my marriage portion or be made to look fools. William has resigned himself, but he refuses to end the marriage – he is still tied to his mother's womb and to the family name. My mother will object because she wishes me to remain wed to an earl and thinks you are a common despoiler of women.' Her brows drew together. 'Why has the King suddenly agreed to buy the ransom – what has changed his mind?'

'A miracle?' Thomas said facetiously, then shrugged. 'I do not know, save that the Prince and the Queen are somehow involved, but I have not pried too closely – I sense that is an affair conducted behind closed doors too.'

Between kisses and embraces he told her about his preparations to visit the papal court to have their marriage validated. In the next room, Edward loudly cleared his throat, and clattered the latch, before re-entering the main chamber. He regarded them with a wry smile and a gleam in his eye.

'Thank you, thank you!' Jeanette cried, her eyes filling again. 'I can never repay you – neither of us can!' She ran to him and hugged him.

'Oh, no talk of that,' he said, patting her back. 'I will think of something you can one day do for me.' He winked to show he was teasing. 'Messire Holland, you should leave, and I must return my dear cousin to the Salisbury lodging before there is a panic in the henhouse and our goose is cooked.' He smiled at the pun.

'Sire.' Thomas bowed. 'I am in your debt, and your loyal servant.' He turned to Jeanette and raised her hands to his lips. 'I will send word as soon as I may. Hold me in your heart and your prayers.' He left the room quickly, and Jeanette heard him murmur to Hawise.

'Come,' Edward said, 'I will return you to your lodgings, and we had better look at those puppies on the way lest you are asked about them.'

'Thank you,' Jeanette said again as they set out. 'From the

bottom of my heart, thank you. You are my dearest, dearest friend.'

He gave her an almost pained smile and after a single, swift glance, stared straight ahead. 'How long have we known each other?'

'All our lives,' she said. 'I remember watching you walk to your mother. She picked you up and cuddled you in her lap, and told you how clever you were. I was perhaps four years old, and jealous, for my mother never cuddled and kissed me like that.' She blinked on sudden tears.

'I remember playing hide and seek with you,' he said, tucking her arm through his. 'You knew the best places and, though I could never find you, you always found me. But you never gave the game away to the others – you still don't.'

She raised her brows at him, trying to fathom his meaning.

'You make me laugh,' he qualified. 'You take my cares away. You know me. I often wish . . .' He cleared his throat and abruptly strode out, his complexion flushed.

An awkward silence developed between them, and Jeanette sensed that one more step might lead to revelations from which there would be no going back. Her heart belonged to Thomas. Edward was her dearest friend even if she was a woman and he a man, but that very detail made for a dangerous line should either of them cross it, even inadvertently. He was the heir to the throne and would marry where politics dictated. His wishes would remain dreams, and she was set on a different path.

'As you know me also,' she said, using a lighter nuance in her voice to restore the equilibrium. 'Thank you again – I hope to repay your kindness one day.'

At the door to her lodging, he stopped, and his smile was a little forced. 'You have incurred no debt,' he said. 'Nor ever shall.' Then he swiftly pecked her cheek, close to the corner of her mouth, and gave her and Hawise into the keeping of the Salisburys' usher.

For the next several days, Jeanette was on tenterhooks as the winter cold slowly yielded to glimmers of spring. The evenings were drawing out and suddenly the shadows were not as deep. She spent a great deal of time in prayer, hugging to herself the knowledge that Thomas was going to Avignon to put their case before the Pope.

Katerine, however, grew increasingly bad-tempered; the King was always too busy with his soldiers, advisers or the Queen to see her and, from what Jeanette overheard, appeared to be deliberately avoiding her.

One afternoon, ten days after her brief meeting with Thomas, a visitor bearing a satchel arrived at the Salisbury lodging and presented a sheaf of documents to Katerine, who sent for her chaplain and, together with Elizabeth, retired to her chamber. When the women emerged, they were tight-lipped and cast dagger looks at Jeanette. William, who had just returned from battle practice, stood, sweaty and flushed, in his padded under-armour, gazing at his mother and grandmother.

'What is the matter?' he asked.

Katerine glowered at Jeanette. 'This has happened, as I feared.' She thrust the pieces of parchment into William's hands. 'Thomas Holland's perfidy knows no bounds. None of it is true – it's a tissue of lies and falsehood.'

William said nothing, but his body stiffened as though he was drawing everything up inside him. He glanced through the documents, some with seals attached.

'You can read it in detail if you wish,' Katerine said, 'but it is of no consequence, for who is going to listen to this fairytale? I shall speak to the King about it and he will stop it in its tracks.'

'It's about my marriage, isn't it?' Jeanette said. 'You can do nothing to stop this from reaching the Pope – nothing! The King won't listen and Thomas is already on his way to Avignon!' Elation and fear surged through her while the women stared at her like a pair of cornered lionesses.

William seized her arm in a hard grip. 'Madam, I will speak with you,' he said, and he dragged her into their bed chamber and shut the door.

Once inside, Jeanette wrenched free of his grip and rubbed her arm, knowing she would have fingerprint bruises later. 'I have told and told you this day was coming,' she said. 'Thomas has the support of the Queen, and whatever your mother believes, the King will not stand in his way. He is on the road to Avignon where he will get a fair hearing.'

'What makes you think the Pope will listen?' William scoffed. 'He has more pressing matters to deal with than paltry disputes like this.'

'Why will he listen?' She tossed her head. 'Saint Silver and Saint Gold, to the tune of eighty thousand florins – that is why he will listen! He will listen because Queen Philippa is involving herself in the case. He will listen because it will make him happy to see the King squirm given the arguments they have had in the past. And the King will do nothing because he will cleave to the Queen in this matter. He needs to keep his own marriage vows sweet. He values Thomas as a proven leader of men whereas you are still in wardship. For all those reasons, Avignon will listen!'

'Do not underestimate my mother and grandmother,' William said stubbornly. 'They always get what they want. Your own mother will fight this too.'

'And you?' she asked scornfully. 'Will you fight it as well, or just drift with the tide?'

He shook his head and began unfastening his quilted jerkin. 'I want nothing to do with it. Let God decide.'

'Do you believe me? Do you think now that Thomas and I were truly married?'

He shook his head and didn't answer.

'You could let me go. You could write to the Pope yourself and say that you agree with Thomas's claim, and that you wish our marriage dissolved.'

'I cannot do that,' he said with weary exasperation. 'It is more than my life is worth. I took you to wife, truly believing in the sanctity of our marriage, and I am not going to deny it now. I will not stand in the way of the decision is all I will say.'

Jeanette puffed out her cheeks. 'If you truly wanted to leave this match behind, you would go out there and tell your mother that you agree to an annulment on the grounds that I was already wed. You know what is morally right yet you dare not do it!'

'I want nothing more to do with any of it – not from you, not from my mother, not from my grandmother. You damned cackle of women can all hold your tongues!' He tugged off his pourpoint, almost getting it stuck round his ears, and emerged red-faced, his fair hair sticking up in spikes. 'Perhaps if you had the grace to see it from my side, you might understand.'

'Perhaps if you had the courage to stand up to those two out there, I would,' she snapped. 'We have both been played false. You have been dubbed a knight, and you have dwelt in the battle camp, and yet they ride over you roughshod as much as they ride over me, as if we are still small children. I will not let them win – will you?'

Without another word, he threw on a clean tunic and stalked from the room, slamming the door. Jeanette sat on the bed, hands clasped tightly together, flesh to bone. Outside she heard the women speak to William and his curt reply followed by the hard banging of the outer door, making the walls vibrate.

Jeanette returned to the main chamber where Katerine and Elizabeth sat muttering together like a pair of witches.

'You will not succeed,' Katerine said to her with hostility. 'I shall go to the King and he shall put an end to it.'

Jeanette shrugged. 'But it was the King who gave my lord Holland the leave and wherewithal to pursue his case,' she replied. 'I do not think you will persuade him to change his mind.'

'No?' Katerine's gaze was glacial. 'We shall see about that.'

The next day was one of relentless drizzle under low skies, grey as old fleece. Katerine had been gone all morning, and returned in the early afternoon, in a mood as foul as the weather. 'Pack the baggage,' she commanded the servants. 'We are returning to England immediately.'

Elizabeth, who had been dozing by the fire, lumbered to her feet. 'Not today, surely?'

'Tomorrow, once the packing is done,' Katerine said tersely.

'What did the King say?'

'That it would be best if I returned there while the Queen is in residence and that he had been meaning to speak with me.'

Jeanette looked down, concealing her triumph.

'Besides,' Katerine continued, lifting her chin in rallied pride, 'the estates need tending – I have to speak with my stewards and factors. The King has given William leave of absence to escort us. We must make haste, for a ship has already been arranged. Perhaps it is no bad thing. There are rumours of a pestilence that is causing great sickness in the south, and it will be safer for us to retire to better air.' She cast a malignant glance at Jeanette. 'Who knows, perhaps it has already reached Avignon.'

After her initial delight that her mother-in-law had received short shrift from the King, Jeanette was unsettled. England was removed from the court, and from Thomas. If she was summoned to Avignon to give evidence, how would she manage it from England in the care of these women who would do all in their power to prevent her?

Talk of sickness frightened her too, lest Thomas and his mother were endangered. She could do nothing about it except pray, and she knew how fickle God could be.

25

Manor of Bisham, Berkshire, April 1347

The first day back at Bisham, Elizabeth appeared in Jeanette's chamber with the usual cup of fertility tisane.

'Pray God that this time he gets you with child before he returns to Calais,' she said. 'I bore my husband eleven children – four sons and seven daughters – and I will not have you diminish our line. You will drink this now.'

Jeanette jutted her chin. 'Your prayers will go unanswered,' she retorted. 'He has no more interest in me than I have in him, and you cannot make barren ground fertile. The papal court will declare in my favour, and all your schemes will come to nothing.' She snatched the potion from Elizabeth's hand, and with her eyes fixed on her, drank it down, shuddering at the bitter taste. Then she handed back the empty cup. 'You reap what you sow,' Jeanette said, venomously.

Elizabeth's hand flashed out, and connected hard with Jeanette's cheek. 'Be careful what you say to me, my dear,' she said. 'There is no one here to protect you now.' Drawing a small knife from her belt, she rotated it in front of Jeanette's face and then polished it on her sleeve.

Jeanette swallowed. 'You are mad.'

'All the more reason to remain on my good side,' Elizabeth replied. 'I hope I have made myself clear.'

Jeanette dug her fingernails into her palms. 'Abundantly.'

'Good. Then we shall wait and see. If you are not with child this time around, then you shall be the next because you will not thwart God's will for ever.'

'Neither will you,' Jeanette said. She knew how to keep William at bay and he was no longer interested in her. Thomas would set the wheels rolling in Avignon and God willing they would prevail.

At the papal palace at Avignon, Thomas waited on a bench as he had waited so many days before. He had presented his petition to the Pope – a miracle that he had succeeded, but letters of commendation from Queen Philippa and Prince Edward had stood him in good stead, as had the presence of an attorney well versed in the dealings of the papal court. That he had fought on crusade and had scars to show for it was to his advantage, as was the fact that he had money and gifts to grease the wheels, including a magnificent black palfrey from the Holland stud herd.

Thomas had not been expecting a personal audience with Pope Clement, but he and his mother had been granted a place in the hall where the Pope dined on several occasions, and all exchanges had been cordial.

He watched a bar of warm April sunlight cross the tiled floor and stripe his boot and thought of Jeanette waiting for him in Calais. His mother, garbed in a dark gown and white wimple, sat quietly at his side, her rosary conspicuous at her belt, her fingers rubbing over and over upon the smooth brown beads. They had been here for a fortnight with their small entourage, staying in lodgings and waiting for a reply. Thomas had had to rein in his agitation and impatience. The papal court was like any other court; the skill was not to make a fuss while not fading into obscurity – a subtle thing of body language and manners. He hoped his gift would find its mark, and that the case might intrigue Clement sufficiently for him to take an interest.

A door opened and Thomas's attorney Robert Beverley emerged, clutching a sheaf of documents. He walked over to them, his dark robe swaying right and left. He was tall and robust, with a fluff of curly grey hair poking out from under his bonnet. His light brown eyes were sharp and shrewd for he had spent sufficient time at the papal curia to know its workings intimately.

'May the Holy Virgin help us,' Thomas heard his mother murmur as she crossed herself.

Thomas rose and faced the attorney, and hung by a thread as Beverley cleared his throat and drew breath.

'His Eminence has agreed to hear your case, and has put it in the hands of Cardinal Robert Adhemar.'

Thomas let out his breath on a harsh gasp of 'Praise God!' He clapped the attorney's arm before turning to embrace his mother.

'This is only the beginning of a long process,' Beverley warned. 'The next task is to assemble the witness statements, and the witnesses themselves. They will be summoned to Avignon to speak, or to have their sworn testimony presented by me as your representative. Summons will be sent to the Montagu party so that they may make their own depositions, and the same for your lady wife. She will be required to appear in Avignon, or have an attorney to act in her stead.'

'When are the depositions required?' Thomas asked.

'Cardinal Adhemar will expect all replies by the last day of December. I know it seems a long time when it is only spring now, but all must be done to the letter and the court has many cases to be heard from all Christian lands, and information must be gathered.'

Thomas swallowed his dismay. 'How soon after that is a judgement likely to be reached?'

Master Beverley spread his hands. 'I cannot say. It depends on any counter arguments from the Montagu family, and we must wait on that information. I would hope not more than a couple of months after that, but I can give you no guarantees. All I can say for now is that our position is strong, and I hope we shall win this case.'

'And thank you for what you have done thus far,' Thomas said, and gave Beverley a purse which the attorney accepted with a bow. 'But if anything can be done to hasten the matter, I would appreciate whatever you can do.'

Thomas and his mother retired to their lodging to dine and make preparations to return to Calais. Sitting across the trestle from him, Maude put her hand over his. 'I hope this girl is worth all this for you, Thomas,' she said. 'I am watching you move mountains for her. There are so many heiresses you could have without any complication.'

He placed his own hand over hers. 'I would move more than mountains. You speak out of your concern for me, I know, but this is the road I have chosen and she is worth a thousand times what I pay, besides which we are married before God, and I would be committing bigamy if I took another woman to wife.'

'Yes, but you have been apart for many years longer than you have been together, and you were both much younger then –

especially your wife. Will you still feel the same if your case is proven and you are united?'

He gave her a pained look. 'You sound like Otto. He has often remarked the same to me and I answer you as I answer him. My feelings for Jeanette have changed over time, but only to deepen. And the same for her. She worries that I will abandon her and take another wife. We lived – and loved – enough in the time we had before to know it is worth moving the mountains. Even if it takes a lifetime, I shall have her.'

'Such a bond is given to very few people, and others must perforce make their flawed way with what they have,' she said quietly, and then smiled at him. 'I do not say such words in bitterness, only that it is the way of the world, and you should cherish what you have. But why this woman and not another?'

Thomas left the table and went to his coffer, returning with a small book he had bought the previous day, bound in exquisite tooled leather with a jewelled clasp, a book of psalms with commentary and explanation. 'I bought this for Jeanette,' he said. 'I know she will appreciate it. She is well read and she has an understanding of everything she reads. When we were in Flanders, she read Emperor Frederick's hawking treatise almost overnight, and was able to debate with my falconer in detail on the subject. She has read Vegetius and Tacitus. Some men mistrust a woman who puts her nose in a book and has a thirst for learning. Some men would rather that their wives could sew a fine seam and be a silent, practical decoration. I would prefer that Jeanette instructs the seamstresses and keeps me company instead, and I do not care if she talks to the servants. A wife of wit and learning can only benefit my household and my career, and better than one who sits over her sewing all day.'

Maude was both surprised and thoughtful. It did indeed behove a woman to be educated, but her own awareness was of household management and accounts, and as an essential need rather than because she especially enjoyed reading. Indeed, she had a preference these days for others to read to her, since her eyesight had weakened as she grew older, even though she owned a pair of spectacles. 'Good,' she said. 'And what else?'

'She is beautiful,' Thomas said, flushing. 'My heart sings when I'm with her. She fills a room with light and laughter – and she challenges me. It will be no milk and water union, but I relish that thought. I want a whole woman who will stand her ground and look me in the eye. I want to see her true self, not a mask put on for others.' He smiled at her. 'You have set a fine example of the mould, Mama, and I will not settle for less.'

'Then I hope matters resolve as you wish,' she said, although her own smile was strained. 'And I shall hope to love her as I love you.'

26

Manor of Bisham, Berkshire, January 1348

Bitter January rain hurled against the shutters, and Jeanette took
the poker and thrust at the logs in the hearth until small flames
licked out along their length. She thought about setting fire to
the room, and imagined those flames crawling across the floor
and up the hangings. How long before the entire room was
ablaze? Nosewyse whined at her. Distracted, she glanced at him,
and the thought receded even if it did not go away.

The chamber was comfortable enough, appointed with cushions and hangings, but it was still a prison where she was held
under strict supervision. Elizabeth had departed in November
on family business. Jeanette had managed to discover from
snippets of servants' gossip that it involved a visit to Avignon to
give evidence to the papal court. No one had told her anything.
William found excuses to be elsewhere when he could, and
Katerine was generally absent on business within the earldom,
and when at Bisham she avoided Jeanette's company. Since the
antipathy was mutual, they rarely engaged with each other.

At Christmas the court had returned from Calais, and Katerine had attended, leaving Jeanette here under virtual house arrest with only guards and servants for company, the monks of the priory, and William's entombed father. To all intents she was cut off from life outside the manor. She was not even allowed to go riding or hunt with Frederick. The most she was permitted to do was to walk Nosewyse around the manor precincts under close supervision. Katerine had dismissed Hawise who had gone to Thorpe to serve the Holland family while her husband John was occupied in Thomas's retinue. Katerine's own maids served Jeanette now, and there was no love lost.

Hearing a shout, Jeanette went to the window and opened the shutters. Through light sleet, she saw riders clattering into the muddy yard, escorting a cart, and her heart sank as her gaze fell on William, and then, stepping heavily to the ground with assistance from two knights, the lady Elizabeth, swathed in her heavy winter cloak, followed by Katerine, also bundled up against the cold. A man accompanied them, wearing a clerical bonnet, his servant leading a pack horse laden with satchels and bundles.

Jeanette pulled back from the window feeling sick. Well, the witches had returned in force, one from court and one from Avignon, but since William was here too, she might be able to discover what was happening. She had no intention of going down to greet them. William would come to see her soon enough. She sat down before the fire to wait, Nosewyse at her feet, and pretended to read a book of Arthurian tales lent to her by the Queen.

The day darkened and she heard the noise and bustle of the cart being unhitched and the baggage unpacked. And eventually, footsteps on the outer stairs from the courtyard. The door opened and William entered, accompanied by a servant bearing a loaf of bread and an earthenware pot on a tray.

The man set down the food, and Jeanette thanked him with a warm smile. She had spent time cultivating the servants. Being considerate to them was good manners and given time would reap benefits in other ways.

Nosewyse ran to William and greeted him with a furiously wagging tail, demanding attention. William obliged with a swift tussle and ear-rub. Jeanette observed his actions. She would never be reconciled to their false union, but the fact that he enjoyed interacting with the little dog and that Nosewyse reciprocated had gradually softened her a little towards him. Dogs always knew. If Elizabeth entered her chamber, Nosewyse would bare his teeth and growl.

'I saw you return,' she said. 'And your mother and grandmother.'

He nodded. 'They are eating in the hall. The journey has been tiring, but they will speak with you tomorrow.'

'I will not be troubled if they do not; I have not missed either of them, and I doubt they have missed me,' Jeanette replied. 'But I am hungry.' Going to the pot, she raised the lid, and an appetising smell of beef and barley wafted up, making her mouth water.

William gave her a dubious look and dismissed her maid. He had broadened out in the last year, and grown again. She understood why people considered her ungrateful and mad not to be attracted to him. He was well liked among his peers at court and had excellent future prospects. But he was nothing to her, and his weakness when facing his mother and grandmother had only consolidated that. Though nowadays she often felt more compassion for him than contempt, she could not muster more than that.

They sat to dine, both so hungry that they said little while they ate, passing morsels of sopped bread to Nosewyse. But once their appetites had dulled, Jeanette leaned a little towards him. 'What news then of the world beyond? I swear I might as well be living on an island in the middle of a lake surrounded by mist for all I know and hear – or am allowed to hear. The servants tell me their tales, but they are all of their families and their cows, and marketplace gossip – but what of the court?'

William wiped his lips on a napkin. 'You hear nothing because there is nothing you need to know.'

She stared at him until he looked away. 'Is there not? And what of what I *want* to know? Will you answer me that? And who is that cleric in your entourage?'

He folded his arms as if caging the knowledge inside himself.

'I will find out,' she said. 'The servants will speak to other servants. Why all the secrecy? What do you think I can do to influence anything – or do I have a great and fearful reputation?'

'You certainly have one for trouble,' he said wryly. 'Even when you are not present, you cause it.'

'Perhaps if I was treated justly, matters would improve.'

He sighed and reached for his goblet. 'You make much ado. My grandmother has been to Avignon to speak with our attorney and with Cardinal Adhemar who is hearing our case.'

'Has there been a verdict?' She didn't tell him she already knew about Elizabeth going to Avignon.

'Not yet. The Cardinal wanted to hear our deposition and my grandmother obliged by providing them with information – in the same wise that the Hollands provided theirs when they visited last year. There is more evidence to gather and the witnesses to the first marriage have been summoned to Avignon to be interrogated. There will be no result for some time yet.'

Jeanette felt as if stones had been dropped into her stomach. She was already at the limit of her waiting.

'What are you not telling me?'

He did not answer, and Jeanette banged her fist on the table in frustration, making the dishes and goblets leap. A startled Nosewyse began to bark.

'It is my marriage that is under investigation!' she shouted. 'Why have I no say in the matter? Why should your grandmother go to Avignon and not me? Am I not a participant and a witness?' She curled her lip. 'Though then I suppose the truth would have to be known.'

'But you are to be allowed to give evidence,' William said, opening his hands. 'It is only that the court has not arrived at that place yet. I have engaged two lawyers to represent our interests – one for me, one for you – and a clerk representing yours is here to take your deposition. He will speak to you on the morrow.'

He had answered without meeting her gaze and she knew he was sliding past her with the truth. All these endless months she had been literally kept in the dark, and she was not about to be shown the light now.

'I know what you are about,' Jeanette said with contempt. 'You and your family are going to try and bury me here for ever.'

He snorted. 'That is not true, and anyway, the key to your freedom lies in your own hands. You know what you have to do.'

'Hah, such a key would just be the door to another prison. You will not succeed, because God sees and knows everything.'

Rising, he dusted crumbs from his tunic. 'I might not succeed,' he replied, 'but my mother and yours are just as determined as you, and more powerful.'

'Yes, but one day they will grow feeble, even if they are not now. You will be given your full inheritance rather than being a ward. If this marriage is judged valid – God forbid – then I shall be the Countess, and I swear they will wish that they had failed to succeed, for I shall remember everything they have done to me, and my memory is long. Perhaps I shall become like them – is that really what you want? What a terrible pattern to weave.'

He moved away from the table and went to the door. 'They will not let you go, and while I am still a ward of court I cannot stop them even if I wanted to. If you say that your supposed marriage to Thomas Holland was a foolish whim and you agree to drop the case, our lives would change for the better, but since you won't . . .' He left the end of the sentence hanging on a shrug and departed, closing the door.

Jeanette picked up Nosewyse and, kissing the top of his head, realised that whatever had happened before, perhaps her battle was just beginning.

In the morning, Lady Elizabeth came to her room. The miles of travel had dropped some flesh from her body, but her jowls remained as pendulous as a bloodhound's. One of the new-fashioned frilled wimples framed the folds of her face and did little by way of enhancement. Her dark woollen gown was embellished with silver buttons down the front, each one sitting on a roll of flesh resembling ridge and furrow plough lines.

'I suppose my grandson told you where I have been,' she said as she plumped herself down before the fire and ignored Nosewyse, who was baring his teeth at her.

'Yes, madam. I know you have been at the papal court.'

'It seems from my discussions there that your marriage to my grandson will be proven without a doubt, and your claim to be wed to Thomas Holland dismissed as arrant nonsense. The King has vouchsafed moneys to William to fight the case, so he is not at a disadvantage. If I were you, I would yield now rather than let the matter drag on to no purpose.'

Jeanette's stomach sank, but almost immediately she rallied. Lady Elizabeth was bound to say such things, whatever the truth of the matter. Stranded here at Bisham, knowing nothing, she could be fed any tale and not know its veracity.

'Well, I am not you, and I hope never to become like you. I trust in God,' Jeanette replied. 'Until the case is heard and the decision made, we cannot know.'

Elizabeth's eyes narrowed. 'My girl, you will live and learn. We have engaged an attorney for you, and his clerk will speak with you concerning your representation in Avignon. You will come to the hall now and give him your deposition.'

'Gladly,' Jeanette said.

Elizabeth raised one eyebrow, but made no comment.

In the hall, the clerk belonging to Jeanette's appointed attorney, Master Nicholas Heath, was waiting for her at a trestle table. Jeanette sat down opposite him, and he acknowledged her with a dip of his head, but glanced towards Elizabeth and Katerine, taking his direction from them. Katerine gestured for him to continue and he opened out a wax writing tablet and took up his stylus. He had watery grey eyes, and he averted them from her.

Having cleared his throat, he began questioning her about the circumstances of her first marriage, but his note-taking was scanty, and he delivered his enquiries in a drab monotone, giving her the distinct impression he had little interest in what she had to say. His lips were thin, his breath stale.

'The marriage was valid, made before witnesses, and it was consummated, not once but many times – I will swear this on oath,' she summarised firmly.

A flush crept up his neck, and again he looked to the other women. 'I think I have all that my master requires,' he said, closing the tablet, and rose to leave.

Jeanette knew, feeling sick, that he was answering not to her but to the Salisbury family, and merely paying lip service to justice. There would be no fair hearing from this.

Elizabeth accompanied him to the door, and she heard the old woman saying that every word was a lie. 'There was blood on the sheets after the wedding night,' she said. 'I saw it with my own eyes and the laundry maid will attest to washing that sheet. You will find my son accords with the matter. Unfortunately, the girl has a weak mind and a tendency to muddle her facts. Make sure that your master knows this.'

'That is not true!' Jeanette shouted, leaping to her feet. 'You know it is not! You are the one who is lying! If she was telling the truth, do you think Thomas Holland would go all the way to Avignon to prove his case?'

Katerine said curtly, 'Master Heath's representative has finished his task. He has sufficient information to make his report – do you not, sir?'

The clerk dipped his head to her. 'Yes indeed, madam, I think everything is clear,' he replied, and hurried out of the door, followed by Elizabeth.

Katerine gestured to two attendants. 'Return my daughter-in-law to her chamber, I fear she is unwell.'

Jeanette drew herself up, and stood tall – taller than Katerine. 'You know my word is true – you have always known. Unlike you, I bear no false witness.' She shrugged off the attendants as they reached for her and stalked away from them back to her chamber.

Having seen the looks exchanged between Master Heath's clerk and the two women, she knew they were damning her with falsehood. He would no more represent her than a fox could be trusted to keep a henhouse safe. She slumped on her bed, and began to cry.

Nosewyse came to her and pawed her skirts, and she scooped him into her arms and cuddled him, comforted, but desolate. She could imagine growing frozen and cold with despair until she became a tomb effigy – an unpainted one, devoid of all colour, naught but stiff folds on a slab.

27

Reading, Berkshire, February 1348

'Sire, may I have a word?' Thomas said to Edward as they stood on the tilting ground at Reading, taking a moment to watch the progress of the carpenters setting up the stands for the spectators. The sound of hammering carried across the field, and the smell of woodsmoke and stew from a workman's fire. Tomorrow was the first day of the Candlemas tourney and tents were springing up like rings of colourful mushrooms around the perimeters. The lorimers and leather workers, the farriers and horse-copers were already busy with customers. Nearby, some squires were sparring with staves and the clack of wood on wood and the youthful shouts added to the melange. The February day was cold but clear and the puddles had dried up after last week's rain – perfect weather for the sport.

'Of course, what is it?' Edward asked.

Thomas cleared his throat. 'Sire, I was wondering if after the tourney you would give me leave to visit my wife.'

Edward's expression sharpened. 'Is that not a little provocative?'

'I have a good reason.'

'Which is?'

A knight rode past, testing a horse's paces, and both men watched.

'Jeanette did not attend court at Christmas. The Countess of Salisbury claimed she was unwell and hinted that she was with child – which I doubt.'

'Even so, that is no reason to visit.'

'There has been no word from her,' Thomas persisted. 'I have heard on good authority that the lawyer's clerk sent to take her statement spoke as much to the Montagu ladies as he did to Jeanette. They say she is sick, but how do we know that? What if she is being held against her will and prevented from speaking? I will not be content until I see with my own eyes that she is whole and well and not being constrained. If there has been interference, then the papal court must be informed.'

Edward frowned. 'You have heard "on good authority"?'

'I heard it from a groom who had gone there to deliver two horses, and who spoke to one of the resident grooms. I am experienced enough to distinguish gossip from truth.'

'Even so, whatever you suspect, you cannot just ride over to Bisham rough shod and cast accusations.'

'I would not do that, sire.'

'Would you not?'

'I only want to know that she is safe and not locked away under duress,' Thomas persisted. 'If I were to visit under your authority—'

'And land the blame on me?' Edward said, but his mouth twitched.

'I give you my solemn oath as a knight.'

Edward pursed his lips. 'I suppose you could have done this without asking at all.'

Thomas said nothing.

'Very well,' Edward said after a moment. 'You may visit Bisham, and take letters and gifts from me to Jeanette, so that the family knows it is at my instigation. Whatever you find, I trust you to act courteously and without violence. You will go unarmed. William Montagu is my friend, and the future Earl of Salisbury, and you will remember that.'

Relief flooded through Thomas. Had he not been expected to joust in the Prince's entourage, he would have leaped on a horse and set out straight away. 'Thank you, sire, I am forever in your debt.'

'Yes, you are,' Edward said. 'I am doing this for Jeanette too, and for William. I do not underestimate either of those women and neither should you. I shall speak to my mother and to Jeanette's brother, for they will wish to know how she is faring.' He looked at Thomas. 'Do not let this distract you from the tourney. I am expecting heroic deeds from you over the next few days, and so is my father. You had better prove your worth.'

From Reading to Bisham was a half-day ride, and Thomas set out on the first morning after the tourney had finished. He brought a couple of knights and squires with him, two yeomen and a groom. Since Edward had warned him against all violence and aggression, he wore no sword and only his squire carried banners – the top bearing Prince Edward's ostrich plume, adopted since the great battle at Crécy, and the one beneath flying the Holland lion. A laden pack horse bore gifts from the court, including a length of rose-coloured velvet from the Queen, a basket of candied fruit and some candles from Mistress Bredon of the royal chamber, together with sweet wine and a goblet from the Prince. Thomas had been desperate to get away, more than half expecting Edward to change his mind or the Queen to put a stop to it. It hadn't happened, but even now his ears were pricked for the sound of pursuit and an order to withdraw.

As Thomas rode, his mind churned upon the details of what he knew and what he did not. He feared that Jeanette had come to some harm, and he had to see and know for himself that she was well. He most certainly hoped she was not with child.

The gate porter demanded to know his business and Thomas told him he was here at the request of his lord, the Prince, and that he came with gifts from the court, since everyone was worried at reports of the young Countess of Salisbury's illness. 'You can see that we are not a big party, and we come unarmed and in peace,' Thomas said reasonably, as the porter regarded him with suspicious eyes. Since there were not enough guards on the gate to force it shut, and because gifts from the court were involved, and the visitors bore Prince Edward's banner, the porter stepped back and let them enter – although he sent his lad running into the manor to raise the alarm.

Thomas rode into the courtyard and dismounted. Stripping his gloves, he followed in the lad's wake, beckoning to his knights Donald Hazelrigg and Henry de la Haye. Duncalfe took the bundles down from the pack horse and followed on with John de la Salle.

The two dowagers were sitting by the fire in the hall, poring over what looked like accounts, and William Montagu was with them. They looked up as Thomas walked in on the heels of the wide-eyed porter's lad. Elizabeth's face turned puce. Katerine abruptly stood up, while William stared, open-mouthed.

'Ladies,' Thomas said, bowing. 'Montagu.' He tucked his gloves through his belt.

'What are you doing here?' Elizabeth demanded. 'How dare you!'

'I am here to pay a visit,' Thomas said urbanely. 'There is

concern at court for the welfare of the King's dear cousin. Indeed, I have brought gifts and messages from the lord Edward, his lady mother, and some of her ladies.' He indicated Duncalfe standing behind him laden with packages.

'The Countess of Salisbury is very well indeed,' Katerine said icily. 'I am afraid you have had a wasted journey.'

Thomas bowed again. 'No journey is ever wasted, madam.' He looked round the hall. 'I am pleased to hear all is well, but as I say, I have gifts from Prince Edward and the Queen, and wonder if it will be possible to present them to her and reassure myself and others that the lady is indeed in good health, that I may report back to her kin.'

'Absolutely not!' Elizabeth spluttered. 'It would be the height of impropriety as you know perfectly well, and that is why I say "how dare you". I do not know what subterfuge you have used with her kin at court, but it will not work here. Get out of this house immediately. You are not welcome.'

Meeting the old woman's gaze was like clashing sword on sword. 'The other reason I am here,' Thomas said, 'is to make certain that the lady is free to speak her mind with her attorney and not be misrepresented. I need to hear from her own lips that this is the case.'

'You go beyond the bounds of what is acceptable,' Elizabeth snapped. 'I understand now why we are faced with this false and disgraceful lawsuit. Of course she is being fairly represented, of course we are looking after her in a manner fitting to her estate, and we need prove nothing to you, for you are not the law. It is no business of yours to be here, and certainly not to see her. We absolutely forbid it!'

'It is our duty to protect this young woman, and maintain her chastity and reputation to the highest standard,' Katerine added. 'You claim to be concerned for her welfare, yet you arrive like a fox to the coop, and you endanger her reputation as you endangered it before.'

Thomas suppressed the furious retort that Katerine was unfit to protect anyone's reputation, especially her own. 'I will see her,' he said, and started forward.

Immediately, two of the Salisbury knights barred his way to the stairs, hands to their swords. Thomas thought he heard the muffled sound of thumping and cries from above.

'Leave now, or face the consequences,' Elizabeth said, and turned to William, who was standing wide-eyed, at a loss. 'Are you the man of this house?' she demanded. 'Get him out of here!'

William looked from his mother and grandmother to Thomas and then wrapped his fists around his belt and jutted his jaw. 'Show him the door,' he commanded the knights.

'Christ!' Thomas said in disgust. 'You truly are tied to the apron strings. Call off your curs, I am leaving. I trust you will make sure that my wife receives her gifts. The papal commission shall hear of this. You cannot hold back the tide when it is on the turn. God help you if you are keeping my wife prisoner.' He cast his gaze towards the stairs again.

'*My* wife is in her chamber and has no wish to see you,' Montagu snapped. 'You will leave, or face the consequences.'

Thomas fought to control his rage, and with clenched fists turned about and strode from the manor, the Salisbury knights clipping his heels, their swords drawn. He could do nothing for he was unarmed, and he had promised Edward in good faith that he would not engage in violence. He only hoped the Montagus would mind their treatment of Jeanette because they knew this would reach the ears of the royal and papal courts. His next course of action was crystal clear.

In the courtyard, he remounted his horse, and glanced up

at the windows above the hall. One of the casements was open and a pale face leaned out, watching him. A hand frantically waved. He waved back, filled with relief, for at least she was alive and full of spirit; but then someone pulled her away from the window which was abruptly closed and shuttered. He reined around, on the cusp of throwing caution to the wind and charging into the hall, horse and all, but the part of him that was a battle commander as well as a soldier kept a grip on such a suicidal impulse. He took a final long look at the shuttered window, circled his horse again to face the gate, and dug in his heels.

Jeanette had seen Thomas arrive, his entourage flying the Prince's banner above his own. She had watched him stride up to the manor entrance and had flown to her door, determined to run down and speak with him, only to discover that she was locked in. She had hammered and screamed and kicked, but to no avail. Dashing back to the window, with wild thoughts of somehow squeezing through the gap, or tying sheets together, she had seen Thomas emerge at sword point and mount up to leave, and she had managed to wave and shout before she was dragged away from the window by a furious Katerine, and the shutters slammed and latched. Her fierce protest that she had a right to see her husband had received a sharp slap and a warning that she would be kept in even closer confinement from now on.

Now the door opened and William entered, looking sheepish. A squire followed, bearing bundles and packages. Jeanette turned her shoulder to show her contempt.

'He should not have come,' William said, trying to justify himself.

She swung round. 'There must have been a reason – an official one. I saw the Prince's banner, I know Edward was involved.

What do you think Thomas will tell him now? What do you think he is going to say to the papal commission?'

William shrugged. 'That is up to him. I can only do what is right for my family.'

'And honourable?' she bristled.

'The Prince and the Queen have sent you gifts,' he said abruptly, to change the subject. 'See, there is some fine cloth for a gown and trim of ermine fur. Do you want to look?'

'What good are such gifts when I am locked up?' she spat. 'Who is going to see them? Do you think trinkets are going to distract my mind?'

'But you have them anyway, so why not look?' he reasoned. 'I will leave them with you. My mother said you should not have them, but even if you think nothing of me, I stood my ground, and here you are. They also said they were going to put bars at your window, but I refused and said that I would not permit it.'

'How brave of you,' she scoffed.

William turned on his heel and left the room – and locked her in.

Jeanette eyed the basket. Doubtless Katerine and Elizabeth had rifled through the contents to ensure no secret messages were hidden amid the gifts. As William had said, there were pieces of ermine that could be used to trim a gown and some velvet in a plush dusky pink. Two embroidered pillow covers with gold laces and a silver dog dish with Edward's ostrich feather device carved on the base – which made her smile. A crystal phial of rose water and some candles from Joan Bredon, and a beautiful small leather-bound book of psalms. Some of the gifts might have been from Thomas, but since they purported to be from the Queen and court, the Montagu women had left them in situ, although for how long was another matter.

Jeanette picked up the book and unfastened the clasp. The pages were exquisite with illuminated letters and curl-leafed illustrations in the margins. A soft pink rose flowered at a line that was a quotation from the Song of Solomon, and moreover, it was written in English. A closer look revealed that the page had been cleverly inserted later and was not part of the original writing.

Her heart quickened as she read the line again: 'I am my beloved, and my beloved is mine. Thou art the fairest among women.'

Tears filled her eyes and she cuffed them away, not wanting to damage such a treasure. Turning the pages, sniffing, she discovered that throughout, here and there, the letters had been changed to be slightly enlarged or diminished and she realised that Thomas had in fact sent her a coded message.

She fetched her wax tablet and stylus, and sat at the scribe's lectern to solve the puzzle, telling the watchful maid that she wanted to practise her letters for something to do. It was only a small book and Thomas's note was short, but he said that he loved her and that he was working towards her freedom and the moment when they would be able to live as man and wife. She must not give up hope.

She kissed the letter she had spent time copying out, but knew she dared not keep it. The maid would find a way to look at what she had been writing and would tell Katerine or Elizabeth. She committed the words to memory, then smoothed them out to blankness, sending up a prayer as the waxy surface lost its waves of writing and became as still water.

A couple of dreary months later, the air turned clear and mild and the trees were suddenly bright with new green leaves. Everywhere was in bud and leaf as spring took hold and raced forward. Jeanette, out in the courtyard throwing a stick for Nosewyse, wanted to race with it, but her constraints remained. Since Thomas's surprise visit she had seen no one beyond the manor servants, officials and guards. She was expected to attend to her sewing and pray. They had grudgingly permitted her to read books on household management and the proper ways of wifely behaviour. She had become very well versed in the habits of poultry and their care. She knew that each hen ought to produce a hundred and fifteen eggs a year and raise seven chicks. That for every five hens there should be one cockerel. There were certainly plenty of the latter. At this time of year their noise began under her chamber window while the stars were still glimmering in the pre-dawn sky. One, then another and another, until the air was raucous and it was time to start the day – but not before she had read her little psalter and kissed its cover in daily ritual.

A shout came from the manor gates, and the watchman and his boy hurried to swing them open. Jeanette shaded her eyes to watch the visitors arrive, scattering the poultry. The banners of Kent fluttered in the wind, and her brother John rode in astride a dappled palfrey. Her surprise and joy flared, but died on the instant as behind the first riders a decorated long carriage came into view pulled by three sturdy bays.

John dismounted, and going to the carriage, helped their mother out of it. Jeanette swallowed nausea. No one had told her about this visit. Indeed, Katerine had returned to court a fortnight ago when the Queen had retired into confinement to bear her latest child, due in the early summer, and only Elizabeth was in residence.

Nosewyse ran up to her mother and danced at her on his hind legs. Margaret batted him away, which made him leap about even more and set up a shrill yapping. John looked on with amusement, stroking his new soft beard.

'Sister,' he said, grinning, 'I see that nothing has changed.'

'That shows you how much you know,' Jeanette retorted.

Before they could embrace, Elizabeth emerged from the manor to greet the visitors. 'Take that dog and shut him in your chamber,' she told Jeanette, her expression pinched with annoyance.

'Shall I shut myself in my chamber too?' Jeanette asked pertly, but picked up Nosewyse and carried him off.

Elizabeth shook her head. 'Come,' she said to Margaret, 'be welcome,' and, leading her inside the manor, called for food and drink.

When Jeanette did not return, Elizabeth prepared to send a servant to fetch her.

'I will go,' John said quickly, and absconded the hall.

On entering Jeanette's chamber, John looked around before sitting down on a cushioned bench by the hearth and fussing Nosewyse. 'You have created a great stir,' he said, fondling the dog's coppery ears. 'In certain places, your name is spoken in a whisper that might as well be a shout.'

'Is it?' Jeanette faced him, her arms folded. 'Well, I am glad, for I have been screaming and screaming to no avail for a very long time.'

'Is it true then? Did you and Thomas Holland truly make a pact and marry in Flanders?'

'Do you think I would be putting this on myself if we had not?' she said irritably. 'Do you think Thomas would be going to Avignon to prove our case just to spite everyone? What do you think we have to gain from such an endeavour?'

'I can see that he has plenty to gain,' John retorted.

'Oh yes,' she snapped. 'He loves living with a threat to his life and reputation hanging over his head. He so enjoys making enemies at court and delights in spending his time scraping

331

together funds to fight the Montagus through the law courts. He stands to lose as much as he gains by continuing the battle.' She shook her head at her brother in exasperation. 'I suppose our mother has been pouring her falsehoods in one of your ears, and William in your other. She doesn't want the scandal, nor the disparagement of having me wed to an ordinary knight and younger son with no title to his name and a disgraced father, when for now I am the Countess of Salisbury in waiting. She will do anything to keep me tied into this marriage – they all will. The lady Elizabeth went to Avignon and perjured herself by swearing I was a virgin on my wedding night, when it couldn't have been further from the truth. She is trying to have the case transferred to England to be heard too.'

John gazed at her with an open mouth, but eventually rallied. 'William has said little to me,' he said. 'He once asked me to intercede with you on his behalf to ask you to look more favour-ably upon him, but changed his mind when I did not understand what he meant. Of late, we have not spoken.'

'William doesn't want this marriage either, but he is glued to his mother and grandmother and the whole business of saving face. It doesn't matter what I want because no one listens whether I whisper or scream. We would not be taking it to the Pope unless there was another way.'

'Mama says you are foolish and that you have no care for your family.'

'Is that what you think?'

He rubbed the back of his neck, which had reddened. 'No, of course it isn't, and I do support you, but in taking up this fight you have put yourself first and your family second – the same with Thomas Holland. He is not just risking himself. He could have married a fine heiress with Raoul de Brienne's ransom money, but instead he is using it to further this . . . this scandalous court case.'

Jeanette tightened her folded arms, wanting to slap him. Despite his remark about supporting her, he was plainly ambivalent. 'The only scandal is that we have to go to these lengths to fight our case, when we are husband and wife,' she said. 'Edward has put his weight behind us. He believes we are telling the truth.'

'Well, that is because he is sweet on you,' John said.

Jeanette shook her head vigorously. 'He is my friend, has been since we were children, and he has a mistress and a baby.'

'And he must marry like all of us in the family interest,' John said pointedly. 'But the way he looks at you, he would be happy to be more than a friend if he could.'

'Don't be foolish!' Jeanette knew she was blushing. 'It is because he knows I am being treated unjustly.'

'His mistress looks just like you – in some lights you could be mistaken for sisters.'

She waved her hand in denial. 'I am done with this,' she said crossly. 'You either believe me or you don't.'

'Oh, I believe you, and I will do what I can to help you. But I confess that I am envious.'

'Envious?' She was astonished. 'Why would you be envious of me?'

'That you have chosen to fight to the detriment of all else including your duty to your family. I cannot do that because, like Edward and William, I am bound by expectations – I cannot refuse.'

'Do you mean to say you are already tied?' she demanded. 'Has mother arranged a marriage for you too?'

He looked down and scuffed his toe on the floorboards. 'Not so much our mother as the King and Queen. That is why I have been given my lands early, to make me a worthy consort. But Uncle Thomas says it is a fine match and approves. I am to wed the Queen's niece, Isabella of Juliers. We are of an age and they think we shall be well suited.' He looked rueful. 'Women, when they gather together in their sewing groups to gossip, arrange marriages for their relatives like stitching secret patterns on their embroideries. I envy you because you have chosen to sew your own colours and to walk away from it all, even at a great cost to yourself and others. It is a brave thing to do among many less positive reasons, and I admire that courage to throw away the good and the steady with the bad as if all of it is chaff in the wind compared to your own desires. Some of us cannot loosen our shackles and do that.'

Jeanette gazed at him, absorbing two things at once – that he was going to be married, and that he was bitter concerning her own choice in dealing with her situation. 'Do you wish to?'

He shrugged. 'There are more advantages than disadvantages. If we take to each other, then well and good. If we do not, I still have my inheritance and may do as I please and take a mistress or two. I am sure we shall manage when it comes to begetting and raising heirs. I have to look at it like that, as do Edward, and William.'

'And the women? What do they think?'

'They make their own lives and their own female friends. There can be productivity and harmony in duty, even if there is not passion and love. Indeed, bonds of affection might grow if they are nurtured. That is what I hope for myself at the least. My bride gains from being the Queen's niece and marrying the King's cousin. I gain from having my inheritance early, a link with the Queen, and an escape from our mother.'

Jeanette regarded him dubiously. He still did not understand because he had a man's perception of the world. At least he had offered his help, although she had no idea what he could do. She doubted his ability to silence their mother. Perhaps he could speak to people at court, and subtly endorse the idea of a union between herself and Thomas – perhaps speak to Thomas himself and organise a strategy.

She drew breath to speak, but John's squire cleared his throat on the other side of the door. 'Sire, my lady, your company is desired in the hall.'

Jeanette made a face.

'We shall be there presently,' John called out, and turned to her. 'Come,' he said, making his tone light to uplift the moment, but not entirely succeeding, 'let us sit at the table, roll the dice and hope to win!'

'I shall keep on throwing until I do win,' Jeanette said grimly. 'They use loaded dice, but then these days, so do I. For I have learned to play them at their own game.'

At the door, she laid her hand on John's sleeve. 'Do what you can for me, John, I beg you.'

He kissed her cheek. 'I promise,' he said, 'but you should help yourself too. For all your talk of playing with loaded dice, it doesn't look quite that way from where I am standing.'

28

Eltham Palace near London, May 1348

Otto set one hand on his hip and thrust out his leg in his tight-fitting hose to show Thomas the effect of his new blue garter. 'What do you think?'

'Fetching,' Thomas said with a grin. 'The women will appreciate you even more than they already do!'

This morning, the King had announced his intention of forming an order of knighthood, a new Round Table of elite knights who would wear a blue and gold garter to mark their prowess and prestige. Details were still being formalised, and robes decided upon, but the King intended the order to outmatch any in the great courts of the other princes of Europe.

Initially some knights had been amused at the announcement, but the King had taken it in good part and said how virile the chosen warriors would look and how their garters would mark them out as men of exceptional military ability, and the ridicule had swiftly ceased. Twenty-four were to be chosen – twenty-five including the King – and garters and robes were to be officially presented in a grand ceremony on St George's Day in Windsor chapel the following year. Otto, however, was trying out the effect already.

Thomas's squire poked his head into their tent. 'Sire, the Earl of Kent is here and wishes to speak with you.'

'By all means, show him in,' Thomas said.

He had encountered Jeanette's brother several times on campaign, and the young man had been residing at court since his marriage to the Queen's cousin Isabella of Juliers. However, John had kept his distance from Thomas thus far, even while being scrupulously polite. His mother, the Dowager Countess, was at court too, keeping the Queen company, which was a pity. Thomas had stayed well away from her, for there was nothing they could say to each other that would not explode into an almighty public feud.

John of Kent entered the chamber. Like Jeanette he was tall, and in his case still growing into his long limbs. His fair hair, a few shades darker than his sister's, held glints of copper and his blue-grey eyes were steady. A new, tender beard fluffed his jaw and chin. Thomas was reminded that he was not a particularly martial man, despite having trained with Prince Edward. Urbane and courteous, he had none of Edward's military passion, and war was a duty to him, not a calling.

'Welcome,' Thomas said, polite but cautious since this was the first time they had sat down together. 'Will you take a cup of wine?'

John nodded acceptance and sat down across the bench from him and Otto. He placed a leather book satchel on the table, keeping it away from the threat of drink spillage.

'I am pleased to see you,' Thomas said. 'We have not had an opportunity to speak, and I have not deemed it appropriate to approach you, although I recognise you are head of your household now and Earl of Kent. I am at your service.'

John flushed and waited while the squire poured wine and placed a dish of almond-stuffed dates on the board before retiring.

'I think it is the other way around,' he said, once the squire was out of earshot, 'and that I am at yours with regard to your marriage claim.'

'I would appreciate any help you can give me, of course, but I understand your position.'

John screwed up his face. 'I dearly love my sister – she is my godmother too. There was no one else and we were under house arrest when our father was executed. She cared for me when I was little, and in our younger years we were close. When I heard Montagu was to marry her, I was pleased, and thought it a good thing for our family. He and Jeanette used to squabble and insult each other as children, but all youngsters do that at play; you cannot take account of such spats when entering into a marriage. I did not understand why my sister was objecting so much.'

'You did not know about her marriage to me?' Thomas asked with surprise.

John shook his head. 'Not at the time. I wasn't involved and I didn't care to be involved – it was a matter for our parents and wardens, and Jeanette never told me. I just thought it was because . . . well, you know how women can bite your head off as soon as look at you sometimes. If I tried to speak to Jeanette she would snap at me, and call me a child. And if I tried to ask my mother, it was the same.' He picked up his cup. 'But recently my sister told me about your secret marriage at Saint Bavo.'

Thomas lifted his own cup, a wry expression on his face. 'It was perhaps not such a fine idea to marry in secret. I wanted to show my commitment to her, but I needed to find grace with

God, and before I openly broached the matter and while I was away, the Montagu match was arranged and your sister was in no position or frame of mind to refuse – which is how we came to this broil.'

'My sister swears you were truly wed before witnesses, and that the bond was consummated.' John reddened.

'Yes, we were. Otto was one of the witnesses.' Thomas indicated his brother. 'The consummation is a private matter between me and your sister, but we will both swear that it happened on many occasions. I love her with all of my heart. I could have abandoned this fight long ago. William Montagu was under-age and incapable of growing a beard when his parents and your mother agreed the match. Like Jeanette he was pushed into it. I fully intended to make my confession to the King and claim your sister on my return from the wars, but instead found her bigamously married to the Montagu boy, and I did not have the funds to challenge the union then. Now I do, and I will continue to pursue the case to its end, whatever that might be.'

John reached to the satchel on the table. 'I have been sorting through family documents since I have come into my majority,' he said, 'and I found these letters in the strongbox.' He removed several strips of parchment bundled together with string and pushed them across to Thomas. 'These are copies of messages my mother sent to the Dowager Countess of Salisbury concerning my sister's marriage with you, and they were written during the negotiations for Jeanette's match with William Montagu.'

Thomas set his cup aside, unfastened the string and read the first one, the brown ink faded along the fold line, but detailing clearly the evidence that Margaret of Kent had known full well about Jeanette's statement that she had been married in Flanders. 'It is a pity that there is no seal to the document,' he said. 'I suspect Montagu's attorney will say it is a forgery, but I shall pass it on to my own lawyer and hope it will aid his case. And I thank you.'

'There is more,' John said. 'The Countess of Salisbury replied to my mother, and her seal is indeed upon the letter.' Triumphantly he produced another piece of parchment, with its wax seal hanging from a folded strip of parchment.

Thomas read it and passed it to Otto, who had already perused the first one. This letter acknowledged Margaret's information and Katerine replied that she had been at St Bavo at the time of the purported marriage and had no knowledge of any such ceremony having occurred. The claim, she said, should be ignored as a fabrication. Neither of them should allow a silly girl's infatuation to stand in the way of a great dynastic marriage for both families.

Sickened, Thomas shook his head. 'They knew,' he said. 'They knew and yet they went forward anyway with a bigamous match.' He looked at John. 'Thank you, I am in your debt for this.'

Looking uncomfortable, John shrugged. 'I am afraid I believed my mother at first, and thought my sister was being awkward, but when I spoke to her recently and I saw the manner in which the Montagu women were treating her, I realised she had been telling the truth – and then I found these letters.' He reached to his cup. 'A man does not want to think of his family acting dishonourably, and I must assume their actions were born from good intentions, but I cannot continue to watch my sister suffer. I have gone against my mother, and it has pained me to come to you, but I felt that in all honour I must.'

'And I am grateful to you,' Thomas said quietly. 'It is no light thing. If there is anything I can ever do for you, you need but name it.'

John finished his wine and stood up. 'See that you follow this through, and make my sister happy,' he said. 'This has to be worthwhile.'

'I swear on my life that until my dying breath it shall be my only cause,' Thomas said fervently.

John nodded. 'I shall do what I can, as I have promised Jeanette too. I wish you good fortune.'

They clasped hands, and John departed with the empty satchel under his arm.

Thomas sat down heavily on the bench and, puffing out his breath, picked up the letters to read again. 'I embarked on this road determined to see it through whatever the outcome,' he said, and looked across at Otto. 'I have often wondered if I was fooling myself – I know you have thought so.'

'Many times,' Otto admitted, 'but the further you have travelled, the more I have realised it is your true path, even if the most difficult. I doubt you would know an easy road if you saw it. Even if I do not always agree with you, you have my respect.'

'Thank you, brother,' Thomas said. 'They will claim the letters are forgeries, even with a seal, but each piece adds to the weight of our evidence and lightens the argument of theirs.'

Robert Beverley, back from Avignon, arrived in Windsor at dusk on the same day that the Queen gave birth to another healthy son, christened William. In the summer evening, banners fluttered from the walls and balconies of castle and town, and the air rang with joyous celebration. The church bells pealed the news, and messengers rode out to declare the birth across the land. The castle wards seethed with people carousing and dancing. The King was already planning a grand tourney to mark the birth and the Queen's safe delivery.

Lantern light gleamed in the long twilight, softening the shadows. Master Beverley took a long drink from his cup.

Although dusty and red-eyed from his day on the road, he was smiling as he addressed Thomas and Otto at a trestle table inside their tent.

'I have good news,' he said. 'The Pope has responded with concern to your information about your wife's confinement. The Archbishop of Canterbury and the bishops of London and Norwich have been instructed to enforce the matter of her right to speak freely and openly without coercion. I travelled from Avignon with the messenger myself, and I have a copy of the letter for your own document chest.' He indicated the bulging satchel at his side. 'I shall do my best to ensure the matter is dealt with swiftly and that your wife is permitted to report her side of the case in a full and thorough manner to someone who is not in the pay of other parties. I shall be at court for the next month, and then returning to Avignon – all being well.'

'Thank Christ!' Thomas said on a huge surge of relief. 'They did not even allow her to attend her brother's wedding, but kept her locked up at Bisham.'

'Well, that will change under this decree,' Beverley said, 'although it does not mean she will have the freedom to come to court unless expressly summoned by the King or Queen. However, her attorney will be expected to make a full accounting without bias or prejudice.'

He sat back as Thomas's squire arrived from a cookshop with a roast hen on a platter, white bread, and a dish of green herb sauce.

'How will that be enforced?'

'A member of the clergy could attend,' he said, 'or perhaps an independent witness, or a family member without a particular bias.'

'Her brother might be willing,' Thomas said. 'He is now the Earl of Kent and wishes to see justice done. Indeed, I have my own letters for you and evidence that the Dowager Countess of Kent knew of the first marriage, and discussed it with the Countess of Salisbury.'

Beverley paused, a piece of chicken halfway to his lips. 'That is indeed useful information.'

'The Earl of Kent will swear to finding the documents in the family strongbox and to handing them over to me.'

'Excellent!' Beverley attended to his food for a moment, then wiped his lips on a napkin. 'I have every hope of winning this case. William Montagu's attorney is accomplished, but he is no match for our evidence.' He laid his chicken bones at the side of his dish and picked up the second leg. 'I should warn you to expect some delay – there is serious pestilence in many of the cities of the south.'

Thomas frowned. 'We have heard rumours, and some say it is creeping closer to our shores. Do you know its nature?'

'I have not seen it for myself, but I have heard from those who have, and two people of my acquaintance at the papal court have died.' He shook his head, his expression sombre. 'If you catch the ordinary pox or the mezils, you have a chance of surviving – sometimes scarred, it is true, but you will live out your lifespan. Some die, some live. But I have not yet heard of anyone who has survived this new disease. It kills whoever it touches, whatever their condition in life. It starts with fever and malaise. Some folk void their stomachs, some do not, but soon swellings like eggs appear in the neck and armpits and groin and they quickly become black and putrid. Other lesions fester on the body and the dying person often coughs up gouts of blood. By the end, and by the mercy and pity of God, they are insensible. A man may come home, eat his dinner, play with his children, love his wife, and within a week every one of them will be dead or dying.'

The attorney crossed himself, and so did Thomas, alarmed, for Robert Beverley was pragmatic and not given to flights of fancy.

'Some say it is God's punishment and we should be better Christians, but whatever the reason this pestilence brings instant death,' Beverley went on. 'Will England escape? I doubt it. For all that we have a moat and barrier of sea, we trade widely, and travel between cities on our business. Sooner or later it will come here and then God help all in its path.'

Hearing this, fear shivered up Thomas's spine. What if all this striving was for nothing? When death came calling, there was no recourse to appeal.

'I say we should continue as we are but take precautions,' Beverley said. 'We should be humbler before God than is our wont, and keep ourselves shriven and in a state of grace. That is all we can do.' He finished his wine and rose to leave. 'I should go. I have much to do and the Queen to attend on the morrow, but we shall speak again soon, and I thank the Earl of Kent for his cooperation.'

When he had gone, Thomas rubbed his jaw and looked at Otto. 'Sobering news,' he said. It made him even more determined to win his case, but he had a gnawing feeling that time was not just passing, it was running through his hands, and running out.

29

Windsor Castle, Berkshire, June 1348

Summoned to the court at Windsor by royal invitation, Jeanette arrived on a glorious June evening and was glad to step from the cart, for riding with Lady Elizabeth was always a trial. Katerine and Elizabeth had been tight-lipped at the summons, but could not ignore a royal command. Jeanette knew she would be closely guarded, but still hoped to find a way to speak with Thomas.

Numerous brightly striped tents crowded the castle precincts, hosting a huge gathering of nobility, here to celebrate Queen Philippa's churching after little William's birth, and to attend a grand tourney to honour the new prince and his mother.

Jeanette's stomach tightened with anxiety. It had been an age since she had been among so many people and it was like going from a diet of bread and water to a vast banquet. It left her feeling overwhelmed and nauseous.

The Salisbury lodgings consisted of three silk and canvas tents erected in front of the castle keep, and Katerine hustled her through the flaps and behind a partition at the back of the tent. 'Do not think that you shall be gadding about the tourney field,' she warned. 'You shall be a proper wife and remain under supervision until expressly summoned by the King and Queen.'

Jeanette deigned not to reply. Something had hardened and matured within her over the past few years as she had realised that even in a state of supposedly being powerless, a disdainful silence was insurmountable, and gave her control and power of her own. They might be constraining her, but she treated them as if they did not exist.

Jeanette approached the Queen, who was preparing to go and sit in her place of honour to view the tournament parade and the first bouts of the day.

Yesterday in the Chapel of St George she had celebrated her churching and given thanks for the safe delivery of yet another royal son. Jeanette had felt a little sorry for Philippa, who had been barely visible, swamped by her robes of red velvet embroidered in gold and pearls and so heavy with gems and stitchery that the garments could have stood up on their own. The mantle, lined with miniver and ermine, was more fitting to a winter's day than midsummer and Philippa's face had been a flushed dusky red, almost matching her costume. There had been little opportunity for Jeanette to speak with her, for the Queen had been occupied with official ceremonies. Jeanette had not seen her afterwards either, beyond a curtsey, for so many others had been waiting to make their obeisance and the Montagus had declined to linger.

Today there was yet more ceremony and expectation to endure. This time Philippa was robed in blue velvet embroidered with golden birds and a ransom-weight of pearls. The display was utterly sumptuous but uncomfortable for its wearer despite her stoical smile. Jeanette, glad to be much more lightly gowned in her dusky pink velvet with a cream silk underdress, curtseyed.

'It is a while since we have seen you at court,' Philippa commented, 'but I am pleased to see you among us again and I trust you are well.'

'Yes, madam, and I thank you and the King for the summons,' Jeanette replied gracefully. 'I have missed being among company; I have missed my friends and my kin.' She smiled at Joan Bredon, standing among the Queen's ladies holding Poppet, who was wearing his golden acorn collar.

Philippa turned to her jewel box to select the rings and brooches she would wear to add to her already glittering array. 'We have missed you too, but we have been aware of your progress. I would not want you to think you were being ignored. Indeed, you have often been on my mind.'

'Madam, I am glad you have thought of me,' Jeanette replied, wondering where this was leading. 'It comforts me greatly and gives me hope.'

The Queen held out her fingers for the rings to be pushed on. 'We should talk further,' she said. 'I hope you will stay at court for a while. You have a new sister-in-law with whom to become acquainted, and of course your brother is here.' She raised one hand to regard the rings. 'A word of warning . . . be careful in your behaviour while your case continues. Much as you might wish to linger in the company of certain courtiers, you would be wise not to jeopardise your future by behaving rashly. I hope I make myself clear, my dear. I have your best interests at heart. Do not spoil the broth for want of a little more cooking.'

'No, madam,' Jeanette said meekly, and thought she would still strive to see Thomas if possible. The broth, as far as she was concerned, had been cooking for quite long enough, and required seasoning!

Not in the least taken in, Philippa held Jeanette's gaze sufficiently long to show how serious she was.

Another young woman arrived, robed in bright brown silk
with striking gold embroidery. Her thick brown hair was plaited
either side of her face in two coiled braids, with an elaborate
veil and circlet draped over. Her dark eyes and the set of her
jaw marked her as kin to the Queen. Jeanette had met her
brother's new wife briefly yesterday, but had only gained a fleeting
impression. The young woman had seemed pleasant enough,
with a sparkle in her eyes, and had spoken affectionately of John.

Jeanette curtseyed to her; Isabella reciprocated, and they
exchanged cheek kisses under the Queen's benevolent eye.

The entourage moved out to the tournament lodges and
Philippa bade Jeanette sit near to her with Isabella. John himself
was among the squires and knights on the tourney field, but
only as part of the parade, not as a combatant, for his skill lay
not in the joust or the sword fight. He was more at home as an
administrator, in which role he could wear his Venetian spectacles and see the world with improved clarity. Still, he looked
very fine, and when Jeanette said so to Isabella, the latter smiled
proudly. John looked up at the stands as he paraded past on a
glossy bay horse and cheerfully saluted in the women's direction.

Isabella cast a handful of flowers at him, and Jeanette remembered how she had thrown her own to Thomas at the tourney
in Ghent. She looked for him now among the arms and banners
and listened as the heralds called out the names of those taking
part. The King was jousting today at the head of half of his
Knights of the Garter; the other half were riding with the lord
Edward. As the King's knights trotted past, gorgeously capari-
soned, she stared straight ahead, her hands in her lap.

Isabella eyed her askance. 'Do you not throw flowers to your
lord?'

'He is not my husband,' Jeanette said. 'Surely you must have heard the talk at court, and John must have mentioned this to you?'

'A little. But it is unwise to believe everything you hear, and John says it is a difficult matter and he does not wish to discuss it. He says the papal court in Avignon shall decide the truth.'

'I have known the truth every day of my life for the last eight years and more,' Jeanette replied. 'Whatever the papal court decides, I will always know it in my heart and how to weigh it against the falsehood of others.'

Isabella's brown eyes widened and she drew back, clearly at a loss.

Jeanette lifted her chin as the Prince's contingent rode on to the field and the heralds cried the names of the knights fighting under his ostrich-feather banner. 'There is my true husband,' she said as Thomas passed their stand on Noir, with Otto riding beside him on his rangy chestnut, both men wearing the blue garters that marked them out as elite knights. 'I do not throw flowers to him either, for we know what is in our hearts, and we have tokens far beyond a moment of public display that would cause trouble for us both.' She looked at Isabella. 'When I married Thomas, we chose each other. How many people sitting on these benches can say that? Some will come to love and some will come to grief, and some will settle for a partnership of estates and children and daily bread. But I know what I have, and I will never stop fighting for it. I would rather die first.'

Isabella looked shocked and Jeanette smiled, albeit bitterly.

'What of duty?' Isabella asked. 'Does that mean nothing? What of honour?'

'They have their place and I do not deny their worth, but there was no honour in the marriage I was forced to make with William Montagu. They told me I had to wed him; they said

Thomas was dead. They said no one would believe us and they tried to bribe Thomas to drop his claim. They said that the marriage was false – that I was a foolish girl, taken in by the blandishments of a man who just wished to have his way. It is their honour that is tarnished, not mine, and I will stand firm unto death in the face of their lies.'

Isabella swallowed, clearly out of her depth, and despite her rancour at the world, Jeanette took pity on her. 'That is my situation. I do not expect your understanding or sympathy, but whatever your path with my brother, I wish you well, and hope you wish the same for me.'

Isabella nodded. 'Of course,' she said faintly.

Joan Bredon joined them, squeezing herself in at Jeanette's other side, her freckled face bright with pleasure. 'I saw Donald in Thomas Holland's entourage,' she said. 'He's got a new horse, one of the Holland blacks.'

'Yes, I noticed.' Jeanette smiled at her friend. People mistook Joan's wholesomeness as a sign of an uncomplicated nature, and Joan played along and learned much in consequence. She and Donald Hazelrigg had been quietly courting for some time; Jeanette expected they would marry, for they were of similar rank and without impediments. But for now, Joan was one of Queen Philippa's ladies, and Donald was serving under the Holland banner.

Joan lowered her voice. 'How goes it with your matter in hand?'

'Slowly,' Jeanette said with a grimace. 'They keep me confined so I barely know what is happening, and my testimony has been ignored. I am only here because Thomas wrote to the Pope and told him I was being held against my will. I have been released, as you see, but now the Archbishop of Canterbury is ailing, and we hear every day of this terrible pestilence that is advancing on us. Avignon has been struck, and it is creeping ever northwards. I fear my case may never be heard, or that I may die, or Thomas may die, God forbid, while we are still in this dreadful limbo.'

'Oh, Jeanette.' Joan's hazel eyes filled with compassion. 'You have always dwelt in my prayers, but I shall mark you especially now – and Thomas. If there is anything else I can do . . .'

Jeanette flicked a glance around to make sure that their conversation was not being overheard, especially by her new sister-in-law of whom she was unsure. 'Perhaps when you are about the court and if you speak to Donald, you might find a way to give Thomas a message he will find comforting or useful. If you do not wish to do so, I understand. I would not ask save that I am closely watched, and they make it impossible for me to speak to him myself. If they suspect anything, they will lock me up and force me to drink poppy syrup.' She made a discreet gesture in the direction of William's mother and grandmother, sitting in the lodges to their right with some other ladies of the court.

Joan's eyes opened wide.

'Yes,' Jeanette said grimly. 'That has been my life for many years.'

'You have my word that I shall do what I can,' Joan said, her lips set in the way they did when she was determined on a matter.

'Thank you.' Jeanette touched her arm in gratitude. 'I will not forget this, I promise you. I know you would never speak of me being in your debt, but I am, and when I am able, I shall repay you, and Donald, ten times over.'

The two teams led by the King and Prince Edward jousted against each other in the lists. The matches were all to prove valour, and once again much of the fighting was for show with moves and moments of drama worked out beforehand to enthral the crowd. There were tricks and feats of skill, near misses and deadly clashes with blows pulled at the last moment. Thomas demonstrated his speed and precision at the quintain, collecting all the rings on his lance, and as always, he and Otto performed a glittering demonstration of fighting skill, their movements a blur, too swift to follow as sword and dagger flashed and challenged, twisted and turned.

Jeanette watched them, her eyes alight, her heart full of love and pride, but trepidation too, given that Thomas had lost the vision in one eye. A single slip could result in serious injury, and their speed was incredible. She dared not show her emotion and had to clench her fists in her lap and remain outwardly calm, knowing she was giving herself away by her very lack of reaction. At least Thomas and William were never pitted against each other, about which she was supremely relieved, and thanked God for the common sense of those organising the bouts.

The contests ended as the light began to fade and the Queen retired from the lists to her chamber to hold a banquet for the ladies, while the King held one for the lords in his own hall. Jeanette had no opportunity to meet with Thomas that night, and impatience gnawed at her, keener than Poppet's teeth on a walnut shell.

In the Queen's chamber the following day, Jeanette gave her statement concerning her marriage to her attorney Master Nicholas Heath, with Joan Bredon and one of the Queen's chaplains as witnesses to her words. Master Heath's clerk, who had taken her original deposition, had been dismissed for accepting bribes, and replaced. A fresh-faced young man with ink-stained fingers and a mop of chestnut hair was now taking notes. Master Heath himself was in late middle age with stiff hips and a cynical, world-weary air, but he listened patiently to everything she told him while the clerk scribbled furiously, his manner in complete contrast to the previous one.

'I shall see what I can do for you,' Master Heath said as he gathered his materials together when they had finished. 'I am sure we can resolve the matter in your favour.'

'Do you truly believe so?'

'Yes, I do. I shall have to go through this again with the other attorneys, and it will be for the Cardinal to decide. However, I have every hope that we shall prevail.'

'When will I hear more?'

'That will depend on the papal court and the state of the hearings. We are due to present ours in September with the depositions from the witnesses and pleas from both sides. I expect to be able to report back by Christmas.'

'And will it be done by Christmas?'

He made a tutting sound. 'I counsel you to patience, my lady. The wheels grind very slowly in Avignon and it will depend on how many protests and challenges we receive from Master John, your husband's attorney, and how we respond to them. Yours is not the only case upon which the Cardinal must give his judgement, and with the disruption of the pestilence . . .' He let the words hang.

'Then when?' she demanded. 'Some time never perhaps?' To her mortification, her eyes filled with tears.

'My lady, I beg you, do not weep.' He signalled to Joan Bredon, who was already on her feet.

'Then give me an answer. Tell me when. I have been waiting for almost eight years! You counsel me to patience. How much more do I need?'

He gave her a compassionate look. 'I cannot say Christmas, because I do not believe it will be then. Let us say before next spring is in full bloom, hopefully by Easter.'

'Easter?' Jeanette cried. 'But that is more than nine months away!'

He opened his hands in apology. 'I wish I could say better than that, but if you begin counting the days now, it is truly not so long. I know it is a burden, and I am sorry. I shall do my best, I promise.' He bowed and rather swiftly left the room with his clerk. The Queen's chaplain followed.

Jeanette wiped her eyes on her sleeve.

'At least he is doing something,' Joan said, 'and at least you have a date.'

'That may never come,' Jeanette said bitterly. 'I want Thomas now, Joan, not at some mark in the future that keeps being moved ever further away.'

'I know, and I wish I could help.'

The door opened again and another lawyer entered – an older man this time, with a pristine white cap and black hat. He had rounded features and hooded, shrewd eyes, the tawny colour of new ale. He bowed to Jeanette and introduced himself as Master Robert Beverley, attorney at law representing Thomas.

'How did matters go with my colleague?' he enquired.

'Well enough, I think,' Jeanette answered, rallying, not wanting to be caught in tears. 'I told him all that I knew, and how matters stood.'

'We will win this case,' he said, his tone matter-of-fact. 'They have little to go on. There are some challenges, naturally, but they will not stand up against our testimonies.'

Jeanette swallowed. 'What challenges?'

'Counter claims concerning the veracity of the evidence of the witnesses. The lady Elizabeth Montagu swears on oath that the marriage was consummated and that there was evidence of your virginity on the sheets the morning after the wedding night.'

'She is lying.' Jeanette's lip curled in disgust. 'The blood on the sheets was planted. Surely you do not believe her above those who were witness to my marriage?'

'Of course I do not,' he said, 'but I am telling you what you need to know. Your mother has confirmed by letter the same story as Lady Montagu, and the Countess of Salisbury.'

'They would all agree with each other,' she said with scorn. 'It is no less than I expect.'

'Indeed,' he said gravely. 'And their word as three ladies of high birth and substance will carry weight in the court. But at the same time, I have a letter in my possession from your mother to the Countess of Salisbury that mentions an awareness of your first marriage and assuring the Countess there will be no impediment. My evidence will show how these ladies have colluded in laying a false trail.'

Jeanette shook her head in contempt. 'What does my supposed husband William Montagu have to say on the matter?'

Beverley rubbed his chin. 'He says he will abide by whatever the court decides and without rancour, but as far as he knew, you were a virgin on your wedding night with him, and he took the women's word for the evidence on the following day, for although he was a man in that way and able to procreate, he was not familiar with the deed as such.'

Jeanette snorted down her nose. 'Nothing happened on our wedding night, and he knows it. If I may speak frankly, I had been familiar with that deed on many occasions with my lawful husband.' She gave him a firm look. 'I am no wanton who speaks out of turn, but I am telling you truthfully how it was – as I told Master Heath, and that first clerk of his who was accepting bribes from the Countess of Salisbury and her mother-in-law.'

'And I thank you for your candour, my lady,' Beverley said, although he looked taken aback, and his neck reddened.

'Master Heath said it might be Christmas-tide before he reported back, or even after.'

'He is probably correct,' Beverley said. 'The meeting will take place at the end of September and the witnesses will be questioned and other matters ascertained. Master John will try to persuade the papal authorities to hear the case in England, and ask why it came before Avignon in the first place. The decision will then go before the Pope. With the sickness that is rife in Avignon and elsewhere, court proceedings have slowed down, and they were never swift at the outset. I am sorry, but that is the way of things. I am afraid that the three ladies opposing you have dug in their heels and will not yield – they have come too far to turn back.'

Jeanette sat up straight. 'So have I, Master Beverley.'

He bowed to her. 'And I shall see it through for you and Master Holland, you have my pledge.' He smiled wryly. 'I know the word of a lawyer may not count for much in some circles, but I have always prided myself on mine.'

Jeanette rose to see him out and felt just a little relieved because she believed in him. 'Thank you,' she said, 'I do trust your word.'

'He seems like a good man,' Joan Bredon said when he had gone. 'Do not worry, you will win.'

'But I do worry,' Jeanette said. 'What if the Pope does pass the case over to the English courts and they do not decide in my favour?'

Joan shook her head. 'The Pope will not hand over that authority, especially at this stage. The Montagu lawyer is grasping at straws.'

The door opened again, and this time Thomas slipped into the room. Jeanette gasped his name, ran to him, flung her arms around him and raised her face to his. They kissed hard and long, and when they drew apart, her lips were tingling.

'I cannot stay, but I had to see you,' he said. 'I am leaving for Avignon again any day. We must be stronger than ever now.'

Jeanette nodded, but thought that she had put so much strength into this already, she did not know how much she had left. Or that a moment would arrive when she would become a burnished column of endurance, without any other purpose except to withstand the storm. Perhaps it was the same for Thomas. What kind of relationship waited for them at the end of all this striving? She had been falsely married to William Montagu for four times longer now than she had known her true husband.

They kissed again, holding each other, rocking. 'I should leave,' he said against her lips, but still he held her, and Jeanette clung to him to feel his body and his touch, trying to make the moment stretch for eternity. 'Stay with the court if you are able. I have spoken to your brother and to Prince Edward. They will do what they can to make sure you are not forced back into confinement.'

The door opened again and they sprang apart, but it was Robert Beverley, who rumbled his throat and gave them a warning look. 'I am not accustomed to standing as a lookout at lover's trysts,' he said. 'Messire Holland, your borrowed time is now looking like a dangerous moment.'

Thomas acknowledged him with a nod. 'Thank you.' He squeezed Jeanette's hands a final time and followed the attorney out, giving her a single glance over his shoulder. Returning it, she felt bereft to the point of pain. Seeing him leave was unbearable. She started forward, but he closed the door, and Joan grasped her arm and pulled her back. Jeanette struggled for a moment and then turned into her friend's arms and wept.

'It is hard,' Joan said, 'I cannot begin to know, but you have friends and good people who will love and support you.'

'Yes,' Jeanette said desolately, 'but they are not Thomas, and I need a respite from staying strong.'

30

Papal Palace at Avignon, September 1348

Thomas stepped forward and faced Cardinal Robert Adhemar and his clerks and officials who had finally gathered to hear the evidence concerning the disputed marriage. The chamber was hazy with smoke from the braziers burning incense and herbs to ward off the miasmas of the great pestilence that held the city and surrounding towns and villages in its grip.

He repeated to the Cardinal the information he had given almost a year and a half ago when here with his mother. 'I married the lady Jeanette, daughter of Prince Edmund of England, Earl of Kent, in good faith and before these people in the April of 1340 before I left to attend the King in England.' He gestured to the bench behind him where the witnesses waited their turn. 'The lady was of an age to consent and did so freely, as Master Heath will attest from the deposition he took from her at the English court. The marriage was consummated – on numerous occasions.' He explained about going on crusade and returning to find that Jeanette had been joined to William Montagu in his absence.

The clerks scratched away, making notes. The smoke from the incense burners caught in Thomas's throat. Behind him, Otto suppressed a harsh cough against his clenched fist. Thomas looked round at him briefly. His brother was sweating, his fair hair lying in dark strands against his scalp. Thomas experienced a frisson of anxiety. The pestilence was rife in the city. Thousands of victims lay rotting in mass graves. Pope Clement himself sat in his chamber between two fumigating fires just like these and allowed no one to approach him closely. Everyone attended church and made confession at least once a day and regular penitential processions chanted through the streets, ringing bells and crying to God for forgiveness, mercy and protection.

Just before he left for Avignon, the English court had been cast into deep mourning by the news of the death of Princess Joan, just fourteen years old. Travelling to her marriage in Castile, she had contracted the pestilence during a stop in Bordeaux. And then the new baby, William, whose birth had been celebrated at the Windsor tourney, had also died – not of pestilence, but of a fever. Perhaps it was indeed the end of days, as many were saying.

He was worried for Jeanette, and his family. A merchant had arrived in Avignon two days ago and told them that the pestilence was ravaging London, and no matter how much people prayed and were penitent, the relentless spread continued unchecked.

Having given his evidence, Thomas sat down on the bench beside Otto. The latter rose to take his turn, and swayed as he adjusted his belt and straightened his tunic. He approached the Cardinal and the clerks and cleared his throat again with another cough. Amid wafts of eye-stinging incense smoke, he gave the papal committee his statement in a hoarse and gravelly voice. 'In all my life I have never been more certain of a fact – that my dearest brother Thomas Holland was married in the presence of all these witnesses at the Abbey of Saint Bavo. I can vouch for everyone here. I know that the marriage was consummated, for my brother told me so, and I trust his word. He would not lie to me, and I do solemnly give my oath to my statement.'

Master John, the Montagus' attorney, raised his brow. 'You may trust your brother's word, but if you were not present in the room, then you cannot vouchsafe that part of the proceedings. All you can say is that you were present at a marriage that was conducted by a friar who is now "unfortunately" deceased.'

Otto flushed. 'I stand by my word. Master Heath will confirm what I say through the sworn testimony of the lady herself.' He turned to look at Jeanette's attorney, and suppressed a bout of coughing.

Master Heath shuffled his documents. 'Indeed, the lady has made such a statement. She declares that the marriage was consummated on several occasions and that she was coerced into the match with William, Lord Montagu.' Master Heath submitted the document. 'I spoke to her in person and she confirmed all this to me in person.'

The Cardinal passed the documentation to a clerk and summoned the next witness, Henry de la Haye.

Otto returned to his seat on the bench and slumped, head down, lips pressed together. When Thomas laid a hand on his forearm in concern, Otto waved his hand in a gesture to say he was all right, but clearly he was struggling.

Henry de la Haye gave his witness statement, then John de la Salle, and then lastly Hawise stepped forward, her chin jutting and her face pale.

'I have attended my lady for many years,' she said. 'I served her in Flanders when she was a lady in Queen Philippa's chamber, and I was present at many of the meetings between herself and Messire Holland before they were married. I witnessed that marriage; indeed I was married myself that day. I attended my lady on occasions when she went to her husband, Messire Holland, and I assisted her when she had need. I state clearly that Messire Holland was her carnal husband and a great wrong has been done by forcing her into a marriage that was beyond her powers to refuse.'

Thomas looked at Hawise with pride and gratitude and swallowed emotion at her staunchness in his and Jeanette's defence.

William's attorney, Master John, folded his hands around his cloak edges. 'I am sure these witnesses all think they know what happened,' he said, 'but we have the sworn testimony of no less than the Lady Elizabeth Montagu – the former Earl of Salisbury's mother – the Countess of Salisbury, and indeed the lady's own mother, the Dowager Countess of Kent, that the bride was a virgin when she married William Montagu. All of these good ladies attest that they witnessed the sight of her virginal blood on the sheet and upon the bride's thighs on the morning after the consummation of the marriage to William Montagu her husband. I would welcome the opportunity to conduct further investigation into this matter, for clearly there are two versions of events very much at odds with each other.'

Thomas stood up again, frustration burning in his chest. 'Then clearly one is wrong,' he said, 'and I, and these people here, know which one. Please excuse me, Your Eminence, with your leave, when I married my wife she was carrying my child, and Mistress Hawise will confirm that I tell no lie.'

'Indeed, it is true,' Hawise said. 'My lady miscarried the

child after the Countess of Salisbury gave her certain herbs in a tisane. The event was covered up, but that makes it no less real.'

Master John narrowed his eyes. 'None of this is reported here.' He turned to Jeanette's attorney. 'Master Heath?'

The latter shook his head. 'I would have to say that the lady made no mention of this when I spoke to her.'

'Then we do not know whether it is the truth, or yet more fabrication,' Master John said forcefully. 'Not until we question the lady herself.'

Cardinal Adhemar surveyed the gathering with weary exasperation and clasped his hands on the table. 'This is a tangled matter indeed. I have listened to the claims and counter claims and must weigh them carefully. I cannot give you a judgement today, for this matter requires further investigation and clearer documentation. I am not satisfied with either testimony and I wish to know the true circumstances without hearsay. I will not require the witnesses again, but I do require further full depositions from all attorneys by Lent of next year. This is too important an issue for mistakes to be made and I want to be satisfied on all counts.'

Thomas pressed his lips together, striving to remain stoical and steady as the Cardinal swept from the room followed by his assistants and scribes. In reality he wanted to upend tables and smash things.

'It was less than I had hoped for, but not a complete disaster,' Robert Beverley said, joining him. 'I think the Cardinal favours our case, but since your wife is the King's cousin and the opposition is the Earl of Salisbury, the judgement must be sound and without room for repercussion.'

Thomas exhaled with irritated anger.

'I understand your ire, my lord,' Beverley said, 'but a sound judgement now without room for error will set matters in stone. Should Lord Montagu choose to wed again, he will need to show documentation to prove that he was never married to the lady. The matter has great implications for inheritance.'

'I have no doubt that it does,' Thomas growled, 'but I do not see why it should take so many more months to sort out.'

He turned at a sudden commotion behind him and saw Otto dash from the chamber, and then an instant later came the sound of heavy retching. Thomas left his attorney and hurried outside to his brother, who was doubled over.

Thomas touched Otto's brow. 'Dear God, your skin is burning,' he said. 'We should get you back to our lodgings.'

'I am all right,' Otto wheezed. 'There is nothing wrong with me – it's all that damned smoke in there!'

'Mayhap, but we should do as I say. There is nothing here for us at the moment.'

Thomas took his arm, and looking at the others of their party, saw the same fear in their eyes that he felt within himself.

Once at their lodging, Thomas laid Otto down on his pallet. His brother's teeth were chattering as though he was frozen to the marrow, but his body was scorching to the touch. Thomas stripped him to his shirt and braies while Hawise fetched a bowl of tepid water and a cloth to wipe him down.

Their landlord was unhappy when he heard that one of his lodgers was sick, and Thomas had to pay an increased rent in order to stay, and eventually add the persuasion of his sword point to the exchange.

Food was left outside the door and they were abandoned to their own devices. Otto turned his head away from the bread and cheese that Thomas tried to feed him, but managed to swallow some water.

'I should make my will,' he croaked. 'My throat feels as though a butcher's been using it to strop his knives.'

'Do not talk like that,' Thomas said furiously. 'And do not think I shall be a tender nursemaid either. I won't let you go, even as you refused me that option in Prussia.'

Abruptly, he rose from the bedside and began pacing the room, too full of restless energy to sit still. Otto had been at his side all of his life. His earliest memories were of playing with him, tumbling like puppies in their mother's chamber. Of learning together, competing with each other, but always side by side, with him the protective older brother, and Otto bound in loyalty. How much he had taken Otto for granted. To think of losing him was unbearable.

Hawise wiped Otto's brow and brought him a soothing tisane. He struggled to a sitting position and took a few sips, even though it was obvious that swallowing was excruciating.

'This will help you rest and sleep,' she murmured. 'My lady used to drink this to ease her if she had an ague.'

Otto forced another swallow of the tisane. 'It is in God's hands,' he croaked.

'Yes, it is, but we should help Him too,' she said. She took the cup from him and straightened the sheet. 'Rest now.'

His lids drooped, and within moments he had fallen into a heavy sleep, his breathing stertorous.

'You should sleep too,' Hawise said to Thomas.

He shook his head. 'No, I will watch him as he watched over me. He is my responsibility.'

'As you wish,' she said, 'but let others relieve you if you have need.'

'You and John,' he said, his voice thick with emotion, 'you are part of my foundation and Jeanette's. I swear I shall reward you if ever I am able.'

'Let there be no talk of that now,' she whispered. 'We know and understand.'

Thomas settled himself to watch over Otto, observing each breath, each twitch and groan. He wiped his brow and packed up the pillows behind him when Otto's throat rattled in his sleep like a bag of rusty nails. As the hours passed in agonising slowness, Otto woke occasionally to cough and retch. Hawise frequently came to check on him, and in between the racking spasms gave him more sips of tisane.

'I'm not dead yet,' Otto managed to rasp at Thomas towards morning. 'You can stop looking at me as though I'm a corpse – but Christ, my throat. Someone's lined it with iron filings!' He drank again, spluttered, and drank some more.

'Take off your shirt,' Thomas commanded.

'What?'

'Take off your shirt. I want to see if you have the marks of the pestilence.'

Otto shuddered. 'No,' he said. 'I'm finished if there are.'

'Christ, man, come on, do it.'

Setting his jaw, his face filled with fear, Otto struggled to remove the sweat-soaked garment, but was too exhausted, and Thomas had to tug it over his head.

Hawise came to the bedside and examined him thoroughly. 'Thank the Holy Virgin, I can see no marks on you,' she said.

'Are you sure?' Otto anxiously peered into a hair-tufted armpit.

'Yes, but you are burning and you are very sick.' She turned to Thomas. 'Keep cooling him with that cloth, while I make a herbal plaster for his chest.'

Thomas grimaced when she returned shortly with a pungent herbal mixture involving a lot of mustard to deal with his racking cough, which she spread on a bandage and wrapped around his chest.

'I know,' she said as Otto added a retch to his coughing, 'I am sorry, but it will draw out the evil humours.' She added a strip of parchment to the plaster on which was written a prayer to St Joseph to intercede and restore Otto to full health. 'See if you can go back to sleep,' she said. 'I will renew the plaster in a little while.'

Otto closed his eyes, and Thomas resumed his vigil, his own good eye burning with fatigue, but not for a moment would he close it. He desperately needed his brother to live; to continue to be his rock, his stalwart, his companion. It couldn't end here like this. When they fought together, they were in complete synchronicity, and he could not imagine doing that dance with a death-shadow at his side when there should be a whole man.

As dawn broke, Thomas stood up to stretch his cramped muscles. His bladder was twinging and he badly needed a piss, but was reluctant to leave Otto even for a moment. Perhaps they could find a physician to tend him, although given the reaction of their landlord, and the state of the city itself, it would take a miracle. All of those educated in treatment and healing of the sick had either already died from the pestilence or were too frightened of contracting it to come to the bedside of a foreigner.

He pinched the bridge of his nose between forefinger and thumb, and when he looked up again, discovered that Otto was looking at him.

'Brother,' Otto said, and was then seized by another heavy coughing fit. Thomas rushed to prop him up on the pillows and had the tisane ready at his lips. Hawise joined them, bleary with sleep, a shawl around her shoulders.

'No buboes,' Thomas said, having checked again, 'and I fancy he is not as hot as he was before.'

Hawise tested Otto's forehead against the back of her hand. 'I think you might be right, thank God.'

Otto slept again, and Hawise took over the watch from Thomas who went to attend to his bursting bladder and then to lie down wrapped in his cloak. He felt as if his vision was filled with sawdust, and his own throat was gritty and sore, the more so when he wept with delayed reaction and relief, choking as he tried to suppress his sobs.

Over the next few days, Otto made a slow recovery and managed to leave his bed and sit by the fire, though still riven by a hacking cough. By this time, Thomas and Henry de la Haye were both suffering from the same malaise. Hawise and John de la Salle were less badly affected and cared for everyone else, although Otto seemed to have had the worst of it.

No one developed the dreaded buboes of the great pestilence, but the malaise still proved to be debilitating, and although everyone gradually recovered, they were left with the legacy of a gravelly cough and weak exhaustion. It was several weeks before they were well enough to face the return journey to England. Seeing the daily procession of shrouded corpses through the streets as they left Avignon, Thomas knew how fortunate they were to be among the living – for now – and gave great thanks to God, while wondering just what they might find on their return.

31

Royal Manor of Otford, Kent, January 1349

Jeanette admired the silver cup Edward had just presented to her as a New Year's gift. Her name, 'Jeanette', was engraved upon it, and beneath it a little dog in the shape of Nosewyse in hot pursuit of a rabbit. He had bestowed fine New Year's gifts on others too, including a silky grey palfrey for his mother, and cups and gems for his siblings and friends, but his thoughtfulness to herself melted her heart.

'For my favourite cousin,' he said, his eyes bright with pleasure, and he kissed her on the lips. It was an easy thing, not beyond friendship, and made her feel happy and warm and loved – emotions that were sparse in her life.

'Thank you, sire, I shall drink from it every day and think of you,' she said.

'And I shall think of you drinking from it, and be glad,' he replied, and moved on to present a pair of embroidered gloves to William, sitting beside her. William received them with gratitude, and showed them to her.

'They are very fine,' she said with polite courtesy. 'They will suit you well, my lord.'

They had reached an understanding. In public they fulfilled the roles expected of them as the Earl-apparent of Salisbury and his wife, performing with dignity, and distance. The former heat and violence had departed their relationship, leaving impersonal strangers trapped in a marriage neither of them desired. But William refused to actively defy his mother and grandmother, and so they waited. If it came to the worst and the Pope rejected Thomas's petition, this, Jeanette knew, was the best they would ever have of their union.

Jeanette had remained at court since the summer in the Queen's household, mostly at Langley with the royal nursery. For the winter feast, the court had moved to Otford, everyone dwelling in fear of the great pestilence and wondering where it would strike, and if they were next.

The King had been making plans to renew his campaign against the French, but the truce had been extended because of the devastation wrought by the pestilence. So many had lost their lives. Fields were going unharvested and untilled. New graveyards and cemeteries were being opened to accommodate the dead, often in mass graves. Along with Princess Joan and the baby William, the Archbishop of Canterbury had succumbed to his years, and his successor had died of the pestilence before he could assume office so they had no senior ecclesiastical leader in England. Sometimes Jeanette felt as though they were sailing off the edge of the world in a rudderless ship.

She had heard briefly from Thomas, who had been serving in Calais with the King's troops but had sent her a message via her brother, that all was progressing well, and she should be hearing from Master Heath on a few final matters and that Master Beverley might want to speak with her again to clarify a few minor details. That had been in late autumn, and she had heard nothing since. Thomas and Otto had then been sent home to their family's estates, and the court was in a diminished state because of the pestilence. For all, it was a matter of waiting out the sickness and hoping that God would be merciful.

Master Heath finally arrived at Otford to talk to Jeanette. He looked worn and tired, his features drawn, but he was stoical as he sat down with her to go over her testimony again. Once more, a little impatiently, she gave him her evidence, and swore to its truth.

Master Heath pursed his lips and consulted his notes. 'It emerged at the court hearing that you had been with child when you wed Messire Holland, yet you said nothing of this to me. Is this true?'

An icy burn shivered her spine and she gripped the edge of the table, feeling dizzy. Master Heath looked round to summon assistance.

'No,' she said quickly, 'I am all right. It is a memory I have tried and tried to forget. I did indeed believe myself to be with child and it was one of the reasons for our marriage. The Countess of Salisbury gave me a herbal tisane to balance my humours, and it brought on my flux. The Countess wished to avoid a scandal, for she was my guardian in lieu of my mother, and she wanted me for her own son because of my royal connections and dowry. She and my mother turned rumours of Thomas's death on crusade into truth to further force me into marriage with William Montagu. If I must, I shall travel to Avignon myself and state all this in person.'

The clerk was staring, pen poised. Master Heath nodded to him. 'Write this down,' he said.

Jeanette stared at her tightly clenched fists, her eyes prickling.

'I think you will win your case,' Master Heath said. 'The opposition is standing on quicksand, and the evidence for the marriage being valid has the greater veracity in the scales. I was not certain at the outset, but now I am convinced.'

'Neither I nor my true husband would have put ourselves through all of this danger and unpleasantness had we not been truly wed,' Jeanette replied. 'My husband could easily have found a new bride with the ransoms he gained in battle had he wished, and even if I am the King's cousin, I would not be worth the fight he has had to sustain to come this far. For my part, I could have dwelt in power and contentment as the future Countess of Salisbury, and been feted at court, instead of being locked in my chamber for months on end.' Her voice grew fierce with determination. 'Every day I pray to God to finish this soon, and grant that Thomas and I may be together. We shall never stop fighting until justice is done – and I hope that is true for our lawyers also.'

'Of course, my lady,' Master Heath assured her. 'You are courageous, and you deserve that courage in your legal representation.'

He gathered his materials together and was bowing to leave with his scribe when Katerine walked in. Jeanette recoiled. She wondered if the Dowager Countess had been listening at the door. Master Heath bowed urbanely. Katerine inclined her head.

'Stay a little while, Master Heath,' she said. 'I have some new sweet wine of Cyprus you would enjoy.' She firmly took his arm and ushered him to sit down again. 'I know you are here to take my daughter-in-law's deposition, and I will not interfere with that, but I thought you might have news of the world beyond the court. Is it truly as bad in France as we hear?'

He had no choice but to accept her hospitality, although his body was stiff and self-contained.

'My lady, I fear so,' he replied. 'Many people have been struck in every part of the land through which I have travelled, and all manner of society in the same way as here.'

'Has the work in Avignon been affected too?'

'It is as anywhere else, my lady,' he answered cautiously, 'but even so it continues – as must we all continue.'

She looked thoughtful, and Jeanette wondered what she was brewing. The wine arrived, presented in a rock crystal flagon that displayed the golden-tawny liquid to its best effect.

'You are a stout-hearted Englishman, Master Heath,' Katerine said as her steward presented him with a decorated glass goblet. 'Indeed, a learned attorney of many years' standing.'

'I do my best, my lady, and to represent my clients to my utmost ability.'

He took a swallow of wine. Katerine tasted hers daintily.

'I am sure you do – but do you not find your long journeys in such difficult times worrying and wearisome? Do you not think it would be better if the hearings were held in an English ecclesiastical court?'

Jeanette sat bolt upright. So that's what she was about! Trying to persuade the attorneys to move the case to England where she could exert her influence and sway the outcome. She cast a glare at Katerine, who ignored her.

'I do not know about that, madam,' Master Heath said. 'The papal court has dealt with the case thus far, and Cardinal Adhemar is familiar with the material. Certainly, the journeying can be wearisome, but I am accustomed to long days of travel, for it has ever been thus. Besides, the papal court, even if it moves slowly, is better than the English one in these matters since it delivers the highest judgements that cannot be disputed. The Pope is God's representative on earth and there is no higher authority, which has to be a sound reason in a case such as this.'

Jeanette smiled with satisfaction at his reply, but then felt a frisson of unease, for Katerine too was smiling. 'The papal court is better? That is your opinion, sir?'

Master Heath inclined his head. 'I would say so, madam, in my experience, and I have sat on many benches and examined many cases. I consider it will be fruitless to move the case to England and would do more harm than good.'

'Well, that is a considered opinion, sir, and I thank you for it. You have been very helpful.'

He gave her a slightly puzzled look, and having finished his drink, rose to take his leave. 'I do not know in what way, madam, but I am glad to have been of service.' He bowed to Jeanette. 'Thank you, my lady, and I hope to have news for you very soon. I pray God to keep you safe.'

'And you, sir,' Jeanette replied, feeling unsettled, for she was certain that Katerine was scheming to no good intent. She looked like the cat that had stolen the cream from the dairy.

32

Manor of Broughton, Northamptonshire, March 1349

At his manor of Broughton, Thomas had spent the morning going over the accounts and discussing the sowing of the fields and other matters of agriculture with his steward. Thus far the village had avoided the pestilence, but he was on constant guard, for this might be the still before the storm. In places, entire communities had been wiped out. Cities had been devastated, with no one to attend the dying, or to say prayers for the dead, and in some cases even to bury them. People were terrified and helpless, for there was no outrunning the disease, and despite fervent prayers and penances, God appeared not to be listening.

He had stayed away from the court; indeed, had no reason to be there. France and England were at truce as they dealt with the pestilence. He had been to Calais a few times on the King's business, but nothing more, and Parliament had been suspended until Easter.

Leaving the accounts, he went to saddle his palfrey, intending to ride him out to check the progress of the ploughing. In the stables, he found his archer Samson spending time with his young colt, now nine months old, Thomas's gift to him as promised during their campaign in France. Samson had named the colt Cygnet, for although the foal was a warm, bright chestnut, his dam was a white brood mare named Swan. When not practising at the archery targets, or tending his plot of land, Samson was usually to be found at the manor stables visiting the colt, bringing him titbits and lavishing him with attention.

'How's he doing?' Thomas enquired.

'Grand indeed, my lord,' Samson replied, his wide grin exposing a missing front tooth. 'He knows his name, and my special whistle, don't you, lad?'

The youngster butted him. He had a thin white blaze running from his forelock to the tip of his nose and two short white socks on his hind legs.

'You have a good one there.'

'Aye, my lord, and thank you.'

Otto arrived and joined him for the ride. Thomas eyed him critically. They had been training less than they should – there had been no incentive in the winter without tourneys to attend. Otto was developing jowls and a soft pouch to his gut, and Thomas knew they needed to get back in the saddle and to their weapon play. While both men had been recuperating from the malaise that had struck them down in Avignon, and Otto especially since he had been hit the hardest, it was time to return to business.

Thomas's spirited liver-chestnut palfrey had belonged to John de Warenne. The Earl had died the previous year, leaving several horses in his stable to Thomas and his family. Two Spanish mares now ran with the Holland stud herd on the main estate. His sister Isabel had returned to their mother following John's death. The Earl had left her well provided for in his will with money, robes and a casket of jewels, but Thomas knew they were no compensation for losing John himself, and Isabel was in deep mourning.

Master Beverley had set out for Avignon again for the next sitting of the council. Thomas had stayed behind to tend his manor and was busy making it his home, rather than a distant source of income. A place fit for him and a princess to be alone for a while and make up for lost time. Pray God that soon he would be able to bring her here.

Riding with Otto, he looked out over the ribbed black soil and the people going methodically about their work. It wouldn't be long before it was time for sowing seed. 'We are fortunate,' he said. 'Here we still have people to work the fields; we still have our priest and the space to bury our dead. No one has perished of the great sickness. In London they do not even have enough linen for shrouds and they are tipping people into the graves, rich man and pauper alike, with no one to say words over them, poor souls.'

'Perhaps we are looking at the end of mankind,' Otto said. 'Perhaps the birds of the air and the beasts of the fields will inherit the earth. Perhaps God's wrath is such that there will be no people.'

It was a disturbing thought, and Thomas decided they definitely needed to take themselves in hand and begin training.

After their ride, Thomas returned to the accounts he had abandoned for fresh air, but still did not feel like tackling them. Going to the hawk perch near the window, he took Empress on his wrist and fed her a few gobbets of raw meat from his cupped fist. The action made him think of Jeanette and their time in Flanders, and he wished he could have those moments again for the first time.

Otto arrived with a jug of wine to share, and Thomas

returned Empress to her perch. The two brothers were standing side by side when John of Kent's messenger dismounted in the courtyard.

Thomas's chest tightened with anxiety. With the pestilence rife, the expectation was that anyone bearing letters might be the harbinger of terrible news.

De la Salle brought the messenger to Thomas's chamber and the man knelt before Thomas and produced a small packet from his belt pouch. Thomas broke the seal, opened the letter, and swiftly read the lines.

'I do not believe this,' he said grimly. 'How can this be?'

'What is it?' Otto asked.

His heart in his boots, Thomas handed him the letter. 'Master Heath has been arrested and thrown into prison for speaking against the King and the King's justice. He is no longer representing Jeanette and will be replaced by another attorney.' He clenched his fist and struck the wall. 'I do not believe this. Christ! I met Master Heath in Avignon and I seriously doubt he would have said such things.'

Otto shook his head in bafflement.

'I suspect someone has been interfering, and since it is by order of the King, a seeker for answers would not have to look very far.' Thomas dismissed the messenger and sat down heavily on the window bench. 'They won't win,' he said grimly. 'When I dig in for a fight, it is to the death – I care not who my enemy is. I have gone too far and too deep to lose it all now.'

On an early April morning, Jeanette arrived at the royal hunting palace of Woodstock in the Montagu travelling wain. The harnessed horses drew to a halt and she stepped from the cart with relief. The journey from Oxford had been relatively short – only a few hours – but it was still too long a time to be confined at close quarters with Katerine. They had been visiting the priory of St Frideswide, founded by Lady Elizabeth, who was lauded there at least for her pious works. If only they knew, Jeanette thought.

They had spent three days at the priory. The pestilence had been gaining ground in Oxford and the city had been cloaked in a vile miasma of smoke and stench. Jeanette had been thankful to leave and return to Woodstock's pale walls and tranquil, rustic surroundings. Elizabeth had chosen to remain at the priory rather than make the journey, bedevilled as she was by her aching hips and increasing infirmity. King Edward was at Langley Palace with Philippa and their family, but the wider court and hangers-on were domiciled here at Woodstock.

Instead of following the others inside, Jeanette clipped a leash to Nosewyse's collar and slipped away, desperate for a moment to herself after the confines of the cart. She drew her skirts through her belt in the style of a farmer's wife so they would not obstruct her and strode out with the dog, taking pleasure in the easy strength of her young body. Nosewyse ran ahead, chasing scents along the woodland paths. They followed the line of a stream and she inhaled the pungent aroma of wild garlic from the early white ransom blooms. The gardeners had been less diligent since the pestilence and many areas had become overgrown and weedy. Not caring that she would be scolded on her return, Jeanette sped along the muddy trail after her dog.

She had heard nothing from Thomas, who was not at court because the King did not require his services during a truce. She prayed every day for his safety. Master Heath's arrest had shocked her deeply – all Katerine's doing, she knew, and stemming from that conversation where she had trapped Master Heath into speaking the words that had brought him down. In the last few months, Jeanette had run the gamut of every emotion from despair, to hope, and back to despair. It was like constantly going up and down a set of stairs. Reach the top, retreat to the bottom, then begin climbing again. Somewhere along the way she had realised, with relief, that she did not need to be in constant motion, but could wait in the middle and be stronger and less exhausted. These days she no longer railed against Katerine and Elizabeth, but showed them her indifference, and that gave her power. The same with William, although he too had reached a similar settlement. His resolve to do nothing had changed from an aimless drift to a point of anchor.

The stream eventually led to another garden with a pool and a spring. Nosewyse stopped to drink, lapping with his swift, pink tongue, and she crouched beside him and scooped the clear, fresh spring water into her mouth. Supposedly a king, hundreds of years ago, had housed his mistress here and this garden and well were dedicated to her. Her name had been Rosamund and she had died while still a young woman and had been buried at the nunnery at Godstow. Jeanette imagined her sitting by this spring trailing her fingers in the water, perhaps with a dog like Nosewyse for company. She made a wish to the lady of the well, asking her blessing to keep Thomas safe, and to bring them together, and promised to light a candle next time she was in church.

'Where have you been?' Katerine demanded when Jeanette returned. 'You look as if you've been walking through hedgerows.'

Jeanette looked down at her damp, muddy skirts. 'I nearly have,' she replied with a smile. 'My legs were cramped and I had to stretch them after the journey, and Nosewyse needed to walk. You wouldn't want him to make a mess in the chamber, would you?'

'Well, change your gown, you look like a hoyden.' Two deep vertical frown lines sat between Katerine's eyebrows, and a light sheen of sweat gleamed on her skin.

'Certainly not the sort of wife you would want for your son,' Jeanette said pertly, and went to her bed space where her garments hung over a clothing pole.

The maids helped her to change into a fresh gown of apple-green silk trimmed with fur and re-dressed her hair, tucking it inside her wimple.

Servants brought food to the chamber, and the women dined there rather than go to the hall. Katerine picked at her food, eating a few flakes of herbed salmon and then pushing her dish aside. Jeanette fed small morsels to Nosewyse, who plucked them delicately from her hand.

Katerine retired to her bed space at the back of the room but Jeanette was not ready to sleep and sat by the open window, watching the stars, while Nosewyse curled up on her coverlet. She remembered the times with Thomas in Ghent. Sneaking out of the ladies' chamber to join him and the other knights, and rolling dice in the tavern. She thought of spring evenings when she was still innocent with the world before her at sunrise, and her eyes stung with tears. Where was that future now?

Eventually, with a sigh, she summoned her maid to undress her to her shift and plait her hair into a soft braid, then, holding the little book of psalms in her hand, she knelt at her bedside and said her prayers, asking God to watch over Thomas and Otto, and everyone she cared for. And then she lay down to sleep with the book still in her hand, and Nosewyse curled at her feet in an imperfect circle.

In the middle of the night, she awoke to the sound of Nosewyse softly growling, and low moans from the direction of Katerine's bed. It was still dark, but a glimmer in the sky hinted at dawn.

Jeanette pushed aside her covers and went to Katerine, to find her sitting up, drinking from a cup, with her maid in attendance.

'Go back to bed,' Katerine said sharply when she saw her.

'I thought something was wrong.'

'Nothing is wrong, go away.'

Jeanette did as Katerine bade her, but being wide awake by now, she slipped her feet into her shoes, pulled a loose gown over her chemise, topped it with her cloak, and left the chamber, saying she was taking Nosewyse to relieve his bladder.

Outside, the dawn was breaking in a glorious wash of egg-yolk gold. She inhaled the sweet air and listened to the twitter of birdsong and the cries of the roosters on the dung heaps. The air smelled enticingly of spring and growing things. She took Nosewyse on a circuit of the smaller garden close to their lodgings. The dew soaked through her shoes and darkened the hem of her gown but she did not mind; indeed, she enjoyed the invigorating sensation of the sparkling cold against her skin.

From the gardens, she walked to the kitchens and purloined a small loaf from a scullion to whom she sometimes talked, much to the disapproval of Katerine and Elizabeth, who considered that fraternising with common people would bring about the ruin of the already precarious world order.

By the time she and Nosewyse returned to the ladies' chamber, replete and scattered with crumbs, it was full daylight. This time no one asked where she had been. One of Woodstock's physicians was leaning over Katerine, and her chaplain stood nearby, looking perturbed, running his prayer beads through his fingers.

'What is happening?' Jeanette asked.

'The Countess has a fever and a headache, my lady,' a maid said, her face pallid with fear.

Watching Katerine toss and moan, Jeanette felt queasy, and

the bread she had just eaten sat uneasily in her stomach. Bruise-like swellings were developing under Katerine's chin, and Jeanette sensed the fear in the room, tangible as a heavy cloak. This terrible thing feeding on Katerine might turn on her next, but no matter the loathing she had for her mother-in-law, she could not abandon her.

Without Katerine, she was the senior lady in the household, and after a hesitation she turned and addressed the head chamber squire. 'Rob, fetch a scribe and find a messenger to ride to Langley. The lord William must know of this immediately. And send another to the lady Elizabeth,' she added, although she did not relish the thought of the old woman coming to Woodstock. 'Langley first, since it is further.'

The squire departed, his gaze wide with shock, and Jeanette turned back to the sickbed.

As the spring day strengthened into full sunshine Katerine's condition deteriorated. Her fever brought on convulsions, and in between them she muttered in semi-delirium through cracked, dry lips. Jeanette had dreamed of gloating, but looking at this woman who was rapidly approaching death's door, she was indifferent beyond a touch of pity.

Katerine's eyelids fluttered open and she focused on Jeanette, suddenly lucid. 'Well,' she croaked, 'all you need do now to win is to survive me.'

'What kind of victory is that?' Jeanette took the cloth, infused with rose water, wrung it out, and laid it on Katerine's brow. 'I will never get back the years that you and others have stolen from me. I shall be glad you are gone, but I shall not dance on your grave. Let God be your judge.'

Katerine stared at her with glazed eyes and licked her lips.

'I shall not forget you,' Jeanette said. 'You have shown me

what I hope never to become in the time that remains to me, and I am grateful. I do not expect you to ask me for forgiveness, nor do I ask any in my turn from you. But I advise you to ask it of your son before it is too late.'

By the following evening, the swollen lumps in Katerine's throat had been joined by others in her armpits and groin. The tips of her fingers and toes had blackened and she had begun to spit blood. The priest had heard her confession and the household had gathered around the bed to wait and to pray.

William arrived at dawn, having ridden by torchlight from Langley as soon as he received the news. He was flushed, sweating, grimy, and stank of horse as he burst into his mother's chamber. Seeing the grief in his expression and the disbelief, Jeanette experienced an uncomfortable wave of compassion.

'Mama.' He shouldered his way to the bedside and, kneeling, took her blotched hand in his. 'Mama, I am here.'

She turned her head towards him, but when she tried to speak, blood trickled from her mouth.

'Do not go, Mama, do not go. We need you here.'

Jeanette swallowed, feeling desperately sorry for him.

'My boy,' Katerine croaked. 'I wanted so much for you . . . everything has been for you. Promise me . . . promise me you will abide by . . .' She fought for breath, and fresh blood gushed over the pillows.

'I promise,' William said. 'Mama, whatever it is, I swear on my soul.'

Katerine shuddered and convulsed again, and ceased to breathe. The priest placed a cross between her hands while someone hastily opened the shutters on the pearly morning light to let her soul fly free.

William stumbled to his feet, tears streaming down his face, and Jeanette's own throat tightened to see his grief. She gently touched his arm. 'William, I am so sorry.'

He cuffed his eyes and pushed her off. 'No, you are not,' he answered bitterly, and roughly pushed past her and out of the door. But once outside, he stopped and put his face in his hands, his shoulders shaking.

Jeanette ordered two attendants to bring a bowl of warm water and some food to the empty chamber next door. Also, to set up a bed there with fresh sheets. Then she went to him. 'Come,' she said. 'You rode hard to get here in time. Let me find you some clean raiment and food.'

'Why should it matter to you?' he spat. 'You have never cared before.'

'I have grown up,' she said. 'I shall continue to fight against this sham of a marriage tooth and nail, but it is my Christian duty to offer you clean clothes and food, and to say I am sorry.'

'I do not want your pity,' he said fiercely. 'I do not want you to look at me as though I am a wounded animal you want to put out of its misery.'

She turned away to compose herself and think of a reply, for that was exactly how she thought of him.

The maids arrived with a brass bowl of steaming water, soap of Castile, and a towel. Jeanette went to rummage in a clothing coffer to find robes that would fit him, and found a soft velvet tunic that had been his father's. Katerine's death had cut him adrift. He would pick up the threads again because he had to, but he was also going to lose the case, and that meant his mother, his wife, his future would all be gone. His grandmother had been a looming presence with Katerine alive, but at one stroke she had become a powerless old lady – as if all her teeth had been pulled out at once.

'You need to rest,' she said. 'When you have slept, we shall do what must be done.'

'I cannot sleep,' he said. 'What about the vigil?'

'Rest for a couple of hours while your mother is prepared for her journey. I will see that the baggage is packed, and I will wake you.'

He swallowed and, relinquishing control to her, lay down on the bed.

Katerine lay in Woodstock's chapel through the day and overnight while Jeanette made arrangements to return the body to Bisham Abbey to be buried beside her husband. She had woken William as she had promised so that he could escort his mother's body to the chapel. She ordered the stained sick-room sheets to be taken and burned, and the floor rushes too. The shutters were to be left open to allow the miasmas to dissipate, and she had had fresh candles lit in the chamber and prayers said. And then she joined William in his vigil and knelt with him until the dawn rose. She had barely slept herself for two days but was too restless, and it didn't matter. Time enough later for sleeping.

Leaving William again, she took Katerine's keys and went to sort out the strongbox and the coffers to ready them for the travelling carts. She did not know their contents, for Katerine had always kept the keys about her person. The two large iron-bound chests nested smaller boxes inside, and several drawstring bags were lumpy with coins and jewels. One chest held clothing, and among the robes, veils and hair pieces, Jeanette recognised one of the King's blue garters with its golden buckles and daisy studs.

She laid Katerine's cloak in the chest. One of the smaller coffers yielded several more pouches of coins, and a box of documents. There were receipts and recipes for herbal remedies and nostrums, some of which she recognised as having been given to herself, and she grimaced, feeling nauseated. These she took and cast down the latrine shaft. Several letters tied together with a piece of ribbon bore her own mother's personal seal, and she caught her breath. She had no time to read them now, but feared they would disappear if Elizabeth or William got hold of them, so concealed them in her own jewel casket beneath the wax casings holding her rings.

By late morning the cavalcade was ready to begin the journey to Bisham. Lady Elizabeth was travelling straight from Oxford to meet them there for the burial. Jeanette was preparing to climb into the travelling cart and William was already mounted on his palfrey when, with a fanfare of horns and trumpets, the King arrived. William instantly leaped down off his horse and bent his knee. Jeanette dropped in a deep curtsey.

Edward gazed at the cortege and the bier on the cart with its pall of red and gold silk draped over the shrouded coffin and tucked around the sides. The courtyard fell silent beyond the tread and snort of the horses and the banners flapping on their poles.

The King approached the bier, removed his cap and bowed his head. 'God have mercy,' he said, and his eyes were wet. He turned to William, bade him rise, and embraced him. 'Your mother was a great lady and will be long remembered with affection and respect by all. I shall have masses said for her in Windsor when the Garter Order gathers, and I will expect you to be there.'

'Yes, sire,' William said huskily, and swallowed.

Edward gave his shoulder a paternal squeeze. 'God grant you a safe journey,' he said, and turning to Jeanette, raised her to her feet. 'I do not know what the future holds for you, cousin,' he told her, and his mouth twisted wryly. 'Even the will of kings is powerless against the will of God. I wish you safe journey to Bisham and I hope you will honour the Countess as befits your rank and hers.'

Jeanette heard the undercurrent of warning in his tone. 'I shall indeed, sire,' she said. 'Whatever differences we had, I shall support the Earl of Salisbury in burying the Countess with honour, and I shall pray for her soul.' She raised her head and looked him directly in the eyes. 'If you will permit me to give you something . . .' Leaving him, she went to the waiting cart, and a moment later returned with the blue personal garter she had discovered. 'She would have wanted you to have this,' she said. 'It was among her treasures.'

Edward took it, looked down at it in his hands, and swallowed hard. Without a word he turned away, his movements stiff and jerky, as though all the joints in his body had seized together.

The royal household troops formed a guard of honour for the entourage, and dipped their banners as the cavalcade made its way out of Woodstock's gates and took the road to Bisham.

Jeanette sat before the fire at Bisham, warming her hands. Spring was taking its time to take hold. The weather had turned chilly for Katerine's burial, and Jeanette still felt cold from the long hours of masses and prayers. She had been forced into the company of the lady Elizabeth, but the old woman had lost her power to bite, and was an irrelevance. William had retired to his chamber, and she was alone.

She picked up the letters she had taken from Katerine's strongbox, unfastened the ribbon and, feeling queasy but determined, unfolded the first one and started to read, and as she did, hot and cold prickles flashed down her spine, for the letters made it clear how much her own mother had colluded with the Salisbury women in keeping her under their regime. Margaret had encouraged Katerine and Elizabeth to confine her and not spare the rod. Her mother declared in no uncertain terms that she refused to have her daughter wed to a lustful household knight with a disgraced father and vowed to assist the Montagu family in any way she could to fight the false marriage claims. She reiterated her belief that Thomas Holland had forced himself on an innocent young girl, thereby robbing her of that very innocence.

Jeanette resisted a powerful impulse to screw up the parchments and cast them on the fire, for this was damning evidence of the scheming against her. Indeed, rather than destroy the letters, she would have a scribe multiply them into several copies and send a set to Thomas.

Hearing footsteps outside the door, she hastily pushed the letters under her bedcovers as William entered the room.

'I could not sleep,' he said. 'I thought you might still be awake.' He was still fully dressed, although he had removed his belt and his hair stuck up in tufts from where he had been lying on his pillow.

'What of your grandmother?'

He grimaced. 'What of her? She has retired for the night and she will return to Oxford to her nunnery in due course.'

Going to her bed, he slumped on it.

Jeanette eyed him. 'Do you want some wine?'

He gave her a half-hearted nod and she sent a servant to fetch a flagon. Then she folded her arms. 'Your mother is laid to rest,' she said. 'Can we now lay our marriage to rest also?'

He regarded her with dull, bruised eyes. 'Not until we have the papal ruling. My mother's dying wish was that I saw it through to whatever end, and I shall do so.'

'Is that what you think she meant by "promise me"?' Jeanette raised her brow. 'Even when you know what the result will be?'

William rubbed his temples. 'I have such a headache; I wish I could sleep.'

'You will not do so until this is sorted out. I do not know why you persevere.'

'Because what do I have if I do not?'

The maid arrived with the wine. He sat up, and the pieces of parchment crackled beneath him. 'What is this?' He flapped back the coverlet to reveal the letters and she darted forward to grab them, but in the same moment changed her mind and drew back.

'They were in your mother's coffer,' she said. 'Letters from my mother to her. Read them if you will, and then tell me you still want to stand in the field with your sword in your hand and not let me go.'

'You took them from my mother's coffer?' he accused.

Jeanette suppressed her irritation. 'Do not make it about that,' she said. 'I was forced into a match that both your mother and mine knew was wrong. You were pushed into it too. Read them and know the truth.' She gestured with an open hand.

He shook his head at her, but did as she suggested; but after he had read a couple, he tossed the rest aside.

'What will you do with them?' he asked.

She saw him look towards the hearth, and prepared to intercept him. 'They should go to my attorney and to Master Beverley,' she said, 'but I do not trust them to arrive safely in the right hands, so I shall keep them for now, and send copies.'

'Put them somewhere safe then, and out of my sight. I do not need to read the rest – I am too heartsick already.'

Jeanette hastily stowed them back with her jewels and locked the box.

He looked at her miserably. 'I do not suppose you will stay here now for there is nothing to keep you, is there?'

She shook her head. 'I need to visit my mother. I have things to say to her face, rather than let them continue to fester within me.'

He nodded wearily. 'But you will accompany me to Windsor for the ceremony of the Garter in Saint George's Chapel, won't you?'

She looked at him in wary surprise. 'The court will be there and the other Knights of the Garter, including Thomas. Are you not taking a great risk?'

William shrugged. 'You hated me at the outset, and I felt the same about you. I even thought you were a little mad, and I listened to others because I was too young to know what I should do – to be a man. But we understand each other better now. I hope you would not smirch my honour, and the same for Thomas Holland, even if for no other reason than that it would hamper due process.'

'I have never been the one hampering due process,' she said shortly, 'and neither has Thomas, but you need not worry about any unseemliness. I shall put the letters in Master Beverley's hands until I have a new attorney, and after Windsor I shall go to my mother.'

'And after that?'

'To the Queen's household until the case is settled.'

William lay back down on the bed and looked at her. 'If not for your match with Holland, we might have made a good marriage eventually,' he said, almost wistfully.

'We would have rubbed along together, perhaps – it does no good to speculate. You should find yourself a wife of your own choosing.'

He snorted. 'I intend to, but until then I shall live very well in Edward's household. But supposing the papal court decides our marriage is valid after all?'

Jeanette shuddered. 'Do not tell me you are still wishing for such an outcome.'

His complexion darkened, and he looked away. 'No,' he said. 'But I still wonder . . .'

'Well, don't,' she snapped.

He closed his eyes and she waited until he had fallen asleep, then left the guest house and walked Nosewyse along the moonlit garden paths. She did not wonder at all: she knew such a burden would be intolerable.

In the morning, William came to her as she was packing her baggage. 'Listen,' he said, setting his hand on her sleeve, 'I want to make it easier for both of us.'

She eyed him suspiciously. 'In what way?'

'You asked me about standing in the road with my sword and I have been thinking about it ever since. I have been defending what in truth was a dishonour from the start. My own attorney knows this is a lost cause and although he has not said so, I know he thinks that attending the hearing in Avignon is a waste of his time. It will have to go forward to a judgement and a conclusion, but I will not encourage the fight. I shall tell him I have no interest in continuing with the marriage and I expect him to concede so that I may wed elsewhere.'

Jeanette stared at him. 'Truly?'

'Truly. Let it be finished.'

Jeanette's heart danced that he was finally ready to give in, but she was angry too. What a shame it could not have been long ago.

His smile was humourless. 'After the trials of recent years, I am ready to dwell at court and serve as a bachelor for a while.'

'Then I wish you well,' she said, and strove to remain neutral. 'And I hope only good things for you.' She sat back on her heels.

'We were both put in an impossible situation. Let us part in mutual courtesy whatever has gone before, and with dignity, so that we may find it possible to speak with each other at court in times to come.'

'Of course. I am sorry for the lost years – for both of us.'

'So am I,' she said stiffly. Her younger self would have thrown one of the portable candlesticks at him, but these days she had more control.

'We can make up for them in how we live from now on,' he said.

It was a comforting platitude, and she said nothing. He leaned over, kissed her cheek, and left her to her packing. She felt pity for him amid the greater emotions of hope at the thought of impending freedom and fear that it might still be snatched away.

33

Westminster, London, May 1349

Feeling as though a heavy stone had lodged in the pit of her stomach, Jeanette stepped from the barge at the jetty and made her way through the orchard to the doors of her mother's house on the banks of the Thames. Harbingers had gone ahead to announce her arrival. While it might have been entertaining to appear without warning, she wanted to do everything with the full power and dignity of her position. Margaret might think of her as a scapegrace girl, and no match for her, and she was determined to show her a different face today.

Her mother emerged to greet her, her garments rich but plain and dark in contrast to Jeanette's plush blue velvet trimmed with red silk. Margaret's cheekbones were blades, her mouth a narrow line. Jeanette curtseyed, observing propriety.

'Daughter,' Margaret said in taut salutation and raised her to her feet, her hands cold and her cheek-kiss as dry as a leaf. 'Welcome, but I was not expecting to see you. I understood you were at court. Certainly, you are dressed for that arena. I am surprised to see you in such array to visit your mother. Where is your husband?'

'At Windsor with the King,' she replied, 'but he will be returning to his estates after Whitsuntide, and visiting his own mother – so I hear.'

Her mother frowned. 'I do not understand your meaning.'

'You never have,' Jeanette said. 'You have never listened to me, or only to hear what you wanted to hear – but enough. Are you not going to welcome me within?'

'Of course.' Margaret opened her hand to gesture her inside, and brought her to the small solar and called for wine.

Jeanette sat on a carved bench by the hearth and ostentatiously arranged her gown. 'Perhaps you do not know,' she said. 'William Montagu's mother died of the pestilence three weeks ago at Woodstock, and has been buried beside her husband at Bisham. I attended her sickbed, and I accompanied her funeral procession to the priory. The lady Elizabeth has retired to Oxford, to Saint Frideswide's.'

Margaret paled. 'That is terrible news! I am grieved to hear it.'

'She has gone to face God at the foot of his throne,' Jeanette said. 'When I speak of my husband, I speak of Thomas Holland, not of William Montagu, who has never been my husband and accepts the fact for himself now. Indeed, he is seeking to make other arrangements for a union that will not be brought into question.'

Her mother pressed her hand to the base of her throat in a gesture of tension that Jeanette remembered from her childhood. She felt no compassion. She was not here to mend fences, but to break them down and to clear away the detritus between them. 'It is finished, mother,' she said. 'But I have things I need to say to you that will not wait another time.'

Margaret sat up straight, her body rigid. An attendant arrived bearing wine and hot wafers and she waited until the dishes had been set down and the servant had retired.

'I cannot believe that Katerine is dead,' she said hoarsely.

Jeanette reached for a wafer, ate half, and gave the other piece to Nosewyse who was waiting expectantly for his share. 'Why should you not? So many others have been stricken.'

'Have you seen your brother?' she asked with anxiety. 'He is well?'

'Yes, he was at Windsor for the inaugural Ceremony of the Garter,' Jeanette answered. 'And his wife. They send you their greetings and their prayers and say they will visit you soon.'

Margaret continued to pat the necklace at her throat, and then abruptly rose to her feet, clearly shaken. 'I have matters to attend to,' she said. 'Make yourself comfortable and we shall speak later.' She made a swift exit from the room, walking briskly, leaving Jeanette staring after her. Before, she had always been the one to run from a situation. Thoughtfully, she drank her wine and ate several more wafers.

Jeanette paced the chamber where her baggage had been brought. The floor was swept and kindling laid ready for a fire. The servants had prepared her bed, layering the straw, the feather mattress, the blankets and sheets. Walking between the window and the door, she thought about her mother. Margaret had been a thorn in her side for so long – she had even looked like a thorn today, all spiky and stiff in her dark clothing. She swore that if she ever had children, especially daughters, she would never do to them what her mother had done to her.

She exchanged her travelling gown for one of fine-grained red silk, with a jewelled belt. The low neckline swooped beneath her collar bone, showing an expanse of milky skin, and skimmed the top of her cleavage. The cuffs were gilt-buttoned to the elbow and she adorned her fingers with delicate gold rings. Her women braided her hair and fastened it around her head in a shining natural coronet entwined with artificial flowers set with pearls. She subtly coloured her cheeks and lips, and darkened her brows. When she looked in her hand mirror, she was pleased with what she saw. Here was no frightened girl, but a powerful woman of the royal court, exactly as she had intended. She would face her mother not in rebellion, but in certainty.

When the usher summoned her, she followed him to her mother's private chamber, where a table had been set up before the hearth. Her mother had changed her own gown for one of dark violet wool with gold embroidery and covered her hair with a clean white wimple simply and severely draped around her face. Her only jewellery consisted of a gold cross around her neck and her wedding ring. The good woman facing the hoyden, Jeanette thought with grim amusement, but she had no intention of being put down this time.

Her mother looked her up and down. 'Your father was a prince,' she said, 'and you are the niece of a king, and the wife of an earl. It is fitting that you robe yourself according to your high status. But if that status were to diminish, you might find yourself in straitened circumstances, without the coin for such . . . garish extravagance.'

'But I would have everything I need and more,' Jeanette said calmly.

They sat down to dine. The sewer poured water over their hands, and the excess trickled into a brass bowl.

'I am surprised though that you are not more soberly dressed as a mark of honour and respect to your mother by marriage,' Margaret continued to jibe as she dried her fingers on a towel.

Jeanette dried her own hands. 'I saw the Countess of Salisbury fittingly buried for William's sake, but I owe her nothing, and it is over now. I shall dress as I see fit, and if it is not as you see fit, then it is your concern, not mine.'

Margaret primmed her lips but said nothing as the servants arrived with bread and tender beef served in a rich cumin sauce. They dined in silence. Margaret picked at her food. Jeanette ate as usual, finding comfort in the textures and flavours on her trencher. But eventually she set down her knife and spoon, washed her hands again and looked at her mother.

'When I went to Flanders, you kept the jewels that my father left to me for when I should be married. And when I was married – falsely – you kept them still. It is one of the reasons I am here – to claim them now.'

'They belong to your father's estate,' Margaret said stiffly. 'Look at all the gauds you have in your coffers already. Why do you want more?'

'We both know my father willed them to me – I have read the documents. They are not yours or the estate's but mine.' Jeanette felt anger rising inside her, and struggled to remain calm. 'I shall never find all the pieces of myself that I need to be whole, that have been stolen by others, but this is one part I can restore.'

Margaret pushed aside her dish, leaving most of her food uneaten. 'You are making a fuss over nothing as you have always done,' she said. 'You have only ever thought of yourself. You do not understand what I have sacrificed for you and your brother. You do not understand what it was like for me to have one husband die in battle, and then to be sold in marriage to your father. Without a say. Without anyone to take my part and fight for me!' She struck a fist upon her chest. 'To begin building again only to have him arrested and executed and know that I was without support with two small children and another about to be born. Do you know the fear I experienced? Have you ever really understood the struggle I had to keep our lands intact as the kites circled and plundered? I had to fight for every single concession. Every yard of cloth, each mouthful of food that you ate.' Her voice shook. 'Whereas you, my daughter, have had every advantage in the world and have thrown it to the ground and stamped on it, for some . . . some tawdry, bestial act of lust!'

The burst of emotion had flushed her mother's face with colour like wine flooding through grey glass, as all the pent-up anger and resentment of years burst through into the present.

Jeanette was astonished, but neither cowed nor made contrite. 'Yes, I do understand.' She stood up. 'I understand very well indeed what it is to be given in marriage against your will – to be coerced and forced into moulds that will never fit your being. I understand what it is to have no one to fight for you and to stand alone. I would have thought that because of what happened to you, you would never want the same for your own children, but I was wrong. You want me to suffer the same, and now you blame me for refusing that harness and desiring a different future for myself with a partner I love and who would move heaven and earth for me. Perhaps you are envious. I do not know, mother, and I no longer care. I do know that should I bear sons and daughters in the future, I shall not do to them what you have done to me. Those jewels are mine. They are not yours by right and I ask for them now.'

They stared at each other, breathing swiftly. Jeanette felt the emotion flowing through her and outward to her mother, and the surge meeting in the middle was like two fierce and powerful bolts of lightning.

Abruptly leaving the table, Margaret went to an iron-bound chest standing against the wall, and taking the keys from her belt, unlocked it, and removed the small enamelled blue box. 'Are these what you want?' She opened the box, to reveal the glint of gold and jewels, her eyes filled with disgusted condemnation.

Jeanette took it from her and looked down at the contents. She remembered running the string of pearls through her fingers as a little girl, and being scolded for playing with them. She remembered adoring the enamelled white doe image on the belt buckle plate. And she remembered it all being taken away, sometimes with a slap, and being told she could have them when she grew up. Well now she was grown up. Her throat tightened and her eyes blurred. 'You kept these,' she said, 'and you took away my childhood.'

Margaret gazed at her dumbfounded. 'I strove with might and main to give you an inheritance and the wherewithal to survive,' she said. 'I took nothing from you. Look at you now, the great lady in all your silks and gauds.'

Jeanette gripped the little box, her knuckles blenching. 'You sold me for silver, mother. You sold me to the Montagus for your own benefit, not mine. You have taken from me my beloved husband, and you have wronged me consistently and knowingly. You tore up my contract, stole my wedding ring, and sold me into false marriage, knowing I was already wed. You stood by while I was imprisoned. You bore false witness to the truth. You forfeited the right to be my mother long ago and I will no longer remain your daughter. This is the end. I shall hold no quarter for you, as you held no quarter for me.'

Margaret opened and closed her mouth, but no sound came.

'I will have my wedding ring too,' Jeanette said.

'I do not have it.' Margaret's voice was a leafy whisper and she set her hand to her throat. 'Why should I have kept such a worthless thing?'

Quivering, Jeanette pressed her lips together, dangerously close to tipping over into full rage. This little box had been a barrel of pitch at the end of a fuse. 'How dare you! It was not yours to do such a thing, whatever you thought of its value,' she said, once she had mastered the urge to fly at her mother. 'I want no more of you from this day forth. You are dead to me.' She turned to leave, for there was nothing more to say and she wanted it to be over. 'I shall return to court in the morning, and I doubt we shall meet again.'

'Dear God, daughter, you will regret this,' Margaret said.

'I think not, mother. My conscience is clear. Is yours?'

She left the room and closed the door. Under her fingertips she could feel each curve and rib of the casket's structure as if it was a living thing. She felt as though she had just walked through a violent thunderstorm. The lightning was still flashing, but she had endured the worst and come through it. She did not regret a single word, but now she was wrung out and trembling with reaction. She had whipped up that storm to bring it into the open, and now she had to let that energy leave her body. Going to her bed, she curled up on the coverlet with the little box folded in her arms and against her heart.

In the morning, Jeanette prepared to depart. She was not expecting Margaret to come out to bid her farewell after yesterday's encounter, indeed she hoped she would not, but her mother was there to escort her to the waiting barge.

'May God grant you a safe journey, daughter,' she said. 'Whatever has passed between us, I will not wish you ill. I have always wanted the best for you – I still do. And if your notion of what is best and mine differ, then so be it.'

Jeanette eyed her mother, standing like a pinnacle of weathered granite. Perhaps in this they were alike, for she too had the strength to withstand whatever was thrown at her. Her mother did not look like a woman defeated. She looked like one who would continue to fight. There would be no truce, no quarter given. Even in the midst of her antipathy, she respected that.

'So be it,' she repeated and, turning her back, stepped into the waiting barge.

34

Papal Palace at Avignon, August 1349

Throughout the summer the pestilence ravaged town and village, castle and cot. Nowhere escaped its decimation. Churchyards filled up with the dead, and in the towns, pits were dug. Entire communities died and fields lay fallow. The truce with France continued, and those who remained clung to a knife edge and prayed.

Thomas travelled again to Avignon in August, hoping this would be the final time. Robert Beverley was present, and Jeanette's new representative John Vyse, but William's attorney failed to appear and sent no one in his place. Cardinal Adhemar, however, had received a letter sent directly to him from Jeanette's mother, declaring that Jeanette's testimony was not to be believed for she had been too young at the time to know what she was doing and advantage had been taken of her.

The Cardinal pushed back his sleeves and threw up his hands. 'We are at an impasse again,' he said irritably. 'Never have I known such a case. We cannot go forward when there is no one here to represent the Earl of Salisbury.'

'Your Eminence, surely something can be done even without his presence,' Thomas said. 'This case has dragged on for more than two years. What if you adjourn it again and Lord Montagu's attorney still does not appear? Is this to continue indefinitely?'

The Cardinal gave him a narrow look that suggested he thought Thomas was being discourteous, but then he sighed. 'I will speak to his Holiness, and we shall see what can be done. For now, we shall adjourn and reconvene here in three days' time.'

Thomas swept out, his fists clenched. Beverley and Vyse joined him in the courtyard, and Thomas rounded on them furiously. 'This is intolerable. I have done everything according to the law. Not once have I overstepped the bounds. I could have abducted my wife on the back of my horse years ago – perhaps I should have done!'

'I doubt you would have lived in peace for very long,' Beverley said drily. 'I do not know why Lord Montagu's attorney has not appeared to continue his presentation. Perhaps he is late, in which case the Cardinal is giving him another three days of leeway, and during that time he will speak to the Pope.' He touched Thomas's arm as Thomas gave a huge puff of exasperation. 'We are very close to winning this. Just one more effort.'

The following day, they were summoned into the papal presence. Pope Clement sat in his great chair between two fires burning herbs and incense to purify the air. Behind him, sumptuous wall hangings depicting biblical scenes decorated the walls. The Pope, in late middle age, handsome and urbane, rested his chin on a long, pale hand and regarded them through a veil of smoke.

'This case has been a difficult one from the beginning,' he said. 'I would have expected its resolution long ago, but Cardinal

Adhemar informs me that the attorney representing the Earl of Salisbury has not appeared, and without him we are at an impasse.' He shifted in the chair and the light gleamed on the gold thread polishing the hem of his robe, from beneath which an embroidered scarlet slipper peeped out. 'Therefore, I have taken the decision to appoint a new cardinal and committee to adjudge this case – I am giving Cardinal Bernard d'Albi full authority to make a ruling on the first day of November.' He made a firm motion with his hand. 'That decision will be final. There will be no more of this journeying back and forth' A signal brought two court officials forward to escort Thomas and the two attorneys away to another chamber.

Thomas had heard these sorts of promises before ad nauseam, but had no recourse to argue with the Pope. Beverley and Vyse were optimistic though. 'We have a date for judgement,' Beverley said. 'And that will be the end of it.' But still Thomas shook his head, unwilling to invest his faith in yet another shift of timescale.

'Why do you think Montagu's attorney did not present himself?' Otto asked Thomas as they sat in a hostelry to eat and drink.

Thomas shrugged. 'Perhaps because he knows the matter is a lost cause and not worth his time to put in an appearance. William Montagu has no interest in fighting the marriage now. There are rumours he is seeking to make another match. If so, then the only protest remaining is that of Jeanette's mother, and given the rest of the evidence, it will carry no weight. I suspect the Montagu attorney has decided there are more fruitful cases to pursue, closer to home.'

'It has been a long road,' Otto said. 'I pray that God has seen fit to finish testing you. I would have given up long before now – I can only admire your fortitude.'

Thomas shook his head. Otto's answer was not one of unqualified enthusiasm. 'I am not admirable, brother,' he said. 'If I have fortitude, it is because others have been staunch and supported me against all odds – I will never forget, I promise.'

Otto smiled to lighten the moment. 'Well, that is good to hear,' he said. 'Be sure I will always be at your side to remind you!'

Several weeks later, Thomas was standing before mounds of freshly dug earth and staring numbly at two graves side by side. His mother and his sister Isabel had both succumbed to the great pestilence during his and Otto's absence in Avignon. So many dead. After he and Otto had been so ill there and survived, he had been lulled into a false hope that God might be merciful. Now he was brought back to reality with the impact of a heavy fall. Never to see his mother again when he was so close to achieving his goal. Never to have her wisdom, or Isabel's pithy observations on his state of grace. He swallowed the painful lump in his throat as guilt and grief surged over him, for he could easily believe it was all his fault. He should have been here, instead of in France. He should have been at her bedside while she was dying. He imagined her waiting for him, waiting for news, and him not being there. And Isabel too, who thought him a reckless fool. She was probably right.

'I do not believe it,' Otto said, wiping his eyes, and Thomas set his arm across his shoulders and hugged him fiercely, silently cursing this horrific, dark and deadly disease that trailed a slime of tragedy in its wake.

Others in the village had succumbed to the pestilence, brought by a travelling haberdasher who had spent the night in the manor. The next day he had been raving, and the following day dead, but not before he had passed the malady to several others.

It had struck lightly before moving on, but had claimed a forfeit of the lives of Maude and Isabel Holland.

A letter of condolence had arrived from the Queen, and Jeanette had sent a message with the royal courier, saying how sorry she was for she knew how close he had been to his mother. She had sent, too, garlands of twisted wire flowers to lay upon the graves, and he did so now, feeling bereft that his mother would never truly know Jeanette or love the children they might have. All she had seen was the heartache and striving, not the fruition, and that knowledge hurt – deeply.

'She loved us,' Otto said hoarsely. No matter what we did, we were still her boys – and we can never have that again.'

Thomas could not speak for a moment because his throat was so tight. 'We should do our utmost to honour her,' he said at last, 'and make all her sacrifices worthwhile. From this day forth, I make that my sacred oath.'

Jeanette had sworn never to set foot in her mother's Westminster house again, yet here she was, about to do so. When the messenger had arrived at court with the news that Margaret too had been stricken by the pestilence, Jeanette had been beset by a storm of volatile emotion. She had believed her mother to be indomitable, capable of outlasting everyone, and yet she had succumbed like so many others, including Jeanette's uncle Thomas, who had died in early summer.

Once again she travelled from the court to Westminster by barge. The sky was grey today with rain in the wind but she sat under a sheltering canopy of brightly coloured flags. The river, opaque and heavy with the tide, smelled brackish. She wished Thomas was here to hold her hand, but he was still absent with his family on their estates, sorting out their mother's legacy. She vowed that as soon as they could be together, they would be as one, and they would make a family without any of the contamination that had bedevilled her own. Instead of thinking about her mother, she conjured an image of Thomas, and of the life they would build to replace everything they had lost.

The sunset was a wide golden band behind her, hemming the sky beneath dark clouds and gleaming in the diamond panes of the windows, when the rowers brought the barge into the landing stage at the Kent Westminster house. Her brother was already there and greeted her as she stepped off the barge.

'Does she still live?' Jeanette asked as he embraced her.

John shook his head. 'She died an hour ago while you were still on your way. I arrived this morning and she knew me, but not for long.' He was dry-eyed, his mouth tight, and his face showed the strain marks that would one day become deeper lines.

Jeanette unfastened her cloak. 'She and I had already said everything there was to be said between us,' she responded, 'and our ways had parted long before then.'

'Do you want to see her?'

She grimaced. 'No, but I shall do so nonetheless.' Only by seeing her could she be certain that it was over.

John led her to the room where their mother was laid out, a silk cover draped over her body. A smell of incense permeated the chamber and the windows were open, allowing the breeze from the river to wind through the room and mingle with the scent of death and corruption. Her mother's hands were clasped upon her favourite prayer beads with the cross uppermost. Her jaw had been bound with a linen bandage and her eyes were closed, but only in the way of the dead, and a glint of pupil showed beneath the lids. Jeanette shuddered. She didn't want to go near her, either to kiss her brow or touch her body. She didn't want to think of any part of herself coming from this woman, but she could not erase that particular truth.

She crossed herself in protection, although outwardly the gesture looked like a mark of respect, and then she bowed her head and sat for a moment, before turning away. She was aware of John observing her with shrewd eyes.

'I cannot mourn for her,' she said. 'I do not grieve that she is dead. Let us bury her and be done.'

'I pity her,' John said with sad compassion as they left the room.

'Then you are better than I am, brother. The best I can say is that it is finished.'

John lightly touched her arm. 'She gave us life, and we can thank her and give her due honour for that gift at least. She did what she thought was best, even if it was sometimes for the worst. I know you suffered, and I am sorry, but until you forgive her, you will suffer more.'

Jeanette said nothing. Let her brother believe as he wished and she would keep her own thoughts to herself.

John dug into the purse on his belt. 'She gave me this while she could still speak, and said you should have it, for it was yours.' He took her hand and dropped her first wedding ring into her palm.

Jeanette rubbed her thumb over the cold, smooth gold and shivered, feeling sick. 'She told me she had got rid of it.'

'Clearly she didn't.'

Jeanette slipped the ring on to her finger. It was too big since it had belonged to Thomas – she would have to resize it by wrapping it with twine – but to have it back in her possession was a miracle. 'Did she say anything more to you?'

'Only that she had always done right by you and this was her last act to be taken as you willed, and that she would answer to God with a clear conscience for the rest – as you must answer to God with yours.'

That was typical, Jeanette thought. She had her own victory in regaining possession of her ring, but her mother had still had the last word that couldn't now be contradicted.

'Let her rest in whatever peace she can find,' she said. 'And while I will not bestow my forgiveness since she has not asked for it, I shall pray for her soul.'

A fortnight later, having dealt with her mother's funeral, Jeanette left Donington Castle to return to the Queen. The day was cold with the first chill of autumn blowing.

As she put distance between herself and the castle, a sensation of lightness filled her being. She truly was riding free, under her own hand and the future rising like the sun before her. No one was going to drag her back, imprison and threaten her if she opened her mouth. No one was going to force her to drink vile tinctures to keep her silent, to make her fertile – to make her miscarry.

She thought of Thomas and how her road to him was open, only awaiting the Avignon verdict. It had been so long since their courtship and love-making in Flanders – such a very long time – and she had been naive and untested then. A petulant girl, she admitted to herself, whereas now she was a mature young woman of three and twenty. Would Thomas have changed after all he had endured? From gallant young buck to an experienced veteran of war and diplomacy. They had barely spoken to each other down the years – except in small moments snatched from scrutiny, hidden and filled with fear and volatile, complex emotions. The young knight for whom she had felt such a fierce, liquid desire might be a very different prospect now. They had changed apart not in unison, and although she was buoyant as she rode, she wondered how it would be. What would it be like, too, to lie with him after so long a time? Would they still want each other? It was such a delicate, fragile thing. All her hopes were like beautiful eggshells, and she dared not tread too heavily for fear that they would shatter.

One of Philippa's dogs had chewed her bedspread again, and the tailors had come to remove it for repair. The scolded dog, a white bundle of fluff called Snowflake, had gone into hiding under Jeanette's chair. Exasperated, the Queen waved her hands.

'Take him, take him!' she cried. 'Enough is enough! The amount of cloth that animal has ruined!' She fixed her gaze on Jeanette. 'You are clever with dogs. You have him, otherwise I will have the kennel keeper wring his neck! I should have kept with squirrels!'

'Thank you, madam.' Jeanette wondered if being given custody of the little dog was a gift or a curse given his propensity for textile destruction. At least he and Nosewyse were playmates, not enemies. She would have to train him out of his fabric-chewing habits and ensure he had bones and sinew instead.

In the two months since her mother's funeral Jeanette was still growing accustomed to a life without constraints. She dwelt at court with the Queen as she had done throughout her childhood, acting as one of her ladies. Sometimes she saw William when the King was at court and he was attending on him, but their contact was distant. Everything was in limbo, waiting. Her brother was absent, busy about the affairs of the earldom and their mother's estate.

She scooped the little dog out from under her seat and stroked his silky white curls. The tailor and his assistant departed with the chewed bed cover, and as they left, a messenger arrived with letters from the court which Philippa retired to read in her inner sanctum.

Jeanette took Snowflake and Nosewyse for a walk along the paths outside Langley Palace. A cold wind was gusting and the last of the autumn leaves swirled inside it. Soon the light would fade and night would press against the buildings. Everyone would sit around the fire, roasting chestnuts, listening to stories, telling them, and singing songs.

Jeanette lingered, enjoying the moment alone, even while looking forward to returning to warmth and food. Nosewyse continued to following various enticing scents, Snowflake trotting at his side. A few spots of fine drizzle freckled her face, and a squire came hurrying towards her, commanding her to return to the royal apartments immediately. Her heart skipped, for she knew the Queen must have received some correspondence pertinent to her situation. It might be concerned with her mother's affairs, or it might be about her marriage.

She hurried to return, and handed custody of the dogs to the squire with instructions to find them some antler pieces to chew on. Then she went to Philippa, curtseyed, and was directed to a stool at the foot of her chair.

'The King has sent me a copy of a letter he has received from the papal court,' she said.

Jeanette sat very still.

Philippa's eyes were sparkling. 'I shall not keep you in suspense,' she said. 'Cardinal d'Albi has ruled that the marriage between yourself and Thomas Holland is valid and that the match you made with William Montagu was unlawfully conducted and all ties to be severed forthwith. You and Thomas Holland are to solemnise your married state before a priest as soon as you may.'

Jeanette stared at Philippa, frozen in the moment. Through so many years of struggle and heartache she had waited to hear this, and now, with the words ringing in her head, she could not respond.

The Queen gave her a perplexed look that was almost an echo of the one bestowed on her when she had told Jeanette she was to marry William Montagu. 'Are you not pleased?'

Jeanette tried to speak, but her vision had whitened at the edges. She felt the Queen's hand on her arm, and then someone was burning feathers under her nose and Jeanette coughed at the acrid stink.

Philippa gave her a drink of sugared rose water in a glass goblet, and as Jeanette took a few sips, her head began to clear.

'It must have come as a surprise even though we were expecting such news,' Philippa said. 'And I hope it is good news . . .'

'Indeed so, madam,' Jeanette responded faintly, 'but I have been waiting for ever to hear it. It is as though I have been pushing a boulder before me for so long that when it suddenly vanishes, I fall flat on my face!'

The Queen laughed at the comparison and embraced her. 'Very true, and I understand. Now the verdict has been declared, we shall have your vows properly solemnised at court!'

Jeanette shook her head, still feeling numb.

'What now?' Philippa demanded with a touch of impatience.

'Nothing is wrong, madam,' Jeanette replied. 'Truly this letter is my heart's delight. I know the wedding must be celebrated so that all may hear the verdict of the Avignon court and acknowledge the validity of my first marriage, but I want a moment for Thomas and I to be together. I know we can do so after our new wedding, but I want to see him and speak to him before that day. I would renew my vows every day for the rest of my life if I could. Even if we must have a public wedding, I want to see him again and have time to make time.'

Philippa's expression softened, and she touched Jeanette's hand. 'And you shall have it,' she said with sympathy. 'I shall make sure of it.'

'Thank you, madam.' Jeanette swallowed tears. 'It means a great deal to me. I have been twisted this way and that for so many years, and all I want is to be still in the moment with the man I have loved from the moment I set eyes on him.'

Philippa's eyes were suddenly liquid. 'Leave it with me, my dear,' she said. 'Let it be my gift to both of you.'

'Also, William Montagu,' Jeanette said firmly. 'None of this is his fault. When Thomas and I are wed, I do not wish there to be any humiliation for him, or people laughing behind their hands. We have come to understand each other, and I want this to be honourable for him too.'

Philippa dipped her head. 'Do not worry, my dear, I shall see that all is in order. Now then, if you are intent on having some time with your husband before you have to share him with the court, I have some thinking to do.'

Jeanette departed Langley five days later under the escort of two of the Queen's knights and several serjeants of the household. Philippa had given her two rich velvet gowns and a chest of wimples, head coverings, belts and various fripperies, almost like a wedding trousseau.

Jeanette had no notion of where she was going, for Philippa had kept it to herself as a surprise. The leader of her escort had letters from the Queen and was smiling but taciturn, and Jeanette gave up trying to tease it out of him and set out to enjoy the journey instead.

She sat in a cart amid piles of bags, boxes and chests. As well as all the finery, Philippa had sent her with pies and pasties from the kitchens and a flask of the best wine. Heaps of furs kept her warm as did hot stones wrapped in blankets placed underneath the seat bench in the cart. The road was reasonable and the potholes they encountered not too deep. Yesterday's rain had only been a brief flurry, and the road was clear.

The journey took them the best part of the wintry day, but they arrived at the royal manor of Havering on the banks of the Thames as dusk bruised the late afternoon sky. Jeanette had known their destination for several miles, having recognised the landscape, and had started to smile, for Havering was one of her favourite places – less grand than Windsor, not as sprawling as Westminster, and the way the light caught the windows always gave her the impression that the buildings were smiling at her in welcome.

Messengers had ridden ahead, and in the courtyard torchlight she saw a man outlined in the carved doorway and her heart began to pound. The last of the dusk and the glimmering flame shone on the gold embroidered damask on his sleeve and belt fittings.

'Thomas,' she whispered, feeling light-headed.

The cart stopped and the horses stamped and snorted, steam rising from their coats and nostrils. Thomas left the doorway and came round to the back of the cart where an attendant was attaching some wooden steps. Taking her hand, he assisted her down, and Jeanette thought she might faint.

'My lady wife at last,' he said, and faced her, taking her other hand too. They stood looking at each other in the courtyard, surrounded by bustle but alone in stopped time. 'I received a letter from the Queen telling me to come here,' he said. 'That she was sending you to me, and me to you, and I almost thought it was a dream.'

'I thought I was dreaming too.' She had to drop her gaze, for the fire was almost too hot to endure.

The escort leader cleared his throat, and with an effort Thomas turned his focus outwards and issued orders with regard to the stabling and dealing with Jeanette's baggage. Then he led her inside to a chamber usually occupied by important guests. Beeswax candles glazed the room with soft light, and a welcome fire burned in the hearth.

Food had been set out on a table spread with a white cloth with all manner of small, tasty delicacies to tempt the palate without being a surfeit. Wafers and tiny marrow tarts, and savoury morsels of pork and parsley with various sauces. Goblets of green glass twinkled, and there were two cups of jewelled silver – all the trappings of the court, but much more intimate.

Thomas took her hands again. They had not kissed yet and Jeanette knew that once they began, they would not cease until they had disappeared into each other and become one, and that it was a moment to savour, for it would never come again in their lives.

'It has been so long since we have been alone,' he said. 'And even then, we knew we were chancing fortune and could have been parted and punished at any moment. But now we have our freedom to be together, and I swear to you that with each breath I take, even to my dying one, you will be free. Whatever you want from me, it is yours. I own the blame for what happened before. I should have stayed, I should have spoken out, and I swear on my oath as a knight that I will never desert you again – never! You are my true wife in chastity and in love for ever.'

Jeanette was so moved and overwhelmed that she could barely think, let alone speak. She touched his face and brushed her fingertips over the scar at his temple and his blind eye. 'This is all that I have ever wanted. If I have this, I need nothing more – no kings and courts, no silks, no gauds and decorations. Just you. I gladly give them all up.'

'Truly? You would follow me across countries and battlefields clad only in your shift?'

She lifted her face to his. 'Yes, I would, and never regret it.' And in that moment, it was true.

He kissed her then, and she closed her eyes, and the world went away.

35

Royal Palace of Havering, Essex, November 1349

Jeanette lay on top of Thomas, feeling his bare skin against hers, the coverlet furs pulled up around them. The only light came from the dim, grainy gold candle flame and the red coals in the hearth. He brought a tress of her hair to his lips and kissed it. 'No thread of gold could compare to this,' he said softly. 'You are beyond beautiful . . . Just this one moment makes it worth all the struggle and heartache, and I would do it again and again and again.'

She kissed his shoulder, his neck, his temple, unable to believe that finally they were together without barriers. 'Would you truly? Wasn't there a time when you thought about giving up?'

'On many occasions, but I didn't – neither did you.'

She left the bed and went to pour more wine and renew the fire. The dogs were sleeping in front of the embers and barely stirred as she added a fresh log. 'No, but it was hard.' She swept her hair behind her shoulders, and returned to bed with their goblets. 'Sometimes there was so much weight crushing me I thought I would die, but each time I found the strength from somewhere to withstand another load and stay alive. In the end, the more they sought to stamp me down, the harder I resisted.'

She took a drink and folded the covers around her body. 'Even now I do not know if we would be here in this bed if not for the pestilence taking my mother and William's too. They were holding on to me like a dog gripping a bone. And William's grandmother added her jaws also. I sometimes think they would rather have killed me than see me become your wife.'

He stroked her hair. 'But God must have been with us. Had I not won that ransom in Caen, and if not for the pestilence . . .' He fell silent again, for although the sickness had brought them their heart's desire it had also destroyed so much in its surge and left tragedy in its wake too. 'I wish that my mother and sister could have come to know you truly,' he said quietly.

'And I am sorry not to have known either of them beyond a word or two,' Jeanette replied, although she wondered how she, Maude and Isabel would have fared together as women of the same family. She had experience enough to be wary, especially of mothers when it came to their sons. 'Now we have to make it up to the King,' she said. 'The Queen is on our side and happy for us, as is the lord Edward, but I am not certain how his father regards the matter.'

Thomas set his wine aside. 'We can win him round. We no longer have to contend with the Countess of Salisbury whispering in his ear. He values my service and Otto's, and now that the pestilence has begun to recede he will be requiring our skills.'

Jeanette rolled her eyes and laughed without humour at the notion that he would think that leaving her and putting himself in danger constituted a solution she would be happy to hear.

But then he was a soldier by trade – an excellent one – and his occupation was part of how they came to be sharing this bed at all.

The court started arriving for the Christmas feast ten days later, with the piled baggage carts rolling in first, accompanied by the servants of the Marshal's department, to begin setting up the household and erecting tents. The weather was one of bright, crisp frosts and skies of enamelled blue.

Thomas and Jeanette helped to oversee the arrangements, and Jeanette was glad for them to have something to do now that well over a week had passed, for they could not spend every day in bed, much as they had enjoyed doing so. They had talked and wept and laughed and come to know each other all over again, but now it was time to allow the world back into their lives.

The King and Queen arrived at the same time by prearrangement, and Jeanette and Thomas knelt to greet them with the rest of the household. Tense and apprehensive, Jeanette was unsure how the King would receive them. Philippa had a warm conspiratorial smile for her and Thomas as she swept into the palace. The King cast a brief glance in their direction, his expression neutral. Prince Edward flashed them a reassuring grin and waved as he followed his parents.

Jeanette was swiftly summoned to join the Queen and her ladies, and knelt before Philippa with her head bowed.

'You are glowing, my dear,' Philippa said, her gaze full of amused mischief. 'I take it that all has been to your satisfaction?'

'Yes indeed, madam,' Jeanette answered, smiling. 'We have been making up for lost time – many years of lost time.'

'Well, I wish you and your husband a fruitful outcome. We shall enjoy the festivities and witnessing your renewed vows.'

Prince Edward took her hand and bowed over it. 'I am glad for you, cousin,' he said. 'I wish you all the joy in the world.' He kissed her cheek and then her lips in a swift salute.

'Thank you, sire,' she said, and although her tone was formal, the look she gave him was full of warmth. 'Thomas and I are indebted to you.'

'None of that,' he said firmly. 'You are my dear kin, my friends, and as necessary to me as I am to you. We shall all go forward together.'

On his knees, Thomas bowed his head before the King. Jeanette curtseyed beside him dressed in her wedding gown of red and gold velvet with ermine trim and her father's belt encircling her waist. Around her neck, exposed now, was the little pendant she had picked up from a muddy tourney field as an infatuated girl, and with it, on a gold chain, the recently polished ruby Thomas had once given her, now in a resplendent gold setting. A new wedding ring featuring two clasped hands gripping another ruby shone on her heart finger, made from the gold of her first one. They had recently come from the church of St Mary attached to the palace where they had been married before the entire court, and then celebrated a mass within the crowded candlelit chapel.

The King, resplendent in robes of gold and silver, gem-set rings on his long fingers, bestowed the kiss of peace on both of them. 'Welcome to court as man and wife,' he said, 'and be welcome in any hall in the land in that capacity.' He smiled widely at both of them, but Jeanette still sensed an undercurrent of reserve in his manner. 'You have my word that this marriage will neither be questioned nor put asunder by anyone in the land now that judgement has been made,' he continued. 'I wish the best for you and may your line blossom and flourish. Let the past remain in the past from this moment forth, and let us feast and rejoice.'

The wedding was celebrated with entertainment, dancing and mumming, joy and laughter. There were mock jousts with one young man playing the horse, the other his rider, and attempting to knock down opponents similarly mounted. By popular demand, Thomas had to bring Noir into the hall and make him bow to the gathering, before taking Jeanette up on his saddle and riding off with her to loud cheers. As she disappeared from the room, Jeanette caught the Queen's eye, and the pair shared a warm and knowing look.

On Christmas Eve, Jeanette and Thomas rode out with the dogs on their own to spend a little time together before yet another round of entertainments and feasting. The air was crystal-cold with frost making ferny swirls in the puddles and crunching beneath the horse's hooves. Nosewyse and Thomas's swift black gazehound Onyx ran beside the horses, although Jeanette had left Snowflake behind in Hawise's custody, hoping he wouldn't chew his way through anything other than a bone during her absence. Thomas had brought Hawise with him in his entourage and she had returned immediately to her former position. Jeanette was supremely pleased to have her in her chamber.

Thomas smiled as they rode. 'I have never seen anything as beautiful as your red lips and cheeks in the winter cold,' he said admiringly.

'You may praise me all you wish, not just my lips and cheeks!' She laughed at him. 'Which part of me do you like best?'

'Oh, I could not say, for there is no part that is less beautiful than any other, and of course there are different parts of me that would consider different parts of you as their ultimate praise!'

She spluttered at his saucy reply and kicked her palfrey into a canter. He rode at her side, matching her pace, across the frozen grass and then into the trees, the trunks winter-black and moss-green, the branches bare. The dogs took off, scouting through the woods like wolves. Jeanette was exhilarated at the freedom. No grooms, no attendants, just themselves and time to do as they pleased.

Eventually they came to a charcoal burner's clearing. Thomas produced a flask of sweet wine and some honey cakes and they paused to eat and drink.

He looked at her again. They had made love in the morning before they set out, and even though there was no urgency of lust for the moment, he still could not get enough of her. 'When we leave court after Christmas, I want to take you to my manor at Broughton,' he said.

Sensing a sudden tension in him, Jeanette raised her brows. 'What of it?'

'It will not be what you are accustomed to,' he said, a flush rising under his skin. 'I am not an earl of the realm. I earn a soldier's wage and whatever I may glean in ransoms and plunder. I have a life interest in a few manors from my mother, but that is all.' He took her hand. 'You are the King's cousin. Your brother is the Earl of Kent and William Montagu is the Earl of Salisbury, and his income is more than four times that of mine.'

'I did not wed you for your money or your reputation.' Jeanette stroked his cheek. 'Had I needed that kind of comfort, I could have chosen it long ago.'

'Even so, I want you to know we shall have to trim our sails to suit the horizon. Would that I could provide you with every luxury in the world, but it is not within my means.'

'I do not expect that,' she said. 'I will not starve for food or clothes unlike some of the poor wights who beg in the streets. Nor shall I want for love or protection, for you shall give me those in abundance – more than I have ever had in my life, and that matters more. I have fine gowns and jewels already. We shall have a sufficiency of everything, love most of all.' She drew away to look at him, her gaze serious. 'To possess the freedom to ride my horse and fly my hawk as I choose and not be a prisoner is the greatest gift in the world after what I have known. Those who matter most to us know who we truly are. I tell you again, I care not, and I mean it with all my heart. I would follow you barefoot in my shift, this I swear.'

He swallowed emotion, and kissed her tenderly, and they remounted the horses to make their slow return to the palace.

'I do wonder if the King has forgiven us,' he said thoughtfully. 'Forgiven us for what?'

'Well, he has surely lost face because I went to the papal court, and because he was complicit in arranging this match with you and Montagu, only to find I had already married you in Ghent without permission. He was accepting when we knelt to him, but I do not know if we shall find favour in future.'

'He is no fool when it comes to playing the great game,' she replied. 'He needs your skills and he is fond of me. The Queen is favourable to us, and he desires her goodwill, and his eldest son's approval. Edward will always speak for us.'

Thomas smiled at her. 'I suspect the Prince is rather smitten by you.'

'It is only that he has known me since he was born,' she said defensively. 'He has had mistresses and the business of being his father's deputy to keep him occupied, and he will make a diplomatic match when it is time. You do not become smitten by someone who stuffs hay down your tunic in the stables and calls you names.'

Thomas arched his brow. 'I am not so sure.'

Jeanette felt her face growing hot. 'Are you jealous?'

He shook his head, looking amused. 'I have no cause. I am grateful for his aid and support and I will gladly serve and support him in my turn. Perhaps I am a little sorry for him because he does not have you.'

She reached across their horses to touch his hand. 'We grew up almost as siblings,' she said. 'One day he will be a king and he will wed to the dictates of duty. I hope he finds love and partnership within it. For me – I am hopelessly in love with my husband for ever.'

He took the hand she had reached out and raised it to his lips. 'For ever and a day,' he said.

Seated at the feast, enjoying roast fowl in the great hall, Jeanette was slipping morsels to Nosewyse and Snowflake under the trestle when she saw an usher sidle up to the King, murmur in his ear, and give him a sealed letter and a ring. Edward glanced at both, then broke the seal and read what was written on the parchment. Then he spoke quietly to the Queen, rose to his feet, and left the table. His exit caused a hubbub of speculation. The Queen clapped her hands and bade everyone continue eating – a matter of business had cropped up that would be dealt with.

'That does not look like good news,' Thomas said.

Jeanette set down her knife. Someone must have died, but she couldn't think who, because the senior courtiers were gathered in the hall. However, the King had gone white as he read the message. She could feel Thomas's coiled tension responding to the hint of a threat.

Other ushers entered the hall. One of them went to Prince Edward and spoke to him quietly, and then to Sir Walter Manny and Sir John Chandos before arriving at Thomas.

'Sire, the King requests your presence in the ante chamber,' he murmured.

Thomas wiped his lips on a napkin, and stood up. He pressed Jeanette's shoulder. 'I shall return as soon as I may, my love.'

Jeanette watched him leave with the other summoned men – all knights of the Order of the Garter and part of the King's inner military council. Something momentous was afoot.

Thomas and his companions found the King conversing with a dark-haired man with a thick beard and travel-stained clothes. Thomas immediately recognised Amerigo di Pavia, an Italian soldier who was serving as constable of one of the harbour guard towers in the port of Calais.

The King beckoned his knights to gather round. 'Gentlemen, we have some treachery afoot in Calais.' He gestured to di Pavia. 'Tell these men what you have just told me. Do not worry, you shall be well rewarded, and you have saved your own skin in coming to us.'

Di Pavia's fists tightened, and Thomas saw that beyond the tension the man was deeply afraid. 'Messires, as I have told the King, Calais is in imminent danger. I wish I was not the bearer of this news, but for my honour, I had no choice.' He licked his lips. 'I have been approached to betray my post as the King's liegeman, and I cannot confront these traitors on my own, so I come to tell you what has happened, and to clear my conscience. The ring I showed you is a token of my good faith and the truth of what I say, for it was given to me by the man himself as you see engraved, who wishes to betray all agreements previously made, and to enter the town by stealth and take it from you. I have no love for this man and the position in which he has put me.' His eyes flashed with indignation. 'I am no traitor and I would rather die than give in to this plot.'

The King handed the ring around the gathering. Thomas took it at his turn and hefted the weight. It was strong, solid gold, set with the private seal of the French knight and adventurer Sir Geoffrey de Charny, a man with a shining reputation for honour and chivalry. The irony was not lost on him.

'What exactly is this plot?' he asked. 'Just how does de Charny intend to enter Calais?'

Di Pavia's brow creased with worry. 'It is the weather and the stage of the moon that holds them back,' he said. 'They are waiting for a light night and low tide. Then they will come across the marshes to my tower and knock on my door. I must give them my son as a hostage for my good intent and in return they promise me riches beyond counting. But it is dishonourable and I do not trust them. I have agreed to their terms, but I would rather die than lose my honour!'

The King set his hand to di Pavia's shoulder and gripped hard. 'I am sure that is the case – I know you for a good and loyal soldier. And in my turn, I promise you will be well rewarded for your loyalty to me in refusing to be a traitor.'

The Italian nodded and looked relieved, although his body remained stiff with tension. 'He broached this plan to me two days ago and I sailed straight here to bring you the news, but he will come very soon – there is not much time.'

'We will have to go over there and counter it,' Prince Edward said. 'We will lose Calais if we do not act immediately.'

'We must decide swiftly what to do,' his father agreed. 'We must go there in haste and hope we are in time.'

'If they see us or discover what we are about,' Walter Manny said, 'they may abandon the attack and try again on another occasion.'

'Yes, we need to be inconspicuous, but with sufficient numbers to be effective, and we should muster now,' said the King.

Thomas had been calculating how many troops they could gather at short notice, and how much equipment. 'We should wear the clothing of the ordinary folk so as not to draw attention to ourselves,' he suggested, 'and if we take horses they should look like ordinary beasts to the casual eye, perhaps being brought in by a horse dealer.'

The King nodded his approval. 'That is a fine notion, Thomas.'

'And if we have to bring in equipment, we should put it in chests and bags and make it seem that we are traders in ordinary items.'

A general rumble of assent followed his suggestion, and the King nodded again. 'We should begin preparations immediately. Thomas, see to the horses. Make sure they are not groomed for the next two days. William, find chests and bags for the equipment that will not look out of place. Edward, set your men to acquiring some plain, common clothing – nothing too new, but not so old and ragged that it will draw attention. Let the owners be compensated and sworn to silence. Tell them it is for a Christmas jape that the King is concocting, and intended as a surprise they are not to spoil. All of you go about your work quietly. No one must know beyond your own trusted enclave for no hint of this is to reach the French.'

The King turned to di Pavia and put his arm across his shoulders. 'Eat and drink, take some sleep, then return to your post in Calais.' He signalled to his senior squire. 'Robert will attend to your needs and find you comfortable quarters.' He gave the youth a subtle signal to keep a close eye on di Pavia, before addressing his knights again: 'Go back to dinner and finish your meal. Say nothing of this and we shall reconvene at compline, and begin planning our strategy.'

* * *

Jeanette looked up as Thomas slipped quietly back into his place and picked up his goblet as though he had just come back from taking a piss. She noted the others, including Prince Edward and his father, returning too.

'Well?' she asked.

He shook his head. 'Just some business on which the King wanted advice.'

She raised her brows, wondering since when had drawing his senior knights away from a Christmas Eve banquet been a matter of nothing. 'Business,' she echoed with a straight face.

Thomas returned her look blandly. 'Yes,' he said, 'business.'

Over the next few days Jeanette became increasingly aware that something was afoot. After the feast on Christmas Eve, Thomas had escorted her to their chamber, told her he had matters to attend to, and had departed forthwith, not returning until the small hours, and saying nothing about where he had been. She knew he would not tell her, no matter what wiles and persuasions she attempted, so she let him be. Efforts to find out from the maids and servants produced tantalising crumbs, but no nutrients, and the Queen herself made it clear that tattlers would be severely punished.

There were comings and goings at all hours of the day and night. She saw people walking the corridors at unusual times and conspiratorial glances exchanged between certain of the men. She saw Thomas sitting on a wall talking intimately with his archers and serjeants. She came across people wandering about with bundles of clothing. One afternoon, returning to fetch her book of hours, she heard voices in their chamber and paused at the door, to hear Otto saying to Thomas that it was irritating to have to dull their fine armour and remove all the embellishments.

'Pretend we are young knights again, setting out on our life's adventures,' Thomas said. 'It will be like the old days when we kept our kit simple and sharp, and were eager for the fray.'

Jeanette heard Otto give a snort of grudging amusement.

Then Thomas said on a quieter, reflective note, 'We were just young men out for the chance when I set eyes on Jeanette on that ship to Ghent.'

'Hah, and look where that got you!'

'Two stolen hearts, exchanged each for the other,' Thomas said, and Jeanette almost melted.

'You're impossible – both of you! Look, I can't take this dagger sheath, it's too decorated.' Beneath Otto's complaint, Jeanette heard the relish of anticipation.

Jeanette quietly tip-toed away. Her book would wait.

That night, when she and Thomas retired to bed, she noticed a leather baggage satchel on which was placed a clean shirt and a serviceable brown tunic that she recognised as Duncalfe's.

Thomas emerged from the latrine, hitching his braies. She indicated the satchel. 'So, this is the big secret, is it?' she asked. 'This is the thing that does not exist?'

He looked at her and sighed. 'It won't be for long.'

'And just when are you leaving?'

'Tomorrow, when the tide turns. It must be done; we cannot delay.'

'But it is too secret to tell wives – and it is going to involve fighting, and pretending you are common men?'

'How do you know that?' he demanded.

'I overheard you and Otto in our chamber earlier today – I came to fetch my book. I was not deliberately listening, and I left you to it, but I am not foolish.'

Thomas grimaced. 'I can say nothing. I am bound to secrecy and I would be breaking my trust if I told you what it was.

We won't be gone long.' He pulled her into his arms and kissed her.

Jeanette kissed him back. 'Just come back to me,' she said. 'I have spent so much time waiting for you, I do not want this to be all we have.' She could not keep the anxiety from her voice, remembering nine years of separation and heartache, but she could not confine him. If you hooded and leashed a hawk that needed to fly, you destroyed its very nature – as had almost happened to her.

Jeanette watched her husband for a few moments as he checked the contents of his satchel.

'I wish I was going with you,' she said.

'Hah, you would be too much of a distraction,' he replied with a laugh.

On impulse, she went to her sewing box, took out her shears, and going to the chemise she had worn yesterday that was awaiting the laundry maid, purposefully cut a large square from the area over the left breast. 'This is my heart,' she said. 'Carry it with you when you go.' She pressed the piece of cloth into his hand.

He looked down, then raised it to his lips and kissed it, before tucking it down inside his shirt. 'I carry all of you for ever, my lady wife,' he said. 'Do not worry, we shall return before you even know we are gone.'

The King and his entourage departed the following morning before sunrise. Horses circled in the courtyard, breath steaming in the frosty air. There were a few carts and sumpter nags, but most of the supplies awaited at the port. The assembled men were keen to leave to catch the morning tide and all necessary farewells had been said in the night.

They took the Dover Road as the day dawned in a peep of

paler grey on the eastern horizon. Jeanette watched, dry-eyed, until they had gone, then returned to her chamber to change her clothes for mass. Looking through a coffer for a fresh chemise, she noticed the folded pile of soft linen cloths used for her monthly flux and bit her lip. She looked at Hawise, who looked back at her. She pressed her hand to her belly. She had not experienced any symptoms and it was still early to think she might be with child, but her bleeds were usually regular, and she and Thomas had been making up for their years of lost time. She swallowed, feeling afraid. He had gone away again and she was on her own, remembering the panic of their early days in Flanders and that first missed flux. Abruptly she sat down, feeling faint.

Hawise stooped at her side, and put her arm around her shoulders. 'It is all right, my lady.'

Jeanette gathered herself together. 'Yes,' she said. 'And I know it should not come as a surprise, because last time it happened swiftly too – but to find out when he has gone into danger . . . it frightens me.' She gave a tremulous laugh, and wiped her eyes. 'I do not want anyone to know – not yet, not until Thomas returns, and until I am certain.'

'My lips are sealed,' Hawise replied. 'As they have always been.'

Jeanette embraced her and, distracted but determined, set about dressing to attend mass.

36

At sea off the coast of Normandy, December 1349

The evening was dark but clear as the English ships steered a course to Calais by starlight. The men's breath whitened the air in the bitter cold. Thomas gazed towards the Norman coast, straining to see the land against the darkling stir of the sea. They were all wearing sombre colours to hide in the night.

At his side, Prince Edward blew on his cupped hands. 'I hazard you did not think you would be sailing to Calais during the twelve days of Christmas?' he said with amusement.

Thomas shook his head as the sea slashed against the vessel's sides and the scent of salt whipped off the water. 'I have learned to plan ahead, but never to assume, sire. My life has been like this boat, sailing in the dark towards a destination, but always the unknown when it comes to the landing. But yes, I would rather be warm abed with my wife or drinking mulled wine with my boots towards the hearth than sailing to war this night.'

Edward laughed. 'You are an ambitious man, Messire Holland.'

Thomas shrugged. 'Only moderately so. I have everything that I need. My only wish now is for your father's goodwill.'

'You have it.' Edward looked at him. 'He is not your enemy. He has accepted the match between you and Jeanette, and you have my own goodwill and support, for I know you are trustworthy and loyal. You have the ability to think, organise and deliver, and such skills are highly valuable, as my father well understands. He also desires my mother's goodwill, and she is fond of you and Jeanette.'

'Yes, my lord,' Thomas said neutrally.

'I mean it. Jeanette was my childhood friend and companion. I want to see her satisfied and happy.'

'So do I, sire,' Thomas said.

'The only reason I would ever turn against you was if you harmed her, or did anything to make her unhappy. She loves you with a pure and faithful heart and you will answer to me if ever you break it.' His eyes sparked with a vehemence that Thomas recognised.

'Sire, I love her with the same heart,' Thomas said steadfastly. 'We are two halves of one whole. You have my oath, even as I give my oath of fealty to you, that I will never break that trust while there is breath in my body.'

'Then we are as one. Care for her well, my lord. She is a most precious jewel.'

He moved away to speak to someone else, and Thomas delved inside his tunic, took out the scrap from Jeanette's chemise and drew in the scent of her body as he kissed it. He did not mind that Edward felt so strongly about Jeanette. He trusted her, and he trusted Edward, who would perforce marry elsewhere. But he felt a little sorry for him, while being glad for himself to have that powerful rock-solid support.

* * *

Under cover of the hours before dawn, the English contingent of three hundred men at arms and six hundred archers slipped into Calais, disembarking at the harbour tower controlled by Amerigo di Pavia which had a gate from the tower into the citadel.

After a swift discussion of plans, the King divided his forces accordingly. Some were to remain in the tower with the Italian to await the approach of the French, who were massing at St Omer, twenty-five miles away. The King's contingent would enter the town and assemble at the main Boulogne Gate, and Prince Edward would have command of the Water Gate on the other side of the town. Thomas, Otto and Henry de la Haye were assigned to the Boulogne Gate with the Holland archers. In ostensible control of the operation was Walter Manny, a former captain of Calais. The plan was to allay suspicions by making it appear as though Manny had arrived to spend the New Year in Calais with a few old friends. Being known for his connections with the town, there would be nothing untoward about him making a visit.

Playing up to the theme, the King had disguised himself as a common knight, and a spark of dark amusement twinkled in his eyes as he acted as Manny's subordinate. This was far better than any Christmas mumming because it was real and dangerous. Thomas joined in the charade, he and Otto and Henry wearing their dulled armour, the blue garters of their elite knighthood stowed away in their baggage. To the superficial observer, the King of England and his knights were common soldiers on routine business.

Thomas and Otto were billeted in a stable with the warhorses that had been shipped across, and made their beds from clean straw with their cloaks laid over. The King, posing as one of Walter Manny's guards, slept in the house attached to the stables, the home of a wealthy English cloth merchant. Thomas's archers had set up their quarters in a couple of outhouses nearby belonging to another merchant family. They had been told nothing thus far beyond their orders to muster, but now Thomas went to sit with them, share a cup of ale and inform them why they were here.

He looked at their eager faces as they sat over their bowls of stew. Swift and keen as ferrets ready to hunt. He sipped the ale – an acquired taste when he was accustomed to wine – and asked after their wives and families. Young Joss's wife had given birth to their first child two weeks ago, and Thomas made a note not to volunteer the lad for any dangerous tasks. He promised him a gold noble for the infant when they returned. Then he discussed Cygnet's progress with Samson and agreed what a strong young horse he was becoming, although not yet ready for the saddle. Thomas enjoyed conversing with his soldiers. After long months of inaction, doing battle with quill pens and relying on lawyers, it was so good to be back in his own arena, in the company of fighting men – like salt on bread. He adored Jeanette with all of his being, but this too was part of who he was.

'We shall be here for a few days,' he said. 'Keep to yourselves and stay low. The French must not know of our presence. Geoffrey de Charny is leading a plot – secret, as he thinks – to seize Calais from us, but it will not happen. It is our task to ensure it does not.'

He drew lines in the dirt with an arrow to explain the plan.

'A group of them will come round by the marshes at the lowest tide and call for Amerigo di Pavia to open the harbour tower to them. He will do so, but only to a certain number, and then we shall drop the drawbridge, trapping the men inside and netting a fine catch of ransoms. The French plan is to enter the harbour tower by treachery and stealth and overpower our garrison. They will then come into the town via the harbour tower postern and open the Boulogne Gate to de Charny, who will be waiting with the rest of the French. Only they will never reach that far, and this is where we shall be waiting, to welcome them instead.' Thomas grinned at his men. 'I expect you to use every arrow you have to its best advantage and sow a fine crop.'

'Sir, how will we know when the time is right to gather at the gate?' Samson asked.

'There will be a signal from the citadel. We shall have runners in place and will have plenty of time to be in position, have no qualms on that score.'

Thomas finished his ale and returned to his own billet where Otto and Henry were still up, playing a game of dice for pennies by the light of a lantern.

'The men know their business,' Thomas said, joining them. He took a swig from Otto's cup of wine to clear the taste of the ale. 'We'll all be ready and eager when it's time.'

'It is still difficult to know who to trust,' Otto said. 'What if di Pavia does not honour his side of the bargain? How do we know he does not have a deal with the French to take us captive?'

'We don't, but is it likely?' Thomas replied. 'It would be a glorious victory for the French if it came to fruition and de Charny took the King of England and the heir to the throne prisoner, or even brought them down in battle – in which case we would die long before the King did. But far better for di Pavia to have a king in his pocket than a French adventurer.'

'True,' Otto agreed, 'but it's still wise to be cautious.'

'Indeed, but this way, if we prevail, we stamp our authority on Calais without question, and no one will doubt the King of

England's abilities or his spy networks again – for a while at least.'

Otto shook his head. 'I confess I am a simple man.'

Thomas rumpled Otto's tawny hair with affection. 'You see clearly enough at need. I'll leave you and Henry to your dice and sleep a while, then take second watch.'

Shortly before dawn on the last day of the year, de Charny's advance party crossed the marsh at low tide and entered through the door that had been left unguarded as agreed. Di Pavia ushered them within, and received the first part of his payment in return for his son, and within moments the English banners had been torn down from the top of the citadel and replaced with the Oriflamme of France. The French soldiers sped down to the portcullis to wind it up and open the gate to the rest of their number who had traversed the salt marsh and crept along the narrow strip of beach revealed by the low tide.

The French piled in through the tower entrance, but moments later, when the net was full, the portcullis slammed down, trapping them, leaving the rest stranded, and giving the English troops concealed in the harbour tower a fine catch of ransoms. At the Boulogne Gate, everyone had been waiting the signal since well before dawn, and it arrived at first light on swift feet and with a shrill whistle.

'The French banner is planted!'

Thomas waited by the gate, mounted on Noir with Otto and Henry either side, and the archers ready to shoot through the arrow slits in the gate towers and bring down the enemy. King Edward was still maintaining the pretence of being subordinate to Walter Manny, although everyone in the troop knew exactly where he was and a stalwart ring of protection surrounded him.

Noir pawed and snorted, his coat twitching. Tension trembled through Thomas's own body as their soldiers swung open the great wooden gates and the early morning light shone upon the massed array of five thousand French soldiers, eager to seize and plunder Calais to the bones.

At the sight of the waiting English, a roar of dismay surged out from the French. Howls of 'Treachery!' and 'Betrayal!' writhed through the ranks.

'St Edward! St George!' bellowed Thomas and Otto in unison, and the cry was taken up and roared from every English throat and the trumpets blared the charge. From the battlements and through the arrow slits of the gatehouse towers, the archers sent their arrows deep into the amassed French, stitching bloody confusion and mayhem.

Many tried to turn about and flee, for this greeting was an utter shock, but de Charny refused to yield so easily and rallied the men around him, exhorting them forward to seize the gate and hold it by their greater numbers.

Thomas, on the King's left flank, was soon hard-pressed. He focused on protecting the King while trying to prevent any French from winning through. His gaze flicked over the enemy banners and livery, checking for fierce and accomplished fighters who were the greatest threat. When the opportunity came to press forward, he did so with intent, but at an angle so that the slant of his attack protected the King, making his own body a barrier.

Arrows thrummed overhead into the depths of the French, but still the battle was fierce and bloody. Thomas, Otto and Henry fought like steady flames, destroying whatever came at them, but it was a never-ending surge. Wave upon wave, even with the support of the archers, and they had to hold the line. The King had engaged several times. Swords, axes, hatchets flickered at him, and Thomas and others beat them aside with desperate strength.

Otto gasped as he took a hard blow and his horse stumbled, leaving Thomas open for a moment. Thomas pivoted Noir, brought his own sword to bear, and forced the big stallion forward instead of retreating. His enemy grunted and fell back, and Thomas pushed his advantage yet again, by which time Otto had rallied and was once more at his side.

Then . . . sweet relief! Prince Edward arrived from his own station, galloping his troops around to seize on the French rear flank. Heartened, the tiring King's men redoubled their efforts, although the archers desisted theirs lest they strike their own. Seeing the tide turn imbued Thomas with a fresh surge of energy and he spurred forward to help pincer the French between the English lines, until those too slow to flee were caught and either dispatched or taken for ransom, while the English trumpets sounded the victory, and the archers cheered from the walls, and shot volleys into the retreating foe.

The command went through the line not to pursue. De Charny had been taken with many other high-ranking knights, and there was no possibility of the French regrouping for a second assault.

Thomas slapped Noir's sweating neck. His sword arm was on fire, but he was unharmed. He looked across at Otto who had removed his helm and was breathing hard, teeth bared.

'I am going to be bruised to hell and back but I will live,' Otto panted in reassurance. 'My own fault, I shouldn't have let the bastard under my guard, but he didn't cut through.'

Thomas gestured in acknowledgement, checked on Henry and the others, and waved a salute to his archers.

Thomas and his household moved to a new lodging in the citadel with stabling for their horses and tents for the archers.

A barrel bath tub was found and hot water for washing. Otto had a spectacular red bruise down one side of his torso, and a dint in his breast plate, but had been lucky. The wound could have been fatal and the moment of battle might have turned on the instant. Their victory had been hard fought. They had many injured of their own, even if the French had suffered far worse.

De Charny had a deep cut to the scalp that had bled profusely and required stitching. The King was treating him as a guest, if not entirely an honoured one, and had welcomed him to a feast held that evening in the citadel for his senior men. It was an opportunity to parade with chivalry the hostages they had taken between them.

Edward addressed de Charny with the air of a cat patting a juicy mouse between its paws. 'Well, my lord,' he said, 'you must relish our company, for you have set yourself up to enjoy yet another protracted bout of English hospitality.'

De Charny bowed in submission, but the glitter in his eyes revealed that he was not cowed, despite his defeat. He sent a dagger glance towards Amerigo di Pavia. 'Sire, I find myself at your mercy once more, and I am glad for it but sorry too, and I hope you will grant me the same mercy and courtesy that I would show to you if our situations were reversed.'

King Edward eyed him narrowly. 'Christmas is always a time for play acting, my lord, and this has been a charade from start to finish. Did you truly think you could bribe one of my most experienced soldiers to yield to you when we have all fought so hard and so long for this town? And did you think I would turn my back because it was Christmas?' He shook his head. 'My back is never turned.'

'But it might have been, sire,' de Charny said.

'Which shows how much you and your countrymen

underestimate me. You have smirched your honour by offering bribes to my men. What does this say about a knight who prides himself on his personal chivalry, when a man who fights under contract for pay has more moral fibre? You tried to buy your way into Calais, and you certainly paid the price.'

De Charny gave no answer beyond another dip of his head. He was whey-faced and clearly suffering from his injury.

'Was it not a fine jest, my lord, to discover that the common hedge knight in his besmirched armour was in fact the King of England and well ahead of you in every way that mattered?' Edward continued, smiling.

'Indeed, my lord, it was a great surprise,' de Charny answered stiffly.

'Hah!' The King clapped his shoulder and then took pity on him. 'Come, eat and drink at what is still my table and fear no treachery. You are my guest, and we shall say no more this night.'

De Charny had no choice but to agree. The feast was also attended by all the burghers and worthies of Calais and their wives. Any who had considered rebelling would now realise it might not be such a good idea after all.

Thomas settled down to enjoy the feast. At some point Otto and Henry disappeared and he knew women and drink would be involved, but he remained at the table and eventually took himself off to bed, detouring first to talk to his archers, who were full of themselves after the day's battle. None of them had been in any danger, but in the plundering afterwards they had acquired a stocky little sumpter horse laden with sacks of flour and beans, and two good iron cooking pots, which had pleased them greatly. Thomas brought them a cloth filled with slices of roast beef from the King's table that he had carved himself, and gave this to them to share, together with three loaves of bread, an extra shilling each, and a gold noble for Joss's baby son.

'God save you, my lord!' Samson said.

Thomas smiled at the men. 'I hope he does,' he replied, 'for I have a wife waiting at home for me, as you have yours.'

37

Royal Palace of Havering, Essex, January 1350

Jeanette was eating in the Queen's chamber with the other ladies. The men had been gone over a week and there had been no word from across the sea since their arrival in Calais. Two days ago, the Queen had told a select few of her ladies what was happening, including Jeanette, but they had been sworn to a secrecy as tight as the men's. Jeanette had rolled her eyes in exasperation. So much for Thomas's reassurances that he would be perfectly safe.

The Queen had received messages from Calais informing her that the troops had arrived safely and were waiting for de Charny to make his move, but nothing since then, and although those who knew maintained a cheerful attitude in the public domain, behind curtains and closed doors and within chapels there were doubts and prayers, and deep anxiety. Jeanette could not help feeling that the King and his knights thought of their clandestine visit to Calais as a fine extension of the Christmas mumming but with swords involved – like squires enjoying a lark, although it was a deadly serious situation. What if the French prevailed?

A strong breeze was blowing outside, banging the shutters and guttering any candles that stood near a draught, and Jeanette was glad of the hot pottage the kitchens had provided rather than the usual evening bread and cheese. Thus far she was still well, but perhaps it was too soon to be queasy.

Eating another spoonful of pottage, she thought she heard a sound outside. The Queen raised her head too, eyes alert. Nosewyse and Snowflake emerged from their place under the trestle at Jeanette's feet and started to growl.

Suddenly the doors flung open and a crowd of yelling men charged into the room, clad in dark clothes, hoods pulled up around their heads and faces, swords brandished.

The women screamed and the squires and household knights grabbed for their swords, but then one of the figures leaped on to the nearest table, tore off his hood and cloak and stood before them – the King, in splendour, his smile as bright as the sun. He gestured, and Prince Edward leaped up beside him. His companions threw off their outer garments too and set their weapons aside, revealing the host of household knights, all wearing the drab, plain garments in which they had originally set out.

The screams turned to laughter and applause, and questions. The King raised and lowered his arms, gesturing for silence.

'Good folk, do not worry at our jest. You are not under attack; indeed, we have saved you! We have secured a great victory, even dressed as we are. Calais was under attack from within and without, and we had need to go there and rescue the town – which we did to great lustre. We have taken much booty and many French prisoners whose ransoms will fatten our coffers this winter. We said nothing, for we didn't want to alarm you or spread panic when we received the news of the treachery. The Queen might have been able to tell you, but she is good at keeping secrets!' He opened his hand towards Philippa and swept her a deep bow, thereby including her in the subterfuge. 'Now, pray continue with your feast and we shall join you, fresh from the fray!'

To further cheers and claps, the King leaped down from the table and took his seat beside the Queen, and a brimming goblet was swiftly put in his hand.

Thomas squeezed in beside Jeanette, the greasy leather shoulder of Duncalfe's second best jerkin rubbing against her gown. She wrinkled her nose as she passed him her cup and he smiled at her while trying to push away Nosewyse, who was more enamoured than she was by the scents adhering to his garments.

'I slept with the horses most of the time,' he said.

'Yes, I can tell.'

'Well, don't worry, I have to give the clothing back,' he said with a grin. 'I would hate you not to love me.'

She studied the motion of his throat as he drained the wine, watched him eat bread with a ravenous appetite.

'The Queen told me where you had gone,' she said.

'Well, that was her prerogative, not mine,' he replied. 'We're home, and Geoffrey de Charny is being called "Geoffrey de Chagrin" now, and rightly chastised for making war in a time of truce.'

Between mouthfuls, Thomas gave Jeanette the gist of what had happened, and she watched the bright animation on his face as he spoke and knew that this was her lot. She had married a soldier, not a monk or a cleric. She had a lion, not a house cat. And it was fitting, for she herself was a lioness by birth and by inclination.

She lightly touched his cheek. 'No matter in what state you return to me, I thank God for it, but as a good wife, I should see you bathed and clad in fresh raiment.'

He raised his brows and smiled. 'Are you saying that I smell?'

'Like a horse,' she said, laughing, but she was already summoning the servants. Everyone would be ordering the same, and if she wasn't swift, there would be neither bath tub nor hot water to be had, no matter the rank of the person involved. 'But I still love you . . .'

'You just want to undress me.'

It was Jeanette's turn to lift her brows. But then her smile grew coquettish. 'Of course,' she said. 'Why would I not? Never judge a man by his clothes until you know what lies beneath them!'

'Does that advice apply to a man considering a woman too?' he asked with amusement.

'You should know.'

'Perhaps I need reminding,' he said. 'Perhaps we should remind each other.' He took her hand and raised it to his lips.

Circumspectly, they made their way out of the hall, the dogs trotting at their heels, Nosewyse clutching half a roast chicken in his jaws for future consumption.

Two days later they left the court to travel to Thomas's manor of Broughton. A large baggage cart laden with gifts lumbered behind them, pulled by a pair of sturdy cobs that were also presents from the King and Queen. Four sumpter horses plodded behind the carts, piled with sacks. There was a smaller cart too for the hawks and their equipment, presided over by John de la Salle.

Jeanette rode along smiling, but quiet, keeping her secret to herself, although several times since his return she had been tempted to tell him. She had said nothing at court, for she wanted the news to be theirs alone for a while.

They approached Broughton in the mid-afternoon, with the late sun gleaming on the roof shingles in a spill of liquid gold, and the whitewashed walls drenched in soft yellow light. The moat glinted and the dry reeds at the water's edge clacked together in the chill breeze, harbinger of evening. Smoke twirled from the manor's chimneys, and as their entourage approached the gate, grooms came to take the horses.

Thomas dismounted swiftly and helped Jeanette down from her mare, then held her lightly against him. He too had been quiet, and she saw the anxiety in his gaze as she looked up at him.

'I would give you a great palace if I could,' he said.

She smiled and shook her head. 'I have told you, I do not need such places. Even when I had every luxury to command, I had nothing without you, and thus I have everything now. This will be a fine home to settle and, come harvest time, begin raising our child.'

He looked into her face. She took his hand and put it against her waistline.

'Truly?' he said.

She nodded. 'Truly.'

His jaw tightened as he strove for control but tears brimmed in his good eye. 'That is the greatest news,' he said, his voice choked with emotion.

'It is the beginning again.' She stroked his face with her other hand. 'We have survived, and we shall show them indeed what it is to love, and let those who doubted now know the truth.' She reached inside her gown, drew out the small enamelled belt pendant on its chain, and kissed it. 'I picked this up from the tourney field the first time I saw you joust and I knew then that it was for ever. They said it was the whim of a girl, but it never was – I knew my mind even then.' She tucked the necklace back inside her gown. 'We shall have difficult times, but none more challenging than those we have already faced.' She nudged him. 'Are you going to show me into my new home?'

He blotted his face on his sleeve. Behind them, a cloud of doves soared up from the cote behind the manor, and in a sudden change of mood, Thomas pounced on his wife. Sweeping her into his arms, he whirled her round until she burst out laughing, and then he carried her through the doorway and into their marital home.

Historical Note

I had been thinking about writing a novel (or more than one novel) about Joan (Jeanette) of Kent for a while. She had crossed my path numerous times on various forums dedicated to medieval history, and I wanted to find out more about this fascinating woman for myself – which led me initially to two biographies of her life, and the realisation that even with a gap of some seven hundred years between the fourteenth century and now, with all the social changes and tremendous leaps in technology, there remain many similarities and points of connection. The fourteenth century was a time of war, plague, excessive consumption and the overturning of what had seemed like a settled world order. The more things change, it seems to me that the more they remain the same!

I became very curious to know more about Jeanette and the circumstances that led her to her first marriage and then to her bigamous second match with William Montagu. There were so many questions, and so few answers. How did it all come about?

What were the emotions and motivations of the people involved? The historical record is not always clear on such details and frequently biased. Jeanette and Thomas must have had gritty determination and a powerful need for each other – dare I say love – to hold firm against all the obstacles thrown in their way by relatives with very different agendas.

To general history, Jeanette is more commonly known as Joan of Kent, but this was probably not the name she used. In 1348 Prince Edward, the King's heir, known to later centuries but not in his lifetime as the Black Prince, presented her with a silver cup with her name 'Jeanette' engraved upon it. He knew her intimately, having grown up with her (he was about three years younger) at the royal court. That he should use this appellation on a personal gift is telling evidence that he had always known her by that name, which is a diminutive of 'Joan'. When I asked her in my writer's mind to tell her story, that is how she came to me, as Jeanette, and I felt that she should have her familiar name restored to her.

Jeanette was the daughter of Edmund, youngest son of King Edward I by his second wife, Margaret of France. That made her a princess, and first cousin to King Edward III, her father and his having been half brothers. Edmund fell foul of the complex politics of the period and was executed for treason when Jeanette was very young. For a time, Edmund's heavily pregnant wife Margaret was held under house arrest at Arundel with Jeanette and her brother Edmund (who was to die in infancy). John, the third child, was born posthumously and Jeanette and little Edmund became his godparents at the font because basically there was no one else. Some historians have erroneously given Margaret of Kent a fourth daughter, also named Margaret, but given the timing, this cannot have happened, and the reason for a mention is a clerical error where the scribe absent-mindedly wrote Margaret's name instead of Jeanette's. We don't know the birth order of the first two Kent children, and there is some evidence to suggest that Jeanette may well have been the oldest child, perhaps born in September 1326.

As Edward III gained control of the political situation, he and his young queen Philippa took in his half brother's children and raised them at the royal court in their households. Margaret remained a widow and was formidable. She spent much of her time restoring the Kent estates from their plundering and misappropriation following her husband's execution and was a force to be reckoned with.

Jeanette accompanied the royal party to Flanders in the summer of 1338 and there became involved with the royal household knight Thomas Holland. His own father, like Jeanette's, had been executed – in Robert Holland's case, he was considered a traitor by the house of Lancaster because he had ignored a summons to support his lord during an important military engagement. Although he was officially pardoned for the act, he was later ambushed and beheaded by representatives of the man he had betrayed. In similar straits to Margaret of Kent, Matilda (Maude) Holland had to strive to keep the family name afloat and maintain the inheritance of her sons and daughters. I have streamlined the Holland family in the interests of the narrative, but Thomas had two older brothers as well as Otto, and five sisters, including Isabel, for a time the mistress of John de Warenne, Earl of Surrey.

Jeanette was in her early teens when she married Thomas Holland in Ghent – he was in his early to mid-twenties. Both swore under oath they had taken marriage vows before witnesses and that the marriage had been consummated – a circumstance that in medieval law locked that marriage securely in place. We know this from the extant details laid before the papal court in Avignon during the hearing of the case between 1347 and 1349. We know they married in the spring of 1340 – probably April – but we don't know the precise date or place, so I have gone with my best guess.

Shortly after the marriage, probably within days, Thomas was summoned away to active military duty with the King, and after that departed on crusade for over a year. During that time, his marriage to Jeanette remained hidden from the world. We can only speculate on the reasons. I have suggested in the novel that Thomas and Jeanette were waiting for the right time, knowing the news would not be joyously received. The crusade might have been a way for Thomas to atone for what could have been perceived as a sin, especially since the marriage had been consummated and his position at court as a household knight, and a younger son of a disgraced father, was precarious.

Whatever the reasons, he was far away when Jeanette's family arranged her marriage to William Montagu, who was one or two years younger than she was and in his very early teens at most. We don't know the circumstances, only that the wedding took place in 1341 before the end of February, and that Jeanette consented. The union would have been agreed by the families rather than the couple themselves. William Montagu's mother, Katerine, Countess of Salisbury, had had some responsibility for Jeanette and other young women in Queen Philippa's household while the court was in Flanders. Again, we don't know whether Katerine knew that Jeanette and Thomas were conducting a clandestine affair under everyone's nose. We do know that while in Flanders, King Edward had been considering marrying Jeanette to the son of a Gascon ally, but for whatever reasons, the negotiations fell through.

Jeanette was later to say she agreed to the Montagu marriage because she had been frightened of what might happen to Thomas if she spoke out at the time. The French chronicler Jean Froissart mentions in passing that in the early 1340s Thomas only had the sight of one eye. Perhaps she was told that he was dead or maimed. News from the crusades would have been difficult to obtain and corroborate.

Around a year after Jeanette's 'marriage' to William Montagu, Thomas Holland returned from his crusade. Nothing is reported in the historical record about that return. Did he meet up with Jeanette? Did he tell anyone that he had married her? How did he find out about the Montagu marriage? There is a deafening silence, so again, both historian and novelist have to make their best guesses.

Thomas returned to military service – perhaps he realised even then that in order to have his wife restored he would need money he did not have, and the only way to obtain that money was through his skills as a soldier in taking rich booty and ransoms. He joined several battle campaigns, at one time serving with William Montagu Senior, the father of Jeanette's teenage 'husband'. Was anything said between the men? We don't know.

One chronicle states that Thomas Holland became the steward of the Salisbury family while Jeanette was married to William Montagu Junior. I suspect that the timing is out on this statement and that if Thomas did do any stewarding for William Montagu, it was for Montagu Senior and on the Scottish campaign that pre-dated the Flanders tour of duty of 1338, and happened before Thomas became a royal household knight. It would have been utterly ridiculous for Thomas to be stewarding in a household where he was in dispute with the family over the legality of the dynastic marriage of their son and heir because he was claiming a prior union with their son's wife!

It has been suggested that Thomas attempted to gain compensation from the Montagus by promising to keep his mouth shut in exchange for patronage and payment, but that the scheme fell through in 1344 when Montagu Senior was killed while jousting in a tournament. This may indeed have been the case, but is modern speculation by one particular historian and does not gel with the detail that both Thomas and Jeanette fought on for many more years with stalwart determination to be together.

What changed the situation for Thomas was the French campaign of 1346 when at the Battle for Caen he took Raoul de Brienne, Comte d'Eu, prisoner and for some unexplained reason was granted the stupendous sum of eighty thousand florins as his ransom payment. These payments were brokered through the King and his son Prince Edward, and one can only assume that the news about Jeanette's first marriage had become known to the inner courtly circle by now, and that the King saw fit to bankroll Thomas's efforts to have his marriage to Jeanette validated. Again, we do not know the circumstances, only that it happened. We can speculate that King Edward highly valued Thomas's fighting abilities, whereas William Montagu Junior, Jeanette's second 'husband', was still an unproven teenager, but we don't know. The King did assist Montagu with funding his side of the court case, but perhaps more in the interests of fair play, and perhaps because he was influenced by his close friendship with Katerine, Countess of Salisbury and her mother-in-law Elizabeth de Montfort. Certainly, he didn't assist William Montagu to the tune of eighty thousand florins – the contribution was much more modest. Raoul was eventually taken to England and returned to France in 1350 to arrange raising his ransom but was executed by his own side who suspected him of treachery.

Thomas set out for the papal court in Avignon in the spring of 1347 to state his case and ask for it to be heard. His mother accompanied him – we know this because she applied for a dispensation to have a portable altar so that she could pray along the way. Katerine of Salisbury did the same thing, and although she probably did not travel to Avignon, her mother-in-law Elizabeth de Montfort certainly did in November 1347, to have her say on behalf of the family.

A protracted court case ensued. Thomas had the same lawyer throughout, one Robert Sigglesthorne Beverley, who had worked for Queen Philippa in the past – dare one speculate that Philippa herself had a hand in assisting Thomas and Jeanette? William Montagu's own attorney (confusingly named John Holland and thus I have called him Master John in the novel) didn't turn up in Avignon during the later stages of the case hearings, and sometimes sent deputies instead – although sometimes they didn't appear either. The attorneys representing Jeanette were woefully inadequate or else compromised (Nicholas Heath, for example, was arrested by the King for untoward practices) until finally, in the closing stages, one Master John Vyse, who had also been employed at one time by Queen Philippa, saw the case through. One might be forgiven for suspecting delaying tactics and under-hand dealings at work.

At one stage in the proceedings, Jeanette was incarcerated without access to an attorney and was unable to give a witness statement. Thomas Holland complained to the Pope about her circumstances, and the latter wrote to the Archbishop of Canterbury and two other English bishops, ordering them to sort the matter out and make sure that Jeanette was not being held under duress. The fact that Thomas himself had to chase up the detail of Jeanette's incarceration shows his determination to pursue the case, and the equal determination of the Montagu family that Jeanette was not going to be allowed to speak for herself. William Montagu and Jeanette's mother, Margaret, were cited as the major complainants, but since William was still a minor, and in the care of his mother and grandmother, it is more likely that Katerine and Elizabeth were the movers behind the scenes together with Jeanette's mother, who seems never to have reconciled with her daughter, and any opportunity to do so was curtailed by the ravages of the plague.

Bubonic plague, known to history as the Black Death, had ripped its way through Europe and arrived in England in the middle of 1348, adding its own devastating impact to Jeanette and Thomas's difficulties and slowing down the court case, which dragged on deep into 1349. Pope Clement VI dismissed the original cardinal in charge of the hearing and appointed a new one, Bernard d'Albi. A cut-off date was set, and Jeanette and Thomas's marriage was finally pronounced valid by a papal injunction dated 13 November 1349. The couple married again before a priest to make it solidly official before the year was out.

Following an overnight dash during the Christmas festivities to rescue Calais from an assault launched by the French, and King Edward's triumph, Thomas and Jeanette retired from court to Thomas's manor at Broughton, where their first son, Thomas, was born some time in 1350, presumably the autumn. The baby was given the christening gift of a silver basin by Prince Edward, who stood as the child's godfather, and who maintained close ties with Thomas and Jeanette throughout their marriage.

It is interesting that in the nine years that Jeanette spent as William Montagu's 'wife' they had no children, suggesting that they either did not cohabit or did so infrequently.

Katerine, Countess of Salisbury and Jeanette's mother Margaret, Dowager Countess of Kent had remained in permanent opposition to Jeanette's first marriage, but both women succumbed to plague. In the fourteenth century it was known as the 'poxe' – as were many other diseases. I have taken an author's decision to refer to it as 'the pestilence'. Katerine died from it in April 1349 and Margaret in September of the same year. Thomas's own mother, who had offered her son every support in his campaign to have Jeanette restored to him, also fell victim to its ravages in the summer of 1349. Also to die of plague was Jeanette's uncle, Thomas Wake, her mother's brother, in May 1349.

Katerine is a medieval spelling of the modern name 'Katherine' but at the time the 'th' was not pronounced, so I have gone with the medieval version. Did she have an affair with King Edward III? The jury is out. Some historians think definitely not, others hedge their bets. She was certainly a very close friend of the King's (platonic or not), as was her husband, and she had duties that kept her at court and within the royal circle. A story written by a French chronicler tells how King Edward, overcome with lust for Katerine, beat and raped her during the Scottish campaign in the late 1330s, but it is thought to be anti-English propaganda without substance. However, it might be a case of no smoke without fire, and there may have been a sexual connection between the two at some point in their lives, even if not a violent or abusive one. Edward III's biographer Mark Ormrod is cautious, but does not discount the detail.

Edward was known to be devoted to his queen, Philippa of Hainault, but even devoted medieval husbands sometimes strayed when a wife was in confinement during pregnancy and childbirth, or otherwise absent from court, and later in life, when Philippa was ailing, Edward most certainly took a mistress for his comfort in the very notorious Alice Perrers. Personally, I suspect it was part of a pattern that had gradually intensified throughout the King's life.

Both Katerine and Jeanette as countesses of Salisbury are connected with the foundation story of the Order of the Knights of the Garter. The legend goes that one of these ladies was wearing a garter that slipped off her leg in public and the King was swift to scold people for mocking the lady – whichever one of them it was – and founded the Order of the Garter to teach his knights about chivalry. The problem with this tale is that the garter at that time was a piece of male apparel and the scene is unlikely ever to have taken place.

The Royal Rebel as a novel stands alone, but Jeanette herself, despite her 'happy ending' of 1349–50, still had an eventful life ahead of her, and a part to play in the power struggles of the long fourteenth century. She was embedded in the lives of the people involved from all walks of society, and she still has so much more to tell me. Her tale is ongoing . . .

Select Bibliography

For readers wishing to delve further into the period via non-fiction I have listed below some of the books I used while researching Jeanette, and I am grateful to all the authors for furthering my knowledge and giving me food for thought.

Benedictow, Ole J., *The Complete History of the Black Death* (Boydell, 2021)

Bliss, W. H. and Johnson C. (eds), *Calendar of Entries in the Papal Registers Relating to Great Britain and Ireland vol. III AD 1342–1362* (Kraus, 1971)

Douglas, David C. (ed.), *English Historical Documents IV 1327–1485* (Eyre & Spottiswoode, 1969)

Froissart, Jean (selected, edited and translated by Geoffrey Brereton), *Chronicles* (Penguin, 1968)

Goodman, Anthony, *Joan, the Fair Maid of Kent: A Fourteenth-Century Princess and her World* (Boydell, 2017)

Hefferan, Matthew, *The Household Knights of Edward III: Warfare,*

Politics and Kingship in Fourteenth-Century England (Boydell, 2021)

Lawne, Penny, *Joan of Kent: The First Princess of Wales* (Amberley, 2015)

Mortimer, Ian, *The Perfect King: The Life of Edward III* (Vintage, 2008)

Munby, Julian, Barber, Richard and Brown, Richard, *Edward III's Round Table at Windsor* (Boydell, 2007)

Newton, Stella Mary, *Fashion in the Age of the Black Prince 1340–1365* (Boydell, 1980)

Nicolle, David, *Crécy 1346: Triumph of the Longbow* (Osprey, 2000)

Ormrod, W. Mark, *Edward III* (Yale, 2013)

Sloane, Barney, *The Black Death in London* (The History Press, 2011)

Stansfield, Michael M. N., *The Holland Family, Dukes of Exeter, Earls of Kent and Huntingdon 1352–1475* (University of Oxford thesis, 1987)

Sumption, Jonathan, *Trial by Battle: The Hundred Years War I* (Faber and Faber, 1990)

Warner, Kathryn, *Philippa of Hainault: Mother of the English Nation* (Amberley, 2019)

Wentersdorf, Karl P., 'The Clandestine Marriages of the Fair Maid of Kent', *Journal of Medieval History*, published online in 2012

Acknowledgements

I'd like to take a couple of paragraphs to extend my appreciation to the many champions behind the scenes who have helped me in enormous ways during the writing and production of *The Royal Rebel* – and indeed of all my novels.

Thank you to the magnificent team at Blake Friedmann, headed by my wise and wonderful agent Isobel Dixon. Between you, you have fought my corner and expended a huge amount of effort chasing down elusive rights and technical contract details, to bring my novels to the widest audience possible. I greatly appreciate your dedication, your professionalism and your friendship. Without you, I wouldn't have a career!

I would also like to thank the team at Little, Brown, especially my editor Molly Walker-Sharp and her thoughtful, enlightened perception which has made a huge contribution to my crafting of Jeanette's story. Jon Appleton on the production side for his lovely good nature and sense of humour, and an especial thank you to Dan Balado-Lopez for the final copy-edit and a tidy up of my dates, spellings, and other gremlins. Any mistakes that remain are all mine and I own them.

Finally, a heartfelt thank you to my husband for providing me with tea and love and making the house a home that's always there when I return from my daily forays into the medieval past. To my dearest friend Alison King for being there whether it be adventuring in history, or going out for a coffee and chat. And to you my fantastic readers. You enrich my life with your humour, your own stories, your love of history, your friendship and engagement with me and my novels. I appreciate every single one of you – thank you.

Elizabeth

New York Times bestselling author Elizabeth Chadwick lives in a cottage in the Vale of Belvoir in Nottinghamshire with her husband and their four dogs. Her first novel, *The Wild Hunt*, won a Betty Trask Award and *To Defy a King* won the RNA's 2011 Historical Novel Prize. She was also shortlisted for the Romantic Novelists' Award in 1998 for *The Champion*, in 2001 for *Lords of the White Castle*, in 2002 for *The Winter Mantle*, in 2003 for *The Falcons of Montabard* and in 2021 for *The Coming of the Wolf*. Her sixteenth novel, *The Scarlet Lion*, was nominated by Richard Lee, founder of the Historical Novel Society, as one of the top ten historical novels of the last decade. She often lectures at conferences and historical venues, has been consulted for television documentaries, and is a member of the Royal Historical Society.

For more details on Elizabeth Chadwick and her books, visit www.elizabethchadwick.com, follow her on X, read her blogs or chat to her on Facebook.

Yet, that's not where this story ends.

Jeanette will be back in 2026.

No longer a royal rebel, but a mother herself and
happy at last.

But fortune's wheel never stops turning . . .

Keep an eye on my website and social media for more!

elizabethchadwick.com
X @Chadwickauthor
/ElizabethChadwickAuthor